Bear Slayer

HAL COLE

Order this book online at **www.trafford.com**
or email orders@trafford.com

Most Trafford titles are also available at major online book retailers.

Printed in the United States of America.

ISBN: 978-1-4269-7254-6 (sc)
ISBN: 978-1-4269-7542-4 (e)

Trafford rev. 08/02/2011

 www.trafford.com

North America & International
toll-free: 1 888 232 4444 (USA & Canada)
phone: 250 383 6864 ♦ fax: 812 355 4082

Bear Slayer

He stood stark naked except for a skimpy loin cloth. The sun glistened on his oiled skin adding emphasis to his angular well muscled frame. He was tall for his age and often associated with older young braves, competing with them in games of strength and endurance. His gaze was fixed on the trail where he anticipated the French half-breed would soon appear. He had been just a lad of ten when the half-breed had left his village for parts unknown. The emotions of his anticipation had a ting of kinship longing, which they rightly should for the half-breed was his biological father. Wapaxo was known as the arrow maker's son but his height belied this kinship as did his extra wide shoulders. His mother knew the relationship and felt pride that the potlatch association had given her this handsome son. It was accepted as natural and Wapaxo belonged to the lodge of the arrowhead maker, who was also the tribe's historian who was known for his faultless memory when he related tales of his ancestors and their deeds.

The huge figure straightened a little as he ambled up from the stream bed and saw the figure that he recognized as his offspring. They embraced as equals with a firm left forearm clasp. Always the left for it was closest to the heart. Jacque asked him, "Have you been practicing with the bow and sling?" "Every day", was Wapaxo's answer beaming when he seen the approval in his father's face. He had turned fifteen a couple of moons ago in the early spring. He had completed his puberty ritual by fasting and enduring the long sleepless ordeal during a thunder storm. The tumbling thunder head clouds had resembled huge shaggy beasts in his Trans like state. When he reported this to the medicine man he was told that he was destined to hunt "Tonka" bison. To fulfill his destiny he would have to cross over the mountains to the east of the continental divide. When he related this to Jacque, His biological father resolved to start him on a rigorous training plan for he knew the dangers and pitfalls of a buffalo hunt for he had been on several before crossing over to the coastal range. The big difference was Wapaxo wouldn't have the advantage of using a firearm. He had become skilled as an arrowhead maker under the tutelage of his lodge father. The northwestern region of the Mother river (Columbia), had several deposits of obsidian (natural glass), that made excellent arrow heads.

Jacque and Wapaxo spent many weeks together honing the young brave's archery skills this enhanced the social position of the pair in the tribe for they supplied a steady stream of fresh meat for the cooking pots. As they tramped the woodlands Jacque instructed Wapaxo in the language of the Shoshone for this had been the language of his mother. Jacque's father Pierre LeBlanc had broken away from a trapper group after he had been forced to kill one of the group's trappers over the possession of several traps. As was his custom he had boldly walked into a Sheep Eaters. "Shoshone" camp with a large buck on his shoulders. In fact this was how Jacque entered the camp of Wapaxo's lodge father and mother. His feet had been in terrible condition from frost bite. Wapaxo's mother had soaked them in a. sagebrush -.bud bath and nurtured him into walking condition. The practice of POTLATCH (sharing) was deeply inculcated in the Klickitat social order and included sharing of wives with travelers. The Klickitat language expresses the size and quantity of something by repeating the noun or verb. For example water would be a small amount; water water would be a large amount.

ThusWapaxo's mother had told her friends of her mating with Jacque and the copious amount of semen, (mullum). As a small boy whenever Wapaxo would pass a group of visiting wives somebody would mention Mullum-Mullum Mullum and they would all giggle knowingly.

The mainstay of the Klickitat diet was salmon. They were excellent fishermen and the Mother River (Columbia) was the source of their seemingly endless supply of salmon. Thru time they had learned to preserve their catch by slow smoking over a variety of woods according to their acquired tastes. They had also learned to increase the preservation of their catches with the use of salt which they bartered for from the coastal tribes who had developed a taste for the smoked salmon. The salt harvested from low coastal flood plains and sea otter pelts collected from the off shore kelp beds were highly prized by the Klickitats. The women of the Klickitats also were excellent basket weavers. They were able to weave willows and grasses so artfully that they held water. The sea otters extra luxurious fur was used to line the tall winter moccasins. The moccasins bottoms were made from wapiti, (elk) hides. Shoulder and rump leather was used for soles and the softer more pliable belly hide was used for the tops. Had Jacque had such moccasins when he made his trek over the high country to the lodge of the arrow maker, he wouldn't have suffered from frost bite and there possibly wouldn't have been a Wapaxo.

In the mid-summer of his nineteenth year Wapaxo was a superb warrior. He stood six feet tall and weighed 180 pounds without an ounce of fat. Jacque helped him pack and re-pack the back pack his mother had made him. Only essentials for his trip were assembled. He would have to live off the land. His hunting weapons consisted of a fine English yew wood bow that Jacque had reluctantly bequeathed him. In his quiver he had a bundle of carefully crafted, obsidian tipped arrows. His prized possession was a spear equaling his height in length and tipped with a huge obsidian blade that was equal to the length of one of his feet. He had become the brunt of many jokes and barbs about his huge spear. The shaft was of myrtle wood which was very hard and durable but extremely rare in straight pieces. He had collected the sinews of the game they had brought into the village. These he had shredded and soaked and used to bind the huge spear point to the shaft. It was truly a formidable weapon. Having never seen a buffalo, he had only his trans-like images seen in the rolling thunderhead clouds during his puberty ordeal to guide him in his design of a suitable weapon. Jacque had drawn maps on the ground showing him how he was to travel up the Columbia to the Snake River and where he could find a pass to take him to the flat country before reaching the continental divide. Another weapon Jacque had taught him to use was the sling. This provided him with small game during his trek.

Following the Snake River forced him to trudge through a semi-arid brush land to avoid the treacherous Snake River canyon. A large stream flowing into the Snake blocked his passage westward so he worked his way up stream to find a crossing. As he topped a little knoll he glanced down toward a beaver pond and to his delight seen five teen aged maidens bathing in the pond. He sneaked down closer to the stream and was startled to hear a couple of bear cubs squealing in alarm. He had no sooner heard the cubs when a huge grizzly sow rose out of the berry bushes, standing up to see what was troubling her cubs. It was apparent that the cubs had been following their mother on the opposite bank of the creek. The beaver dam had formed the pond increasing their distance from the sow. this plus the five maidens had alarmed them and they were calling for their mother. Recognizing the danger facing the girls Wapaxo fitted a stone into his sling and wafted it on its way to a direct blow to the base of the sow's spine. She wheeled, spotted her tormentor and charged... Wapaxo dashed for a close by ponderosa pine but was unable to attempt to climb when the sow charged., her hind legs driving her front legs up swinging in a mighty blow, but not before Wapaxo had rested the but of his big spear against the trunk of the large tree at an angle that met the sow's chest. Her weight and forward motion drove the super sharp blade deep into her chest cavity. As she swung her right paw at Wapaxo's head the shock of her wound affected her accuracy and her large claws tore a sizable chunk of bark and wood out of the tree before striking Wapaxo and sending him flying into the berry bushes. The squeal of the cubs gave the sow an adrenaline rush that carried her to the edge of the beaver pond even though each step she had taken on the way had driven the point of the spear deeper into her chest and ravaged her heart and lungs. The Indian maidens huddled together against the beaver dam, caught between two large grizzly cubs and their enraged mother. Prepared to suffer untold mangling they were astonished to see the sow drop dead at the edge of the pond. While scrambling up the bank and putting on their clothes they noticed the crumpled figure of Wapaxo. Their analytical minds saw that it was obvious this handsome young brave had delivered them from unspeakable disaster. Disregarding their baskets of berries, they dispatched the youngest to the village to seek help while the elder four attended Wapaxo. They stripped off their shirts and stretched them over two slender lodge pole shafts. Rolled Wapaxo on the makeshift stretcher and started toward the village hoping their baskets of chokecherries and service berries would still be there when they returned. Several strong young men met the maidens and took over the task of bearing Wapaxo to one of the large lodges. Several others went to the berry patch encountered the two cubs, dispatched them and quartered the big sow after skinning her and collecting the claws and teeth believed to have great spiritual significance.

It was several days before Wapaxo was alert enough to appraise his whereabouts and attempt to communicate. He tried first in his native language then he switched to Shoshone which was partially understood by these Digger Indians a branch of the Nez Perce Nation... They had been so named because their main staple was camas root which of course was dug. Wapaxo's first utterance that was understood was "where am I" The Chief answered, "You are with the Ponocs, O' Bear Slayer. Here you will be honored and cared for". Wapaxo was about to ask about his belongings when he noticed them in a pile to the side of the lodge. Surprisingly his spear had survived the sow's lung toward her cubs. It had been cleaned by admiring warriors He knew each item of his possessions. Had been thoroughly inspected and appreciated by the admiring warriors.

As he lay weak from the loss of blood and the concussion he had received from the grizzly, the maidens who had carried him most of the way to the village took turns attending to his needs. All four were attractive but the one that introduced her self as Milliwana "Willow Flower," seemed most attentive. She is the daughter of a Sub-Chief and understood Wapaxo's Shoshone dialect better than the other three. This put her in his presence more often as she interpreted for the others.

It was weeks before Wapaxo could make his way about before succumbing to dizzy and weak spells. When he finally overcame these maladies he started a rigorous regime of exercise to tone his body to its former condition. Time was his enemy. Jacque had warned him that the high mountain passes would soon be impassable. The tribal elders encouraged him to stay with them until spring. He was eager to comply for they had horses and he was learning to be an accomplished horseman. The advantage of traveling horseback was as obvious as his courtship of Milliwana as she rode with him on hunts and assumed the tasks of preparing the animals he brought to the village.

After a successful hunt Milliwana's father Sub Chief Wild horse brought Milliwana to Wapaxo and placed her hand in his saying", "it is good and right that she should belong to you for without your slaying of the bear she would not be here to belong to anybody." The wedding was a joyous occasion with much dancing and feasting. The wedding gifts included two appaloosa horses, a fine large 15 hand stud and a gentile mare broke to pack. Milliwana brought her own horse a startling white mare that she had tamed as a colt. These were extravagant gifts for the wealth of the tribe was their horses, essential to their nomadic life style. One of their food staples was camas root. The preparation of camas flour is a precise routine of milling and washing the root several times before grinding it to flour and made into cakes. It is essential to do it precisely for without the correct amount of grinding washing the meal would be hard to digest... The tribe did not cultivate the camas they simply traveled from one established patch to another, taking only the fully developed roots and leaving the immature to grow for their next visit... The use of the travois intrigued Wapaxo.

In the spring after the streams had receded enough to make fording possible, Wapaxo started preparations for his journey over the divide. It was a crisp spring evening when a young lad brought a message to Wapaxo that his presence was needed at a council with the Chief and his council. After refreshment, smoking of the pipe formalities, Sub Chief Tall Man asked Wapaxo, "Where can we acquire more of the white sand (salt) that makes food taste better?"Wapaxo replied," It can only be bartered from the coastal tribes." Tall Man asked, "What can we trade". Calculating carefully Wapaxo replied," Two of your worst ponies loaded with camas bread should buy the weight of a fat woman in good clean salt." The discussion lasted late into the night. It was finally decided that Beaver Boy would accompany Wapaxo and Milliwana back to Wapaxo's home village. Beaver boy's accompaniment was essential to shortening the trip as much as possible since he had scouted the route to the mother river several times. This was agreeable to Wapaxo for it would give him an opportunity to show off his bride, tell the tale of the bear, and load up with salt that will be needed with his expected harvest of buffalo meat

With the help of Beaver Boy the trip was uneventful. The reception at his reunion with his tribe was a call for celebration and Milliwana was warmly embraced. She found the main fare of smoked salmon to be especially delightful. Wapaxo and Beaver Boy left Williwana with the tribe while they journeyed on to make the trade with the coastal natives. Beaver Boy was amazed with the expanse of the Pacific Ocean and couldn't comprehend that nobody had ever gone to the end of this body of salty water.

Wapaxo was able to trade for as much salt as they could pack and also several sea otter pelts for gifts to Williwana's and Beaver Boy's families. The trip back to the village was interrupted only to visit a site of obsidian where Wapaxo gathered some shards he knew would make good weapon points. Fearing the loss of valuable traveling weather the three adventurers made a hasty departure from Wapaxo's village and headed up the mother river. Each evening when the travelers stopped to rest and feed the horses Wapaxo would spend some time teaching Beaver Boy the art of making arrow head points. Williwana not interested in arrow head making would spend her time gathering food plants and medicine herbs.

Upon arrival at the Digger camp, Wapaxo was delighted when Beaver Boy asked to accompany him on the trek to buffalo country. He reasoned that he wouldn't have to leave Williwana alone when he hunted for meat. Happy with the salt and otter pelts the tribe arranged for a pack horse for Beaver Boy.

July found the trio following the Salmon River into what is known now as the Bitter Root country, way north of the Snake River route Wapaxo's father had plotted out for him. Game was plentiful with an abundance of mule deer and mountain grouse that Wapaxo was able to collect with his skillful use of the sling. At this edge the Bitter Root country they came upon a burnt out area. They had plenty of meat and decided to travel until dark when Milliwana asked to pause. Not knowing the extent of the burn they agreed with her and camped where there was grazing for the horses. Leaving the warriors to set up camp, Milliwana said, Dig a deeper fire hole and took a stick to draw a circle to indicate the fire pit size. She then took a small basket and walked into the burnt area. When she returned she lined the fire pit with fist size boulders and dug another pit along side. This pit she lined with a cured deer hide this she filled with water adding wild carrots, onions, and morel mushrooms complimented with venison and salt. When the fire was burnt down she took a green forked branch and extracted several of the fist size boulders, dropping them into the water, meat-vegetable mixture. She repeated adding stones until she had the water boiling and giving off a delicious odor.

After they passed through the burnt out area the trio chose to camp by a lively stream. It was Beaver Boy's turn to hunt for the evening meal. Having seen several cotton tail rabbits he took his sling that he had become quite proficient with and was confident that he could bring back two or three young ones. .Yelping while at a full run he attracted the attention of his companions. At first they were alarmed until they seen that Beaver Boy was out running a large silver badger that was in a hissing angry mood It seems that Beaver Boy had killed a cotton tailed rabbit that the badger had chased out of its hiding place. Not about to give up its prize he charged Beaver Boy. The bear slayer and Milliwana found the scene quite amusing. Having no argument with the badger Beaver Boy simply continued his hunt until he had collected three plump, this year's rabbits. Wapaxo quipped, "We should change your name to bagger runner," They all laughed...

The next day found the travelers in heavy timber and only scattered deer trails could be seen... They tried to advance up a dry draw only to be blocked by heavy downfall. They back tracked and tried to go around the fallen timber turning south only to find themselves rim-rocked with no passage for horses. At Beaver Boys suggestion they stopped in a little clearing, unloaded the horses and he set out on foot to find a passable route. When it started to get dark Milliwana prepared a quick meal and they settled in for the night. Beaver Boy arrived telling them they had made a mistake when they turned south. He had back tracked and found a good trail to the north of the blow-down.

Beaver Boy led them to the well worn trail over the mountain range and they dropped into the Big Hole country. Jacque had spoken of this land calling it the land of many rivers. The bear slayer saw several small herds of Tonka (buffalo); He was eager to stalk them but kept himself in control wanting to see the herds that Jacque had told him about where tonka flowed over the prairies like salmon in Mother River. They skirted the southern end of a large body of water, Flathead Lake. This he remembered was Kootenai-Salish territory. These were known to be peaceful tribes. Later he knew he would be in Blackfoot country where they would have to be alert to protect themselves and their horses.

A large stream that was choked into a mini canyon provided them an opportunity to change their diet. They gathered a large bundle of willow shafts and constructed a fence at one end of the little canyon. At a mid point they built a funnel shaped fence. When their construction was finished they went down stream and thrashed the water as they waded toward the funnel shaped fence. When they reached the opening of the funnel they placed a woven mat that blocked the opening. With this completed they waded into the trap they had constructed and scooped the congregation of trout onto the banks of the stream until they had enough for a feast. This maneuver had its price. The water of the stream was almost too cold to flow. Shivering they gathered wood and soon had a big fire going. When they and their garments were finally dry and warm they turned in for the night.

The following day brought them to the foot hills of the Rocky Mountains and the continental divide. There had only been one short pause when Wapaxo took advantage of a large fat mule deer buck's interest in a rutting doe. They would eat well for several days. It wasn't time to camp for the night when they heard the sound of drums and singing. Sneaking to the top of a hill over looking a park like meadow they saw a village and people celebrating. They boldly rode into the village and presented the fine buck as an offering. Communication was difficult and mostly sign language but they got the drift of the celebration. It was a huckleberry festival. The harvest had been exceptional and they were partaking of huckleberry wine from last year's harvest. The women were not allowed any of the wine but there was a lot of giggling that indicated that they had a source of their own. It didn't take many drinks of wine until Beaver Boy and Wapaxo were joining in the dancing.

The next day was a day of recuperation. The fine deer was history. The village ladies had butchered and roasted it right away. Like Jacque the Kootenai tribe drew maps in the dust and gestured directions for the travelers to follow to pass over the Rockies. They also warned the travelers to be aware of the Black Feet. Two Sleeps from the Kootenai party the trail was plain to follow but the north sides were often blocked with snow in the high country.

There had been no easy game on the upper reaches of the continental divide. Mt goats and sheep could be seen at a distance but it would be extremely difficult to get close enough to bag one of these wily beasts. Following a stream down the eastern slopes made for easy travel and the trio were able to find a good camping spot that was sheltered and had good grazing for the horses. While Williwana and Beaver Boy set up camp Wapaxo gathered his weapons and set off for a cops of trees in a lower valley. Unbeknownst to Wapaxo he was being watched by three young braves hidden in a patch of aspens. They had scouted the camp and decided to try and eliminate Wapaxo, steal his horses and capture Milliwana.His size exaggerated by his grizzly coat gave them cause to be cautious. When Wapaxo entered the grove of evergreens he moved as stealthy and alert as he could... However this didn't prevent his detection by a big very old grizzly that was lying in a pool of hot mineral water soaking his arthritic joints. The odor of Wapaxo's coat alerted the old male that a female was approaching. Disgruntled he lumbered out of the pool and headed away from Wapaxo in the direction of the three young braves. Already in a foul mood the grizzly charged. Only one of the three was able to save himself by climbing a tree. Wapaxo found the mineral pool, read the sign and knew that there wouldn't be a chance for a deer with the bear around.

He made a half circle turn headed toward a thicket of chokecherry bushes having no idea of the action a few hundred yards behind him. Picking up some fine dusty soil, Wapaxo let it sift through his fingers noting the direction the breeze blew it. Satisfied that his scent was blowing away from the thicket he moved cautiously from clump to clump of brush. Just out of bow range stood a large prime cow moose. Her size was astonishing but what was unusual were the two large calves accompanying the cow. Moose seldom bear twins and to have both of the large juvenile calves still with her was really unusual. The larger of the calves was standing at an angle facing away from the hunter. This put it in the desired position for the shot Jacque had taught him was best for a large animal. Wapaxo inched his way slowly toward the calf until he was close enough to insure good penetration and accuracy. He let fly the largest tipped obsidian point with deadly accuracy hitting the calf just below its left ear. The sharp blade went deep penetrating a nerve center and severing a large artery. With a small bleat the calf's legs collapsed under him, twitching as his life blood spurted from the wound. The cow alarmed rushed to her calf's side and nuzzled it until she got a good smell of blood. Then she whirled about with her hackles raised, sniffed the air and looked for the source of her calf's affliction. Unable to detect the hunter's position she turned to the other calf and dashed across a beaver pond into a thick grove of aspen and out of sight. After an interval Wapaxo decided that it was safe to approach his kill. Determining that his accurate shot had achieved his goal and that the blood flow was sufficient to insure a well drained carcass he removed the arrow and headed for the camp site. Arriving at the camp he was pleased that Williwana and Beaver boy had everything in order and hated to tell them that he wanted to move the camp to the kill site. This of course angered Milliwana. They had built a lean-to, gathered wood, hobbled the horses and plucked spruce boughs for bedding. Compounding the problems was Milliwana's condition. She was pregnant and exhausted. She had not told Wapaxo of her condition for she had waited until she was sure. Surprised at her lashing out at him he angered and started to read her the riot act when he noticed how tired she was. Instead he told them of the large moose calf he had killed and that the new site that he had picked would be easier to protect from the huge grizzly that he had seen signs of. At the news of the grizzly Milliwana had flash-back memories of her last encounter with the sow Wapaxo had saved her from and reluctantly agreed to the move.

Wapaxo tried to convince Milliwana to rest that he and Beaver Boy could break camp. She replied with a coy smile, "I should be able to work harder for there is two of me." When the realization of what she was telling him hit him he felt both elated and anxious for they still had a good distance to go to reach the valley Jacque had described to him.

When Lame Wolf felt it was safe to climb down from the large spruce that he had escaped the old grizzly by climbing, he didn't waste much time inspecting the mangled bodies of his party. He simply took their amulets from around their necks and cautiously headed down the mountain. His Kiowa lodge was settled near the head waters of the Sun River. Exhausted he dropped to his knees in front of the main lodge babbling incoherently Grizzly Spirit Man. In order to explain the loss of his two comrades without looking like a coward he declared that he had seen the Grizzly Spirit Man change into a Grizzly bear in front of his eyes. After re-telling his story several times the Grizzly Spirit Man grew in size and the Bear that he had transformed into became larger than a horse. This was the camp Wapaxo, Beaver Boy and Williwana rode into. They didn't understand why the people and children ran and hid when they rode in until he heard Lame Wolf's story. By stating that he was a brother to the Grizzly and remarking about the huge size of the old grizzly, he made a friend for life in Lame Wolf.

The Kiowa were cousins of the Shoshone and there was frequent intermarriage between the two tribes. This made communications simple. When Wapaxo explained that he was on a hunting expedition and asking directions to buffalo territory, he invoked a long dissertation from Eagle Turns About, the tribe historian. The historian said, "you are early the big herds haven't journeyed toward the high mountain country yet. When they do there will be many tribes here." "Why many?" asked Beaver Boy." It is always so," answered the historian. Seeing the disbelief in the visitors eyes, the historian went on to explain, "Many winters ago before the horse, before the white man, during the time of the Dog People, the Ancient Ones followed watonka (buffalo), as the moon cycles made them restless and the Rain Gods brought flooding and drought. The buffalo were everything to the Ancient Ones. They provided food, shelter clothing, tools, and spirit guidance. Only Manitou, the Ruling God of Nature received more reverence. In order to have a successful hunt the hunters must "ten- sleeps" before the hunt perform hunting rituals? These include fasting, dancing and sweat-house purification." Anxiety settled over Wapaxo and Beaver Boy when they asked if the historian would help them with their preparations. After agreeing the historian said," they must erect the sweat lodge themselves. And the women must sleep in a separate lodge during the ritual to prevent distraction from their cleansing and invocations. The Medicine Man was consulted and the cleansing would begin in twenty days. The sweat-house cleansing would be the last ritual performed. The hunters would endure the sweat lodge for two hours. Counting Wapaxo and Beaver Boy there would be thirty hunters occupying the lodge in three shifts, ten to a shift. Wapaxo's logical mind told him this was probably the most important ritual of them all. By hanging their hunting clothes in the sweat lodge they would be penetrated with the scent of the balsam branches placed in the water that the heated stones would be immersed in to produce the steam. He chose the last shift so that Beaver Boy and he would be the last to receive the odor suppressing benefits. The sweat lodge construction was rapidly completed with thirty eager hunters pitching in with every phase. A thirty foot circular ditch was dug in a smooth flat area. A group of the hunters went to a near by grove of lodge pole pine and brought back many long slender green saplings that they placed but end into the ditch. Once the saplings were well packed into the ditch their tops were bent into the center and tied with ropes made from swamp grass. Leaving an entrance flap the frame was covered with buffalo hides leaving a vent hole at the top center. The outside of the shelter was circled with large round boulders to ground the buffalo robes. The floor was covered with spruce boughs leaving a 40 inch depression that was lined with a waterproof hide. The depression was filled with water and balsam boughs. Out side the entrance flap a large fire ring was placed handy to the entrance. This was lined with medium sized boulders gathered from the banks of the nearby Sun River. The hunters not first to enter the lodge remained in calling distance to replenish the heated stones as needed Meanwhile there was a buzz of activity around the women. When asked as to the occasion of the excitement, Milliwana was told that since there had been a heavy frost the previous night. The buffalo berries would be ready for harvest. "What are buffalo berries?" Milliwana asked. ": They are the best berries to make pemmican, they are sweet but tart and they preserve the meat", She was told by one of the older women. Asking further Milliwana was taught how to prepare pemmican. First you must dry the meat, pound the meat until it is fine, add tallow, (the best marrow), and mix with berries. Choke cherry berries make good pemmican, but they do not keep as well. This mixture is stuffed into the thoroughly cleaned small intestine of the buffalo and smoked to preserve. Milliwana remembering what she had learned from Wapaxo's family wondered how this could improve the variety of diet of the Klikitat using roe instead of tallow. The absence of small intestine casings would have to be solved. She planned to try and bring some of the berries home with her. Her pregnancy was becoming quite apparent, but it didn't slow her down or suppress her resolve to complete the hunt and butchering. At this time the western trio had not revealed to the Kiowa tribe that they had the precious salt cargo. Milliwana felt sure that the addition of salt to the pemmican receipt would improve its palatability and preservation.

The Medicine Man called all of the hunters together and said, "In three sleeps we should be in the valley of the Pishkun (Deep Blood Kettle.)*. What is The Pishkun"? Asked Wapaxo.The Story Teller stepped forward and told the tale of the Buffalo Jump.The ancient People that lived mainly from the buffalo didn't have any sophisticated weapons not even the spear throwing stick. To bring down even one buffalo was a major accomplishment. This meant that they had to hunt in groups armed with stone weapons. Many were injured and killed trying to kill enough animals to feed their families and tribes. The Pishkun site was a remarkable discovery for them! A gradual slope led to a bench land that was skirted on the south by a cliff that had broken away leaving a wedge shaped crevasse that trapped any animal that fell over the cliff. With much trial and error and lots of hunters they devised a buffalo drive. On the bench in front of the cliff they created a safety point where a young brave could dive into a shallow trench behind a large boulder and keep from being trampled to death This highly honored brave designated a "Buffalo Boy" would cover himself in a buffalo calf skin and entice a matriarch cow to approach him as he stealthily moved toward his safety trench making calf sounding calls. When the old matriarch was followed by the rest of the herd the drivers would begin chasing the main herd in her direction. If needed they used fire and anything that they could make noise with. The result was a stampede that forced the leading animals over the cliff unable to stop, being pushed by the panicking herd.

The more seriously injured with broken legs, dislocations and other injuries were hazed as far from the cliff as possible before they were slaughtered. The prairie land leading to the Missouri River bank was littered with butchering sites. Drying racks were erected and smoldering fires were set under them to aid in the drying and elimination of flies and other insects attracted to the raw flesh and blood. As the tribes learned they began to select non-resinous hard woods for smoking. These tended to impart a desirable flavor to the dried flesh making it more palatable. Smoke woods and rack material were gathered long before the drive began. With the advent of the horse the hunting parties became much smaller. The kills were not so messy and were more scattered.

*Montana Outdoors magazine; "Deep Blood Kettle" by Bruce Auchly July-August 1993.

The Kiowa Council Chief led the hunting party to their historical hunting grounds near the Sun River only to find his favorite camping grounds occupied by a Crow band. At first he was inclined to force them out, but there were plenty of choice spots so he considered the additional hunters as an asset since the Crow and the Kiowa were not antagonistic towards one another. The Crow War Chief came out to greet them and they agreed to have a smoke and make a plan of action. Beaver Boy saw the buffalo in the distance and asked, "Why are we camping so far from the game?" Running Fox one of the mature hunters explained, "We have learned that it is much better to let Tonka come to us closer to the river where we will have plenty of water to clean with. When the hunt starts the other tribes will push the buffalo toward us." The men set up the drying racks using the lodge pole they had brought with. The women were busy organizing the camp.Wapaxo accompanied several hunters across the river to hunt deer. They went a good distance from the camp before they attempted to bring down any of the white tailed deer that browsed amongst the willows and cottonwood saplings. After dressing out the deer, (normally women's work), they dragged them across the river to distribute. The women waited until the evening breeze was blowing from the south east away from the big herd in the distance. The buffalo (Tonka, Bison, Watonka), are wily beasts and have survived and multiplied by sensing every possible threat to their existence. To have a successful hunt the tribes learned to be as inconspicuous as possible. Before the hunt started the women, children and dogs were sent up river away from the hunting grounds. There they would remain until the killing ended then they would rush down to help with the butchering and meat preserving, when one of the younger hunters told them to come.

The early morning, before daylight, hunt was initiated by the movement of the herds. They are coming our way shouted one of the hunter look- outs. Excitement grew like a wild fire among the hunters. The women immediately began their departure from the area. The rumble of the drumming hoofs alerted everybody to the eminent size of the herd.

The formidable hunting group placed themselves in position to interdict the herd in a semicircle with a left and right flank.Wapaxo chose the left flank. Being right handed he wanted to be in position to inflict the lance like thrust to the lower intersection of the animals ear and neck. As taught to him by Jacque, this was a location where a principal nerve and an artery were adjacent. Severing of the nerve interrupted mobility and opening of the artery insured demise. Three buffalo had fallen to this strategy. It was the fourth one that created a problem for Wapaxo. His thrust hadn't been true and the yearling turned away with such force that it wrenched the spear from Wapaxos's grasp he had evidently missed the nerve. He lost his balance and fell from his pony. Seeing the peril of his hero Beaver Boy swung about and kept Wapaxo from being trampled. With three buffalo to his credit Wapaxo retired from the hunt. It wasn't until he heard of the Crow Hunter's claim to have killed a prize yearling with a spear in its neck that he went to investigate. At first what appeared to be a confrontation was settled when the elders declared that the arrow shot was not a fatal one... Wapaxo claimed the carcass and his spear.

Milliwana was exhausted trying to keep up with the butchering. Her pregnancy was a burden that was obvious to everybody. As the evening shadows settled on the camp the Council Chief approached Wapaxo's group, with him was a comely maiden. He introduced her as" Girl who belongs me". He offered her in trade for three bags of salt and a buffalo. After some haggling Wapaxo agreed to two bags of salt and one buffalo carcass as a fair trade for the "Girl Who Belongs me" The convincing argument of the Council Chief's position was that the girl was an accomplished mid-wife.

The butchering was completed and most of the flesh was sliced into strips for smoking. Wapaxo had gathered a large quantity of alder. This he knew would impart a desirable flavor to the smoked dried buffalo meat. Several of the camps had experienced raids by grizzly, wolves and coyotes. Most of the scavengers were attracted to the offal piles discarded as unusable by the hunters. All of the smaller intestines had been cleaned for casings for the pemmican. The large bones had been broken for the marrow used in the pemmican stuffing. The hides had been scraped and worked with brains and ashes to soften and tan them...

It was a brisk autumn morning that Milliwana assisted by Gee-Gee (the shortened name for the "Girl Who Belongs Me"), presented Wapaxo his son, promptly named "Buffalo Hunter". Celebrations were in order. The tribes feasted danced and smoked in joy for the success of the hunt and the advent of the new buffalo hunter.

For five days the small tribe prepared to travel while Milliwana attended to" Buffalo Hunter and allowed her body to accustom itself to the rigors of riding horse back .Wapaxo had been told about the Pishkun but he hadn't seen it. He asked the story teller to show him the famous buffalo jump. It was almost a days' ride from their camp to the Pishkun.When they approached the cliff from the prairie side. Immediately Wapaxo could feel the magic of the place. He could visualize the masses of buffalo streaming over the cliff. Smell the death and the following smoke fires that followed a successful kill." This isn't all", the Story Teller told him, "See the large flat topped butte in the distance"? Before there was a Pishkun the ancient ones attempted to solve their feast and famine cycle by herding buffalo to an area where they had built a stone fence to direct the buffalo to the top. The Idea was that they could more successfully hunt them in a smaller area as they needed fresh meat. Satisfied Wapaxo led the way back to the camp. There was an immediate problem. The pack horses and the riding horses were over loaded. Gee-Gee would have to walk. Beaver Boy said, "I will change off with Gee- Gee and walk half of the time." They had bonded and without ceremony they became a couple. The ceremony would have to wait for the proper time. They were several days out from the Kiowa camp before they noticed one of the Kiowa dogs had followed them. At first he was shy and only approached when food was offered him and only if it was offered by Gee -Gee. It was apparent that he had become attached to her when she was a member of the Kiowa clan. They promptly named him Gee Dog.

It was late autumn when the travelers awoke to a light snow covering. They were in the valley of the joining rivers. Just as they were breaking camp they heard a shout, "HOIKA."

There was no mistaking the broad shoulders and regal bearing of Jacque. With him were two women each riding fine horses and leading two pack horses. The bond between Wapaxo and Jacque was instantly seen through the clasp of their left hands and arms in greeting...

After the formalities of introduction the group settled into a circle of discussion. Jacque wanted to know all about their trip and hunt and Wapaxo had questions about what Jacque had been doing and why he had two women with him? Jacque explained that he had returned to the Shoshone tribe of his mother and there had married Pillar. When they left Pillar's sister Neena had asked to join them. Her husband had recently been killed by a buck deer that he had approached thinking it was dead." Speaking of buck deer ", Jacque said as he went to the last horse of his train and unloaded a fine two point.

While the women prepared a feast the men smoked and told stories. Jacque showed Wapaxo and Beaver Boy his buffalo gun a sharps 45/70 .Cautiously the two younger men hefted the heavy weapon and asked many questions. Jacque took them aside away from the horses and demonstrated the abilities of the rifle. Picking a rock about 300 yards away Jacque set the rifle on its bipod and blasted away. The two young bucks and the women at camp jumped at the booming sound. The shattered rock was a marvel to the bow hunters. The two young hunters begged to try their hand at the astounding weapon, but Jacque told them all in good time that he planned to travel with them back to their home grounds

Jacque brought new excitement to the group when he told them of seeing a white buffalo two sleeps back on the trail.

That night Wapaxo and Beaver Boy couldn't sleep they had to see the white buffalo

With the women settled in, the horses hobbled and the large shaggy dog on guard the three men made a hard dash back to the valley of the white buffalo. As calculated by Jacque they topped the ridge of the valley early of the second morning. The first objects to come into view were the three large wagons. To the right of the wagons two women could be seen working on hides stretched out on the ground. Hanging further to the right was the hide of the white buffalo. In horror and disgust Jacque said, "The lowest of man creatures the hide hunters have killed the Spirit Buffalo." He went on to explain the nature of the hide hunters, "they kill watonka just for their hides, leaving the rest of the animal to waste." Why?" asked Wapxo. "Money" answered Jacque. "What is money?" asked Beaver Boy. There being no words in Indian language that depicted money Jacque answered, "Trade goods". The three warriors tethered their horses and crept closer. ".Look", exclaimed Wapaxo, The women seem to be captives they are tethered to the tree by their working area."Jacque just grunted and told Wapaxo to creep closer while he went to the top of a little knoll that would give him a better overlook of the total area. The two young braves crept stealthily toward the flat area that seemed to be the center of the encampment. When they stood up two startled men grasped for their weapons, but not soon enough, Beaver Boy and Wapaxo had them dead to rights and they fell in their tracks each with a well placed arrow protruding from their backs. The third hide hunter had observed the deaths of his two companions and was bringing his rifle up to focus on Wapaxo when his chest exploded outward, followed by the boom of the sharps 45/70 Anticipating more trouble the two younger hunters scrambled for hiding. It was only when one of the young girls shouted in glee, "You have killed all of them", that the bow shooters relaxed and stepped forward.

...

Not hearing the maiden's remarks Jacque continued to scout the perimeter of the camp until he was satisfied that there was no more danger from the hide hunters. Beaver Boy sliced the tethers of the hide scrapers. They massaged their ankles and wept with joy at their freedom. Both of them were speaking at once and only Beaver Boy seemed to understand them. Wapaxo tried to get them to slow down and only one at a time speaks. The maidens went back to the hides they had been working on. Jacque explained that they didn't have to do this, but they insisted saying, "It would be wrong for Tonka to give up his life if his hide does not make a good robe"

Jacque began to explore the camp area and was astonished at the richness and variety of the possessions of the hide hunters. The eldest of the group had possessed a sh45/70 like his and hundreds of rounds of ammunition, loading tools, powder, and primers to reload spent shells. With the sharps were six repeating Henry rifles and at least a thousand cartridges. There were many knives some very good ones and lots of trade knives. There were hatches, axes, a cross cut saw and a jack saw. In one of the wagons were trade goods consisting of beads, bright colored cloth, needles, scissors, trade mirrors, pots, pans and a large cast kettle and a smaller one. In a separate bag there were two dozen beaver traps. Some of them were stamped with PL, (Jacque's father Pierre Leblanc's traps). It was evident these men had been more than just greedy hide hunters, they had been robbers. They had waylaid traders, emigrants, and soldiers as was evidenced by the army revolvers and holsters they were wearing and had in the trade wagon.

On the way to the spot where Jacque had met Wapaxo's group and after sighting the white buffalo Jacque had scouted a cave with a large overhanging shelf rock. He had anticipated camping there but had decided to move on for his information about Wapaxo's whereabouts was patchy and he had to spend a lot of his time scouting from high places to determine the hunters trail. Believing he could pull the smaller of the three wagons to the cave he discussed it with the two younger men and it was decided that Wapaxo would head immediately back to his camp. Break camp and join Jacque and the others at the cave as soon as possible. Jacque, Beaver Boy and the two maidens would go to the cave. This place with the hide hunters and the crying spirit of the white buffalo had a bad aura. They loaded the three skin hunter's bodies on one of the wagons, pulled the other along side of it in the middle of a clearing. Covered them with brush and downed timber and set it on fire. When they were sure the fire would not spread they loaded the small wagon, placed the white buffalo hide on top in a place of honor and broke camp. Four horses pulled the wagon two of the work horses and two of the saddle horses were trailed behind. Wapaxo had taken one of the saddle horses for Gee-Gee to ride. They arrived at the cave before dark and set up camp. Wapaxo and the women arrived at mid day. When Milliwana saw the backs of the maidens she shuddered in horror. They were raw from the beatings they had taken she went immediately to her medicine bag; made poultices applied them to the girl's backs and forced them to retire. After the morning meal and a tea made from juniper berries and wild rose hips the two captives rebounded to good spirits. Sitting in a circle the new comers recounted how they had been captured when they were gathering fire wood. There were three of us. "They beat my aunt to death because she wouldn't touch the white buffalo's hide." explained the eldest of the two, "we were not so brave or strong". The white buffalo had special significance for them. Their Council Chief was revered for saving his tribe during the "Starving Time." It was three winters ago that the tribe had run out of food. Game was very scarce because of the droughts and the severe weather. They had eaten their dogs and their horses. Chief Che He Kahakichee (Little Fox) was hunting for anything they could eat when he came upon the tracks of tonka. The snow was deep and the air had a sharp bite as he plowed forward, weakened from hunger. He didn't see the animal that had made the tracks until he topped a small rise and spotted the white buffalo joining a small herd at the edge of an aspen grove. Immediately he turned back to the village for help. All of the able hunters gathered and pursued the buffalo while the women and those left behind broke camp and followed. The hunt was successful and the tribe soon regained their stamina. The white buffalo was never seen again and the doubters began to think the Chief had hallucinated.

The captive girls were named Zena and Kallila; Zena was the elder and did most of the talking. She said, "Now they will know the Chief spoke with a straight tongue." The girls didn't know what direction their village was, but they did remember it was to the north of a tall mountain that had snow on its peak year around. .Beaver Boy remembered such a peak from their trip to the Pishkun area. He stated that he believed he could lead them home.

With three riding horses and a pack horse they set off for the village. It had been agreed that the white buffalo robe should go to Chief Chee He Kahakichee (Little Fox) they were only gone for two sleeps when the camp was hailed with a "HOIKA". Riding into camp was the strangest native Jacque and Wapaxo's group had ever seen. He was a strapping young brave normal in appearance except for his hair and his eyes. He was the result of partial albinism. His hair was black except for a large shock of white hair on the back of his head. His eyes were a pale blue. He had something in common with the white buffalo and was considered a Medicine Man with great powers. His was an unusual message. Chief Little Fox, being familiar with the cave Wapaxo's party was occupying was requesting permission to winter with them. Wapaxo looked to Jacque for guidance. He told Wapaxo to ask, How Many, deferring to Wapaxo for the decision. Thinking about the security of Milliwana and Buffalo Hunter, Wapaxo went over to speak to Milliwana. Jacque thought this strange for his culture didn't include women in decisions. He was glad he had spoken to Milliwana for she asked, "What is the general health of the village's people?" Only then did Jacque see the knowledge in consulting Milliwana. "How are you called?" asked Wapaxo. "I am Peelee Denko, named because of my hair looking like a white tailed deer." answered the brave. "There are 37 men and women and some elderly and children. Most of the elderly and

small children died during the starving winter he explained."
There was one consideration that both Jacque and Wapaxo
had thought of. It was their weakness in numbers. They were
in the fringes of the Black Foot country. Who were noted to
be war like and often taken to raiding parties. After further
discussion Wapaxo said he would consult with Little Fox and
Make a decision then." We will need all of the horses you can
spare," Said Peelee. Milliwana wanted to go and see for herself,
but that wasn't practical with her nursing responsibilities. In
her place Gee-Gee agreed to go and look the women over.
Peelee led off leading the string of horses. Wapaxo brought up
the rear wearing a pistol and carrying one of the henry rifles
and plenty of cartridges.

There were plenty of warm greetings. The intent was
evident when Chief Little Fox seen the horses. They rested
and smoked. Gee- Gee went immediately to the women and
studied them for signs of disease. Seeing none she reported
back to Wapaxo. Wapaxo had noted that the white buffalo pelt
had been given a lodge of its own. He thought this to be a
good sign. That is when he told Little Fox that there could
only be one Council Chief and one War Chief. Little Fox said,
"I can be happy as a Sub Chief under you. It is plain that you
are of good heart as proven by your gift of the Spirit Buffalo's
pelt. Even with the horses Wapaxo had brought with him the
trip would be arduous. All of the walkers had to carry burdens.
The trip took five days. Milliwana had prepared a feast that was
simmering in the largest of the cast iron kettles secured from
the hide hunters. Chief Little Fox's people set up their camp in
one side of the huge cave overhang. The white buffalo hide was
fastened to the back of the cavern in a place of prominence.
It began to rain and everybody was glad for the shelter of
the cave overhang. The morning came early for the village.
Wapaxo assembled a crew and they went to a distant forest and
cut lodge poles to cover the front of the cave. He had been
anxious to use the jack saw as demonstrated by Jacque. For a
stone- age warrior this was a miracle tool. The work horses had
been able to drag all of the needed poles back to the village in

one trip. Anchoring the bases of the poles with large stones, leaning them against the face of the overhang, and covering them with buffalo hides, the cave was secure from bad weather. Gee Dog was the first to detect trouble. He growled and went to Gee- Gee while .looking out over the face of the incline leading into the cave. She went to see what he was complaining about and saw nothing.Peele had been interested in the traps from the hide hunters. In addition to being the Medicine Man for Little Foxes' tribe he was the trapping expert. His traps had consisted of snares and dead falls. None of which could successfully be used to capture beaver. The two streams below were full of beaver as was evidenced by the multitude of beaver dams.Beaver Boy and Peelee went to scout the area and look to the horses. Armed with only one of the henry rifles they were disturbed to see the tracks of a large grizzly. That the bear was a large one was evident by the fresh print in the mud of the creek bank. With caution they inspected the print and noticed that water was still seeping into the track. It had just passed .Concerned about the horses they went to the corralled area to find the horses gone except for the oldest of the work horses. It was dead and partially eaten. Fortunately Wapaxo had kept two riding horses hobbled near the cave. This is one of the times the cave dwellers were glad to have a sizable force to track down and capture the runaways. Again they had to cut more lodge pole and build a corral near the cave. Using the trade knives men, women, and large children set about harvesting meadow grass for animal feed. They twisted the grass into ropes and bound the bundles and stored them in the back of the huge cavern.

The big male grizzly stayed in the area, but he didn't re-visit the dead horse as if it seemed to know that Jacque was waiting for him with the sharps. Just as the hay gatherers were quitting for the day the horses began acting up and the harvesters knew the grizzly was within their scent area. He was thoroughly irritated by the presence of this strange group blocking his traditional hibernation den. He had been born there and had re-visited it every year and intended to do so this year too. The mixture of smells confused the big male and he stood up to survey the area. This was his last mistake for Jacque seen him and the big sharps rifle spoke. A deadly ear shot dropped him in his tracks.

Not knowing when they would need the wagon again Jacque, Beaver Boy and Peelee dismantled the wagon and greased all of the parts with bear grease. Inspecting the wagon Jacque noticed something strange. The bed seemed too thick. Out of curiosity he pried a couple of the bottom planks off and discovered a hidden storage area. Carefully packed under the false floor was a treasure. Carefully wrapped were a surveyor's compass, a sailor's brass telescope, and a bundle of surgeon's tools. Toward the back of the wagon were shovels, gold pans, rolls of soft wire, six more Henry Rifles, a small buckskin bag holding twenty double eagle gold coins and another with gold nuggets. Jacque was astounded at the wealth. Wapaxo asked what the gold coins were and again Jacque tried to explain money to him. When Jacque showed him the nuggets Wapaxo told him that he had seen yellow rocks like these in a stream bed on his way over the mountains. When questioned where? He replied, "I know approximately, but Beaver Boy will know for sure"

Without an election or council meeting the camp accepted Wapaxo as Council Chief, Jacque as War Chief, Beaver Boy as Guard Sub-Chief, and Peelee as Hunting/Trapping Sub-Chief. The white buffalo pelt hanging high on the back wall seemed to have an influence on everybody's attitude and actions. Jacque selected six of Little Foxx's braves for guard duty. He issued each of them a henry rifle and set about training them in its use and care. Beaver Boy gave each of the guards an appointed time of two hours to protect the camp. The tribe made sure they were adequately dressed and that they had buckskin scabbards for their henry rifles. It wasn't one of the guards that noticed something was amiss. Gee Dog alerted GeeGee that there were strangers in the woods at the edge of the valley below the camp.

Jacque picked a good vantage point to overlook the timber edge. Settled out of sight he studied the area through his newly acquired telescope. Although very cautious the six war painted braves below didn't know the advantage Jacque had with his telescope. He presumed they were Black Feet and mentally chuckled when he thought about how they had obtained their tribal name. It was actually Peds Noir, French for Black Feet. They had been so named by French Trapper Explorers who came upon them after they had crossed a burnt out stretch that covered their feet with black ashes. Suspecting that this was an unfriendly scouting party, he doubled the guards watch period to four hours and two guards per shift.

In the slope in front of the cavern he had the people dig five fox holes. These had a breastwork in front of them that would hide the occupant and still allow him to see his portion of what Jacque figured would be the attack frontal. Expecting the attack would be at day light so the fox holes were not occupied at night. Jacque and Wapaxo took up positions above the cliff overhang. They both had 45/70 sharps and henry rifles in case the raiding party came from that direction.

It was four days before the raiders attacked. Again it was Gee Dog that gave the alarm.

Everybody was in place. Jacque gave a tug on the string that alerted the fox-hole guards. It was a large war party and when they came into rifle range they were mowed down in a bitter cross fire. The Blackfoot warriors hadn't expected guns and were completely demoralized.

Jacque located the high ground where the cowardly War Chiefs had positioned themselves. Motioning to Wapaxo to take the one on the right he sighted on the left Chief. The two big 45/70s boomed at about the same time and both adversaries were blown from their horses. When the attackers saw their Chiefs fall they lost all heart and melted into the woods, not even collecting their dead and leaving the abandoned horses to be collected by Little Foxe's tribe. Only one of the tribe was killed. It was the one that in the rush of battle deserted his fox hole and rushed forward to count coup.The abandon horses were quickly rounded-up and the area was scouted for any sign of further aggression. There would be heavy mourning in the Black Foot tribe for the next week and little chance that they would attempt another attack.

Peelee resumed his trapping and his success had many of the women busy cleaning and curing beaver pelts. There was one pelt that he cared for himself. This one he brought to Milliwana's gathering and presented to Neena saying, "If you use this to cover your braids you will look like me. The pelt was a fine pure white weasel pelt... Neena blushed and now everybody knew why Peelee had spent so much time with the women that clustered around Milliwana. It wasn't as they had supposed that it was his interest in improving his status as a Medicine Man that he was learning Milliwana's collective wisdom about the use of herbal treatments that she had known as a young girl and what she had learned from Wapaxo.It was his interest in Neena. He had looked at her and she at him. Milliwana had known but she was glad that Jacque had declared that her mourning period had passed and that she was free to form another association. Winter had become boring. The hunters had been able to keep the people fed. The cattail roots that Milliwana encouraged Peelee to look for had provided a supplement to their diet.

With everybody morose and bored Jacque suggested they learn a new game. The men were divided into teams of four. A plan was drawn in the dirt of the cave floor. A box was placed at each end of the forty foot playing field. Two lines were drawn in front of the boxed ends. The braves were sent to collect strong forked willows from the valley; Jacque cut and shaped the sturdy ones into shuffleboard shafts. Next he sent them to gather thin flat stones

From the edges of the sedimentary stones that sloped away from the cave entrance. These were worked into flat stones of about the same size. In the large boxed ends he placed four arrows in each far corner. In the subsequent spaces he put two arrows in the corners of the first, (narrowest space) and one arrow in the next larger one. Using the forked sticks the object was to scoot the stone into the box. Credit was given for stones that didn't make into the end box according to the amount of arrows placed in their corners; a stop line was placed at about twelve feet. No feet were allowed beyond.

The challenge was accepted and the games began A problem was detected early. The lines became undistinguishable. Jacque solved this problem by having flat stones driven into the lines making them distinct and permanent. Rivalry became rampant and the chiefs had to remind the participants and their boosters that it was only a game.

Game animals from the local area were depleted so a hunting party was formed. Taking off with two pack animals the four hunters headed in the direction chosen by Peelee. There was no sign of buffalo and deer were scarce. Three days out they struck sign of wapiti (elk). They dismounted and studied the tracks. They were not fresh so Jacque didn't expect to see any as he scanned the valley and the edges of the timber. The telescope was a godsend. With it he could normally distinguish the different animals but also their sex. They crested the next ridge and spotted movement in the distance. Fading in and out of the timber was what looked like a herd of twelve animals. Jacque dismounted and scanned the herd with the telescope. It appeared that the herd consisted of only cows. It was Peelee that remarked that the bulls had not left the cows yet but soon would as they started the new growth of velvety horns.This presented a problem for the cows were most likely full with calves. They were hunting with the henry rifles which didn't have the range of the sharps. The hunters splitting into two pairs approached the herd from opposite sides, picketed their horses and stalking the animal to get into range close enough to distinguish the small protrusions of future horns. They didn't want to kill any cows. When they shot only three animals dropped, it appeared that one of them had been hit twice... Beaver Boy was surprised by a large bull charging directly at him. Not having a chance to carefully sight, he snapped off a shot that brought the bull down but didn't kill it. When he stepped forward to slice the jugular vein he was met with a flying front foot. Bruised but not really injured he grabbed his rifle and dispatched the elk with a well placed behind the ear shot. Skinned, dressed and quartered the elk were divided into loads and packed on the horses. The hunters were forced to walk back to the village. It soon became apparent that they could not make it back without walking all night. Picking a sheltered spot they camped for the night. They rear- hobbled the horses so that they could paw through the snow for grass. Smelling the fresh meat, wolves and coyotes could be heard calling to one another. The fire and human smells kept them at bay but they caused the horses to be restless and the hunters had to take turns patrolling the herd.

With the cooking fires busy and an atmosphere of celebration permeating the camp it was decided to have a double wedding. Everybody had accepted Beaver Boy and Gee-Gee as a couple and her pregnancy was known, but Peelee and Neena hadn't announced their betrothal even though Jacque had released her from her mourning period .The ermine skin covering Neena's braid spoke louder than words and the rejoicing began. Che He Kahakichee (Chief Little Fox), being the eldest Chief automatically accepted the charge of performing the ceremony.

Jacque had chosen for himself one of the draft animals taken from the hide hunters. She was a smaller version of the Belgian breed a pale brown with the buckskin characterization of a dark streak down her back and a dark mane and tail. Jacque was walking around her and he noticed the roundness of her belly. She was carrying a colt. Without a doubt Wapaxo's appaloosa stallion had done what comes naturally. She whinnyed and to Jacque's surprise a young long legged moose calf came to her and began nursing. Jacque smiled in recognition of Manitou's power. She was pregnant and started lactating before giving birth to satisfy the need of the moose calf. Peelee had told them of finding the remains of a moose kill by wolves.

Evidently the calf had remained hidden and sought out the company of the horses when it couldn't find its mother.

Beaver Boy was boasting that he would soon be the father of a future supreme hunter.

Milliwana didn't agree; she predicted Gee- Gee would have a girl as beautiful as her mother.

Her accurate prediction enhanced Milliwana's reputation as a Medicine Woman and her services became in great demand. Peelee was glad that he hadn't made any predictions for he had mentally agreed with Beaver Boy. The baby was as beautiful as her mother and Beaver Boy vowed to teach her to hunt. This was not a far fetched idea for Wapaxo had been teaching all of the young people in the use of the sling. As a result Milliwana's medicine practice increased dramatically as carelessness and inaptitude resulted in several injuries. Practice paid off as the youngsters increased their skills the tribe's diet was enhanced with an increase of small game, rabbits, squirrels, and grouse.

The advent of warm weather meant that the snow in the high country would be receding and the passes would be opened for the travelers. The preparations were not frenzied rather slow and deliberate. A sizable amount of the cured buffalo pemmican and jerky was left for the trip. Wapaxo was a little concerned about Jacques actions. He seemed especially concentrated on the shovels, gold pans, and a log he was keeping. He had gold fever.

The travelers took two of the large draft horses that they had equipped with special packs. The remaining four were left with Little Fox's tribe. These and the horses that the Black Foot party had abandoned left the home tribe in good condition. Jacque left them with six of the henry rifles and a hundred rounds of ammunition. He cautioned them to hunt with bows in order to save the rifle ammunition for possible attacks

After the good -bys and Little Fox's entreaty for them to return, they left. It was an odd caravan for the moose calf remained at the Belgian's side. Badger Boy led off for he had an uncanny ability to be a path finder. He remembered all of the landscape features that he had passed on the way to the buffalo hunt. They made their first camp early in the evening of the first day. Each settled into their routine of chores. Peelee took over the chore of looking after the horses. Wapaxo intrigued with the jack saw gathered poles to make lean-tos. The women built fires and prepared meals. When ever they camped by a stream Jacque took a shovel and gold pan and worked the streams gravel. When evening light permitted he would take his bow and look for a deer.

They made another early camp when they reached the eastern edge of the bitter root range. That evening Beaver Boy and Wapaxo took Jacque down a narrow deer trail to the floor below the bench that they had camped on. They brought the two gold pans and shovels. The stream was crystal clear shallow and as wide as three tall men lying down.

Jacque was in Heaven. He waded into the cold water and began working the gravel, digging in the crevices of the bed rock and shouting with glee. There was lots of color and grain sized nuggets. It was only when it became too dark to see that Jacque gave up. The next day he grabbed a handful of jerky and headed down the trail as soon as it was light enough to see his way. Peelee completely baffled by this queer action remained with the women and hunted for small game. There were plenty of grouse and some snowshoe rabbits. When Wapaxo and Beaver Boy joined Jacque they found him next to a large fire. He had fallen in the creek and was blue with cold. As soon as he was warm enough that his teeth didn't chatter he was back in the creek. Each evening Jacque gathered his small pouches of yellow rocks and stowed them secretly in one of the Belgian's packs. It was the fifth day and Wapaxo and Beaver Boy were fed up. That evening they were going to confront Jacque and tell him they wanted to continue the trip. Even the horses were restless and skittish. There was thunder and it started to rain. The bench they were camped on seemed to lift and shake and there was a loud roar. The slide area on the opposite side of the small canyon tumbled down into the creek bed. The creek water went underground. The travelers contributed the earth quake to action of Manitou. It had somehow been wrong to extract the yellow stones from the creek bed so Manitou had covered them and sent the creek away.

Being somewhat more sophisticated Jacque only seen an opportunity lost. He had intended to return and had been taking compass readings and marking prominent land marks in his log book. Brooding about the lost of the gold bonanza made Jacque morose and uncommunicative. His moodiness and preoccupation was felt by all of the rest of the travelers. It was only when the moose calf came into the camp and went directly to Jacque and nuzzled him as if to sympathize with his loss that Jacque's mood changed. Manitou had sent the calf to forgive the travelers for their transgression. Everybody smiled and settled in to enjoy a good breakfast before continuing on their way. On descending the western slopes of the mountains Beaver Boy began to feel the exhilaration of going home. Game was plentiful and the horses were belly deep in forage. Milliwana was especially pleased when she found a patch of camas, (quamash). The blue star shaped blossoms could be found in the low marshy fields. She quickly instructed the strangers to this plant on how to gather it. The bulbous roots were roasted in beds of hot stones. The Nez Perce Indians had harvested this plant for many generations it being a main staple of their diet.Milliwana inspected every bulb gathered, discarding those, (death camas) that didn't confirm to the food plants configuration. Since this was an exceptional patch of camas Milliwana asked Beaver Boy to remember it for future harvests.

The Ponocs were not in the camp where Wapaxo had been nourished to health after his encounter with the grizzly sow. locating them wouldn't be a simple task for they selected each camp by the availability of camas. Since the camas harvesting had to done when the plants were in bloom, for the blue flowered camas was edible and the white blossomed was toxic. . It was up to beaver Boy to locate them by scouting previous sites and areas that he had known to be productive in the distant past. .

Milliwana wanted to accompany him but it wasn't practical since she still was nursing Buffalo Hunter. It was decided that Peelee should go with Beaver Boy and that he take one of the henry rifles with. Beaver Boy took his bow and arrows and one of the good hunting knives. After three days rest and much palavering the two young braves headed south. Jacque had sent the telescope with them and they took turns marveling at the instrument

Beaver Boy knew that recent camp sites wouldn't likely be their present location for as much as they practiced conservation the camas plant was slow to recover after extensive harvest.Camas is a member of the lilly family and prefers low moist grass lands, this deprived the scouts of high places so they often had to climb trees to scope out large areas.

Peelee was high up a large tamarack tree when he spotted an unusual altercation. A big boar badger and young black bear were both claiming a deer carcass that was either a winter kill or it had died of old age. The black bear was several times the size of the badger but the badger made up in ferocity what he lacked in size. His advantage was the carcasses proximity to his hole. The bear would pull the carcass away and begin to eat and the badger would pull it back. Not seeing any sign of the new village he started down the tree when he noticed a mountain lion stalking the horses they had tied to a sapling. The lion crouched and Peelee shot it just before it sprang... Alarmed Beaver Boy shouted, "What is going on?" After jumping the last few feet to the ground Peelee took Beaver Boy to the lion." Do you think he was after me?" inquired Beaver Boy." NO! Way," answered Peelee laughing, "You wouldn't be near as good a meal as one of the horses." During a lunch of pemmican and camas patty, Peelee told Beaver Boy about the bear and the badger. Why don't I get to see anything good like that when I climb a tree?" he asked.Peelee answered laughing, "You are probably too busy hanging on". Using their slings the two scouts were able to bag two plump cotton tailed rabbits. After five days into the search a camp was spotted. They rode in only to find another tribe, but they knew where the Poncos were camped so they continued another day north, glad it was in the direction they had started from. One of the young braves from the camp had spotted the rifle and decided to steal it. He followed the two scouts to their next camp. Fearing something like this Peelee had set a trap. To the surprise of the teenager he found himself hanging from a sapling. At first they were going to kill him but Beaver Boy simply cut off one of his ears. "Let him explain that", he laughed.

In the tradition of Jacque and Wapaxo the two scouts brought a prime buck into camp with them. The two young scouts were feted and praised. The questions were fast and furious.Peelee did manage to tell them the story of the bear and the badger. Who won out? Everybody wanted to know. When Peelee told them that he didn't see the end of the struggle the old chief said, "It was the badger. And he went on to explain that the bear in disgust would reach his paw into the beaver's hole and receive a painful wound that would cause him to withdraw"

Early the next morning the two scouts left for the old camp site to rejoin Wapaxo's tribe. It only took them two sleeps since they knew the way. When they came into camp they were surprised to see only a few of their travel companions were there. They didn't even get a rest and they were off again. Milliwana not wanting to waste time waiting on the scouts had asked Wapaxo to move back down the trail that Beaver Boy and Peelee had just traveled. She knew of a small patch of camas and wanted to harvest it during the wait. .They were in before night fall and were bombarded with questions about the Poncos tribe and their trip. On leaving the Poncos village Jacque asked everybody not to speak about the creek that is no more. To talk of this would bring bad luck to them and the Poncos.

Milliwana's father agreed with the other chief concerning the bear and the badger. He said there were few animals that will attack a badger that has backed into his hole. The lion pelt was of no value since it was too warm for the fir to be well set. After the feasts, dancing and smokes they settled into story telling. Milliwana asked if they had hunted Prong Horn, (antelope). When they stated that they hadn't he said, "You missed the best meat." When they spoke of how fast the antelope were he asked, "Did you know that an antelope doesn't have any dew claws?" The story came out. In the ancient times the deer and the antelope were arguing who was the fastest. They agreed to have a race the antelope bet his dew claws and the deer bet his gall bladder. The antelope picked a valley with small rolling hills and of course the deer lost his gall bladder. The deer complained that it wasn't a fair race since the antelope had picked his home territory. So they agreed to hold another race this time in the woods with downed timber. The deer jumps over obstacles and the antelope ducks under them. Thus the antelope lost his dew claws and to this date the deer has no gall bladder and the antelope has no dew claws. Amused at the story everybody turned in for the night.

Story tellers are the heart of tribal society. Not only is tribal history passed to the following generations so is myth and lore.Minikopa the story teller of the Ponocs was a revered member of the tribe and his evening dissertations were attended by all. This evening he spoke of the "Bear People". The recounting of Wapaxo's tribe of their cave settlement had reminded Minikopa of the ancient myth of the Bear People. Among the ancient people of the far north was a tribe of people that were relatives of the black bear. They were great hunters and gatherers. As the snow receded in the spring the Bear People seemed to spring from the ground like the new years growth. They went forth in the woodlands and sought out plants and small animals for sustenance One of the staples of their diet was the under bark (cambium). They practiced good conservation by not girdling the deciduous trees that they preferred. They were peaceful people but very reclusive. They always built their shelters in front of cave openings. After the first heavy snow, usually in December they seemed to disappear.

The belief of the neighboring tribes is that they hibernated like bears. It was known that in their foraging they searched far and wide for fungi, (mushrooms). There was a special mushroom that they cultivated and harvested in November. It is believed that eating this mushroom put them into a hibernation mode and they slept through the months of December, January, February and the first part of March. It appeared that when they awoke in the spring that they had not aged any during their sleep and in fact seemed to have rejuvenated from any aging they had done in the previous year. This extended their lives considerably and baring any accidents they were thought to live in excess of one hundred and fifty winters. They were often seen in the company of pet black bears. With this to think about the people retired for the evening.

That next morning Milliwana brought a package to Jacque asking him, "What kind of needles are these?" Jacque looked in surprise and answered, "They are fishing hooks." Not familiar with the term Milliwana asked him to explain. It being easier to demonstrate than to explain, Jacque took a long piece of her strongest thread and tied the hook on the end. He then took the largest of her beads and put it a distance of the length of her foot above the hook. Wapaxo was watching this with amusement and curiosity. Next Jacque went to the nearby stream bank and selected a long willow branch. This he trimmed back to a small tapered pole. Next he brought out from the plunder of the hide hunters a roll of soft wire, (bailing wire).He laid the wire on a rock and cut off two lengths by pounding it with another rock. With a small hard twig he made a loop that he fastened to the end of the pole with several twists of the wire. Moving down the pole he fastened another loop. Threading the thread through the two loops and tying the end a short distance of the large end. He had a fishing pole that would allow him to control the length of line. They went down to the stream and he began turning over rocks on the bank next to the water until he found a water bug. With it on the hook he tossed the hook into a pool and pulled out an eleven inch cut throat trout. Fascinated Wapaxo wanted to try. Before long he had a nice mess of trout and he himself was hooked for life. From this time forward Wapaxo spent every spare minute at the stream.

All of the stories had been told and re-told and Wapaxo wanted to head west to his tribal grounds. Milliwana however wasn't finished visiting with her family and friends and friction arose between them. This was the second time they had serious differences. When they had left Little Fox's people Milliwana wanted to bring the large cast iron cooking pot with them and Wapaxo had said no it was too large and heavy to be hauled such a long distance. Milliwana had visioned giving it to her tribe where it would be cherished for cooking camas.

Milliwana was torn between her attachment to Wapaxo and her longing to remain with her tribe. Leaving Wapaxo's bed and wrapping herself in a robe she moved to the other side of the Hogan. Wapaxo was unable to fathom her mood and became withdrawn and morose. Seeking advice he went to Jacque and unburdened himself. Jacque in his knowing way went to his bag of gold coins; extracted one bored a hole in it, threaded a leather throng through it and told Wapaxo, "Go put this around her neck." After showing off her necklace she was cuddled to Wapaxo the next evening. Three days later the hunters were on their way west. Much to Beaver Boys frustration the trek was interrupted every time they came to a prospect creek. Jacque would grab his shovel and gold pan and head down stream. Wapaxo would grab his fishing pole and start looking for insects and trout. Milliwana thought this was very childish, but at least the diet was supplemented with trout. This was all great as far as Peelee was concerned. This left the hunting to him. He was as skilled with the bow as any of the others. The use of the bow to hunt was a necessity to preserve ammunition for the rifles. Jacque had the most disappointment for seldom did he strike any color. His memory wouldn't let the excitement leave him when he thought of the creek that was no more. It had been a prospector's heaven. Beaver Boys skill at path finding helped alleviate the divergence of the prospector and the fisherman's dalliance. Peelee had acquired a handsome four point buck to bring into the Klikitat camp. Again it was celebration time; after smoking, eating, and dancing came story telling time.

This had been a good year for the salmon run. The tribe's larder was overflowing much to Wapaxo's delight for he savored the delicious familiar repast. The story that most interested the travelers were the reports of the large ship seen when the trading party had gone for salt. It had appeared only at a distance because the sea was too rough for the large vessel to approach the shore. Jacque had seen the big ships on what is now known as the Oregon coast. Anxious for a chance to see such a sight, Wapaxo immediately began a plan for a trading expedition.Beaver Boy remained with the women as Wapaxo, Jacque, and Peelee assembled their trading goods and headed for the coast. This time Wapaxo deviated to the obsidian deposit on the way to the coast. He was able to accumulate lots of arrow making shards and two large slabs that could be made into duplicates of his big spear point.

The Puyallup tribe that was the traditional traders with the Klikitats was delighted to see Wapaxo and welcomed him in a true potlatch fashion. Much to Wapaxo's surprise the leaders of the tribe were most interested in the obsidian knives and shards he had collected... Of equal interest were the trade knives secured from the hide hunters. As tradition dictated it was party time. Feasting, dancing, and smoking brought everybody to a point of exhaustion

After the sweat hut and purification rites the trading and haggling began. Jacque being the most sophisticated of the group had fixed on the idea of the value of the sea otter pelts. The salt was the main item for Wapaxo and the only consideration with it was its weight. A plan was forming in Jacque's mind. The salt and the sea otter pelts would bring big rewards at the white man's trading post on the coast south of the mother river.

There had not been any more sightings of the big ships much to the chagrin of Wapaxo.The was the point where

Jacque planted the thought seed for a trading expedition to the coastal area south of Mother River. With everything traded the Puyallup council insisted upon another feast. Along with the feast they gave their visitors a large supply of candle fish. They had an over abundance from this years catch.

Wapaxo stopped the trading party at a beautiful little park with plenty of feed for the horses. This was a point where he could go north to the obsidian outcropping and the rest of the traders and horses could recuperate While he was gone Jacque took the time to look after the horses hooves. He had wisely brought a hoof rasp with him. This was a new experience for Peelee and Jacque taught him the proper way to trim the hooves

Wapaxo was a day over due and Jacque was about to go looking for him when he topped the crest of the ridge to the north and headed into camp. Peelee noticed that Wapaxo was riding peculiar. When he got closer they noticed he was carrying a wolf pup. The pup's mother was lying at the mouth of her den, close to death, suffering from a snake bite. There had been four pups but this one was the only one still living... Wapaxo had been able to revive it by feeding it jerky and pemmican he had chewed and forced in its throat with water. There was no lactating female to feed the pup so she would have to survive with what they could provide.

When they reached home Milliwana immediately took over the care of the wolf pup. One of the new mothers in the camp the Belgian mare provided the milk after much coaxing by Jacque. You would think Jacque was the father of the beautiful appaloosa mare colt the way he strutted and bragged about how beautiful it was. She had the markings of Wapaxo's stallion and very long legs. Moose had left. With the advent of the new mare colt, moose had felt neglected or maybe she had been lured away by another moose.

Eager to start on the next trading expedition, Jacque and Wapaxo gathered their clan together and drafted some of the young braves of Wapaxo's home tribe to build a dug-out canoe. Jacque had fashioned an adz from one of the hatchets taken from the hide hunters.

Luck came their way as they searched the banks of Mother River for a large cottonwood that would be adequate to build a freight canoe. In an excellent location they came upon a large cottonwood that a beaver had been working on. It was halfway eaten through on the river side of the bank. With the cross-cut saw Jacque and Wapaxo felled the tree in short order. Everybody was keeping watch for the beaver that had gnawed the notch in the tree knowing it must be a giant for the chips it had produced were larger than a man's palm. Ten steps from the base of the log the cross-cut saw topped off the upper branches. This portion they rolled away to give them room to work on the body of the canoe. Since it was probably the top branches that the beaver was seeking they hoped he would find their work a bonanza. The next process was the trimming and debarking of the log. After debarking they rolled the log to find the proper side to make up the top of the canoe. The cross-cut saw again came into play. A job that would have taken Stone Age tribes days to accomplish, slicing the top slab off, was done in less than a half hour. Jacque's makeshift adz was used to cup out a long bowl in the center of the log. From a large fire they had burning close by they scooped out large embers that they placed in the hewn bowl. While they were letting fire do its job they rested, ate, and took care of the horses. The charred center of the canoe was easier to remove that hacking through the tough wood to give the canoe a cargo space. This process of burning and hacking went on all of the next day. When an adequate man and cargo space was finished they turned the bottom up and shaped it to provide a balanced shape to plow through waves. The last steps were to polish the hull with stones and make paddles.

When they arrived back at the village they were surprised to see Gee dog and the wolf pup playing as if they were long time friends. The belgian's milk had done wonders for the wolf pup. Because of the source of his nourishment he was named Horse Wolf. Wapaxo's mother had been teaching Milliwana and

GeeGee how to make water tight baskets which they proudly showed off to the would be traders; what Jacque and Wapaxo didn't want to hear was Mlliwana's and Gee Gee's desire to accompany the men to the trading post. When the men finally acquiesced the two women set to work preparing for the trip in high spirits. All of the tribes' women helped in making baskets to pack the salt in. The otter pelts were wrapped in buckskin and food was packed for the journey. The trade goods were packed into the dugout which Wapaxo and Beaver Boy were going to cross the river with. Jacque Peelee and the two women took the horses up stream where there was a wide spot that they could ford.

It was three days before Jacque, Peelee, and the women joined the men with the boat. Wapaxo had scouted the area and discovered a good sized stream they could pull the boat up, secure and hide it. Dropping back down to the trail that paralleled the river, they set up camp.

All four men were armed with henry rifles and Jacque was wearing a pistol. He led off with Beaver Boy and Wapaxo and Peelee brought up the rear. The two pack horses were heavily loaded, but Jacque wasn't worried for they only had a short distance to go. With extra caution they circled the small trading town and selected a hidden meadow to set up camp. Figuring the camp well enough hidden the four men walked into the village. They brought with them a sample of the salt and a few otter pelts. Jacque in broken English showed the trading post owner what they had to trade and bartered long and hard. Both items were in demand, but it was the otter pelts that seemed to be of most interest. Wapaxo stayed by Jacque's side while Peelee and Beaver Boy examined the proprietor's goods. There was also a ship's store down the street that seemed to be in competition with the trading post. Speaking in Shoshone Jacque assembled the four and they headed for the Ship's store. They were about to enter when GeeGee came running disheveled and crying. When they managed to calm her down she sobbed "he took her". The complete story finally came out. A stinking bearded man had grabbed

Milliwana, took the gold pennant from her neck, stripped her and used her brutally. He made her put her clothes back on and drug her off. The description of the man would fit most of the men they had seen in the village. Jacque seemed to know where to look. He headed for the saloon. He went around to the back and Wapaxo followed by Beaver Boy and Peelee went in the front door. Stepping in Wapaxo scanned the look alike scrofulous riff raff and finally settled on one that gave off a glint of gold from his beard as he guffawed to a soiled dove at his table. Moving with feline speed, Wapaxo slung his rifle over his shoulder, pulled his scabbard knife stepped to the man, cut the thong and pressed the blade to his throat.Where you get this he demanded? Startled and shaken the loud mouth said, "from a squaw for services rendered." Where Squaw"? Demanded Wapaxo. Still shaken but somewhat more sober, he replied." In the wood shed behind the hotel" This was the last spoken word from the crud; the next sounds from him were a gurgle as his blood poured from his throat. Wapaxo had practically cut his head off. .He dropped the double eagle coin in the soiled dove's lap saying this is an evil cursed thing. This all happened so fast nobody had moved. Somebody shouted, "We can't let him get away with that. Then he looked to the front door and seen the two braves with henry rifles at ready and the back door into the eyes of Jacque and now Wapaxo had his rifle at ready. Another voice said, "He had it coming. He has been bragging of his rough sex with this man's woman"

Wapaxo dashed out the rear entrance of the saloon followed Jacque, Beaver Boy, and Peelee. They quickly found the hotel's wood shed. The door had no lock and was rickety. With one pull Wapaxo practically tore it from its hinges. There they found Milliwana, half naked, gagged, and bound to a supporting post. With a few quick motions Wapaxo cut her loose and removed the gag. She was bruised, had a black eye and was weeping profusely.Wapaxo picked her up in his arms and carried her to the camp where they had left her. When she finally calmed down, she related to them how the filthy smelly white man had used her ".He won't ever do that again", Said

Wapaxo. "He is lucky he died a swift death. If had known about how he treated you he would have died a hundred deaths before going to the great beyond for evil people."

Jacque, Beaver Boy and Peelee went back to the village with their trade goods. The ship's stores had offered them the best prices for the salt and otter pelts. Jacque did all of the talking and bartering. His selections consisted of some colorful cloth, blankets, cooking utensils, tools, and cartridges for the henry and sharps rifles. Several different thickness of rope, some fishing line, sinkers and hooks and hard candy filled out his must order. They loaded up the pack horses and headed back to camp. The next day Beaver Boy and Peelee stayed in camp and Wapaxo and the two women went into the trading post to let the women pick out something they would like to have. Here began Wapaxo's first lesson in money for much to the surprise of the shop keeper Jacque paid for the purchases with gold coins. The next lesson was the value of the yellow sand Jacque had collected from the creek that is no more. Jacque stepped up to the cashier's cage and questioned him about buying raw gold. When Jacque pulled out his buckskin pouch and poured the nuggets and fine gold on the scales you could see the excitement in the clerk's eyes. Since they were done with their purchases Jacque asked for some of his gold coins in payment for the raw gold, refusing paper money. Before they could depart with their purchases the clerk called a young lad that worked for him over and told him to follow the Indians. This maneuver was noticed by Jacque who suspected that something like this would happen. Forewarned the group collected their possessions and quickly broke camp when Jacque spotted the lad heading back toward the trading post. He knew that with all of their horses it would be difficult to cover their tracks. In order to confuse the men that they new would be following them they split into two parties. Wapaxo with Beaver Boy and the two women took the main trail staying on the road way. When the opportunity came about Wapaxo and Milliwana left the trail and circled around to the timbered area where they had ditched the dugout. Beaver Boy left the road going in an opposite direction until they could circle back and head for the dugout. Jacque and Peelee went back into the village and circled to the trail going south before they headed across country toward the dugout. When Wapaxo and Milliwana reached the creek where the dugout was hidden Milliwana ripped off her clothes jumped in the creek and began scrubbing herself with sand, all the time sobbing how dirty she felt. They had been smart to cover their tracks as much as possible for the Thrackets four brothers and two cousins were working hard to locate them. The Thrackets were the younger brothers of the trading post Proprietor. They and their cousins worked the Thracket ranch and it took a while to assemble them. Greg Thracket had told his brothers of Jacque's wealth and the raw gold he was carrying. Greed spiked their larcenous nature. They wanted to find out where the raw gold came from.

Jacque, Wapaxo and the two women headed upstream to the ford as the dugout loaded with their trade goods headed into the stream. The Columbia is wide at this point and the current was strong. Beaver Boy and Peelee threw their weight into the paddles and were quite a ways out when the Thrackets rode up. Bud Thracket the eldest disgusted that he was loosing them pulled his rifle from its scabbard and was about to shoot when the heavy 45/70 slug tore him from the saddle .The delay in the report from the rifle told the raiders that the shot was from a long distance. Not wanting to mess with whoever was shooting from that distance they dashed into the woods not wanting to be the next. Slim Thracket said, "Damn a buffalo gun! And he must have been a mile away. They hadn't expected this for all he knew they were armed with henry rifles that would be dangerous at close range, but buffalo guns! By the time the Thrackets had regrouped Peelee and Beaver Boy were out of range for saddle guns.

The ford had been smooth and exhilarating. Milliwana seemed to be refreshed, but she still had a strained look and Wapaxo spent as much time as possible comforting her. The dugout had drifted down stream about as much as it had across. Beaver Boy and Peelee had the dugout unloaded by the time the horses arrived. The two women had to help the men pull the dugout up the bank and covered it with branches to hide it until they could come back with more horses and bring it to the Klikitat area.

After a council smoke, feast and rest the Wapaxo troop divided up the trade goods. They set aside goods to trade with the coastal tribes and the tools Jacque had a purpose for. The. Shovels, picks, bars, and gold pans Jacque planned to take back to the stream that was no more. While the tribe was receiving gifts from the trade goods Milliwana was consulting with Wapaxo's mother. She was the healer of this Klikitat clan. Milliwana told of her rough encounter with the filthy white man and asked Wapaxo's mother to help her insure that she had success in her up-coming monthly woman's time. Wapaxo's mother was away for over an hour. When she came back she gave Milliwana some crushed roots and told her to make a strong tea from the roots and take it three days before her last months period day. The time was right. Milliwana made and drank some of the tea. It was bitter beyond belief, but that didn't stop Milliwana from drinking the small clay bowl of tea. The miracle was that her stomach didn't repel the bitter root tea... Four days later she cuddled up to Wapaxo and thanked him for his support during this difficult time. Wapaxo thinking her move was of a sensual nature was surprised when she told him no that this was her moon time.

After a successful hunt Wapaxo's clan was surprised to see a new face in the Klikitat camp. He was a small Tillamook brave. Jacque nick-named him Weasel because of his instant distrust of the middle aged brave. True to their warm hospitable nature the Klikitats made the stranger welcome and gave him shelter. The next time Wapaxo's clan went on a hunt they held a little council away from the camp and agreed to take turns watching the Weasel. The Weasel told a story that he was looking for a brother of his and asked questions about other tribes in the area. On a dark night the Weasle left without notice and was gone for two weeks. When he returned he said that he had discovered that his brother had died a year ago.

Wolf and Gee Dog had formed a bond somehow this bond was extended to the Belgian mare. Perhaps wolf's nourishment from the mare had brought the attachment. The Weasel had found the mare attractive but the attraction was not mutual. She would not let him near her and Wolf helped by showing his dislike for the visitor as did Gee Dog. All of this was noticed by Jacque, increasing his mistrust of the visitor. While the Klikitat tribe was planning for the coming fishing season and a trading trip to the coast Jacque, Wapaxo, Beaver Boy and Peelee were planning to return to the creek that is no more. Wapaxo, Beaver Boy, and Peelee had seen the look in the trader's eyes when Jacque had poured the little nuggets and gold dust to be weighed. They had planned to be traders using the Klikitats fish harvest and the salt and otter pelts as bartering items. Now they took into consideration that a little gold was much easier to carry and care for. They had caught the gold fever.

Everything that had to be done in preparation for the trip to the creek that is no more couldn't be done in secret. Weasel deduced the goals of the Wapaxo clan and approached Gee Gee to ask where the men were. It was a mistake. Gee Dog and Wolf launched themselves at the Weasel to intercept his approach. Gee Gee couldn't stop the canines and it was lucky for Weasel that the men were close by and heard the ruckus.

Unbeknownst to Wapaxo's tribe, the Little Fox tribe in the cave settlement was prospering. Much of their good fortune came from the presence of the albino buffalo hide. The story of the spirit buffalo had spread far and wide bringing curiosity seekers and those that wanted to pay respects to the buffalo spirit. These generally brought gifts that enriched the Little Fox tribe. The resounding defeat of the attacking Black Foot raiding party had prevented further troubles from this quarter. The large cast iron cooking pot that Milliwana had so revered was the center of many good feasts adding to the fame of the Little Fox Tribe. One of the visitors to the cave was a weather-beaten wizened prospector. His looks belied his abilities and energy for he moved with alacrity, bouncing in his step and robust in attitude. His abilities with Indian Languages made him welcome wherever he went. He had been a victim of the hide hunters and absorbed the tale of their demise for it was his pouch of nuggets and fines that Jacque had found among their possessions. The Indian name adopted by the prospector was Bob Cat Bob. As a trapper he excelled in catching bob cats. The bob cat used its excellent sight to hunt for food. After a good rest, a generous gift to the White Buffalo Spirit, and a jovial good time, Bob Cat Bob set out to see if he could intercept the Wapaxo Tribe.

The time was ripe for Wapaxo's tribe to head toward the creek that is no more. Two of the Klikitat young braves asked if they could accompany the expedition. Weasel wanted to accompany them also but Gee Dog and Wolf had changed his mind about being in their company. The trade trips to the coast gave the trekkers a good supply of salt and otter pelts for gifts and trade for camas and horses. With Milliwana's insistence they headed directly for the Ponoc's camp. Jacque was a little irritated about this for he was eager to prospect the area of the creek that is no more. Finally a compromise was reached. Jacque, Peelee, Gee Gee, Broken Branch, Up River (the two Kilikitat Brave new comers), Gee Dog, and Wolf would camp at the creek that was no more and wait for Wapaxo, Milliwana and Beaver Boy to return.

They had been followed and they knew it. It wasn't only the dogs that aroused them it was also the horses. The new colt was especially sensitive to the smells of the western breeze. Jacque decided that he wouldn't make any moves to search for the source of the color they had found in the creek that wasn't there anymore. In fact they moved a mile or so away and camped by a little stream in order to have a fresh supply of water. It was a delightful place and Gee Gee found many of the herbs that had delighted Milliwana. There was an abundance of grouse and rock chucks which were good fresh meat supplies. They were all experts with the slings and found the daily harvest entertaining. Shaggy Main mushrooms grew in abundance everywhere the ground had been disturbed. June berries provided a sweet addition to the meat diet. The small stream was full of west slope cut throat trout. Wapaxo would have been in heaven. Gee Dog was raising a ruckus and wolf wasn't around in fact they hadn't seen him for two days. Jacque had thought that he had heard a wolf howl and surmised that she had also heard the call of the wild and had left to return to a natural life. It was an odd sight, Bob Cat Bob leading two burros hailed the camp. Jacque almost laughed when he saw the little prospector and took an instant liking to him. B.C Bob had always had this effect on people that lived off of the land. He knew from Little Foxe's people that Jacque spoke fluent Shoshone so they were immediately compatible.B.C Bob told him of his visit with Little Foxe's tribe, that he had been tracking him and of his loss of his poke to the hide hunters. Jacque told him of his encounter with the hide hunters and that he had found the poke in their possession. He explained that he had figured that it had been stolen and that he had sold some of the gold. "You did dispatch them"? Queried B.C Bob. When Jacque answered in the affirmative, BC Bob said, "We are even then" and they shook hands.Jacque couldn't explain why but he told B.C. Bob about the creek that was no more and delighted in the excitement B.C. Bob showed when he showed him some of the gold taken from the placer operation they had worked before the earth quake. "Nuggets of this size indicate that the mother lode deposit is close by", said B.C. Bob. "I don't understand" replied Jacque. B.C. Bob went on to explain that gold came to the surface of the earth from the earths core by way of what he called a "Pipe". It turns out that B.C Bob was an

educated geologist. He went on to explain that the earth was a dynamic living morphisim and like any animal or plant in the aspect that it was growing, changing, and shrinking in all areas of its existence. He went on to explain that diastrophism (mountain building), evidenced by earth quakes produced cracks in the mantle which allowed magma and gasses to push to the surface. Water is in the form of superheated steam and minerals in the form of gasses. This combination of gasses and steam is forced vertically or horizontally through the weakest places in the existing rock forming a pipe. At the edges of the pipe the steam and gasses are forced into cracks of the country rock. There they cool and the minerals are deposited. Silica is turned into quartz and the minerals permeate the quartz. Weathering over time exposes the quartz and minerals to erosion. Gold being heavier than most other minerals settles to the bottom of streams in cracks of bedrock and the closeness to the source of the deposit is indicated by the size of the nuggets. The difficulties of the language and all of the new terminology left Jacque's head in a spin. As their friendship grew in strength B.C Bob continued his lessons and Jacque grew to almost worshiping B.C Bob.

With the disappearance of Wolf G Dog assumed the position of guard dog and resented the invasion of Perrro the shaggy companion of Esel the burro and B.C. Bob. G Dog didn't push his position as top dog when he discovered Perro was a female. Both dogs kept looking to the west with nervous actions. "You know somebody is scouting us" asked W.C Bob? "Yea I know they are doing it from a distance", answered Jacque. "We had better not do any prospecting until we eliminate this problem," commented Bob.

When Jacque had sold some of the gold at the trading post he had stirred the imagination of Lem Thracket and his criminal mind and avaricious nature. With the idea of riches for the taking the Thrackets began to plan how they could obtain more of the gold so blatantly displayed by a Half Breed Fenchman. The plan was solidified when Bud Thracket was so foolish as to get blown away on the bank of the Columbia River. The first step was to identify the holder of the gold. The weasel was engaged without knowing the purpose of his assignment. He only thought it was to keep track of the traders so that Lem Thracket could extract revenge for the death of his brother. Thracket had a good handle on the weasel for he had saved him from a lynching mob after he had ravaged a settler's young daughter. Lem had hidden him away at one of the ranch line cabins and kept him in spending money for various chores, this being one of them that he had performed to perfection when he had reported back to Lem everything he was able to observe. Of special interest was the packing of mining tools when the Wapaxo's bunch had headed out to Milliwana's tribe country. On further orders he had tracked the group to the Bitterroot country. When he thought they were settled into their camp he reported to Lem and guided the Thrackets to the area where they situated themselves out of sight in a secluded box canyon. Wolf and G-dog had detected the weasel during one of his first reconnoiter maneuvers. Not trusting him Lem had sent the weasel back to the ranch. With wolf gone G dog hadn't paid too much attention to the little spy parties that were keeping track of the traders. Since the arrival of Perro the nervousness of the two dogs became heightened and was noticed by B.C. Bob. Having lived with his dog in several situations where paying attention to him had saved his hair. Under the pretense of hunting Peelee, Broken Branch and Up River scouted far and wide until they located the Thracket gang. They had a big advantage with the use of the old brass telescope.They were able to hunt close to the camp of Jacque and BC Bob using bows and arrows thereby avoiding any firearm noise to alert the Thrackets of their presence. In their attempt to avoid detection the Thracket gang had to hunt a good distance to the west of their camp to prevent the weapons from alerting Wapaxo's clan. The six members of the Thracket gang being lazy by nature were hard pressed to keep themselves supplied. They had not allowed for the distances that they had to travel to catch up with the traders. The one thing they had in good supply was whiskey. Growing impatient with the constraints of not being able to prospect W.C. Bob asked Jacque to take him to the creek that was no more so he could scout the land and see if he could find the source of the ore they had panned. Leading one of the burros the old prospector made a wide circle before heading in the direction indicated by the map Jacque had drawn in the dirt. Upon locating the earthquake camp Bob went down a gentle slope to a ridge that had once been a small canyon. Seeing the scared face of the huge mountain that had tumbled into the canyon he knew at once that further exploration here would be useless. The choices were go in the direction that the stream had flowed downward or attempt to find the headwaters of the stream that was no more. The down stream direction was blocked by a vast area of downed timber. Bob thought to himself, "The only thing that would clear this area would be a lightening caused fire." To complicate matters his burro was acting mighty skittish. He hadn't brought Perro with him so he had to surmise for himself that there was a bear or a mountain lion in the area. He decided to camp for the night. Before dark he took his hunting knife and hacked a bundle of grass for the burro since he didn't feel it would be safe to hobble him. After gathering a large bundle of wood he started a small fire and set the coffee pot up.Jerky and dried berries would be all there was for an evening meal. With the burro picketed close and his henry rifle at hand he settled down by the fire, wrapped a blanket around his shoulders and attempted to grab a few winks. The burro snorted a couple of times but the fire seemed to keep what ever was visiting him away When morning broke he was up and had a cup of left over coffee. Securing the pack on the burro he headed south paralleling a high ridge that looked like it was too steep to climb. He felt he was on the anticline portion of an up heaved structure. There wasn't anything to do but to work his way around the large boulders and shale. He was thankful for the sure footedness of his burro. Six hours of this brought him to a small stream that cascaded through a large ravine. Bob stopped and took some samples from the rock outcroppings of the ravine walls. What had attracted his attention were the white quartz outcropping. There didn't appear to be any coloring in the quartz other than some rust stains. These and the quartz indicated that the deposit in the form of a sill contained some minerals but nothing exciting. The stream had some good holes so Bob unpacked his gear sorted out his fishing tackle, cut a slender willow and tested the waters for trout. It wasn't long until he had a nice mess of west slope cutthroat trout. Before settling into camp and starting a fire he put out several snares on some active cottontail trails. With some of Milliwana's camas bread and trout Bob had a good meal. With the burro hobbled he settled down for a good nights sleep. The next morning he checked his snares. Two had cottontail rabbits in them. One was still alive so he turned it loose since one would make a meal. After breaking camp Bob continued along the face of the syncline stopping occasionally to break some interesting rock samples finding no indications of more mineralization he doubled back and headed down the little stream where he had camped. The going was rough and impassible near the bottom. Attempting to find a trail going north left him rim rocked. Again he had to turn around and head south. It had been four nights since he had left Jacque at the camp. He was used to loneliness but he missed the companionship of the big Half Breed. Another day passed before he found a place where a rock slide had broken over the rim south of the camp creek. At the edge of the slide was a well used deer trail that led to the bottom of a heavily brushed canyon bottom. Back tracking to a small clearing he stopped and set up camp. He hoisted his camp goods up into a large cottonwood tree and led the burro to water taking his small shovel and gold pan. Finding open water was no easy chore for there were beaver sign everywhere. This was a trapper's heaven. With the burro watered he worked his way around a big beaver dam and found a small tributary to the main stream where he could get to a gravel bottom. He waded out into the cold water and probed the cracks in the bed rock. It wasn't long until he found color (gold). This was no bonanza and working this stream was going to make every ounce extracted worth a barrel of sweat. Satisfied that he had found a clue as to the general neighborhood of the source he decided to head back to the main camp.

Before leaving he had a good dinner of beaver and cattail. After dinner he reached as high as he could up the trunk of the big cottonwood, consulted his compass and blazed the north side.

A good distance to the north east Wapaxo, Milliwana, Beaver Boy and GeeGee were preparing to travel to Jacque's camp. Their visit had been joyous but they were anxious to help Jacque fulfill his dream with the yellow metal. They constantly reassured themselves that they were traders and that the yellow metal was much better trade goods than salt or sea otter pelts. With the gold they could reduce their burden, travel light to trading posts and increase their advantages in trading. The camas, cattail, and berry harvests had been excellent for the Poncos. Wapaxo's group had been able to add two more well built appaloosas to their pack train. It is a rich caravan that headed west for their rendezvous with Jacque.They would be missed by the Poncos for Beaver Boy had been a prolific provider of fresh meat. His archery skills brought success on practically every hunting excursion. The henry rifle ammunition was held in reserve for trouble. Their sojourn was not without incident. Several opportunist scouting parties had attempted to relieve them of their horses only to be dispatched or discouraged by the response of henry rifle fire. It was late summer and the travelers were blessed with an abundance of mountain grouse, nicknamed fool hens. They seemed to have no fear and could easily be dispatched with a sling loaded with small stones.

Near the crest of the Bitter Root Mountains they ran into Mountain Lion problems. The horses had to be corralled and they had to post guard. The spooked animals smelled and sensed the visits of the big cats. One such evening a large male cat was a little too bold and Beaver Boy shot him with a clean shot to the head. They made camp the next day by a mid- sized stream while the women prepared the hide for transport. Wapaxo took advantage of the stop to catch several nice brook trout for the evening meal. Since they had pushed into the mountains the travel was an ideal experience of a nature vacation. .It was late summer and the temperature was refreshing in the mountain atmosphere. At early evening the barks and howls of the coyotes were almost a melody occasionally an owl let them know feathered hunters were about... The feeling of the nearness with nature gave Wapaxo and Milliwana a feeling of content as they bundled together in their sleeping robes. Milliwana had been able to suppress her horror of the encounter with the crud that had taken advantage of her at the trading post and accepted Wapaxo's advances with relish. The morning brought refreshment with a bath in a beaver pond's cool waters. The horses were given additional time to graze and the two couples sought out succulent vegetation for their additional nourishment. Beaver Boy ever the explorer hiked the hills and sought out the high places to memorize the landscape. Gee Gee busied herself with basket making. Selecting supple willow branches for frame work and entwining tough marsh grasses in tight compacted weaves. In the evenings the women went about the forest seeking mushrooms and edible plants to supplement their fish and meat diets. Rose hips were ground and made into tea. The cambium layer from selected trees made cakes with a camas root paste. The idyllic pace of life was laconic and they felt no urge to push their way to the base camp.

Jacque and Peelee had kept track of the stalkers and were mystified as to their intentions. The Thrachets seemed content to bide their time and hunt and fish and to maintain their vigil. Broken Branch and Up River were antsy and wanted to confront them. Jacque counseled them explaining that alertness would keep their camp at an advantage. From the descriptions that the two scouts had brought back from their observations Jacque knew that they were the men from the trading post. However he thought they were after him for revenge for his shooting of the Whiteman on the bank of the Columbia. Not knowing that Wapaxo's party was bringing an abundance of food back from the Poncos camp Jacque had been busy smoking meat and fish for a sustaining larder. When not stocking up on food he built several hogans. He used the method that the buffalo hunters used. He selected places in the young lodge pole coppice where he could thin them out leaving a circle of five to six saplings standing. These he topped, bent together at the top and bound them to form a frame work that he covered with deer skins fur out. The bottom hides were left folded out and weighted with stones. The bottom pelts were well treated with salt and pitch where they met the ground. With time on his hands Jacque was tempted to take his gold pan and check out the neighboring streams for color. Figuring that they were being watched he instead started gathering fire wood and stacking it where he could protect it from moisture. With the camp established he thoroughly checked out their weapons and set up an alarm system for the perimeter. The plan was simple. A comfortable platform was set high in a predominant fir tree. It provided a comfortable seat and supplies that allowed the occupant refreshment and ease of position. One of the henry rifles and ammunition had been stashed in a protected case. When not in use the telescope was handy. A line was threaded through the branches of the surrounding trees to three of the hogans. The guard had only to jerk the line and a clatter of deer horns was sounded.

B.C. Bob was experiencing his own problems. A thunder storm was moving in and it looked like a violent one. He seemed to be the center of the violence of the storm. Thunder and wind forced him and his burro to seek shelter under an overhang. It provided sparse shelter but it did block the stronger wind gusts. The creek below him changed to a turbulent river. Trees were uprooted and brush was washed out into the raging stream. Bob was thinking of the beaver dams below and actually felt remorse that the ambitious animals were loosing all of the work they had done to establish their ponds and homes. When the storm subsided Bob started a small fire with the moss he had collected from the conifers and stored in his pack. All of the surrounding wood was too wet to burn except for the packrat nest material under the overhang. A pot of tea and a warming up saw him on his way to the base camp. When he reached high ground he was able to position himself and with the aid of his compass he set off toward the base camp. The good news of the color that he had found at camp creek was clouded by what had happened with the violent storm. He couldn't be sure that he could re-locate the creek source. This didn't dampen his expectations of discovery for he read the signs telling him that his was a mineralized area. Fatigue and longing for companionship forced him on. He was three days out when he had a lucky shot at a fine deer. This made him decides to stop and recuperate.

Wapaxo's group was a week away from the base camp when the violent storm hit. Their problem wasn't shelter it was fire. Several lightening strikes had started blazes on three of their sides. Crowding into a small steam basin seemed to be their only chance of survival. The natural tendency for fire to burn uphill left them safe in the creek depression. The horses were panicky and forced the group to tether them to saplings close to water. Again nature made a choice and a deluge of water drenched the flames and made the fuel unburnable.

Wapaxo remembering his puberty experience and questioned his destiny. Why had he been sent on his quest to hunt buffalo and then be revisited by a violent storm on his way forward in life? Why had Manitou appointed him to lead and then presented him with these obstacles? There were many spirits to be consulted. Why did the streams and creeks seem to laugh in their dash amongst the boulders and obstacles? And why did the trees moan when disturbed by the wind? Why were so many of the beautiful plants poisonous to the touch? How was one to determine what was wrong from what was right? Be it as simple as to which berries were edible and which were poisons? These questions weighed heavily on Wapaxo's mind and Milliwana detected the depression he was feeling and felt she had done something wrong. When disturbed in his thoughts he would answer her gruffly and remain morose for long periods of time. It was only when she brought him an owl with a broken wing that he seemed to escape his reverie and lighten to her concern for the bird. How he solved his dilemma remained for future cogitation. At present was the desire to advance to the base camp. Drying out was a long process for the sun seemed to have less heat shining through the clouded skies. A brisk rub-down seemed to revive the spirits of the horses and it was contagious. Soon the group was on their way excited that they were only about three days from the base camp.

Far west of Wapaxo's group the Thracker gang was becoming agitated at their inability to move on what they determined to be a discovery of the source of the gold Jacque and the trading party had brought to the trading post. They had no suspicions that they had been well scouted and watched. They had been diligent in their forays and had not noticed any placer activity. They had no clue as to the activity of Bob Cat Bob. Because they had been so vigilantly observed they didn't know of the preparedness of the base camp expecting their offensive. Food was scares and monotonous and boredom prevailed. Greed was their only motivation and visions of wealth kept them from abandoning their quest. They figured that if simple Indians could extract so much gold that they with their expertise could glean much more. They had no way of knowing of the advent of Bob Cat Bob. The violent rain storm had almost washed them out. They had been forced to seek trade with villages that they had encountered on their way to confiscation and control of the source of the gold they had observed. They were obsessed with their superior knowledge believing that they were superior in intellect compared to the simple natives. They hadn't observed the acumen of Jacque in demanding the gold coins instead of paper money for the placer gold he had sold them. They Might have fared much better if they hadn't brought as much liquor with them that they felt free to go to bed every night drunk. Living off of the land was not their forte and every day they stumbled over plants and herbs that could have supplemented their diet. Their waste of game body parts as a result of their enculturation was evident in the collection of scavengers that accumulated around their camp site. Of particular note was the raven. It wasn't by chance that the Native Indians observed the raven with particular interest. They believed that the black eagle had special powers and that it was able to communicate as well as humans. Their alertness was well observed by Indian tribes and many were able to translate their actions and calls to signals to be observed. Broken Branch and Up River had been raised in circumstances that made them well aware of the raven's calls and activities. The pursuits of the Klikitat Indians in gathering salmon and care of the catch enticed the attention of multitudes of ravens. As children they are told tales of ravens. Most of them were fanciful but many of them portrayed the raven as a mystical animal guided by spirits. This led the youngsters to be observant resulting in an awareness of the signals the ravens gave one another and alerted the young braves to the activities of the Thracker gang.

One scavenger attracted to the Thracket Gang's camp was truly undesired. He was a big male wolverine. It wasn't what he ate that caused so much consternation. It was what he claimed as his alone by marking all of the stores with urine of a special odorous nature. Forced to abandon their meat supply the Thrackets set forth to hunt ranging in wider and wider circles ranging from their base camp. Every day two of the Thrackets would scout Jacques camp hoping to find him panning gold.

It had been a very rainy day and the Thrackets had just returned from a scouting expedition observing Jacque's activities. Wet disgruntled and low on whiskey they had just settled into camp when a young Indian Brave and his new bride rode into camp. At first the Thrackets made a mad scramble for weapons. When they saw there was no danger to themselves they began to speculate how they could possibly acquire a change of their diet by using the native's knowledge of the availability of herbs and plants of the area .With enough whiskey in their guts they began to speculate on how they could acquire the two fine appaloosa ponies the natives had ridden in on. Small Pony drew his knife when one of the thugs grabbed Tallena, (Valley Flower). This was all they needed, a shot rang out and Small Pony was half blown away. All of this was observed by Up River and it wasn't long until he had reported back to Jacque. Jacque and the two Klikitat braves grabbed rifles and hurried to the camp. They were too late the Thrackets had all taken a turn with Tallena and she had managed to escape into the brush. Ravaged, sick and saddened she stumbled up stream away from the camp. All she had was the clothes on her back and they were torn from misuse by the thugs. Jacque and the two young braves tracked her and found her huddled in a hollow of the creek bed. Assuring her that they meant no harm, they fed her from their trail supplies and asked her if she wanted to accompany them to their camp where Jacque's wife could administer to her. She insisted that she only wanted to return to her Nez Perce family. Up River volunteered to accompany and guide her. "First", said Jacque "We need the horses." When night had fallen, Jacque and Broken Branch circled back to the Thracket camp. Silently they gathered up all of the picketed horses. They reasoned that why not? It was small compensation for the harm they had caused Tallena besides it would hamper them from following. The raid had been easy for the Thrackets had been whiskey soaked and passed out. They haltered the horses and tied the lead ropes head to tail. Quietly Broken Branch led the horses single file out of the camp while Jacque gathered all of the rifles he could without disturbing the drunken gang. Their pistols he left for they slept with them and would awaken if disturbed. Tallena seeing they meant no harm agreed to accompany them to their camp. The raiding party arrived at camp at the same time as Wapaxo and his group returning from the Digger tribes harvest location. Milliwana immediately gathered up Tallena and took her under her wing. Her experience with the crud that had assaulted her gave her understanding and sympathy that was recognized by Tallena. Gathering her herb collection she ground the root that had been given to her by Wapaxo's mother and gave her the same instructions she had needed to insure her next period. Beaver Boy accompanied Up River to the Thracket's camp and scouted the activity. The hung over white men concerned with the loss of their horses and rifles were blaming each other for their predicament. They were too disorganized to attempt any thought of pursuing the horses not knowing how large the raiding party was and considered the loss of their rifles. The attempt to follow Jacque and the others to their gold discovery was a bust. They gathered their possessions and set out on the return to the trading post planning to gather a larger force and return for what they perceived as a bonanza of gold. They threatened to kill every red skin they come across.

With preparations under way to return Tallena to her tribe the camp was greeted with HOYKA! And BC Bob came into the camp with the good news of his placer find. Tallena's home village was in the general direction of the placer location Beaver Boy was familiar with the country so he proposed a plan that allowed them to travel as a group to the crossing of the Selway River.Millewana insisted upon accompanying Tallena to her home tribe. Wapaxo and Up River remained at the base camp with the other women. It was apparent that Broken Branch was interested in Tallena for he was at her beck and call. With the recent death of her man he knew that it was inappropriate to make his feelings known. The powerful Nez Perce tribe would most likely go in pursuit of the white trash. The rifles and the four good quarter horses were welcomed as was Tallena and Milliwana. Broken Branch was not warmly accepted for the fishing Indians were considered Squaw Braves since fishing was a labor below hunting and warfare. It was only when he was given credit for the theft of the horses that the other young braves warmed to his friendship. His skill with the sling made him welcome at Tallena's father's lodge because of the steady stream of small game. After ten days at the Nez Perce village Milliwana and Broken Branch made preparations for departure. Milliwana and Tallena had formed a strong friendship and so it wasn't a surprise when Tallena asked to join them on their return trip. However Milliwana had noticed the exchanges between Broken Branch and Tallena. The fact that Broken Branch didn't attach any stigma to her encounter with the white men gave Tallena warmth at his attentiveness and she accepted his advances with pleasure.

At the beaver pond valley BC Bob was finding it very difficult to locate his placer stream. The large cottonwood tree he had so carefully marked was no longer there. The violent flood that had accompanied the cloud- burst had stacked lodge-pole pine and other bush against the mighty cottonwood uprooting it and the stream carried it miles down the valley plane. The only recourse was to find bed rock bottoms in the split stream and pan the cracks and crevasses for signs of color. They found gold but in only the deepest crevasse and most of it very fine in black sand. Jacque was the only one that was willing to put in the back breaking labor to pan the gold. Beaver Boy and Broken Branch found a multitude of excuses to hunt and fish to avoid shoveling and panning.BC Bob decided to take off on his own and prospect upstream. Before leaving he sat around the evening fire educating Jacque in the geology of gold's origination. "Gold" he said, originates in the center of the earth with all of the heavy minerals. Here in the core of the earth all matter is in a liquid or gaseous state. The make up of most igneous rock is primarily silica and as such is in a liquid form." It is only when the liquid gaseous mixture which is enclosed in a cooler shell forces its way to the surface through a crack in the shell brought about by movement of the earths mantel during an earth quake that the minerals are brought to the surface. The crack can be vertical or horizontal and any combination of structures. As the molten rock oozes through the crack it carries the metals in the form of gasses on the outside of the intrusion. These are deposited in the existing rock cracks and condense to their pure state. This is known as a contact area. The appearance of fine gold is the result of overburden being weathered away and water washing the gravel and soil to the stream beds. The gold being the heaviest of minerals finds its way into the crevasse and cracks by the rushing water, the closer to the source the larger the nuggets. "What I want to find is the source", explained BC Bob.

As he headed up the stream in a north westerly direction he stopped and sampled the stream bed every mile or so and found color as was noted in the beaver pond valley. When he came to the large spring surging from the bottom of a cliff he realized that he had discovered the original find of the creek that is no more. This pleased him for the direction he had been traveling brought him closer to the base camp established by Jacque. Swinging wide to the west he skirted the former canyon area and headed higher up the sub mountain chain.

Unable to get the young braves to work hard enough to achieve a recognizable quantity of gold, Jacque decided to follow BC Bob's lead and head up stream. When they arrived at the stream's source Jacque realized they were not far from their base camp. It wasn't hard for the women to convince Jacque that they should return to base camp and re-group for another try at finding the gold. Two days later they were back to their snug hogans and the happy women settled into preparing a good meal.Wapaxo was glad to have Milliwana back and surprised to see the warm beauty of the tribes new addition. The last he had seen her she was bedraggled and despondent. It didn't take him long to notice the connection between Broken Branch and Tallena. The aura of happiness here took some of the edge off of Jacques disappointment over not finding workable gold deposits. Everybody chipped in and soon there was a new hogan built. The evenings were growing cooler and the early mornings had a hint of frost. Recognizing the harbingers of winter the tribe began spending all of the daylight hours gathering feed for the horses and preserving food for cold weather.

WC Bob arrived in camp just in time for the wedding ceremonies. Broken Branch settled into his new hogan with his new bride. The tribe was growing. To the west the Thrackets were anything but comfortable. They had lost their horses and rifles. The only weapons they had were their pistols. While adequate for defense they were almost useless as hunting arms. Dejected, hungry and despondent they headed back in the direction of their crossing of the Columbia. They were several days if not weeks away from their goal when they came upon a group of Indian women gathering herbs and wild vegetation for winter stocks. The older women were instructing the younger girls in the selection and care of mushrooms. The women that had stayed in camp had started a large stew of rabbit, squirrel, cattail root, wild onions and carrots. They were just waiting to add the mushrooms. When they inspected the collections of the young girl's they were startled to find several amanitas, known to be poisonous... This was the scene the Thrackets were observing from cover. When they saw no men about they were embolden and rushed in to overpower the women. With the women secured they scooped up the discarded mushrooms and dumped them into the stew and prepared to feast. With their stomachs full they began to molest the women. The younger girls had been able to scatter into the woods so they were spared the sexual attacks of the filthy men. The older women gave the men no problems and accepted the advances smiling within when they thought of the stew. Satiated the Thrackets retired for the evening only to awaken at midnight with severe immobilizing stomach cramps. They never left the camp.

When the younger braves had retired to their hogans BC Bob called Jacque and Wapaxo aside and took them into his hogan. When they were seated around the small smokeless fire he brought out a large buckskin pouch and poured out a pile of nuggets. These he explained he had been able to pan from the stream. From another bag he produced several large chunks of quartz. "Here", "He said are samples from the mother load or the source of the nuggets. The problem is that it took me two days to gather these three samples. The gold is there but the deposit is very tight. We will need explosives and work horses to develop the mine. I suggest that we work the stream until it freezes over, take what we can collect and head for a large trading center down the ocean coast." "And leave the main deposit for somebody else?" asked Wapaxo. "With the tools we have and no explosives we have no choice," explained BC Bob. "Our only chance of working the main deposit depends on complete secrecy," said BC Bob. "Of the others only Beaver Boy would I bet my life on," said Wapaxo. It was decided Wapaxo, Jacque, BC Bob and Beaver Boy would work the stream until fast ice prevented further placer operations. This being settled Broken Branch and Up River were informed that they would have the responsibility of taking care of the women and the camp. This was no easy chore for they had to prepare for winter.

Wapaxo, Jacque, BC Bob and Beaver Boy began meticulously to prepare for a hard trip and establishing a placer operation. After a good meal and goodbyes the four prospectors headed for bed with plans to leave at day break. Broken Branch and Up River were glad to dive into winter preparation for they hadn't caught the gold fever and couldn't understand the excitement of the prospectors. Gathering fire wood, stacking it and covering it with deer pelts was mostly men's work while the women kept camp and gathered grass bundles for the horses. Several times a week the two braves hunted and butchered game for the women to cure and dry.

The trip to the placer stream was expedited with BC Bob's guidance for he had visually plotted and mentally logged landscape markers each step of the way. Jacque eagerly stepped into the stream and panned for color. Delighted at a good show he was ready to immediately work at panning. "Hold up a minute", called BC Bob. " You won't last long if you work in the water the cold will soon have you cramped and your whole body will shut down", he explained.. "I have chosen this place for a good reason. If you will notice the stream has previously run over against the bank.

See the dry curve?" He asked. When the others acknowledged the presence of the old creek bed He said'" That is what is known an ox bow. In time past this creek washed against the cut bank above us. Due to earth movement or flood the creek changed its course and runs straighter as we see it now however when it was wearing down the cut bank it was carrying ore as it does now. First we will build a sluice shoot. And some carry boxes; with them we will wash the tailings above bed rock in the ox bow. He went to the packs and brought out the saw and axes. Soon everybody was busy making lumber and BC Bob was constructing a long wooden trough below some rapids up stream. The carry boxes would have been wheel barrows but they didn't have any wheels so it took two men to transport the diggings to the sluice boxes which had ripples in the bottom. The next day he gave each man a crevasse tool, which was a rod with a flattened end that formed a spoon. He showed everybody how to work down to bed rock and to dig the finer gravel from the bed rock cracks. The next day they began working the gravel in earnest. Taking turns in carrying the carry boxes to the sluice while BC Bob worked the gravel down the ripples in the sluice box. When they took a break to eat they gathered at the sluice and Bob showed them their successes. It was rich as they gathered the flakes and nuggets in small deer skin pouches they had prepared for this day.

The lazy beginning of winter was noted by the silent appearance of snow flakes as the men tiredly continued their extraction and washing of the stream's fine gravel extracted from bed-rock crevasses. Determined to extract the gold bearing sands and gravel until the stream froze halting their washing capability. Their food supply was low so they called a halt to their placer activity and rested and hunted for meat. The average temperature had lowered enough that hung meat would keep without preservation. Not wanting to take a chance of revealing their location they agreed to hunt with bows or slings. Paring up, Jacque and BC Bob took off up stream and Wapaxo and beaver Boy cut off at an angle to a high meadow to the south east. Checking the wind direction they shifted their approach to a more northerly direction. As they approached an opening in the timber around the meadow they simultaneously spotted a large heavily antlered buck weaving in and out of the woods. They enjoyed his regal appearance, but they were meat hunting so they made no move to disturb his meandering. This proved to be a good decision for within arrow shot a young plump dry doe stepped out following the big buck. Both warriors let fly an arrow, Wapaxo's arrow as his father had taught him struck the doe just below her left ear. Beaver Boy's arrow made a good heart shot. The two old timers came into camp with two rabbits. Needless to say much to their embarrassment Jacque and Bob had to listen to the guffaws. With comments to the effect that maybe they had better stick to shoveling gravel.

The stream hadn't frozen, but the snow made extraction almost impossible calling for a decision to break camp. With only a hind quarter of the doe left, the foursome broke camp and headed to the base camp. After spending a miserable night and two long days the sight of the snug hogans was truly welcome. After seeing the small stack of buckskin pouches the women were perplexed as to why anybody would put forth so much effort for so little prize. It was only when BC Bob picked up one of the pouches and told them this would purchase everything they owned and more, that they began to understand. Milliwana and GeeGee brightened up as visions of all of the things they had seen at the ships store danced before their eyes. Comfortable with the knowledge that they were well supplied until spring the clan settled into a routine that concentrated on taking care of the horses and keeping the fires going. Communication was their most pressing problem. With four different languages and different dialect variations of three of them it became burdensome to divide the chores and keep continuity with their activities. B C Bob went to bed mulling over the problem. Early the next morning he asked for a consultation with Wapaxo and Jacque. The three of them settled in BC Bob's hogan and lit up their pipes. "Do you think it is possible for our clan to all learn to speak English", he asked. The question stumped Wapaxo and Jacque voiced his doubts. "If we reach a large trading center together it is only fair that everybody has a choice in the selection of goods to be bartered for," he explained. Wapaxo mulled this over and commented, "Let us ask some of the women to join us and ask if they are willing to learn". It wasn't easy to gather the working women into the council. It wasn't normal to include women in decision making, but this was about selecting trade goods that the women should be able to choose. This meant that they needed to know the value of their choices and be able to substitute when one thing had a priority over another. Milliwana's enthusiasm was contagious. Her alert mind convinced the others that this was something they could do and should do. With the matter settled BC Bob started getting teaching materials together. Jacque helped him make a bunch of frames that they stretched bleached deer skin over. They used these skin covered frames as slates. With charcoal Bob printed the alphabet in capitals and lower case letters. Not familiar with written words the natives couldn't grasp the difference between capital letters and lower case letters. Bob explained that they were like people some grown and some children and that children were often required to do the work of adults.Milliwana's alert mind grasped the concept and she began instructing the other women. The men were the biggest problem. When trying to explain to them the advantage of being able to send written messages, Up River asked why he just couldn't tell the receiver of the message what he needed to know. Bob said, "Maybe I didn't want you to know the message." Why did you ask me to give it to Broken Branch if you didn't want me to know what it was?" This open minded logic made instructions very difficult. How do you convince a native that learning a language and being able to read and write will help him hunt and live off the land? The first month or two was very difficult especially for the men.

This is where Jacque's sophistication came in handy. He made up stories and the students began to grasp the language through the imagination of make believe events. He often asked, "If you wished to hunt an animal wouldn't you study as much about the animal as you could"? Like learning to use a thunder stick, (rifle), if the very first one you ever saw wouldn't give you the knowledge to use it properly how would you learn. Could you make one? The Wasichue (Whiteman) isn't any more intelligent than you but he can use words to do things you never have thought of. BC Bob had several books with him. Most of them were on geology and mineralogy, far too complicated for beginning learners. He resolved to purchase picture books and grade school text when he reached a trading post. This brought up the problem: how to prepare his student for the experience of dealing with the white man and reaching conclusions as to the value of items they might want to purchase. Immediately he encountered a conflict of interests. The women assumed a position of liking things of beauty and functionality to their everyday lives. The men looked to knowledge about things that would give them an advantage over an adversary. Realizing the conflicts of interests B.C. Bob separated his classes into two groups. The women were the earliest risers since they prepared the cooking fires and morning meals. This left the men to the first morning classes. After tending to the animals they gathered after much grumbling and complaining. Wapaxo soon settled the complaints by asking the men if they wanted to take over the women's chores. B.C. Bob was stumped as to how to gain the attention and interest of the young braves, put on his gunbelt and stepped before the group. He had arranged six large pine cones on a rail fastened between two saplings. With lighting speed he drew and dispatched all six pine cones to the amazement of the awe struck braves. They all eagerly voiced their desire to learn to perform this task. He explained that after six days of English classes there would be a class in quick draw and pistol shooting for those that earned the right by learning the new language. He had found the touch stone. Every day thereafter the young braves were patiently waiting to struggle with the reading, speaking, and writing classes.

With the streams becoming fordable and the mountain passes opening up, the clan broke camp. They had wintered good. The horses were in good condition and the food supplies were adequate to get the group through the higher country to the more bountiful low lands.

Breaking camp was mostly women's work and they energetically tackled the tasks from early morning to dusk. However the tranquility of purpose didn't extend to the three younger braves. The competition created by their drive to excel in the use of the pistol had led to disagreements as to which of the three, Beaver Boy, Broken Branch and Up River would carry the pistol for the day. Wapaxo had cut off the issue of ammunition because of the shortage. This didn't hinder the constant practice of drawing and dry firing that filled every moment of opportunity. B.C. Bob and Jacque took solemn notice of the rivalry and wondered if they hadn't opened a can of worms that would later lead to a confrontation and somebody suffering a serious if not a mortal incident. The problem was the inherent drive in young male natives to excel in every contest offered them. This was a contest that didn't lead to mere dishonor, but death. B.C Bob anguished over his selection of an incentive to induce the young men to learn a new language.

The mountains broke away to low hills and valleys. Milliwana returned from a plant gathering excursion with excitement, she had discovered a large patch of camas and urged the leaders to halt and harvest as much as possible. At first the young men grumbling and slacked off from the women's work until they observed Wapaxo, Jacque and B. C. Bob pitching in and gathering roots to be dried and pulverized into camas flour. When given the opportunity to break away from this manual labor and go hunting they scrambled to gather their bows and arrows. The rifle ammunition was held in reserve for possible confrontations. The lack of success in stalking the plentiful herds of deer reminded Wapaxo of the elaborate ritual the buffalo hunters went into to prepare to harvest the prairie beasts. He ordered the preparation of a sweat tent and evening feast. Balsam was plentiful and the hunters were able to approach the deer within bow and arrow range and soon the camp was well stocked with choice venison. Wapaxo decided that it was time to think of the trail ahead and instructed the women to dry and jerk as much meat as was possible. With this goal in mind Beaver Boy, Broken Branch, and Up River set out on another hunt. On their last hunt they had seen signs of other hunters in the area so they decided to take a couple of the henry rifles and some ammunition as a security precaution. On their second day out they bagged two white tailed bucks in good condition. Beaver Boy hadn't seen anything but pregnant does and was returning to the hunting camp when a big dry cow elk stepped out of some tall willows in front of him. The obsidian point caught her behind her left ear and she dropped without a step. After bleeding the cow Beaver Boy left her to get his two comrades to help dressing out the large animal. Upon returning to the kill site Broken Branch and Up River went right to work disemboweling the cow. They were rigging a hanging cross pole between two saplings when a grizzly sniffing at the gut pile charged them. With two swipes the two young braves were sent flying. Beaver Boy slid the henry out of its scabbard and placed three slugs in the bear's neck at the base of its skull. It wasn't luck, it was skilled marksmanship. The two young braves weren't seriously injured just some scrapes and bruises. After thoroughly cleaning the open wounds Beaver Boy bound some moss bandages over the cuts to stop the flow of blood. Up River was the least injured so he rode off to bring back more help and the larger horses as pack animals. Beaver Boy hobbled and tethered the skittish horses left behind. The smell of the grizzly and the blood had panicked the horses left behind. . Almost completely bushed, Beaver Boy started a fire and gathered what he could to make a meal. Placing the deer tongues and the elk tongue in a hide bucket with some herbs and chunks of camas root, he soon had them boiled by adding hot rocks to the mixture. The contents of the upper stomach of the elk were eaten as a nutritious salad. The elk being more of a grazer than a browser, its stomach contents were finer more adaptable to the human digestive system. With balsam boughs as mattresses spread over the ground warmed by the fire and the henry rifle close at hand they settled in for the night.

At day break Beaver Boy led the horses to water and picketed them in a grassy meadow. The sun was high in the sky before the tribe help arrived. Two of the women came to take care of the hides since this was women's work. Only the bears hide, teeth, and claws were taken since the clan had plenty of meat and the bear was old. With plenty of hands the work was completed in short order. They camped for the night and traveled at day break. The dust from the horses hooves had hardly settled when the women began setting smoking fires and stripping the meat for curing. Salt was used very sparingly their supply was low and no prospect of being able to replenish their stock. There was a silent mood change in the tribe. The two younger bucks were no longer in intensive competition with each other and an unseen halo seemed to have settled around Beaver Boy. Wapxo's tribe began to see the superiority of Beaver Boy's abilities which included his instinctive ability with the fire arm. He seemed to be more aware of his environment. Wapaxo had seen him circling a large tamarack tree and touching the bark in many places. When Wapaxo asked, "What are you doing?" Beaver Boy answered, "This is a grandfather tree that has seen many years of this area and I am attempting to gain a little of its knowledge. Notice the twisting of the trunk. The branches have been paying homage to the sun. The wind Gods has given it a particular slant, indicating the most prevalent directions of their forces."

They had been on the move for over a month when they came to desert country. The natives panicked .They had been used to an unlimited supply of water and couldn't believe any place could be so dry. They soon learned why B.C. Bob had them clean and cure the stomachs of the slaughtered animals. Before turning south- west every available container was filled with water at the next stream. It was several days before they reached the foothills of the Cascade Mountains. Heeding Beaver Boy's advice they headed more westerly than south. Although the route was a little more arduous the water was more plentiful. With the advent of more water came a boon in the form of multitudes of sage grouse. With the tribe's skill in the use of the sling came a feast of a welcome diet of delicious poultry seasoned with a delicate flavor of sage.

Beaver Boy, who was always on patrol, came into camp and reported that the Wapaxo group was being scouted by a hunting party. Always alert Wapaxo issued additional ammunition for the henry rifles and sent Upriver and Broken Branch with Beaver Boy to gather information and select a site that would afford the warriors and the clan the best possible defense posture. From a good vantage point Beaver Boy was able to discern that this was not a hostile group. In fact the group consisted of women and children and Beaver Boy thought that he recognized one of the braves. With Upriver and Broken Branch keeping watch he approached the leaders. His observations were correct these were trading Chinooks and the one he recognized had been part of a party he had traded camas to for salt. They were loaded with superbly made baskets, otter furs and salt. Their destination was a port on the coast in what is now California. The women were delighted with the merger that was formed and the group set off the next morning as a stronger cohesive trading party.

No mention of gold was made so the Chinooks were stumped as to what the Wapaxo clan was going to trade their stores of camas were not significant. It was the possession of henry rifles that secured the bond between the two groups. The braves of the Chinooks were allowed to handle the rifles and were completely fascinated by the hunting advantages the rifles afforded. The Chinooks were baffled by the Wapaxo clan's preference for the use of the traditional bow and arrow for collecting game. Beaver Boy finally was able to convince the Chinooks of their need to conserve the ammunition by telling them that the bullets were like the arrows to the bow. They were able to make arrows but not bullets.

Millewana was disappointed there was no camas to be found during the next weeks of travel She and the women were forced to harvest cat tail roots for basic food.Pinenuts were in abundance but as a steady diet they created digestive problems for the tribesmen that seldom ate them, resorting to more starchy foods for basics. As they followed a main stream down the west slope of the Cascades berries were harvested to add to the meat diet.

Upon arrival at a cliff overlooking the Pacific several of Wapaxo"s clan were astounded at the magnificence of the great body of water. Of special note was the sighting of the migrating whales. When they came to a break in the cliffs the Chinook tribe made for the beaches and commenced to harvest clams. Milliwana and the rest of the Wapaxo clan's women delighted in digging, and shucking the tender morsels from the shells. Soon there was a feast provided and everyone settled into a festive evening meal.

The traders moved back inland to avoid the rugged coast line for ease of travel their next experience involved the northern fringes of the Sequoia forest. The giant trees were unfathomable to the woods Indians of the northern regions.

Wapaxo was delighted to find myrtle wood bushes in abundance and spent many hours searching for straight branches to make weapons from. To avoid the almost impenetrable forest and brushes the traders were forced to head back toward the coast and work around the many jetties formed by the drainage from the land and wave actions of the ocean. Topping the ridge of a large jetty they were delighted to see a cluster of buildings and two large sailing vessels anchored in the harbour.Manny Horses's clan was eager to rush down to the village.Wapaxo called for a conference advising everybody to stay out of sight. It was decided that they circle and enter from the south after establishing a defensible camp. Beaver Boy headed out with a half dozen scouts. After several hours they chose a rise that seemed possible to defend. It was hard to contain the young braves of Manny Horses' tribe but the women were told of Milliwana's experience at the Columbia trading post and understood the need for safety and protection. A little stream provided water and ample lodge pole pine was soon cut to build two horse corrals and wickiups.They reasoned that two corrals would provide them with horses to capture any that managed to escape. The young people were sent out to harvest grass for the horses. Hunters followed the stream into the woods and they soon returned with several small coastal deer. Jacque suggested another conference. His knowledge of alcohol's affect on his brother Indians led him to convince Wapaxo and Manny Horses that it would be wise to give the braves a lesson. They still had several jugs of whiskey taken from the hide hunters; they had a party. With all of the weapons secured the only results were a few bruises and lots of sick stomachs and head aches. The next day was lost. It was Jacque, in his position as Lead Warrior who decided the entry and defense plan. The village was organized to block any entrance to the living and council area except for two point's one leading to the trail to the village and an exit route to the timbered area. The in- between areas were blocked with lodge pole and brush. The younger members of the party had been busy at each creek and dry creek crossing gathering stones for their slings. Piles of these stones were at both entrances of the camp and in dispersed places between the lodges.

With Beaver Boy and Broken Branch left to guard the camp the trading party consisting of Wapaxo, Jacque, B. C. Bob, Manny Horses, Up River, and a Sub- Chief to Manny Horses; Wolf Runner. To prevent too much attention they split into two groups with three entering from the north and three entering from the south. They slowly scouted out the lay of the town from opposite sides of the street. Unlike the Columbia trading town there appeared to be three active trading posts. According to an earlier agreement they assembled at the north end of town in a coppice of quake aspen trees to discuss their approach to trading. Jacque agreed to accompany the Manny Horse tribe to assist in bargaining. B.C. Bob and Wapaxo had noticed a bank like building and decided to feel out their exchange approach for their gold dust. When B.C. Bob was able to determine that the town had a script arrangement with the trading posts they decided this was the best approach to the exchange of their gold. Jacque wasn't having as much luck with the trading of baskets, fish, pelts and salt. There appeared to be collusion between the trading posts. Their bids were too close to not be coherent. The sea otter pelts seemed to be of the highest value. With Jacques coaching the Manny Horses traders they separated out their pelts and offered them in smaller bundles it was soon apparent that the Russians were most eager to buy the sea otter pelts. The trade in salt appeared to be consistent. Evidently the coastal tribesmen of this area had depressed the demand for salt.Many Horses tribe was pleased with the value placed on their baskets by the Russian traders. The unique ability to weave baskets that held water was significant. The designs were artistic and recognized for their value as art objects

Suspicious of the script Bob Cat Bob and Wapaxo only exchanged a miniscule amount of gold for script which they took immediately to the trading posts and purchased supplies. Satisfied that the script was valid they returned to the exchange and purchased a substantial amount of script. The quantity of gold created an immediate excitement and interest as to its source. Ignoring the attention of the gathering of the crowd following them from trading post to trading post, they were startled by an aggressive young man that rushed forward and shouted," Doctor Mc Namey". Startled by hearing his proper name, B.C. Bob wheeled about to confront the young man that thrust forth his hand in greeting. "Ivan Utzeph!" He exclaimed, "You're a long way from home". "I was about to say the same thing to you", replied Ivan. With brief explanations the friends agreed to meet later and hash over old times. It was at this point that Wapaxo, B.C. Bob and Jacque crossed paths. Jacque had heard the young man call Bob," Doctor." He commented that he didn't know B. C. Bob was an MD. Bob's reply was, "It isn't a medical title but an academic one, explaining further that he had been a professor at a university in Scotland and that the young man Ivan had been one of his students".

The port village was bereft of females of all ages. This led the sailors and traders to surmise that the newly arrived Indians had brought their women with and were camped in the vicinity. With a universal belief that female companionship could be obtained with trade or liquor, three sailors stumbled into the trader's camp. Alerted, the women and children hid out in their hogans. The camp was ghostly quiet when the three men drunkenly stumbled down the main path between the shelters. After passing several shelters the men were about to search one of the hogans when a young maiden of fifteen years of age stepped out to see them out of curiosity. The smallest of the group was the first to see her. She wrinkled her nose in disgust when she seen the dirty clothes and messy beards. He yipped in delight as he grabbed for her and she cringed in fear. His two friends turned to see his prize when they witnessed the sudden pain and shock as he fell forward loosing his grip on the maiden. He had been struck in the back with a stone the size of a goose egg. Angered and instantly sober he turned and reached for his holstered pistol. It never cleared the leather before his wrist and hand was shattered with a similar well placed stone. Suddenly all three sobered up and beat a hasty retreat from the camp. There had been no need for the two rifle men to fire a shot. As disgruntled as they were, they felt lucky to escape the "Stone Throwers" camp. It wasn't long until the news of the women hunter's experience was spread throughout the village. The barterers laughed and felt no need to interrupt their buying since there had been no gun fire involved. Not to be dissuaded one of Manny Horse's warriors dashed back to the camp and learned of the encounter. The humor evoked when he returned to join the traders, bringing loud guffaws and much merriment to the gathering of traders. The revelers Including Beaver Boy, Up River, Broken Branch and B.C. Bob stepped into the largest of the bars. B.C. Bob had reclaimed his revolver and holster from the young braves who now wore their own pistols with pride, slung in buscadero style holsters that had wide skirts that hugged their slim hips and were tied down with leather thongs. Immediately there was tension amongst the mountain men and woodsmen at the bar as the four settled at a table selected by B.C. Bob. Four bearded tough looking customers turned their backs to the bar and faced the table where B.C. Bob and the three young braves had seated. Remarks were made to the effect that Red Skins didn't have the right to come into a bar with white men. In an attempt to prevent a confrontation B.C. Bob got up and went to the bar and bought the house drinks. This however didn't appease the four toughs. They were looking for trouble. B.C. Bob gave instructions to the three braves, He then picked up the shot glasses emptied by the loud mouths tossed all four into the air and in one rolling roar the glasses exploded simultaneously. The display was all it took. The bar maid brought the two pitchers of beer and glasses to the table and everybody turned to their drinks. B.C. Bob gave the bartender enough gold to pay for the damages then he went to the town marshal and arranged for a shooting contest the next day. His plan was to convince the town that the traders were not to be messed with.

Dr. Mckamey and Ivan Utzeph pushed their chairs back from the hotel dinning room table, lit their pipes and began talking at once. They were both fluent in six languages. It was a toss up Russian or English. English won out. Dr McKamey urged Ivan to begin with his graduation from Scotland's most prestigious college and return to Russia. In Smolensk he continued his higher education in Geomorphology and made several field studies in the Ural Mountains and Siberia. It was the culmination of his Siberian trip that brought him to Sevastopol where he signed on with the Russian ship Kodiak carrying fur hunters, "promysloviki" to Alaska and down the North American coast to Ft Ross. The highly sought sea otters were becoming scarce and the Russian fur men were forced to turn to farming and live stock raising to put food on the table. When it became B.C. Bob's turn to relate his past life that earned him the name of Bob Cat Bob, he explained that he had accompanied a wagon train to Wyoming Territory where he became interested in the mineral outcropping in the Shoshone Mountain area of Wyoming. There he lived with the Shoshone people also known as the "Sheep Eaters". His attentiveness to language sounds aided him in becoming fluent in their jargon. He had been living on mostly cotton tail rabbits. The hind legs and backs were the fleshiest portion of the carcass. He used the entrails and front of the rabbits as bait for Bob Cats. This he suspended above a trap that the bobcat landed in when he sprang up to snare the food. Arriving in the Shoshone camp with a large number of bobcat pelts earned him the name of Bobcat Hunter which was shortened to Bob Cat Bob and later to B.C. Bob.

It was when the conversation centered on the subjects most dearly to the two geography educated men that they lowered their voices and B.C. Bob explained to his old student about his discovery of the sill deposit of gold ore that he had discovered. Ivan had instant gold fever and asked;" Is it possible for me to join you in your return trip?" "I don't have the authority to grant you the permission", explained the Professor." Wapaxo is the tribes Chief and it is a decision he would have to make. I can speak on your behalf, but he has been moody lately. There is a feeling of discontent. There is too much happening that he has lost control of and he might refuse" There is another aspect that would have to be considered ", Ivan conjectured. The Kodiac Captain's daughter Tatjana and I are going to be married here at Ft. Ross. I would of course want to bring her along." This brings a whole different aspect to the scenario, Milliwana,"Wapaxo's wife has a strong influence on Wapaxo and without her endorsement it wouldn't be possible, replied the Professor.

The shooting contest was staged. Beaver Boy, Upriver, and Broken Branch were the clear winners of all events because BC Bob did not participate. Several pistoleros and toughs were more than just the losers in the contests. They had bet large sums on the out come and consequently they were spending a lot less time in the bars buying drinks. There was another side affect influencing the tribe's tranquility. Wapaxo resented the attention paid to the winners of the shooting contest .The emphasis on fire arms achievements diluted his stature as the master hunter (Bear Slayer). His mighty spear became a lesser symbol. The lack of elk sinew prevented him from re-lashing the large obsidian point to the myrtle wood shaft. .

He called for an audience with the three braves; berating them, calling them white men squaws, he directed them to leave immediately for the eastern hills and to take only bows and arrows. They were not to return until they had killed large game and brought it back to camp. When word of his actions reached Jacque and B.C. Bob they knew their plans to add the local blacksmith Igor and Ivan to the expedition was in jeopardy. If they were going to try extraction of the gold ore from the rich sill they would need drill bits that would constantly need sharpening and repair. Jacque went to the blacksmith and asked him if he could permanently fasten the obsidian to the shaft in a decorative fashion. Assured that he could, he explained to Igor the history of the spear and its significance to Wapaxo.

Igor had been working hard to construct a large wagon capable of hauling his tools, equipment and stock of iron and other metals to the ore deposit. They had procured eight oxen to pull the wagon, but no roads and a paucity of terrain information made the task seem impossible. Chief Manny-horses had learned that the sailing ship Kodiac was planning to dock near the mouth of the Columbia on its return trip to Sevastopol. Jacque and BC Bob arranged transport of the wagon to the mouth of the Colombia They feared that not including Wapaxo in these decisions was a mistake, Igor was delighted he could add much needed supplies and the problem of transporting explosives could be solved. The Kodiac carried a large supply of Chinese constructed explosive devices consisting of improved black powders packed in bamboo tubes.

Beaver Boy, Up River and Broken Branch were still smarting from the dressing down handed out by Wapaxo when they ventured into a collision of cultures. Southern California in the early 1800s was a cauldron of people, cultures and power struggles. At the top if the pyramid were the Hidalgos, which had been given large land grants from the royals of Spain. Not necessarily in the order of social rank, but in consideration was the percentage of Spanish blood line. The Mestizos, (those with mixed Indian and Spanish blood), that had attached themselves to the Hidalgos of wealth and power. Many of the large land owners, (those holding thousands of acres, proceeded to stock the land with as many head of cattle as they could buy,(regardless of source). The results were huge herds. The big influx of beef depressed the market and barrels of corned beef sought by the shipping trade were unprofitable to produce. It was the hides that seemed to hold their value. The big outfits branded their cattle with large brands that could be easily distinguished from a distance. The large brands disfigured the hides and the prices dropped. To combat this they began artistically cropping the ears. The problem with this is that they were hard to distinguish at a distance and were easy to alter.

Enter another element to the melting pot. The Anglos, (these came from different back grounds mostly from European extraction). The Civil War spawned a deluge of resentment created by political differences and actions of combat. Under the guise of justification for atrocities real or imagined, reasons, were established for criminal activity. Without any allegiance and a lack of organized civil law, the criminal element found the huge herds of practically unmarked cattle easy pickings especially the herds of the arrogant Hildagos'.The Hildagos biggest losses weren't the bad Anglos but their own suppressed, scurrilously treated vaqueros. They had created amongst themselves a colorful dashing image that they worked hard to portray as dashing and carefree. The advent of a fiesta brought out their expensive wardrobes for the benefit of the senoritas. Strutting, dancing, playing of guitars and the consumptions of copious amounts of pulque, cerveza, and for those that could afford it tequila. Envying the flamboyant life styles of the Hildagos that treated them like dirt under their feet, they plotted to elevate their standards by relieving the big rancheros of as many un- marked cattle as they could sequester. Working at night they moved small bunches to northern valleys just out of the bounds of the big estates. When they accumulated a herd of around a hundred they moved to more northern areas planning some day to establish their own estancia. Marcos Degoro, Alfredo Blanca, Angel Rubio, and the Hernandaz brothers seldom had the opportunity to work together since they were indentured to three separate rancheros. The political pressures had caused the Hidalgos to heed the call of Mexico's Hierarchy to assembly for consultations on the Nord-Americano movement into California. This provided an opportunity for the movement of sequestered cattle north to a holding area where they could later drive them to land they had squatted on and establish a ranchero. It was late evening when the rustlers, exhausted and hampered by lack of daylight settled in and set up camp. The previous evening had been arduous as the result of a predator spooking the one hundred plus head of the mixed trail herd.

About a half mile north of the rustlers camp Beaver Boy, Upriver and Broken branch had also had a strenuous day, only able to bag a small coast deer they had butchered for camp meat. The elk they sought had moved to higher country. Still smarting from the rebuke of Wapaxo there was little communication as the warriors checked their weapons and settled in for the night

The Ft Ross community awoke to a beautiful autumn day as Tatjana stepped from the dory that had brought her to the dock from the four- masted Russian cargo ship her father Boris Sheppenov captained. It wasn't an easy circumstance that brought her to this foreign coastal village. When her father had informed his crew that she would be aboard he almost lost his crew to rebellion. It was a prevalent superstition that women on board a ship were bad luck. It was only a week before the scheduled departure that the crew became totally disabled with a virulent intestinal malady. Tatjana lacked only her internship to be a full fledged medical doctor. The ship's crew had all consumed a shell fish stew. Recognizing the symptoms' Tatjana scoured the countryside around Sevastopol for rose hips, high in vitamin C content. She made porridge and force fed the crew. The result was an instant bowel cleansing and she became their saving angel. To the men came the realization that she would be a life saving asset on any voyage.

The image of an angel fit Tatjana Sheppenov with only the wings lacking. She was five feet five inches tall, one hundred eighteen pounds, with shoulder length bright blond hair, and light blue eyes. Most people found it hard to look deep into her eyes they were so penetrating. She had been in Sevastopol for a year and had met Ivan Utzeph as a natural circumstance since he was attached to the Russian council and attended the high level social functions. With his Doctorate in Geomorphology and Masters in Mathematics Ivan was often asked to speak about Geography and couldn't help seeing her in his after audience, formal introductions, they became frequent companions at embassy functions. When he was asked to sail with the Kodiak to the western American coast and submit a dissertation on American geomorphology he gladly accepted with the stipulation he could terminate his assignment at his choosing. Captain Sheppenov approved of his daughter's association considering Ivan an equal in the Russian hierarchy. He reluctantly watched their attraction grow into full blown love during the months at sea.

Greeting Tatjana at the dock, Ivan whisked her up into his arms and they embraced. She had wanted to observe Chief Manny Horses' basket makers constructing the beautiful baskets she had seen brought on aboard the Kodiac.Milliwana greeted the couple and accompanied them to the hogans of the basket makers. Tatjana immediately became a serious attraction. The young Indian maidens couldn't believe her hair was real. They had seen the dirty blond hair of some of the sailors but none with the radiance of Tatjana's. Milliwana had to chase them away as they tried to feel to see if it was real. As they made their way from hogan to hogan Tatjana marveled at the deftness of the basket weaves as they selected the different fibers, tapping them into shape, maintaining lovely patterns. She ordered several colorful baskets and asked Ivan to bring them to the ship later.Milliwana picked up one of the water tight baskets and presented it to Titjana. She told her that this was the most perfect sample of the basket weaver's skill and only had one small flaw. After repeated use the strain on the fibers caused the baskets to leak at the junction of the handle.

Tatjana couldn't help notice that the two basket weavers were totally identical twins. She asked their names and Milliwana answered, "Diannee and Diannaa". "How do you tell them apart?" asked Tatjana. The reply was, "nobody can". They were like one person with two bodies and identical in every way. Their parents had died of small pox when they were twelve years old. They were raised by their grand parents that had passed away six years ago making them in their early twenties. They were quite attractive tending to be well built on the voluptuous side. Very light hearted they seem to be laughing all the time. Delighted Tatjana said goodbye and informed Ivan that she wanted to go back to the town and visit with the blacksmith Igor.As they exited the basket maker's hogan they were met by Tallena. Milliwana made the introductions showing her pride in Tallena. When B.C. Bob was conducting classes in Shoshone and English Tallena was his star pupil. She had a natural talent for languages Pleased to learn that the couple planned a visit to the blacksmith she asked to accompany them. Ivan thought to himself," where could you find three more beautiful women?"

Igor seemed to never sleep. When he wasn't working on a big project he was making small articles for the women and metal arrowheads for the braves. His knives were treasures to those who owned them. Delighted for an excuse to leave his forge and anvil he greeted them in his gruff but gentle manner. His large six foot six frame and two hundred sixty pounds was a body builders dream. Despite his huge bearing he moved with the grace of a professional dancer. Tatjana said," I have come on behalf of my father, Captain Boris Sheppenov, he has agreed to haul your blacksmith tools, metal, and wagon to the mouth of the Columbia river. ". This was music to Igor's ears. He had been filled with worry and consternation over the prospect of moving the huge wagon he had built and the tons of tools and working metal north to the mining site B.C. Bob had told him about. Complicating the voyage is the movement of the explosives Jacque and B. C. Bob had purchased from Captain Boris. This consisted of two hundred bamboo Chinese explosive devices. Using the natural hollow structure of bamboo the Chinese had developed a modified more powerful black powder and packed it tightly onto bamboo tubes. Realizing this all depended on Wapaxo's acceptance of him on the trek Igor hurried back to his shop to work on his special project. Almost forgetting about Tallena's query. "Can you build me a potter's wheel?" she asked.

Since he had never seen one, Igor demurred, "Not for a while", he answered." Where can I see one? "Tallena answered, "When you have the time I will take you to the Mexican part of the village and show you one." Igor noticed the beautiful basket Tatjana was carrying and asked to look at it. As he was examining the basket Tatjana explained what Milliwana had told him about the one flaw in the exquisite art work. Stepping out into his shop for a moment, he came back with two short pieces of copper wire. These he wove into the handle area, taking the stress from the fibers holding the handle to the basket. Handing it to Tatjana he said, "This should take care of the problem." Laughing she said," You will have to show this to the makers yourself. Typical of female nature she was match making and knew it.

With only his work on his mind Igor had neglected his personal hygiene and his surroundings. Although his shop was well organized his dwelling was a boar's nest. Not knowing how to approach Igor's personal hygiene problem Tatjana enlisted the help of Ivan.

Ivan deferred to B.C Bob who concocted a story when he went to visit Igor concerning the transport of the wagon and supplies aboard the Kodiak. Starting with a complement he said," Igor you remind me of an old Scott at home. He was of royal blood and yet he had no friends for he truly loved garlic. So that he reeked of the pungent order about his person and his dwelling. He died a lonely man regardless of his good attributes. Embarrassed Igor spent the next day bathing, washing clothes and cleaning his dwelling.

Tallena's fascination was focused on the skills of the Mexican pottery makers. Her natural attribute of language skills soon had her speaking passable Spanish. Her first trip to the Mexican quarter made her uncomfortable for she couldn't miss the attention of the vaqueros as they eyed her beauty. The next trip she was accompanied by Broken Branch her husband who was recognized as being one of the expert shooters, "known as the deadly trio". The interest in Tallena gave way to thoughts of preservation. After closely examination of the different pottery wheels in use Tallena located one that seemed to be the best. This she showed to Igor. Igor had brought writing material which he used to sketch a picture of the devise. Within the week he summoned Tallena and showed her the improved version of the pottery wheel. The big improvement was the two opposing pedals that gave momentum to the wheel without the need to use the hands to spin while shaping the clay. He accompanied Tallena back to Manny Horses cluster of hogans to bring the reinforced water basket to D and D as they were now known as. There was no doubt that Igor was prepared for this, his clothes were clean and his person almost glowed with his trim beard and well washed body. At first D and D were shy, but their interest in the huge blacksmith permeated the atmosphere and they giggled like two blushing teenagers. In thanking Igor they placed their hands on his well muscled upper arms in caressing motions. Tallena glowed in observation of blooming love.

In the center of the grass meadow stood an excellent beef heifer. Beaver Boy circled around to the opposite side of Up River and Broken Branch, remaining out of sight staying in the timbered edge, Broker Branch circled to one side and Broken Branch the other. Almost simultaneous they loosed an arrow into both sides of the heifer's neck behind the ears. The stricken animal dropped in its tracks with hardly a quiver. With practiced efficiency the three hunters had the hide off and the offal dispatched. As they arose from their chore they found themselves surrounded by the five vaqueros with rifles trained on them. Unable to understand the Spanish chatter they stood dumbfounded. Their first thoughts were chagrin over their nakedness without their pistols. It was evident to them that these funny jabbering riflemen were tempting to steal their game.

The Vaqueros were in a different dilemma. The Hernandaz brothers wanted to string them up. Their argument being "they" were rustlers! "Go find their horses and gear first", shouted, Alfredo. Gathering up the bows and arrows and not finding any firearms puzzled the vaqueros. Fastening their lariats around the necks of the hunters, they back tracked to where they had tethered their horses. Puzzled as to why no firearms were found the discussion as to what to do with the rustlers was brought up again. The cool head of Marcos seemed to prevail. He recognized the trio from the shooting contest and wondered if a hasty execution wouldn't bring reprisals from the tribe. Alfredo and Angel remarked about the tribe having gold and wondered if they couldn't find some way to make the tribe pay for the beef the vaqueros had stolen in the first place. They had done an excellent job in skinning and fleshing the hide this being the most valuable part of the heifer added reason to their argument.

Wapaxo called a council meeting. Jacque sitting to Wapaxo's right knew that one of Wapaxo's concerns was the inclusion of Igor and Ivan as members of the trek to the home camp. Concealed to his right was a heavy porcelain base made to hold the shaft of Wapaxo's spear. He leaned over and whispered to Wapaxo, "We have a guest" He signaled to the brave at the council Hogan's entrance, who stepped aside to allow the big frame of Igor to stoop and enter the council room. He marched up to Wapaxo knelt to his knees and in a memorized speech in Shoshone said, Oh Bear Slayer, I hope this meets with your approval as he laid Wapaxo's spear before him." He had formed a brass clasp that held the large obsidian blade to the myrtle wood shaft. One side if the clasp was engraved with a buffalo figure and the opposite side was a grizzle bear. Igor stood up as Wapaxo picked up the spear and grunted his approval and set it into the porcelain base. It was no longer a spear it was now a rulers scepter with three white bald eagle feathers hanging decoratively below the clasp... Wapaxo almost smiled as he seemed to sit a little straighter. He said, "The two waisachu and their women will be welcomed to the trek home. Again the half smile appeared knowingly as he thought about Igor's two wives to be. Manny Horses had told him that Igor would have to take both sisters as wives since they were inseparable.

Between Wapaxo and Chief Manny Horses to his left was one of the more fancy baskets. Wapaxo withdrew from the basket a large ear of corn. He plucked one kernel from the ear and held the cob and the kernel for all to see. "This", he said, "is the true gold. As you can see every cob has a multitude of kernels, each of which can produce a stalk with one to four cobs. When properly dried and stored the kernels will keep for years. This is true wealth, there doesn't have to be a hungry time. The women, with escort will go amongst the farmers of Ft.

Ross and trade or purchase as many four ear stocks as possible. When they have all of the four ear stocks they can trade for three and two ear stocks. The cobs of the four ear stocks will be sorted out and kept for seed. Wapaxo was performing genetic selection.

The meeting was closed when a teen aged brave from Manny Horses tribe brought news of the Vaqueros bringing the hunters into camp. BC Bob and Tallena hurried to the center of the Manny Horse camp. The Vaqueros were tense when they noticed that they were many times out numbered by rifle carrying braves and B.C. Bob with an efficient looking pistol. The Vaqueros hadn't been able to communicate until Tallena appeared on the scene. B. C. Bob listened as Tallena questioned the vaqueros and translated for him. Upon hearing the story his first reaction was one of anger but when he heard the demand of thirty dollars for the meat and hide he realized this was a simple transaction and added a bid for an additional beef and hide in the same condition for, the same amount to be brought in the next day. With a tightness of fear in their throats the vaqueros were glad to depart as quickly as possible.

Cupid had been busy. Chief Manny Horses had two couples seeking matrimony and it was apparent Diannee and Dianna wouldn't be happy until they had corralled Igor the blacksmith. It was amusing to the two tribes the excuses the two basket weavers cooked up to give reasons for visiting Igor. Never had any bachelor received so much attention and had his dwelling kept in spotless condition. Housekeeping had been a burden for him, stealing time from his shop projects. By some quirk the tools and gadgets he spent an inordinate time on were those that would please women. His latest tool was a pair of scissors. He had worried about the size and utility. The DDs had small hands and yet they needed to cut leather. The DDs had secretly measured one of Igor's shirts and were in the process of making him one out of bleached, fringe trimmed deer belly hide. It was to be his wedding garb. The DDs had matching dresses. There hadn't as of yet been any ceremony, but the blacksmith was known as Igor two wives, generally followed with a chuckle. Tatjana and Ivan were married by her father the ships captain. Since they had been accepted to join the trek by Wapaxo he felt they should join in the two tribe's ceremony. The die was cast. Manny Horses and Wapaxo had announced that they would start the trek in thirty sleeps. Hunters from many horses tribe and the deadly trio of Wapaxo's tribe had been successful in their hunts, deer and elk meat would be added to the beef bought from the rustlers. New delicious bread made from camas flower and ground corn was baked and ready. The Alcalde, the Magistrate, and Tatjana's father were included in the assembly. A Mexican guitar ensemble joined the drum beat of the tribes, making the festivities a truly colorful. Event. With only a small amount of pulque available there was a little lifting of the spirits without drunkenness.

Thirty one days after the announced departure there was an eerie silence about Ft Ross. The trek had left the day before and they had left very little evidence of having ever been there. The five rustlers entered the former camp of the tribes to seek the possibility of selling more beef. The hogans had been moved with only the rings left behind. The barrier and the corrals were the only evidence of having been a community. Leaving their horses in the corral the five vaqueros circled the area and decided that this would be a good location to establish their ranchero. They had Fort Ross and the ocean to the west and a rugged cliff to the east with plenty of good pasture to the north and south. They sought out the magistrate and queried as to the ownership of the property only to be told there was no patented land outside of Fort Ross. The surrounding land was claimed by the Russians and Mexicans There was no way of either of them enforcing their claims. With aside deals, i.e. agreements for payment of beef for life, the Ft Ross officials with the aid of a scribe drew up papers of title to Ranchero Sonoma naming the five as holders of land described as bounded by Ft Ross, The Pacific Ocean and specified leagues north, east and south. Feeling secure with their phony papers the rustlers celebrated. By trading beef they soon had a large crew cutting lodge pole and putting up jack fences. Ranchero

Sonoma didn't rely on normal calf crops to expand their herds. They continued to raid the big southern California ranches and bought stolen cattle from anybody that could herd them north. The result of their accumulation made a glut on the beef market. It was only the hides that held their value. Soon the ranchero began to experiment with leather tanning and this soon grew to be their best product with the trading ships.

Since the traders trek couldn't just return the way they had come they had to search out and mark a new trail north to rendezvous with the Kodiac at the mouth of the Mother River "Columbia." By agreement the new trail would be marked by two stones one on the other of sufficient size as to prevent accidental dislodgement. Three stones would indicate next marker would indicate a change of direction. The change would be marked by a forked branch with another branch in the fork to indicate direction. Beaver Boy urinated on the change of direction indicators to prevent animals from disrupting them.

Bringing up the rear of the trek Igor was driving the only wagon. His two wives were herding the six extra oxen. Every horse carried a pack or pulled a travois. Two teen aged braves were with Beaver Boy, two with Wapaxo and Manny Horses at the head of the trek, two with Igor and two bringing up the rear guard headed by Broken Branch. The trek was being followed was without doubt. However there was no concernment since the tribes knew they were merely trying to find their gold strike. In the mean time Broken Branch scouted them day and night to find out as much about the trailers as possible. He even assigned them names according to their appearance. There was Baggy Pants, Brushy face, Limper, and Too Tall. Broken Branch found the trailers humorous. They were careless, clumsy, loud and totally out of sync with their environment. One of them had chosen a poison oak bush to relieve him self. He even used the leaves to clean up afterward. Broken Branch knew in two days he would be in serious trouble.

Still laughing to himself he led his horse across a small stream right into the path of a mother skunk. She got him good.

He stumbled back to the stream leapt in and began flushing his eyes and scrubbing himself with sand. It would be days before he could leave the odor behind him. Even his horse shied away when he tried to mount.

In the main group of the trekkers the poison oak came in a different form. The tribe's dogs chasing after rabbits and other forest creatures became covered with the noxious resins which were passed to the children as the dogs sought them for affection. Milliwana was consulted and she recognized the symptoms immediately. However the limestone clay of her home territory wasn't available. When she told Tatjana of the problem the two of them went to Ivan who remembered seeing limestone outcroppings a days journey back. With haste he rode as fast as possible back to the limestone outcropping and gathered as much as he could carry. When he returned to the main camp, that was stalled to attend to the problem, Tatjana and Milliwana immediately crushed the stone and made poultices for the affected children.

Beaver Boy topped a small ridge and gazed upon a mighty fir tree before him. As was his usual reverence he dismounted and embraced the tree after he tethered his mount. Noticing the nervousness' of his horse he climbed up the mighty fir and scanned the area with his the field scope he now carried with him every where. About twenty five yards to his left he discovered the problem. A large male mountain lion was scenting the bushes next to a beaver dam. He wasn't interested in the horse because the breeze was from him to Beaver Boy's mount. A female had marked the bush next to the dam before she crossed it. The problem was a large bald faced hornets nest was now directly over the path across the beaver dam. Hoping to follow the female and not interested in dashing his adoration with a cold water bath, the big cat flattened his body to give clearance to the hornet nest and started across the dam rather than swim the pond. Smiling Beaver Boy fitted an arrow to his bow and let fly clipping the bindings holding the nest to the branch just as the cat passed under it, the result was instantaneous. In less than a second the cat was covered with vicious hornets as it dashed for the brush on the other side to avoid the onslaught.

From his position high up the big fir tree Beaver Boy could see that to swing east down from the beaver dam wouldn't be a good route for the coming travelers. As he descended from the big fir tree, Up River joined him. They laughed over the cat and the hornets and Up River told him they were going to have to go west to find decent passage for the following travelers. After leaving the proper sign they headed up stream away from the beaver pond. The sun was setting when the two scouts entered a nice little meadow with a small stream winding through. They hobbled their horses, lit a small fire and supped on pemmican before settling in for the night.

Up River left at day break marking his route, he followed a small stream flowing to the west. The sun felt good on his back. About three hours after leaving Beaver Boy he topped a small rise and saw a small village clustered on the bank of a small lake. He tethered his horse on the trail so Beaver Boy knew he wanted to meet. The two runners had joined Beaver Boy bringing messages of the traveler's progress and stories of the poison oak episode. Beaver Boy climbed the rise and scanned the village with his telescope. The occupants seemed to be elderly, women and children. The scouts were cautious of the absence of adult males. This could be danger if the absent men were a war party. Deciding on the side of caution, Beaver Boy crept in close to the village to spy out as much information as possible. Making special note of their dwellings and clothes he briefed the sharpest of the runners making him repeat the message to make sure it reached Manny Horses. There was little remained to do but wait. The security of the main party was the utmost objective. The main party was a hard one and one half days ride behind the scouts.

A new scout arrived at the scout's camp. He told Beaver Boy and Up River that they need not have any concerns about the absence of men in the camp. This tribe were Hupa (Hoopa), well known as spirit dancers. This time of the year they danced to thank the Gods and Spirits for the past good year and to ask for blessings on the coming year. This was a function of the young most vigorous of the male members of the tribe. The women were not included in the activities.

Beaver Boy and Up River went hunting. Before dark they both had a large dry doe. After skinning and cleaning the animals they let them hang for the night. Cautiously but not apprehensive they entered the camp. All of the children had disappeared and only several old women and a pack of snarling dogs greeted them. When they presented the meat four older men approached and admired the fine animals. The meat was divided up and fires were started to prepare a feast.

Beaver Boy, Up River and the runners couldn't help but notice the skin of the older people and the children. Most of them were covered with scales and some had open sores. It was a sign of malnutrition. No wonder they were delighted to see the fresh meat

It was two days before the main party arrived. Milliwana and Tatjana immediately noticed the skin condition of the camp and came to the same conclusion; malnutrition. This astounded Milliwana for she had seen, much to her delight, large patches of camas along the edges and in the coves of the lake. Leaving the men to set up camp next to the stream, Milliwana enlisted the women of the tribe to join her and several of the trek's women to accompany her to the camas plots. Camassia, "camas", later to be known as camas was in abundance. However there were two varieties. It was too late in the year to distinguish the blue camas from the white camas from their blossoms. The blue flowered camas being edible and the white flowered camas toxic. However Milliwana was a camas specialist since she had lived with and harvested it all of her life. Taking several of the Hupa ladies with her she showed them the differences. Most of their conversation was in sign language and would have to be repeated with Manny Horses present to stumble his way through the difficult language.

Wapaxo didn't object when Milliwana asked to stay with the Hupas a little longer. They were ahead of their schedule to meet the ship at the mouth of the Columbia. He anticipated that they would soon be in Manny Horse's country so going should be easier. The camas harvest almost turned into frenzy. Milliwana looked at almost all of the tubers to make sure none of the white blossomed variety was collected. The children seemed to assimilate the fastest. The exchange of games brought screams of delight. It was the old stick ball game, that seemed to be ubiquitous, turned out to be the favorite.

It was early evening of the fifth day that the dancers returned to camp. Their arrival had been anticipated and a feast had been prepared. Milliwana had prepared a large quantity of her camas/corn bread that she had perfected. Fresh meat and camas boiled and baked was in abundance. The trek's children were horrified and ran to their mothers for some of the dancers were still costumed in the spirit garb used during the dance. The dancers couldn't help but notice Wapaxo and his scepter. They were impressed and some of the elders were allowed to handle the obsidian tipped spear. Some of the elders had traveled into the Klamath territory and communications were easier for them. Two of the Hupa elders that had traded to the north agreed to accompany them to the mouth of the Columbia. This delighted Wapaxo because of his concerns for the heavily laden caravan.

After an exchange of gifts the trekkers left the Hupas in good spirits. Beaver Boy, Up River, and the two runners accompanied by Spirit Dancer and Wolfman had left at day break. As the trekkers approached the west coast they began to encounter sea otter trappers. Knowing these pelts to be highly prized by the Kodiak Captain and crew Wapaxo bartered with some of the prizes he had accumulated. Fortunately the biggest demand was for the knives crafted by Igor "With Two Wives". Sea food was easily exchanged for camas flour and fruit.

When they arrived at the delta of the Columbia they were disappointed that the big ship was not in sight. They prepared to camp and await the ship when they learned that the large vessel had sailed upstream to a better harbor and dock, "Portland". After sending runners ahead to let the captain know they were here they headed up the southern banks of the Columbia to a meeting place.

The meeting of the trekkers and the ships crew was climactic. Captain Sheppenov as pleased as he was with the otter pelts was enthralled with his daughter's radiant appearance. He soon grew to understand as he learned of her experiences with what she described as the beautiful natural existence of the American Indians. When asked if she wanted to return to the ship and Russia she declared," the story has just begun there is no way I can not continue to the climax whatever it brings".

When the local inhabitants learned of the trekkers plan to pull the large wagon up river to the confluence of the Snake they laughed and said" impossible". Wapaxo knew of The Dalles and knew he would have to swing south around them to continue going east. .This brought the problem of crossing the Columbia. The north of the Columbia was Wapaxo's home territory. Though rugged he felt it was passable. Just south of The Dalles the river widened and was shallower. It was obvious they would be forced to lighten their load. With the help of Chief Manny Horses they were able to enlist the help of the tribes owning boats on the south side of the Columbia. Wapaxo insisted that his seed corn be given highest priority only the most reliable and safe boats were loaded with the seed corn, All of the blacksmith's iron was loaded on the heavier barges The oxen were forced to swim the river. Once on the north side of the river, the oxen were harnessed and made ready to pull the wagon on shore. In the middle of the river was an island that had a large tree at its western end a medium sized skiff towed a rope from the ship's cordage to the island and secured it at the base of the tree. Two medium sized logs were fastened to the sides of the wagon. By steering the wagon at an angle they were able to use the rivers current to swing the wagon close enough to the north side that they could paddle and pole it to the shore. The balance of the trekkers and the small wagon were easily brought to the northern shore. Delighted to be in home territory Wapaxo declared a holiday and the travelers set about resting and feasting.

During the second day of the rest period Broken Branch joined the party. Manny Horse's runners had rejoined his tribe as they headed to home territory. He was not a bearer of good news. There was a party of ruffians that had managed to stay on the Wapaxo tribes trail regardless of their clumsiness. Wapaxo called Beaver Boy, Up River and Broken branch into council. Remembering the Thrakets he decided to make elimination of this threat a high priority. The deadly trio accepted the assignment with enthusiasm.

The home coming to the Klikitat village of Wapaxo was a joyous occasion especially since Wapaxo was burdened with gifts for all. For Wapaxo the feast of fresh smoked salmon was a veritable treat. In a serious note he called for a council. In an unusual attendance he included the women and children. He then introduced them to the cultivation of corn. Showing the cobs and explaining how to husband the crop He generously endowed them with seeds from the three cob plants, reserving the four cob seeds for himself as royal seed.

Remembering the Russian greed for sea otter pelts he advised them to gather as many as they could in trade and keep them for the next meeting of the Russian freighter. He was pleased that they had accumulated a good supply of salt and traded for as much as they would freely expend.

The next topic to come forward was the five men on their trail. With good descriptions Broken Branch was able to make sure they would recognize the culprits. The story of the Thrackets was told and re-told many times. The women especially enjoyed the mushroom consumption episode. It exemplified the superior intelligence of Indian women. The basket skills of the wives of Igor were noted and the Kilikitat women marveled at their artistry. However their admiration of Igor drew more than a little jealousy. Igor, typical man enjoyed the attention and for a brief moment all was not well with the two wives. A particularly attractive Klikitat maiden had admired Igor's powerful biceps by rubbing her hand over one of them; two pair of brown eyes glared their unacceptance.

With the feasting, trading, and reunion celebration ending Wapaxo's tribe assembled their group and prepared to head for home. The deadly trio back tracked to try and find the followers. Running low on supplies the nefarious five had committed several petty crimes and were sought by their victims. Living off the land was their nature so they sought to steal whatever they could to enable them to follow the traders. With this in mind Broken Branch had left a trap. They had brought several of the white flowered camas bulbs with them. At one of their camps they left some roasted white camas behind as if they had been eating from them and had a fill. It could have been disastrous for the nefarious ones but they had luck in snaring a few rabbits earlier and only tasted the camas and not eaten enough to cause them any gastronomical problems. It was easy to track the white men since they were crude and arrogant in their dealings with the local people. Broken Branch hadn't been able to determine which one of the five was the leader. He assumed that the one that rode the beautiful very large white mare was in command because she was an outstanding prize. Upon reaching camp Broken Branch told Wapaxo about the big white mare? The next day at dawn Broken Branch led Wapaxo to an advantage point where they could survey the camp and Wapaxo would get a chance to see the elegant horse. Watching the mare dancing in exuberance delighted the Chief and he resolved to acquire the steed. Knowing that the future would bring a conflict with these unscrupulous characters Wapaxo cautioned Broken Branch to prevent any injury to his desired possession. Departure day was both joyful and sad; they were headed home to activities dear to their individual hearts. B.C. Bob, Ivan, Igor and Jacque were anxious to exploit the rich gold deposit. Wapaxo dreamed of preparing the ground of the fertile valley and planting corn.Milliwana had during her close examination of the Hoopa area camus , noticed the seed pods and had carefully collected some that she was sure had come from blue flowered tubers. Wapaxo's concentration with corn cultivation had wondered if she couldn't revive some of the old camas areas of her childhood. Tatjana was eagerly looking forward to experimenting with the clay B.C.Bob had told her about. Igor was anxious to drill and blast the rock. He needed to get his shop established to make the drills to work with the bamboo explosives that had yet to be tested. Two big stalwart Klikitat braves and their women were allowed to join the tribe. When they had made their desire known B. C. Bob queried the two young men and found that their main reasons were to obtain henry rifles. He made it plain to them that they would have to work for them. He also informed him that the work would be hard mostly breaking stones.

The deadly trio scouted the followers from dawn to dusk. They had chosen an ambush spot ideal to eliminate this threat. Igor and his two wives assumed the big wagon's journey problems. At every halt the young people gathered grass to feed the horses and oxen. Despite the difficulties of the passage the Wapaxo tribe made good progress. Three days away from camp it was obvious the five men following the traders were scouting them to locate their gold source. Wapaxo decided that he would try and buy the big white mare. The nefarious group had fallen for the trap as Beaver Boy and Broken Branch had expected them to. They set up camp in a secluded meadow with a small stream meandering through its center. Branching off from the meadow were three coulees that were flanked by small cliffs. Jacque assumed the leadership roll and assigned five braves to participate in converging on the camp site. He took one of the cliff positions with his sharps, Wapaxo took another and Beaver Boy took the third cliff position. Moving up the bottoms of the coulees were Broken Branch, Up River and one of the oldest Klikitat newcomers. Working up stream Bob Cat Bob hailed the camp when he was sure the others were in place. Three of the nefarious ones grabbed their rifles and headed for cover.

When called in B.C. Bob remained in sight of his cliff watchers as he approached the campers. He was armed with his revolver and hunting knife. When ordered to drop his gun belt he simply complied making sure the hammer thong was loosened and the pistol was ready to draw. Believing him to be alone, the three that had sought cover stepped out with rifles trained and ready. "What you want?" asked the bearded one. I would like to buy the white horse", answered B.C. Bob. "You don't have enough money to buy that horse", answered the bearded one and the others guffawed. B.C Bob slipped a buckskin pouch from under his belt and said," there is ten ounces of gold here far more than the price of half a dozen like it". The bearded one held out his hand and B.C. Bob let him heft the pouch and pour some of the nuggets from the creek that is no more, into his palm." It's a fair price agreed the bearded one, but it's not for sale and I'll just keep this for my trouble." And again came the guffaw this time louder and with knee slapping animation. That would be robbery" said B.C. Bob. "No! Shit", replied the bearded one followed by a guffaw. B.C. Bob shifted his weight and one of the rifle bearers lifted his rifle and levered a cartridge into the receiver.

This was his last action as his head exploded followed by the loud report of a sharps buffalo gun. B.C. Bob ducked and rolled toward his pistol belt. With lightening speed he palmed the revolver and shot out one of the bearded ones eyes as he reached for his own pistol. B.C. Bob said," you are surrounded and completely covered". Upon hearing this three of the remaining gang members melted into the timber. Not believing B.C. Bob but not taking any chances they moved up the coulee to where they had their horses corralled. The timber was thick and the three could easily conceal them selves however they were pinned down afraid to move. B.C. Bob scooped up his pistol belt and moved into the timber away from the three headed toward their corralled horses. A heavy silence settled over the camp.   The sight of the nuggets had built determination into the remaining three. With their determination they managed to cluster and whisper ideas as to how they could survive their predicament. They could hear the five horses and two mules stirring around in the makeshift corral. They had selected this particular coulee to build their corral because it had a sloping path and an escape route at the upper end of the coulee. Beaver Boy and Broken Branch guessed at their plan for escape and circled around to block their escape. Remembering Wapaxo's admonition to not endanger the white mare they held back figuring the three would select their own horses to use in their attempted escape. The gregarious mules determined not to be left alone pushed themselves between the horses and shouldered the escapees away from their horses interfering with the attempts to saddle-up. When Beaver Boy called for them to surrender they dove for a pile of downed timber and brought up their rifles blasting away without definite targets. It was no contest. Broken Branch had joined them and no one fired a shot until they had definite targets. After a period of deafening silence, Wapaxo's bunch gathered up the possessions of the nefarious ones, burned what they didn't salvage, assembled the ramada, laid out the five corpses with their heads pointed south west toward the Spirit Mountain, " Mount Hood." Wapaxo explained, "Even bad people have a right to seek the spirit world. With their bodies pointed toward the spirit mountain. Their spirits can climb the mountain and seek the spirit world beyond. " It was an impressive appearance as the traders entered the valley where Wapaxo planned to establish his corn fields and set up his permanent camp. Leading the group was Wapaxo riding the large white mare with his scepter thrust forward. Assembled to greet him were the elderly members and those not fit for the trading expedition plus the Poncos, Milliwana's original tribe. Her father had moved into the head chief position. The association was to Wapaxo's liking, but he hadn't planned on the people being on the fields where he planned to grow corn. This wasn't a real problem since the Ponocs were a nomadic people that followed the camas harvest and therefore held their position on a temporary basis.

Wapaxo had a plan. He called for a council. With most of the tribe assembled he spoke," I feel the bite of winter in the fall air. We must prepare. Basket weavers are to gather reeds from the marsh area below. Weave the reeds into large mats. The warriors the oxen tenders and every one capable shall gather loge pole timbers. Construct a lodge forty steps of a tall man wide and sixty steps long. Set posts and braces. Make a roof with a steep pitch. Cover the roof poles with the mats. Cover the mats with clay soil and grass. Build racks inside to store all of our seed and perishable possessions". Jacque, B.C. Bob, and Ivan reveled at Wapaxo's decision and appreciated his show of intelligence and leadership. With bow saws traded for at Fort Ross the men were able to fell the lodge pole pine close to the valley and drag them to the building site. Using bunch grass from the swampy area below they were able to bind the log pole into a gable shape after setting the stringers to the supporting posts and the ridge pole with pegs bored into the supporting posts. With the wall posts fastened up the sides held by swamp grass and pegs the building was ready for the mats. After lacing the mats to the roof and walls a mixture of clay and pine needled was spread over the mats and worked into every crack and space. They were ready for snow.

With the big storage building sitting up from the proposed corn field Wapaxo set aside a site for the blacksmith. Further up the slope he laid out a plan for the dwelling area. There was a sense of urgency and everybody rushed to get ready for winter. Igor made a stone boat to bring in heavy flag stone to build the blast furnace area and his forge base. Using the same techniques Wapaxo had directed for the storage area he built a workable smithy area and added comfortable living quarters for him and his two wives. Milliwana was able to coax some of her old tribe to assist with the work. The men of the Poncos were reluctant to engage in any type of manual labor. They considered this women's work and put forth a minimum of effort when bribed with trade goods. With the advent of snow the travelers were settled in and gave thanks to the Gods with a feast. Work was suspended and the hunters went forth. Beaver Boy, Up River and Broken Branch were a little apprehensive thinking Wapaxo might ask them to leave their firearms. But Wapaxo remembering the encounter with the rustlers didn't wish to leave his warriors in a vulnerable position.   This was home territory for the terrible trio. They agreed to take the two new Klikitat braves along. Mitwask the older of the two Klikitats was most eager to join in the hunt for he was sure he would be given one of the henry rifles. When they found out that they had to prove their worth before the rifles would be theirs Mitwask and Yatum felt that they were going to be no more important than the two mules taken to haul the meat in. Mitwask was known as the Boat Builder and Yatum was titled Master Swimmer.having earned their names as young Klikitats. Beaver Boy having learned the importance of the preparation ceremonies led the group to the sweat lodge. In order to save time Beaver Boy had the lodge ready with the attendants of several teen aged young bucks they skipped the hunting dance and voiced the chants as they sweated profusely and beat their skin with balsam branches. With Beaver Boy in the lead, they headed for high country searching for elk. They had been riding for two days before they found snow deep enough to provide tracks of the elusive big animals. With the aid of the brass telescope they spotted a herd of thirty elk that they could circle and get down wind from. Beaver Boy and Up River paired up with the new hunters and stood ready to back up their shots. It wasn't necessary they proved to be good bowmen each downing a dry cow with well placed arrows. When it came time to dress and quarter the elk it was a different story. To Mitwask and Yatum this was women's work and they were unskilled. Beaver Boy ridiculed them saying that they must be even less than a woman if they couldn't even do women's work. With two big cows packed on the mules and front quarters on the saddle horses they headed back to the village planning to pick up a couple of deer on the way.

Mitwask and Yatum were a little miffed. They felt that they were established braves and should be treated as such. Gathering wood for fires and water hauling was beneath them. Beaver Boy saw which way their sticks floated so in a muffled conference with Broken Branch and Up River they decided to teach the new comers a lesson. They ignored the duo and went about the camp chores as if they weren't there. When they cut the meat they only cut portions for the terrible three. The camas/corn bread was divided into three portions. Without speaking they took their food and settled into enjoying their meal. When the newcomers saw that nothing had been left for them they inquired, "where is ours?" Broken Branch answered, with a question, "What have you prepared?" Dumfounded there was no answer. Beaver Boy, Up River and Broken Branch cleaned up their preparation chores and went to bed. It was dark when Mitwask and Yatum managed to wash down a couple pieces of camas/corn bread with water and rolled in. The next morning Mitwask and Yatum were out of bed early they started a fire, skewered a few pieces of meat and roasted it over the coals. Beaver Boy, Up River, and Broken Branch said nothing as they munched on the bread and meat they had sequestered from the evening meal before readying their horses to continue the trip. Sheepishly Mitwask and Yatum had learned their lessons and for the rest of the trip stepped forward to accomplish what had to be done.

Jacque, B.C. Bob, and Ivan had been busy they had set off the first series of charges and loaded the manageable ore onto the stone boat Igor had built to haul his blast furnace and forge stone to his shop. Only pieces 20 pounds or less were loaded. The plan was to have the weaker members of the tribe breaking the pieces into blast furnace fodder.

Ivan with his calculating mind had been shaping dried hardwood spindles into a size that if it were gold it would weigh 10 ounces troy weight. These he had covered with bear grease and given to Tatjana to make clay moulds. Filled with gold they would be what he had learned to know as smugglers bullion. They had been used for centuries by thieves to smuggle their ill-gotten gains across country's borders. A little larger in diameter than a pencil and approximately 11 inches long they could easily be stitched into clothing and concealed in other objects.

Ivan helped Igor develop a plan to smelter out the precious metals. Igor had developed a practical method of determining the temperature of iron by color. A few experiments with some of the placer gold from" the creek that is no more" proved that gold which melts at 1063 deg Celsius was the same temperature the cast iron ladle turned a light orange color. The next problem they had to solve was finding a fuel source to run the blast oven and forge. Without coke or coal they had to depend on charcoal. A short distance from the village was a grove of maple trees. Maple being a hard wood would make good charcoal. They cut down a medium sized dead tree blocked it and split it into chunks. With a good supply of kindling they set the maple on fire in a scooped out area excavated with the oxen team, covered the fire with green branches and dirt and let it smolder. It took several days before they had sufficient charcoal to run the blast furnace.

Tatjana and Milliwana were getting lots of medical practice. Having the younger people and women breaking the ore chunks into fines was creating a multitude of injuries and wounds. The two women made a wonderful team. Milliwana with her knowledge of native herbal medicines and Tatjana with her formal medical training kept everybody taken care of. In addition to the usual maladies and injuries was the advent of pregnancies. Both of the care givers and Igor's wives were in the family way. The biggest speculation was would both of Igor's wives have twins? And when the babies arrived how would they distinguish who was whose? The happiness that prevailed in the blacksmith's camp was unparalleled.

Jacque and B.C Bob had exposed the seam of mineral bearing quartz. They were able to use the three sizes of bamboo charges to the best results due to Igor's ability to keep the three drill sizes in good shape. The snow was actually a god send. It gave the stone boat a smooth path to transport the ore chunks on.

The only unhappy camper was Chief Wapaxo. He was anxious for spring to arrive so he could get his corn planted.

The injuries that occurred from crushing the ore angered him but his pride in Milliwana's medical practice gave him additional status. When a pouring was completed the smugglers bullion was divided according to a formula worked out by Jacque, B.C. Bob, and Ivan. When Wapaxo was brought a smugglers bar he buried it in a corner of his hogan with a smirk to himself, "Let's see this grow"! Although the mine was a considerable distance from the camp, the explosions were heard and this also disturbed Wapaxo. In February Wapaxo noted that the fodder for the animals was in short supply. He ordered every able bodied person to stop what they were doing and canvas the country side for horse and oxen food. Jacque, B.C. Bob, and Ivan were in a rich pocket of ore and didn't want to pause in their excavations. B.C. Bob suggested that they feed some of the corn in storage to the animals. This was sacrilege. Wapaxo summoned Beaver Boy, Broken Branch, and Up River and sent them to the mine site to order the mining halted and the foraging expedition carried out. Jacque, B.C.Bob and Ivan were angered, considering Wapaxo short sighted because of his lack of understanding of the value of the gold. It was B.C. Bob that brought the discussion to a head when he said, "What we are talking about isn't gold or corn but time. If we put as much effort into gathering forage as we do mining we should be able to collect enough to see us through the winter. Agreeing they scattered to the stream banks and forests of deciduous trees. At the stream banks they collected young willow shoots. In the forest they stripped the bark from the saplings taking care not to girdle the trees. They separated the cambium layer from the bark. When they had collected as much as the mules could carry and what they could stack on the stone boat they headed for the village. Wapaxo was mollified to a degree that he allowed a small portion of the stored corn to be added to the animal diets. The basket weavers reluctantly relinquished some of their craft supplies to the need of the animals and life returned to normal

Igor was the only tribe member that wasn't expected to gather forage. This didn't keep the twins from doing their part. When back from foraging feed it was delightful to watch them trying to out do one another in taking care of Igor. He didn't have to worry about slighting one or the other since he still couldn't tell them apart. Igor had a plan. He knew that platinum melted at 1773.5 deg. This was a temperature higher than his ladle could handle.

The only solution was to form a ladle out of clay. With this plan he heated some of the slag he had cast aside and poured two bracelets of platinum. Secretly he shaped the bracelets to fit his wives He put a simple design on each with only a slight difference. Now when one of them did something for him he could tell which one it was. The only problem was that the sisters had been working with intricate designs in their baskets and they detected the difference so they periodically exchanged bracelets.

Knowing how important the corn was to Wapaxo Milliwana enlisted Tatjana in a plan to jump start the spring planting. They had both been involved with experimenting with the potters wheel Igor had made for Tatjana.Bored with attempting to make intricate vases they started making simple clay pots with drain holes to jump start the spring planting with corn plants. It wasn't long until they had over a hundred seedling pots ready. All of the big storage sheds floor space was in use so they had to devise shelving to arrange the pots. Wapaxo in his rounds observed their activity and questioned them." Why you make shelves of little pots?" he asked. Milliwana artfully answered, "We hope to be able to plant before Mother Nature brings us warm weather. Grunting his approval he continued his rounds grumbling when he heard another blast from the mine. At the mine Jacque and B.C. Bob had excavated the rich pocket they had opened earlier and were now into some denser rock formations. Complicating matters was the approach of warmer weather. Transportation of the coarser less mineralized ore was becoming more difficult. The stone boat wore out and mining activity had to be suspended to spend time on the road. Frustrated with the lack of interest by the native braves they called a halt on the extraction of ore.

Occasionally they would run into a rich deposit only to run into large sections of non bearing ore. Continued injuries by the natives breaking the ore down to workable blast furnace material had almost brought Igor's blast furnace operations to a standstill. They came to a complete halt when they had to cook another batch of charcoal.

The Ponocs camping spot was becoming a mud flat. They broke camp and moved up next to Wapaxo's tribal grounds. As they moved they organized their possessions in preparation to heading to the next camas flat. They had a routine that put them in position to harvest the camas when the blossoms indicated the edible from the toxic.Milliwana had a different plan. Her people had always harvested the mature bulbs leaving nature to re-establish each patch by leaving the immature bulbs to vegetate. With the seeds she was able to harvest from the Hoopa camas beds she was planning to increase the beds close to their home camp. Enlisting the women to assist her in her plan she provided each with a pointed planting prod. They waded into the marshy ground and probed into the soil dropping seed as they progressed. This proved to be wasteful since the seeds floated instead of settling into the mud. Regrouping the women began making smell balls of clay and soil around the seeds. These being denser dropped into the mud and stayed down. Next summer would tell the tale.Milliwana could hardly wait for the seedlings to appear. This was probably the first attempt to farm camas. The women's actions hadn't missed Wapaxo. Remembering the Mexican farmers of Ft Ross he was eager to start seeding his corn fields.

Jacque, B.C. B ob and Ivan had run into an outcropping of mostly granite with only traces of quartz and scant color. With the core rock denser than what they had been excavating they drilled with the larger drills and packed the holes with the larger bamboo charges. They cleared the area and crouched behind an outcropping to set the blast. It was a mighty one felt throughout the area the ore moved as they had planned and the dust had hardly settled when the overhang above the excavation broke loose and crashed down over the mining area burying the operation under hundreds of feet of rock and dirt. None of the miners and animals were affected but the operation was brought to an abrupt halt. The hand tools, drills, and equipment were lost. .

Wapaxo was angry. He called a council and decreed that there would be no more blasting. His decree was easy to adhere to since the bamboo charges had been buried with the drills. Wapaxo said, "Mountain has been wounded and is angry. It will be no more. The miners went to the tailings pile, high graded the ore and proceeded to bring it to the smelter. With the last of the ore rendered and poured B.C. Bob, Ivan, Jacque and Igor double checked their records of distribution to make sure those that had worked in the production of the smugglers bars received an equitable share. The young Klikitat braves that had joined Wapaxo's tribe were given their rifles, a ration of ammunition and as a bonus Igor had made each of them a handsome hunting knife. Tatjana was included in the bullion distribution for her part in making the molds to pour the smugglers bars. Wapaxo remained reserved and unconcerned with the distribution. There was enough gold to make the principals of the operation wealthy.

The tribe knew what was needed to bring Wapaxo to a joyful mood. Igor readied the oxen and the plow. B.C. Bob went back to the mine site and surveyed the creek with the intention of building a diversion dam to irrigate the corn field. The slide had built a natural basin across the creek and a little reservoir was filling. A ditch along the hill side was easily formed to carry the water above the field. Jacque and Ivan spelled Igor at the plowing and the oxen teams were rotated so the field was getting twelve to sixteen hours of working every day. They didn't have any fencing wire so they had to devise some means to keep the deer from eating the corn as it came up. Beaver Boy suggested that they put lodge pole posts in and around the field. Then assigned the posts to each of the men to urinate on knowing the deer would shy away from the human smell. When the weather warmed enough to preclude a killer frost the women transplanted their corn starts from their clay pots.

When the corn stalks began to reach for the sky Wapaxo reacted as if he had fathered a new nation. The urine marked posts were doing the job of keeping the deer from the field but they were ineffective in keeping rodents and rabbits away, there was no alternative somebody would be needed to patrol the field at night. Since the children of the Wapaxo Tribe were skilled with the sling their employ seemed to be the natural

Every morning at day break Wapaxo would circle the field and when nobody was watching he would water several posts. The transplanted corn was growing exceptionally fast. Having observed the Mexican farmers at Ft. Ross Wapaxo knew that with care there would be no more starving time.

Milliwana was also well pleased with her seeding of camas. She also true to her tradition was eager to start an expedition to some of the camas valleys she had known all of her life. She voiced her desire to Wapaxo and he called Beaver Boy and directed him to take two of the new Klikitat warriors and accompany the women to a harvest. The two mules were made ready to bring the tubers back to the camp. As the five women and three escorts were about to depart three young braves riding three fancy appaloosa ponies rode into camp. They had messenger stripes painted on their upper arms and carried coup sticks and bows and arrows. Beaver Boy sent a young lad to fetch Broken Branch and Up River. Through sign language the three messengers were able to convey their desire for a conference. It was determined the three messengers were from the famous Chief Joseph.of the Nez Perce.

Wapaxo bade them to alight and squatted before his lodge and started a conference with a Smoke Ceremony. Beaver Boy spoke the Nez Perce dialect and it was soon revealed that the messengers were here to visit the Spirit Woman (Tatjana) Healer. Chief Joseph's youngest grandson was ill with an undiagnosed sickness. The three messengers rose to their feet and took a defensive stance when Ivan approached the council. Waisachu (Whiteman) spat out the leader of the messengers, with enough emphasis that Ivan understood their meaning even if he didn't understand the word. He spoke with Wapaxo, "Tatjana is not going anywhere". He stated. Wapaxo bristled, and sent a young lad to fetch Jacque and B.C. Bob. Again the bitter word Waisachu was heard. Jacque turned to the messengers and told them that the Spirit Woman was the wife of the white man and that the white men were loyal members of The Wapaxo Clan. He also stated that he was familiar with the famous Chief Joseph and respected him as a powerful leader. Next he addressed Ivan, Why not let Tatjana decide"? he asked. Ivan sat in silence, finally agreeing, he said," go and find her. But first I need to know how long the trip will be" he added." You know she is three months pregnant". When Tatjana was brought to the council the three messengers were awed by her beauty. When they explained their mission she stated, "Only if Milliwana goes with me" When Milliwana learned of the direction they were going she agreed. There were several camas plots along this route and they would only be gone three days. Since the camas expedition was already set it was simple to assemble and depart. Both Milliwana and Tatjana took their medicine packs with. They had only been gone a day when Wapaxo sent for Up River and Broken Branch. Painted for a council meeting the two braves and Wapaxo headed for Chief Joseph's camp.

On good horses, Wapaxo on his large white mare and the two braves riding appaloosas they made good time and soon caught up with the Nez Perce and the camas party. When they came to a camas patch familiar to Milliwana Beaver Boy and the camas harvesters split off and set up camp to harvest the roots. Wapaxo assumed the lead and looked regal with his scepter and robe. The reception wasn't cordial. In a rapid burst the Nez Perce told of the hated Waisachu (white men) in Wapaxo's tribe. Adding to the tension was the large group of Nez Perce warriors in war paint. The women were taken with haste to the sick boy. Tatjana observed the yellow in the boy's eyes and his high fever and diagnosed kidney stones. She called for cold water and applied cold compresses to the feverish boy. She reached into her medicine bag and took out several juniper berries which she crushed. Calling for boiling water she made a tea with a mixture of two teaspoons of crushed berries steeped from boiling to a drinkable temperature. She urged the boy to drink a pint of the tea.

She told the mother that he would have to urinate frequently through the night and that she would be there at dawn for another dose of the tea. When the fever broke to chills they covered him and he slept fitfully through the night. She asked the mother to keep the urine and was pleased when it appeared cloudy the next morning. At dawn she gave the boy a weaker tea and not a full pint. At noon they fed him a robust soup and he began to recover.

Chief Joseph and Wapaxo held a private conference and Wapaxo told the story of his tribe and why they had white men as members. When asked by Chief Joseph to join him in an assault on the white man's army, he skillfully declined but pledged his support of Chief Joseph with a shipment of trail food to assist him on his campaign to the Big Hole country.

On the third day the crisis of the boy's illness was over and a feast was planned. Milliwana made some of her camas-corn bread and the Nez Perce were converted to farming corn. This of course was just an added burden to the women of the tribe for farming and food preparation was woman's work. Wapaxo and Tatajana were escorted to a pasture of fine looking horses. Tatjana was told she should select a horse for her service to the grandson. Thinking of Wapaxo's large white mare she looked in askance to Wapaxo as she pointed out a large beautiful appaloosa stud horse. Wapaxo beamed as he discerned her intent .With an understanding that belied his young age Wapaxo knew that it was the nature of woman to practice matchmaking that even extended to the animals they were associated with. His mare had to have a deserving mate and bear colts.

The acceptance of Wapaxo's tribe to Chief Joseph's camp still wasn't cordial even with the apparent recovery of his grandson. Several factors were the cause of the distrust and coolness of the meetings between Wapaxo and Chief Joseph. One of the differences was the age of Chief Joseph. He could easily have been Wapaxo's father. Wapaxo's acceptance of waisachu (white men) into his tribe was incomprehensible. Chief Joseph's contact with white men had only been confrontational. Topping Chief Joseph's apprehensions was the henry rifles carried by the braves accompanying Wapaxo. Thunder sticks were feared and completely mysterious to him and his braves.

Chief Joseph called for a departure conference. With the pipe smoking ceremony completed the meetings atmosphere was still loaded with apprehension. Chief Joseph rather briskly asked, "What tribe you come from?"Wapaxo answered, "My lodge father is the arrow maker/ historian of the Klikitat tribe." I lived in the shadow of Mother River," (Columbia) Wapaxo answered. "You say lodge father, Why?" asked Chief Joseph... "I have been told that my Sub-Chief Jacque is my blood father and I see the resemblance." "Why do you ask these questions now that your grandson is cured"? asked Wapaxo. "The healing performed by the white spirit woman is acknowledged and rewarded, but I need to know that your people are not spies for the waisachu. " Would a true warrior bring his wife to a confrontation"? Asked Wapaxo. "Your wife with spirit woman?" asked Chief Joseph. "Yes she is Poncos" Replied Wapaxo. "Poncos!" Exclaimed Chief Joseph! "She is Nez Perce." "Where you find Nez Perce wife"?Wapaxo recounted his exploits leading to his receiving Milliwana as a bride, omitting his mad dash for the pine tree making him sound more brave." I am known as Bear Slayer amongst the Poncos", stated Wapaxo. I had wondered why one so young could raise to tribal chief" mused Chief Joseph. "I was first an arrow head maker" said Wapaxo. Handing his scepter to Chief Joseph, he remarked. "I made this bear killing spear point." He went on to say; "When you see how the point is fastened to the shaft, you will see the work of a white man. There is something to learn here. When you noticed the rifles my braves were carrying you knew that it was white man's work. I have learned that across the great waters

to the east, (the rising sun country); there are many large nests
of white men. They are like the tonka of the plains, too many
to count. They are also like the bald faced hornets. When their
nests are disturbed they storm out fighting and when there are
many nests the attacks are deadly", I will not send my warriors
to attack the white men, but I will support you with food to aid
in your battle". At this point Wapaxo showed the large ear of
corn to Chief Joseph and told him how each kernel of corn
could produce four cobs on each stock grown.

The next morning Wapaxo's troop departed Chief
Joseph's camp. Milliwana was anxious to meet up with the
women who had stopped at the camas patch to harvest. She
had brought several baskets of seed s in clay pods she wanted to
plant in the harvested area. Beaver Boy's group had a successful
harvest and was disappointed to hear they were expected
to re-seed the area harvested. .The harvest was so successful
the load had to be distributed amongst Chief Joseph visitor's
packs.

Beaver Boy and Milliwana were in deep discussion.
They had both seen two large cottonwood trees that appeared
to have honey bee nests. The trees were large and it seemed
impossible to harvest the honey. When they arrived home
they discussed the honey problem with Jacque. He simply
stated, "Why don't we cut the trees down?" The big cross
cut saw taken from the hide hunters had been forgotten
.   The basket
weavers were given a task. They were to make six bee proof
helmets to be worn by the hive raiders. Several water tight
baskets had to be constructed to carry the harvested honey in.
There was one constriction. Several of the basket weavers were
pregnant including both of Igor's wives. The question here was
which would give birth first? To complicate matters both of the
medicine women were also pregnant. Igor didn't know if he
should celebrate or what. What if his wives had twins? Cutting
down a big cottonwood tree and harvesting honey amounted to
a lot of work. For some mysterious reason Beaver Boy, Up River
and Broken Branch came to the conclusion that they were low

on meat and they should strike out to see if they couldn't find elk. When push came to shove the honey harvest crew ended up being Jacque, Igor, B.C. Bob and Ivan. The braves wanted no part of stirring up a bees nest. The women since most of them were pregnant were not asked to assist in the honey harvest.B.C. Bob and Ivan made several torches of dry twigs and green evergreen branches. The intent being to create smudges to quiet the bees. Arriving at the bee trees the decision was made to tackle only one tree, saving one for later.

With the ax Igor notched the tree in the side he wanted the tree to fall. The vibrations of the ax blows stirred up the bees. Jacque and Ivan were soon covered with angry bees when they started to saw into the opposite side. Their helmets and buckskin wrappings protected them from the attacks. Not so with Igor. Two bees had managed to invade his helmet and he was stung twice. When he first noticed the bees he was tempted to remove his helmet. The second sting convinced him this was a bad move. Both stings were on the cheeks which immediately swelled and turned red. He knew that no matter how much the bees buzzed they only had one sting each. His only hope was that more bees didn't find the opening into his helmet.

With baskets of honey the gathers trekked home to a welcoming party of gleeful children and happy wives. Igor showed the only ill effects of the harvest. His wives at first decried his ill fate which quickly turned to gleeful laughter when they saw his large puffed red cheeks. Beaver Boy, Broken Branch and Up River having just arrived from a successful hunt dug into the honey. When Wapaxo noticed that they had not skinned and dressed their game he harshly called them to task. "Skin and dress your game before you enjoy the harvest of those not afraid to confront the bees." he commanded. The women stepped forward and cleaned the intestines in preparation for making pemmican. Wapaxo had directed the increased pemmican production to coincide with his promise to Chief Joseph that he would provide the army food supplies for the big chief's intended battle with the white man. He knew Chief Joseph would like to of had his rifle equipped warriors in his intended skirmish. He had tried to convince Chief Joseph that this would be to his advantage since Wapaxo's trade connection furthers his war efforts.

Wapaxo's tribe had pressing domestic problems with the multiple pregnancies in the clan. His wife tribal medicine woman, Tatjana, Igor's wives and several women were with child. The women of the tribe were the backbone of their existence. Harvest of the corn was coming. There need be more gathering of camas and berries if the dream of a prosperous winter was to exclude the feast and famine of past years.Wapaxo and Milliwana had made note of the California tribe's and Manny Horses' people's use of pine nuts.Wapaxo and Milliwana had noticed the improvement in pemmican when pine nuts were mixed with the meat, berries, and tallow. In conference with Beaver Boy, Up River, and Broken Branch Wapaxo asked them to look for pine nuts. When they reported back to him he assembled a Tribal council. Members able to gather nuts were directed to gather as much as possible. Special care was given to saving the intestines of all of the game. These were cleaned with sand in a running stream and used for making pemmican. The promise to Chief Joseph would be kept.

One of Igor's wives was first to give birth. It was a beautiful girl. The rejoicing was muted by the competition between the twins. The second twin was two weeks behind her sister and anxiety increased when her water broke and labor didn't produce the necessary dilation for normal birth. Jacque heard of the problem and remembered the satchel full of surgeon's tools and supplies taken from the hide hunters. He went to the locker where he had left the satchel and brought it to Tatjana. She looked up and paused in her massaging of the twin's abdomen and sorted through the surgical implements. She was not a trained surgeon and despaired at the thought that both the mother and child would expire if she couldn't dilate to allow the infant to arrive with a normal vaginal birth. To attempt to remove the baby surgically without anesthesia was a last moment procedure. She resumed her massaging and alternated forcing her legs apart. With a loud scream a fine baby boy was born. When everything seemed to have returned to normal Milliwana and Tatjana noticed the baby's extra wide shoulders; truly the son of a powerful blacksmith.

Wapaxo and Beaver Boy had walked to the far end of the corn field. There was a tall ponderosa pine that had been topped by a lightening strike. When the bee tree was cut down, Wapaxo had a chunk of the log cut out. It contained most of the larva and the queen bee, surrounded by honey combs and bee bread. Wapaxo and Beaver Boy (the consummate conservationist) were building a platform to support the log chunk on the top of the snag.   With all of the domestic occurrences settled the tribe had gained eight new members, four boys and four girls a good balance. The harvest work continued and the tribe made preparations for their next trading quest.

Planning ahead is what had made the two well educated members of the tribe so successful. Dr. Mc Namey and Ivan Utzeph were enjoying coffee; they were both excited at visiting what would soon be called the "Golden Gate".

Not to disparage their native tribesmen, they knew they would not be able to manage their wealth. The Native American could not understand ownership of land. They reasoned that if you couldn't take it with you how could you own it? Jacque had asked Wapaxo, "Do you own this hogan"? When asked if he owned all of it, he answered, "of course", Jacque said, "let me see you take the floor with you." Ivan noted that their native brothers didn't understand the concepts of rent or interest. The fledging city of San Francisco promised opportunities of great enterprise. Ivan had noticed Tallena as an extremely alert young lady and proposed that she be groomed for business later.Milliwana was consulted and agreed that Tallena was very sharp and agreed to ask her to work with Ivan. Broken Branch curious about Milliwana's questions attended the first few sessions of Tallena and B.C. Bob and Ivan. They put in long hours with finance problems and English language. Broken Branch had become interested in working with wood. He started by making the carrying boxes used to bring the ore to be crushed and smelted. He was instrumental in building the flume that was carrying water from the pond (created by the land slide), to irrigate the corn field. When Jacque told him of water wheels and saw mills he spent long periods studying the diagrams drawn in the dirt by Jacque. How he found the time no body knew, but Igor build a model water wheel for Broken Branch and they spent hours playing with it.

Chief Joseph and his warriors were on the move. He sent a runner to Wapaxo that any supplies that could be spared should be sent to the big meadow just south of Trapper Peak east of Nez Perc Pass. Beaver Boy knew the area.

The camp buzzed with activity. The two mules and three pack horses were loaded. Beaver Boy, Broken Branch, and Up River left at dawn. It wasn't far but rugged. Trapper Peak reached above 10,000 feet. Maneuvering for the battle of The Big Hole was in progress.

The Nez Perce were a mighty force and high tension could be felt in the air. Pressure from all levels was put on the Wapaxo warriors to join in the attack on the white men. Beaver Boy acting as spokesman refused to agree even when called cowards or white man lovers. "We are not afraid but we are honorable", he replied. We gave our word to bring you supplies and we have. He agreed to leave the two pack horses behind but insisted on taking the mules back with him. There had been no agreement on the livestock. The mules were very dependable and needed for the next trading expedition. The horses could be replaced and there were no good mules available. After a short rest The Terrible Trio headed back to their camp. As the trio descended from the high country they jumped a small herd of elk. Glad to have the opportunity to harvest the meat they deployed and brought down two big bulls. It was dark by the time they skinned and dressed the carcasses.

The load of meat was all the two mules could carry even with the front quarters divided up amongst the saddle horses. They made early camp, rubbed down the live stock and hobbled them close by. The meat had to be hoisted up into the trees. There were just too many predators to not protect it any way they could. Remembering the honey incident they stretched the hides and fleshed them out; grumbling about women's work. When the travelers rode into camp they were greeted with great joy and bombarded with questions.

Wapaxo silenced the welcomes and took the three into his hogan for a conference. "Did they try to get you to join them," he asked. When Beaver Boy told him how they tried to shame them, Wapaxo said, "It is hard to make friends with a skunk or a porcupine. Even to hand feed them can be troublesome."

Tallena was having a difficult time understanding rent and interest. Listening to Ivan trying to explain it from a time perspective was just too complicated. B.C.Bob poised the question." If a friend of yours wanted to use your horse to collect camas would you expect this friend to share the collected camas with you when she returned?" When Tallena agreed this would be proper. B.C. Bob said, "If you had agreed to this and the division of the harvest a forehand it would in effect be rent."This Tallena could understand. She then asked," "If I sleep in another persons hogan, why should I pay rent?" This was a hard one. Ivan asked her. "If she was someplace and had no place to sleep out of the cold and no friends about, would she be willing to trade one of her fine pottery vases for a night in a stranger's hogan?" She agreed that this was agreeable. "Then you are paying rent" said Ivan. "I have another thought for you," said B.C. Bob. "Suppose you had a hogan between your brother's and your sister's they gave their hogans to you. Now you don't have need for them but they are valuable so you don't want to give them away. These hogans are so valuable that nobody can buy or trade for them, but they want to live there. They have something that they are willing to give you to let them live there until you sell the hogans. Would you be willing to do this?" When Tallena said yes to this supposition. Ivan said, "Then you are renting it to them. One big stumbling block for Tallena's instructors was the concept of money. She had learned the rudiments of reading and writing and understood that a written promise was to be considered valuable if it represented something tangible. The use of colorful sea shells for trade was common to the coastal Indians but wasn't used much by the plains Indians. Wealth was generally held in the form of horses. Horses were generally traded one-on-one. The concept of something that would be worth ten horses wasn't considered. Vases and baskets were considered items that could be traded in quantity.

Tallena was a skilled pottery maker and she knew that it took considerable more time to make vases with intricate designs than it did plain ones so it reasoned the intricate vases were more valuable than the plain ones. The leap from the value of vases to the value of horses involved time, space and mobility. Ivan posed a question to Tallena. How would you trade forty fine vases for two horses that were three sleeps away? She agreed that this would be a big problem. Ivan said the white man has solved this problem with what he calls script. At this point Ivan produced some script he had picked up in Ft Ross. With this white man can ", what he calls buy", anything, horses, vases, food, cloth, and many other things you can think of and much that you can't comprehend. Something has to make the script valuable. If the man who owned the horses had established a value of the horses couldn't he write this value on a piece of paper and sigh it as a guarantee value? Tallena understood but she qualified her answer by saying;" the man must be known to speak with a straight tongue". "This is why money was invented." Ivan answered. "What is money?" asked Tallena. "Money comes in two forms, coins and bills (script)" said Ivan as he reached into his pocket and pulled out some change to add to the script (dollars) he had laying on the table. Several sessions such as these were needed for Tallena to grasp the understanding of purchasing and selling. Then she was given the task of explaining it to Milliwana.

The harvest of corn, pine nuts, and camas was coming to an end. All of the hunters were dispatched in four directions. Men and women were busy butchering and curing the game.

Strips of flesh were salted, dried and smoked. Trimmings were finely chopped, mixed with corn or camas and berries and packed into the cleaned intestines with salt and herbs. This was pemmican. The final process was to slow cook the stuffed intestines over smoke pits. Women, children and warriors were all busy gathering and stacking firewood. The children six years or older gathered grass for the live stock. This they spread out to dry and then twisted into small bundles. After the first frost preparations were underway to prepare for the trading trek. Trade camas, corn and hand craft items were packed in baskets. B.C. Bob and Igor distributed the smuggler bars to those who had worked in the mine or processing, The exception being Wapaxo; he had received his share as the bars were formed. Jacque had convinced Wapaxo to let him and B.C Bob exchange his share of gold into goods that were of use to him.

The first leg of the trading trip was to be to the Klikitat camp where Wapaxo was born. The home camp was to be occupied by the Poncos with Beaver Boy looking after the Wapaxo tribe's interests. Igor made the large wagon and oxen ready. He had shod the oxen and they were in top condition. Runners had been sent to Manny Horses camp to inform him of the beginning of the trek

Mitwask and Yatum were the most excited of the trekkers. They were going home as full braves armed with henry rifles. They still held positions inferior to Broken Branch and Up River but only they knew that. In actuality they were very efficient with their new fire arms. It was only the paucity of ammunition that kept them from being true experts. Up River was the chief scout and he was autocratic in his instruction and assignments of the scouts only giving deference to Broken Branch. With Beaver Boy left at home camp Up River and Broken Branch took the lead and trail guard positions, alternating Mitwak and Yatum between the two experienced scouts. With Wapaxo and his scepter riding his magnificent white horse at the head of the procession, there was an electric feeling as they turned west down the Mother River's (Columbia) northern bank. The previous trips had been guided by Beaver Boy but now Wapaxo and Igor knew the way.

It was mid-day of a beautiful early autumn day when they broke the crest of a small hill and headed into the Klikitat village. A huge crowd of children, women, and even the fishermen came to greet them. Eager hands took care of the horses, mules and oxen. It was plain that Wapaxo was the prodigal son. His large white mare and his scepter seemed to call for homage. A big feast had been planned. Large whole baked salmon as the main dish which was complimented with beaver tail, mountain grouse. Camas, cat tail bulbs, and corn bread were served as side dishes. Everything was piled on large and individual wooden trays. Wapaxo had forgotten how delicious the baked salmon was. He was in epicurean heaven. Mitwask and Yatum were basking in the adoration of the young braves around their ages and the young maidens that openly flirted for their attention. As evening drew near the elders assembled and proceeded with the smoke ceremonies and story telling. B.C. Bob, Ivan, and Igor made special note of the fine full flavored tobacco produced for the rituals. Igor asked, "Where did you obtain this fine tobacco?" Mietwataka the tribal historian spoke up, "We trade smoked salmon for tobacco grown on one of the islands. Very tricky traders here," he explained. "They hide poor quality coarse leaves in center of bundle". You want to trade for tobacco I go with", he added. B. C. Bob and Ivan had immediately seen a chance to earn huge profits in the bigger southern trading posts. Cured tobacco pound for pound was as valuable as the sea otter pelts.

When the subject of trading came up Wapaxo was told that a big water canoe had come into the port across the mother river. It was much larger than the one that had carried the wagon north for the last expedition. Excitement arose; Tatjana leaned over and asked Ivan to find out if it was her father's ship. Observing protocol, Ivan asked Jacque to broach the subject. Mietwataka answered Jacque's question. The big canoe is called "The Czarina" they had sent a runner to ask about you." Tatjana was sure this meant her father was the captain. Igor was also pleased with this information. He had asked Tatjana's father to bring him lots of metal and supplies.

After three days rest the coast trading party headed west. Several traders from the Klikitat village joined bringing their trade goods and looking forward to increasing their salt supply. This time Wapaxo didn't digress to the obsidian deposits. Igor's arrow heads were too superior to spend the time and labor to fashion obsidian points. The only deviation was the search for myrtle wood. The bushy shrub seldom grew any straight stalks, but since Wapaxo had found one he had hoped to find another.

The trading was fast and furious. Otter Pelts, salt and this time candle fish. Whale oil was available but transportation and storage was difficult. Jacque noted that there was a deep inlet that would allow the passage of a large sailing vessel. This he would inform Captain Boris Sheppenov about the availability of whale oil and that he would interested in getting as much as he could haul to the permanent Wapaxo camp. There was a big advantage to the deep water port for trade in land. It wouldn't be difficult to construct a wagon road to the Klikitat village and smooth sailing from there on. On the way back to the Klikitat village a visual survey was made and notes taken for expansion of the route to the future port.

Back at the Klikitat village the traders regrouped and set plans for the trek to Portland. With considerable more goods to trade, they had to construct another dug-out. Moving the wagon from the north bank of the Colombia to the south bank was only a reversal of what they had to do to move from the south bank to the north bank. The trek west to Portland had also been improved. Now there was a graveled road. The only depreciating factor was the presence of hide hunters. They had discovered the more lucrative market for buffalo hides and had moved in en- masse. Their total disregard for nature and the environment was apparent in their camps and rough shod treatment of the native inhabitants. When Wapaxo's group passes by one of their encampments they attempted to run rough shod over them. The beauty of the treks female members brought forth aggressive propositions. When one of the hide hunters moved aggressively toward Tallena he found himself facing Broken Branch. He reached for his pistol and that was his last mistake. He ended up with a third eye in the middle of his forehead. Noting Broken Branches speed several others moved in a threatening position only to find themselves faced by Up River, Mitwask and Yatum's ready henry rifles. After Broken Branch's proficiency they backed off and dispersed thereby saving their lives it was a good decision for had they looked further they would have seen Wapaxo and Igor looking down the barrels of two buffalo rifles at their group. Word had reached the port of their arrival and a reception was gathering. Captain Boris Sheppenov ordered the traders piped aboard. After the ohs and awes they scrambled up the boarding ramp. All except Wapaxo came aboard. Wapaxo would not budge. He wanted nothing to do with this enormous frightening contraption. In recognition of his status Captain Sheppenov descended the boarding ramp and extended his hand. Wapaxo took his hand but would not budge toward the ramp. Jacque joined them and questioned Wapaxo and all he would say was "too big". Big it was over twice as big as the Kodiac that Wapaxo also wouldn't board.

The Czarina was almost twice the size of the Kodiak. It had passage space for fifty and a large dinning and galleria area. The cargo carrying space was doubled. Captain Sheppenov explained that the last trip had been so profitable that he had purchased the Czarina from his own funds when she was only two thirds completed in the docks at Sevastopol. Captain Sheppenov informed them that his crew consisted of fifty men. Many who were builders busy constructing warehouse space and dock for him here in Portland. Igor was doubly pleased when he scanned the manifest of arriving cargo consigned to him. Captain Sheppenov told him his cargo would be warehoused until he returned from California as the new land was now being called. He also stated that his next port of call would be San Francisco. All of this was discussed before Tatjana had a chance to introduce her father to his new granddaughter. They all withdrew to the galley. Refreshments were served. Captain Sheppenov couldn't understand Wapaxo's refusal to come aboard. Jacque was at a loss for words. He has never been where he wasn't in command since he was a young man. For him to enter a large structure he didn't understand was like entering a confinement. "I think I understand said Captain Sheppenov, I suppose I would feel the same in an open space he controlled.

After a tour of the ship Captain Sheppenov explained that he intended to establish a presence in Portland and in San Francisco. Jacque, Dr McKamey, and Ivan expressed their desire to invest in establishing a financial base in San Francisco. A verbal agreement was reached. They would collaborate. At this point the Wapaxo group revealed to Captain Sheppenov that they had considerable wealth in gold. Captain Sheppenov revealed his desire to build a dock worthy of being a birthing place for the Czarnia.

Since the Czarina would reach San Francisco before the trekkers Ivan, Tatjana and Dr Mckamey decided to sail with the ship. Being in San Francisco two weeks before the trekkers arrived would allow them time to establish accommodations for the traders.

With no concern over the value of the gold aboard the Czarina Wapaxo's troop headed south to meet up with Manny Horses people. It was a festive reunion. Familiar routes were taken and a stop at Ft. Ross was enjoyed by all. The Ranchero Sonoma had grown due to theft of herds of cattle from the hidalgos. They had employed the skills of the Mexican population to tan and produce leather. The quality of the leather was good and the traders were able to make good exchanges. Due to the weight of the pottery products they selected only the most delicate. The smaller pottery was packed in intricate baskets that were in themselves works of art. Re-supplied, rested and anxious to be on their way, they broke camp and headed south. Their activities were routine until they reached Bodega Bay country. There they took advantage of the rich clam flats. Wapaxo was particularly fond of clams and was in no hurry to leave these rich diggings.

The Czarnia had good sailing time, winds had been favorable and there had been no storms to impede the sailing. They had reached Yerba Buena a good two weeks before Wapaxo and the land traveling traders were expected to arrive. Docking the huge sailing vessel was a problem. After several soundings a cove was located south of the bay entrance. The bay belonged to one of the Spanish/Mexican Hildagos. The huge ship was impressive and it was an advantage to have a permanent docking facility there. Negotiations secured the area for the Czarina and twenty adjoining acres. Over night the additional laborers aboard and all of the Indian workers were busy building the dock and a warehouse. Timber was procured from the Hidalgo. Igor sectioned off a portion of the warehouse space for a shop. The activity in the docking area was hectic. Dr Mc Kamey, Captain Sheppenov, Ivan and Jacque rode into what was soon to be the center of San Francisco. They couldn't believe the chaos. Saloons, gambling establishments, and disorganization were the most obvious of conditions. When they entered the different establishments it was apparent the only medium of exchange was gold dust. The bars were equipped with scales where patrons could deposit gold fines for purchasing libations or food. Anticipating this Ivan had cut pieces of smugglers bars into one ounce segments. These being unfamiliar to the recipients they immediately tested the pieces with acid to determine their gold consistency. Comparing the prices of drinks and food they established gold as being sixteen dollars an ounce. The lack of viable currency was noted.

The ships maintenance room gave Igor a work shop where he could experiment with forming gold coins. He cut the smuggler bars into one ounce pieces. Formed them into coins that he stamped on one side 20 and on the other X-X... These became known as double X's which later became double eagles. Because of ease of use the double eagles costing 1 and one-half ounces of gold became universal methods of exchange. The work shop section of the Czarina warehouse became a mint.

Wapaxo and his troop of traders arrived at the southern end of the Marin Peninsula. Jacque and B. C. Bob met them with two large barges to carry them across to the San Francisco peninsula from there they made a loop to Yerba Buena to rendezvous with the Czarina. They were delighted to settle on the acreage north of the warehouse. Fresh water was a problem. The stream running through the meadow was polluted by up stream squatters. Captain Sheppenov had anticipated this and filled several ships hogs heads of water for their arrival.

Wapaxo as ever exuded an aura of superiority as he agreed to board the Czarina. Accompanied by Jacque he circled the deck, glancing frequently over the rail to the water below. He frequently stomped his foot and listened for reverberations. He felt of the big hawsers that held the ship to the dock. It was only after examining the deck thoroughly that he agreed to go below. He wrinkled his nose as he inspected the crew quarters it was the gallery that seemed to impress him the most. As is the sign of a good ship the gallery was immaculate.

With the animals taken care of; the trekkers settled in for a good nights rest. After the morning meal Wapaxo, Captain Sheppenov, B.C. Bob, Ivan, Igor, and Jacque held a conference. Wapaxo was brought up to date on the money problem. When shown one of the coins minted by Igor, Wapaxo was baffled when told one of these coins could buy a horse.

Land ownership still wasn't comprehensible to Wapaxo. He was glad that he hadn't used any of the smuggler's bars on his way to the rendezvous. He turned them over to Igor saying make me twenty horses. Igor laughed and told Wapaxo that the group present was going to earn him hundreds of horses. The council from Captain Sheppenov to Wapaxo agreed to pool their resources and invest in San Francisco. Without legal council the percentage of ownership was determined as follows; Captain Sheppenov owner of the Czarina would hold three shares and three votes. Wapaxo as Chief would hold two votes and two shares. Ivan and Tatjana would share two votes. The burden of record keeping and dispersals would give Tatjana a vote. Igor's production of the smugglers bars gives him one vote. Jacques work in producing the gold and counseling Wapaxo gives him one vote. Dr Mckamey (B.C.Bob.) was granted one vote for his expertise and work on extracting the gold. Tatjana drew up the papers and everybody signed, Wapaxo made his mark a big arrowhead.

Captain Sheppenov. Jacque and Ivan were at the Hidalgo's ranchero. They had just completed an agreement to take all of the lumber his small saw mill could produced He was bragging about how loyal his people were, remarking about a coastal bark that had just docked when all of the crew deserted to go the gold fields. When the Czarina Captain heard she had a ship load of window glass they went to talk with him. He was truly bitter complaining that he didn't have anybody to un-load his ship. They asked to look at his manifest and after a short conference made him an offer to take his cargo and his little ship off his hands. When they agreed to pay in gold it was a closed deal. It didn't take the new owners long to bring a crew from the Czarina and re-dock the little ship along side the larger vessel.

Tatjana spoke to several of the syndicate's members and asked, "What do you plan to name your group?" She explained the difficulties encountered when she needed to identify the group in some acquisition or expenditure." We have one thing in common" She said. The Russian people identify with the bear and Wapaxo is known as the Bear Slayer. Why don't we call our concern Ursus Enterprises?" "Ursus is the scientific designation for the bear species." Jacque explained this to Wapaxo and everybody agreed. "Now that we have a name; what are we going to do with the hundred acres north of here that we purchased?" asked Captain Sheppenov. In Keeping with the present development, we should lay out streets sidewalks and commercial buildings. "We need a bank," said Igor," Our exchange of double XX's for dust has been well accepted at two and one half ounces of fines for each one ounce XX coin.

." The prospectors know that when they pay for drinks with gold dust they are shorted and prefer the coins. Some of the laborers brought over from Sevastopol were Shipwrights and knew how to draw blue prints for construction. The die was cast and Ursus Enterprises buzzed with activity. Ship builders were unfamiliar with masonry work so it was necessary to seek out masons for the timber- stone structures planned. It was known that limestone and clay when fired and pulverized made mortar when mixed with sand and gravel. The small bark that brought the glass was on its way back to the southern California ports to obtain more.

Weeks ran into months and Wapaxo was ready to return to his normal existence and his corn patch. About to leave, he remembered one of his latest finds, "The Good Tobacco", He brought it out and they had a parting smoke. Wapaxo disappeared and came back with a pannier he could hardly carry. When he emptied it in front of Jacque and Captain Sheppenov they drew a sharp breath. Wapaxo explained that he had buried the smugglers bars and they didn't grow as his corn had. Jacque asked him if he remembered making his mark on the paper. Wapaxo grunted an affirmative. Jacque said this will make it grow. Wapaxo appointed Jacque as his spokesman and they departed the next morning. Igor and his two wives remained and concentrated on furthering the plans of Ursus Enterprises. The twins were busy with their babies and Igor was glad they weren't trying to please him all of the time.

The shipwrights had to move a bulkhead to make room to bring the huge safe out of the captain's quarters. They set it on wheels and moved it into Igor's shop area. The smugglers bars were buried as Wapaxo's had. The safe held only papers and Double XX's coins.

Construction had begun following the shipwright's plans. The two story building was laid out to position the bank portion in the center of the complex. The huge safe was positioned and the building was built around it. The center of the plan positioned huge cut stone blocks around the safe and timbers framed the teller and clerk positions. High vaulted ceilings allowed for second story office spaces framing the lobby. It was impressive.

Wapaxo and the trading caravan trudged into Portland stopping at the big dock- side warehouse. It had been raining for three days. Captain Sheppenov had given Wapaxo a bundle of letters. One was addressed to the Portland based supervisor. When he opened it he recognized Captain Sheppenov hand writing. It directed the Portland office to grant all courtesies and wishes to Wapaxo explaining his importance to the company. Reading this the supervisor quickly ushered the caravan into the big warehouse. He had two large metal hogs head barrels to be positioned about twenty feet apart and fires be lit in them. Two men were assigned to keep the fires going and to monitor them for danger to the rest of the warehouse. The animals were rubbed down and taken outside to the old camping area corral and fed.

Communications were difficult. Wapaxo called Milliwana to interpret. She had grown quite proficient in English and the Portland Supervisor was pleased not to have to stumble verbally with Wapaxo who made a comment on how wonderful it would be to have a big warehouse like this in his village. The supervisor cleaned a space in the dust on the floor, handed Wapaxo a stick and asked Wapaxo to draw what he needed. Still not sure what was going on, Milliwana coached Wapaxo and made modifications to the drawing. What had been a whimsical wish grew into a command. A water wheel and a saw mill had been arranged by Igor and Jacque when they were in Portland the last time. Warming and drying off, the women of the traders began preparing food over the fires. Wapaxo expecting to trade for the accommodations shared some of the treasures from San Francisco with the Portland crew. When the rain let up Wapaxo was ready to assume his trip. The supervisor asked Milliwana to have Wapaxo stay for a while. This was not to Wapaxo's liking, but he agreed out of gratification for the shelter they had received when they were so miserable upon arriving in Portland. When several days had passed Wapaxo grew impatient and prepared to leave. Working day and night the supervisor was ready in two more days. With everybody assembled Wapaxo brought out some of the good tobacco and they held a smoking ceremony, blessing the up- coming trek. Wapaxo still didn't comprehend what was happening when he was met at the Colombia river ford by three huge wagons pulled by six oxen each. Ten men trailing pack mules followed behind the wagons. Exasperated with the slow moving caravan Wapaxo rode up and down checking and re-checking all of the activity. Finally he summoned Milliwana and met with the millwright heading the wagon train and they had a conference. After listening to the millwright she turned to Wapaxo and said, "You wanted a warehouse, you are getting a warehouse and a saw mill". Stunned to silence they trudged on.

The weather was not kind to them the rain had turned to snow. The oxen teams had to double up to make it up some of the hills close to the main camp. Tired cold and hungry the greetings by Milliwana's father: "Moose That Walks on Water"? Wapaxo asked him how he received his name. When I was young my family was headed for camas country and I saw this big Bull Moose standing in a blue lake and told everybody about it. The blue lake turned out to be a field of camas. So everybody called me Moose That Walks on Water. I have a brother that is named "He who Brings Bad Weather", I Guess this tells you about the day he was born ".Now tell me why you are called "Wapaxo", asked Chief Walks.? Wapaxo laughed and said," "Hunter of Tonka" was too long to say so my family shortened it to Wapaxo. Now I have another name given to me by you, "Bear Slayer". It is easier to just say Wapaxo. The good rich tobacco served as a catalyst to humor and good conservation.

The weather had grown cold and the completed water wheel driven saw mill could not operate; the stream that propelled it had turned to ice. Unable to build the warehouse the Portland crew packed and left. They took only the wagons and the oxen, leaving the mules behind. .

The Portland crew had no sooner left and a scraggly starved group of Nez Perce rode into camp. They had trekked over the Bitterroot Range from the Flathead country where they had been forced by the white man's army to relocate after the defeat of Chief Joseph just south of the Canadian border. The Wapaxo tribe took them in, fed them and gave them shelter. The women and children settled in and the men left with mules loaded with, food headed back to the Salish-Kootenai country. Wapaxo's wisdom had been proven again. Chief Walks' people had just completed a good harvest of camas. This with Wapaxo's bounteous harvest of corn took up the slack. With all five hunters scouring the area for game and permission to use the rifles granted, meat was also plentiful. Snowed in and comfortable the dejected braves were ready to listen to Wapaxo.

Wapaxo called a conference. Crowding in as many Chiefs and Sub-chiefs as possible, with the rest of the room filled with braves. He began: "You are all strong braves. You have been defeated in battle, but don't let this defeat you in spirit. Open your minds; the white man is human like you with one exception. The white man's braves and family heads are not afraid of physical work. They are willing to work in adverse conditions to achieve strength and status that enables them to manipulate the environment to their advantage. When the trees and flowers bloom the white man is going to return to this sanctuary and improve it. Stay and learn. You have the blood of great people flowing through your veins. Let it nourish your brains to advance our people.

Tatjana had joined the staff of what was soon to be a major hospital. The administrators gave her credit for the time she had spent as a rural/native care giver as internship. This shortened her educational period and she would soon be an accredited physician. Ivan worried about her over extending herself in the Ursus business. At a conference they decided to seek an accountant and clerk to take up the slack. It was touch and go with the recently formed city council. The need to set parameters for construction was evident. The Ursus group had exceeded any goals they had so far set.

Adjacent to the bank an emporium displayed the goods available which included merchandise brought in by the Czarina. Two areas developed from the construction efforts were the demands for glass and cement.

The first load of glass brought in paid for the bark and its shipment, leaving the glass used in Ursus programs as pure profit. The big financial gains were made in the bank. The council had petitioned the congress to establish a mint in San Francisco. Ursus applied for the contract and received it hands down. Somebody made note that Ursus being the generic or scientific name for bear was appropriate for California the Bear State.

Ivan as real-estate vice president was constantly looking for suitable investment opportunities. With a well established office Ivan approached the Hidalgo on selling his holdings. With reservations the Hidalgo agreed. Holding back ten acres of high panoramic view property the deal was consummated. The Ursus Bank carried the contract and quietly began developing the property.

Los Angeles was booming. Ursus purchased several light fast ships to ply the coast for cargo and passengers. Agriculture expanded and produce was in big demand in San Francisco. To the north the harvesting of redwood was reaching dynamic proportions.Ursus was awake and envolved.On the newly acquired Hildagos properties a new large hotel was springing up in an idyllic setting. Staying with the bear reference it was named: The Grizzly Arms. The hotel was staffed by Chinese immigrants from the developing China Town section of San Francisco. They were hard working and very neat people. The uniforms of the house keeping staff were embroidered with the likeness of a grizzly bear. This evoked a multitude of jokes amongst the entrepreneurial and traveling merchants.

The Czarina set sail on a gloomy November morning with only one stop at Ft. Ross and then Portland. She was loaded with trade goods from southern California and leather from Rancho Sonoma. Igor and his family were aboard. Igor felt needed by Wapaxo. A coach line had been established between Portland and San Francisco. Milliwana had sent a letter about the activities at "Camaize" as Wapaxo's village was being called. Igor had ordered the waterwheel sawmill to be built in the spring and he wanted to be there for this.

Igor's wives were delighted with the huge ship, showing no sign of sea sickness. Their only problem was the lack of activity. They had been use to running from daylight to dark all of their lives. Washing clothes by trailing the laundry behind the big ship in nets was a novelty. Added to the richness of their lives was the newly gained knowledge of cold-packing vegetables and meat in glass jars. They had brought on board a large supply of the glass topped jars of various sizes and the rubber bands used in sealing the food to keep it fresh. Pots, pans, and skillets were waiting the new stove in the hold of the ship. Every day in San Francisco had brought them a new delight. It was equivalent to the awakening at the end of the dark ages.

Two days out of Ft. Ross a violent storm hit the California coast. With the entire yardage hauled in, the hatches battened down and deck cargo tied securely. All there was to do was hunker down and ride it out. Even the sea worthy stomachs could not withstand the pitching and rolling. Everybody was sea sick. After twelve hours of turmoil the sea calmed and the sails were set as the sun made a feeble attempt to raise the human spirits.

The estuary of the Columbia was a welcome sight. Due to the size of the Czarnia, pilot boats were sent ahead to guild the large ship to the up-stream harbor. Every docking is an event, but somehow this was more fortuitous given that the Czarnia had survived the violent storm to arrive on a spectacularly beautiful day. Each passenger and crew member disembarking felt a need to give thanks for the solid earth under their feet. Anticipating Igor's arrival the dock supervisor had ordered a suit at a Portland hotel. It caused quite a stir when the bell hops escorted the Igor and the twins to their suit. Their luggage was brought up by the stevedores of the ship. Amazed at the opulence of the suit; the twins inspected everything asking Igor a multitude of questions that he couldn't answer. When it came time to eat, Igor boldly waltzed into the dinning area with his two wives and children. An alert waiter ushered them to a large table brought high chairs for the babies and stepped back. Igor having had some experiences with San Francisco restaurants made selections from the menu. The head waiter believing they were some foreign dignitaries stepped forward and helped with the selections. Igor with his broken English managed pork steak dinners for all three. Tea seemed more appropriate for drink. The babies were given small bowls of graham crackers and milk which they delighted in. When it came time to leave the waiter gave Igor the bill and a pen. He signed not exactly understanding what he was doing. Feeling that he had not done right he placed a XX coin on the table.

Back in the suite the three adults each took a bed and the babies were bundled into one crib. After a while as Igor was feeling the stress of the day melt away he felt a warm body snuggle up to him. It was loving time. In the morning Igor was awakened by the crying of the babies. He looked for his wives and found them in the bath room in the shower. They had mastered the spray and were chortling as they scrubbed each others bodies. He stripped off and joined them. The babies continued to complain until finally somebody heard them and rushed to their rescue.

In Portland Igor knew he was going to have trouble shopping with his wives. He only had XX coins. He went to the Portland bank and talked with a teller. Finally after confusing the teller she called the bank manager. Igor explained these were 1 Oz gold coins Using a postage scales the manager determined the weight to be correct. Common sense told him that they were gold because this agreed with his knowledge of the density of gold. Next it was Igor's turn to be skeptic. The currency offered stated $20.00. Igor had traded in San Francisco money, but was this the same as Portland money? He reasoned if he could procure what he wanted from the merchants of Portland it didn't make any difference. His wives wanted mostly frilly things and things like towels and yardage. The exchange of twenty XX's gave them money to burn. When the women had finished their buying Igor spent the balance on pocket knives. The boys of Camaize were about to be bribed into working.

With the ox cart loaded with the cook stove, fence material, some specialty wire copper and iron and blacksmith specialties, they were ready to head home and the storm broke The wagon drivers conferred even with six oxen they weren't about to tackle the muddy road ahead. Igor conferred with the millwrights that had started on the water wheel and he said that he would send for them when the creek was manageable. A single runner on a good horse could make the trip in two days.

Wapaxo was anticipating the return of Igor. Everything was broken or needed improvement. The tribe's women were equally excited about the return of Igor's wives. They had always been such a cheerful addition to the tribe's activities. And the stories they knew they would bring forth about San Francisco and Portland. Little did they know about the gifts to each and every one of them? Their big prize was the cook stove and the pots and pans. The tribe was about to make giant steps into the white man's world. Whale oil lamps and candle fish were coming to help them explore the large collection of children's school books.

One of the hardest tasks of the tribal women was the preparation and tanning of leather. A portion of the leather obtained from the Rancho Sonoma was secured for the village of Camaize. The delight of the women of Camaize could not be measured. Moccasins and children booties were in production in every Hogan. The women knew the feel of the leather as to what it should be used for. The soles were of course the heavier of the back leather while the belly leather made the tops and straps. The fine goods were dealt out to the women that had helped with the reduction of the ore to smelt- able fines. The Nez Perce visitors could not help but see the richness of the Wapaxo tribe. It was a hard adjustment of the Nez Perce warriors but facts were facts and they slowly accepted the realization that Wapaxo's people had a better life.

Theirs were not only adjustment to thinking that had to be made. Wapaxo began to realize that the gold had been what had made much of this possible. He went to the old mining site and looked at the slide that had covered the diggings and wondered if it could be possible to recover the past workings. Without the guidance of B.C. Bob and Ivan it was impossible for him to conjecture the possibilities.

As spring and warmth released the stream to flow the workers from Portland appeared to work on the water wheel. They brought with them the necessary pulleys, belts and axels to drive the large saw blades. Only the carriage and slides needed to be manufactured at the site. It was a joyous day when the first log was placed into the shoot and forced through the blade.

Through all of this, Wapaxo had one concern. The mill was going to occupy the meadow that he had intended to plant with corn. To the west of this meadow was a strong stand of tamarack. When they told him that this would be cleared to produce saw logs he was mollified.

The timber was selectively cut and only the standing dead or cured timber was taken. The site for the warehouse was selected by Wapaxo. It was a rocky knoll not suitable for cultivation. The Nez Perce braves observed the activity and were astounded at the accomplishments of the white men. Wapaxo mingled amongst them remarking," Do you see why there is no chance to defeat this adversary when they have so much determination for improvement?"

The Nez Perce grew rebellious. They refused to participate in the work and they chastised their wives for their acceptance of help from Wapaxo's tribe. One of the sub-chiefs confronted Wapaxo and threatened him. Wapaxo said, "You are a fool. Take your people and leave." Give us horses and supplies and we will return to the Flat Head," they said... Wapaxo said, "Take with you what you brought and I will give you food for five days. "It is a seven day trek", replied the sub chief. "And you call yourself warriors! Hunt your way." replied Wapaxo. The sub chief's move toward his knife was cut short by the clatch clatch of the rifles held by Beaver Boy, and Up River.

The bitter and dejected Nez Perce left the next morning... The terrible trio followed them for several days to make sure they had really left the Camaize area. Wapaxo pondered the situation and couldn't rationalize the conduct of the Nez Perce. The clash of the white men and the native Americas could have easily been condensed to economics. The Native Americans were established in a culture of living off of the land. The Whiteman involved himself in exploitation of the land.

Wapaxo pondered the differences in the approaches to survival. It only took a catastrophic event of weather to emphasize that man be he aboriginal or highly cultured to realize that some things are beyond man's comprehension. Not all of the Nez Perce had left. Hanging around the trading post were several neer-do-wells. One named Manny Coups. Came up to the veranda, where Wapaxo was sitting in his chair, demanding," Me want tobacco!" Wapaxo reached in his pouch and took out a generous pinch of tobacco and offered it to Manny Coups. Manny Coups sneered, saying "Me want much tobacco". Wapaxo asked him, "What do you have to trade?" Manny Coups replied "Me warrior not trade man," "Warrior is also good hunter. I haven't seen you bring any meat into the village" answered Wapaxo, causing Manny Coups to loose face. Angry Manny Coups pulled his knife and lunged at Wapaxo. Ever the cool head, Wapaxo had only to lean his scepter spear outward and Manny Coups impaled himself on the sharp obsidian point like the grizzly sow had done years ago.Manny Coup's knife clattered to the deck and was covered with blood, Manny Coup's blood.Wapaxo pulled the spear out and said, "Manny Coup has just counted his last coup, himself." Wapaxo wiped the spear on Manny Coup's clothes and walked regally away leaving Manny Coups for his acquaintances to take care of.

The arrival of Igor and his two wives was an auspicious occasion. Igor's wives couldn't wait to set up their new stove and cook with the pots and pans from San Francisco. They had also brought a large quantity of exotic fruits and vegetables from Southern California.Wapaxo couldn't help feel the happiness in the atmosphere. What a change from the dour influences of the Nez Perce. With out resting Igor went immediately to the waterwheel construction area. Hoping to convince Wapaxo that they should try to re-open the mine, he had purchased an ore hammer mill to reduce the high grade to manageable smelt ore In fact he was taken back when it was Wapaxo that brought up the suggestion that they should try to produce more yellow iron. They agreed that Dr McKamey would be needed to survey the area and make the decision.

Dr McKamey had become involved in the fledging local university and wouldn't be available until the spring break. Igor wrote a letter and sent it to Portland to be forwarded on the shuttle to San Francisco. The burgeoning success of Ursus had produced huge dividends. Knowing Camaize's need for a medium of exchange the executives of Ursus prepared an outline and procedure instructions with one hundred thousand American dollars with Dr Mc Kamey to establish a Camaize financial base. The new currency reminded Dr. Mc Kamey of the script he had encountered at Ft. Ross.

Wapaxo sent for Beaver Boy. Since Up River and Broken Branch were with him the terrible trio met with chief.Wapaxo had a lunch packed and the four headed for the little lake that had formed as a result of the earth quake and slide. Picking a nice spot on the shore of the lake next to the old mine entrance they squatted and Wapaxo brought some of his special tobacco saying, "let us smoke". As the four friends inhaled deeply the rich smoke the serious nature of this meeting hung in the smoke cloud about their heads. Wapaxo spoke, "This is sacred ground. Father Mountain expressed his anger over our digging and blasting and created this little lake". A silence settled over the group. Beaver Boy spoke, I have walked this area many times since the mountain shrugged and I believe that the mountain shrugged to please a beaver family that had asked for his help in creating the lake" he said. Since that time the beaver family has raised two sets of young ones. This has been a joyful place. "This I did not know about and think about", replied Wapaxo. Up River spoke, "We have been hunting two sleeps from our main camp so as not to deplete the local game supply and maintain the serenity of this lake". "There are a few elk drinking from the lake and a bear has denned up a sleep up the creek," said Broken Branch. Wapaxo said, "The blasting and digging for yellow iron has brought us prosperity. Do you think Father Mountain would become angry with us if we continued this?" Beaver Boy said, "Not if it didn't disturb the beaver family." Up River and Broken Branch agreed. They had their lunch and prepared to leave. Wapaxo told them he had sent for B.C. Bob to consult him.

Wapaxo sent Up River with a big fresh horse to greet B.C. Bob. He told him to remember B.C. Bob had been leading a white man's life and to take his time coming back. He even suggested that they try out some of the trout streams along the way. The stage route between San Francisco and Portland was well established and this was Dr McKamey's choice for the trip. In addition to Dr McKamey's luggage the stage coach carried a large cast iron kettle. As B.C. Bob Dr McKamey remembered Milliwana's disappointment at being forced to leave the kettle at Little Foxe's cave camp. He purchased a large mule and had a special pack made to carry the heavy kettle. Up River met with B.C. Bob the next day. In the list of wants from the women at Camaize was a fishing reel and fishing line. Wapaxo had seen brook trout in the beaver pond. His success there would insure that the lake wouldn't be disturbed by mining activity.

White Owl Omen

Thirteen year old Rabbit Runner stood outside Chief Moose Who Walks On Water's; hogan. Rabbit Runner had no father or he wouldn't have dared to attempt to see the Chief and address him in person. He announced himself loudly, "Oh mighty Chief I am an orphan without a father and I seek counseling. After a brief pause Chief Waters, Milliwana's father said enter. The boy said trembling, "I bear news of great importance". "Speak", said Chief Waters." I have been told that to see a white owl is an important omen", said the boy. "Who has seen this owl?" asked Chief Waters "Only me," said the boy." "Who else?" asked Chief Waters? To see a white owl was a very powerful omen. As to whether it was a good or bad omen depended on many things. Chief Waters was worried. He had never encountered this omen. He dismissed the boy and told him to be here the next day at mid day. After the boy had left Chief Waters looked for Wapaxo. In a hushed voice he told of the boy's sighting of a white owl. He had found Wapaxo inspecting three deer that Beaver Boy, Up River and Broken Branch had just brought into camp. He was glad to have the terrible trio here especially Beaver Boy for he seemed to be able to commune with nature. He was the closest in character to be a shaman. Beaver Boy said that they must consult with the oldest woman in their area. Since there were no old women in Wapaxo's tribe the ball was in Chief Waters'court.When Rabbit Runner came the next day Chief Waters sent him to find the oldest woman in his tribe. When the many times grandmother arrived with Rabbit Runner they cowered trembling before Chief Waters and Wapaxo. It was Beaver Boy that put them at ease. Addressing the old woman he said, "Grandmother we are merely seeking your advice." "What do you know about the "White Owl Omen"?

The White Owl Omen

In a clear strong voice the old woman answered. "To see a white owl can be a good sign or a very bad sign." "When is it a good sign?" asked Wapaxo ".There are many indicators", answered the old woman. ".What time of the day was the white owl seen?" And who saw it"? Asked the old woman.Wapaxo answered," The young boy that brought you here saw the owl in early evening". "These are both good signs", said the old woman. "Was the owl flying, perched or eating?" asked the old woman.Wapaxo deferred to the young boy who answered. The owl was perched and seemed to be studying the area and not eating", said the boy. "Did the owl fix its gaze on you?", asked the old woman. "I don't think so", answered the boy. "There are no bad points", answered the old woman. Because the owl didn't fix its gaze on the boy the up coming event will not affect him. Thanking the old woman, Wapaxo gave her a bundle of rabbit pelts.

The event of the evening was the expected arrival of B.C. Bob. All of the arrivals from the mother river port were greeted with excitement since they usually brought new goods and interesting people.Milliwana was in the forefront of the visitor greeting crowd. At first she couldn't believe her eyes. B.C. Bob was leading a mule that seemed to bearing a large cast iron kettle. This one was even larger than the kettle she had been forced to leave with the cave tribe of Chief Little Fox and it had a lid. She rushed forward and exclaimed her excitement. Approaching from a different direction was Igor. He had been privy to the iron pot surprise and had made a tripod support with a length of chain hanging from the apex. This would make it easy to adjust the pots distance from the fire...Milliwana immediately became a believer in the white owl omen.

At first Wapaxo was perturbed but when he saw the enthralled look on Milliwana's face he mellowed and accepted his being left out of the surprise. It was a cinch that the next evening would be blessed with a large feed of a camas specialty by Milliwana.

THE CONVENT

Her position with the hospital in San Francisco had put Tatjana in contact with The Sisters of Marialata Charity. There were several aspects of the sisterhood that impressed her. They ran a little clinic where they treated disadvantaged people to simple Medicare. They conducted schooling for children, ran a dairy, a library; and were almost self-sufficient for their daily needs. The advantages to the village of Camaize were apparent. Tatjana had spelled this all out to Dr. Mckamey. His was the job of informing Wapaxo and convincing him of the advantages. Wapaxo mulled over the information and was reluctant to accept the religious aspect. He was afraid to offend his Natural Gods and called for a conference with Beaver Boy, Up River and Broken Branch. The heart of the consideration was in reference to the respect that should be given the natural revered Gods. Beaver Boy spoke up," They are women, what can they know of the woods, the mountains, the streams, and the wild life? They dress funny said Broken Branch. He remembered seeing them on his trip to San Francisco. Wapaxo spoke, "We all have something to learn. Should we try to teach these women the understanding of our natural Gods? It was a challenge, a chance to count coup.

Tatjana received the go-head with delight. URSUS would finance the expedition and agreements were set forth. The engineers of URSUS consulted with the Mother Superior and plans were drawn. Where the sisters asked for forty square feet they were given sixty.

Czarnia II sailed from San Francisco on an early April morning. Aboard were all of the building materials except lumber. The saw mill at Camaize was running long hours every day. The Town was growing. Twelve Nuns were aboard with twelve dairy cows and one bull. The crew joked "the Nuns were going to have to find their own bull".

Glass was not new to Wapaxo but he rebelled at his use of it for dwellings. He rationalized that if somebody wanted to look out side they should merely step out. And if somebody wanted to look in they should enter if permitted to. Concrete and its uses were a complete mystery to Wapaxo. Only Mother Nature could build rocks. To break rocks and shaped them was understandable, but to shape and mold them was hard to believe. Wapaxo sent for Beaver Boy, Up River and Broken Branch. It is time to hunt watonka he said. They selected two new tribal members and set forth.

The hunters carefully prepared for an extended hunting expedition. They trailed four mules with packs to bring home the buffalo meat. With only the objective of bringing home the greatest possible amount of meat they took only modern weapons. Wapaxo relinquished the lead to Beaver Boy, trusting his natural instincts of nature and path-finding. When they

were four sleeps out Beaver Boy doubled back and reported that he had tracked a couple dozen bison and believed they could be taken. There was only one problem. They were not the only hunters tracking the herd. As close as he could determine twelve other hunters were on the trail. They seemed to be Nez Perce. Not wanting a confrontation Wapaxo sent Broken Branch and Up River to scout them out and see if they couldn't have a cooperative hunt. When they returned their report wasn't good the Nez Perce were in war paint.Wapaxo knew that his was a superior force with two buffalo rifles and four henry repeaters. Beaver Boy had brought his quiver and bow with and agreed to ride into the Nez Perce camp and ask for a cooperative hunt. Wapaxo didn't like this idea but he trusted Beaver Boy. As Beaver Boy rode into the Nez Perce camp Wapaxo and the four hunters snuck into close rifle range around the Nez Perce. Just as he had feared one of the Nez Perce recognized Beaver Boy and called him one of Wapaxo's Squaw- warriors. They surrounded Beaver Boy taking his bow and quiver. They immediately recognized the steel tipped arrows as being Wapaxo equipment. They laughed and told Beaver Boy the Tonka were theirs and theirs alone. Beaver Boy said, "we only need four animals and there were over twelve in the herd". One highly painted warrior stepped forward saying, "You Squaw –Warriors can clean the entrails and carcasses.

And scrape our hides for us." He forced Beaver Boy against a tree and started to tie his hands behind him. Why Wapaxo decided to use the buffalo gun even he couldn't tell you. The well painted brave's head exploded spattering blood and flesh on several others including Beaver Boy. Calm and collected Beaver Boy stepped back and said, We made you a fair offer now it is better you leave this area before the only meat you will be taking is your own carcasses In. shock and confusion the party of sixteen gathered their horses and equipment and dashed from the area. Up River and Broken Branch followed the Nez Perce with the telescope making sure they were riding away from their hunting area.

The bison had made a U-turn and headed west. They had evidently picked up the odor of the Nez Perce hunters and were evading them. Beaver Boy knew of a lush valley that lay in the general direction the bison were going. The hunters counseled and decided to swing wide and see if they couldn't intercept the game at the narrow entrance of the valley. A wind out of the south west was not favorable to their plan. Wapaxo was reminiscing of the preparations he and the hunters had made for the Pishkun hunt. The chants and rituals had a ting of a spiritual aspect however the sweat lodge and balsam smoke served as a cover-up of their human scent. As tired as they were it was decided that they should begin their circle as soon as possible so that they could at least be in position to build a smug fire to alleviate as much human and horse smell as possible.

Beaver Boy had been right. The bison were following a large regal bull on the trail of the lush valley. This shift by the bison was a good deal for the Wapaxo hunters since it put them closer to home when they finally arrived at the kill zone. Well situated they settled in and chose the four animals they needed. Two each two year bulls and cows were grouped together. When they chose the time to kill the shots were almost one roll of rifle thunder. Only the henry rifles were used since they were within fifty yards of the animals. The dressing was new to the two new bucks in the party but they followed the lead of the terrible three and did the woman's work in silence. Turning the entrails inside out and scrubbing them with sand was necessary to clean them properly for the stuffing with pemmican

Camaize had visitors. Four young Salish Kootenai braves with their wives and children had arrived to petition Wapaxo to join his tribe. They arrived just as the hunters were entering the village with their load of bison meat and hides. The young braves received a welcome and a surprise when Wapaxo directed them to assist in the preparations of the hunt's meat. They had expected to work but working alongside women taking care of game was not normal behavior for their tribes and only the attitude of the hunting party and their willingness to step up to the tasks made it possible for them to humble themselves and do the women's work. They marveled at the hand operated meat grinders imported from San Francisco, These machines could well be men's work since they had never seen them before.

In celebration of the successful hunt Milliwana's large pot was loaded with heart, liver, sweetbreads, and kidneys. The evening meal would be late but it would be a sumptuous one.

The next morning there were more surprising visitors; Ivan and Reanna, Igor's brother and wife had arrived on the Czarina II. They were both educated people having graduated from a St Petersburg Catholic university.Reanna was here to do her Doctorial thesis on Native American Languages. Ivan was a mechanical engineer. Igor's two wives were at first a problem for the two devout Catholics. However the longer they became acquainted the more the practicality of the situation was accepted. Ivan's hobby was horticulture and this endeared him to Wapaxo who was eager to try the multitude of seeds he had brought with him.

Camaize was not like any Native American village Ivan and Reanna had read about. The trading post where the locals brought their products to trade for white man's goods and their neighbors produce was uncommon. Ivan and Reanna were settled into a temporary wigwam. They had hardly unloaded their luggage and articles when the tribe began to bring them all sorts of hides and food stuff to add to their comfort. Igor insisted they take their meals with him. After a tour of the tribes activities Ivan remarked that the camp could use a water system. Igor took Ivan to the little lake above the village and the two laid out a water system that employed a windmill and water tower. Planks from the sawmill could be made into main line pipes. After the project was discussed with Wapaxo who didn't understand it but conceded to the two mechanical types and the system was on its way. Valves were discussed and a message was sent to San Francisco and Ursus engineers soon had them on the way.

Dr McKamey (B.C.Bob), Igor, Ivan, and Wapaxo began planning on the possibility of re-opening the mine. The sill deposit had shifted and it wasn't easy to locate the direction of the shift. B. C. Bob had Igor make two ell shaped iron rods. These he held out in front of him as he crisscrossed a grid pattern to locate the severed seam of mineralized aggregate. The tremor had not only shifted the sill laterally it had also dropped vertically. Digging test holes and driving rods into the rocks caused vibrations that disturbed the beaver in the pond.

They got busy and dammed up the pond outlet that supplied the sluice that drove the water wheel, that ran the sawmill. Every morning four or five men were busy cleaning out the beaver's work. It was conference time. They gathered in Wapaxo's meeting room Wapaxo, The Terrible threesome, Igor, B.C. Bob, and Ivan. When the problem was explained Wapaxo found it amusing. He stated , " you mean to tell me that it takes five men to clean out what a few beaver did in a nights work?" and laughed. Ivan spoke up, "Why don't we just trap the beaver out?" Beaver Boy slowly shook his head. Wapaxo rose to his feet angry, saying loudly "NO! The beaver are Gods favorite people. Without them we wouldn't have many fine little valleys and water would wash away everything. There would be no camas plots or ground to grow corn. You cannot eat your yellow iron." Do you forget so soon! Father Mountain shuddered when your Boom Boom injured him and threatened the beaver's pond. To help the beaver people he sent some of his rocks to strengthen their dam.

It was an impasse, Wapaxo had spoken. The white men withdrew and gathered at Igor's.

It would be impossible to explain the value of gold to Wapaxo. The problem had to be solved without disturbing the beavers. They cleared off a large table and began building a model of the beaver pond/mine site. Above the beaver pond was a small waterfall. They measured and calculated and came to the conclusion that they could divert some of the water above the waterfall and pipe it to the waterwheel flume. With this in mind they began hauling plank from the sawmill to the work site. Just when they think they have enough timber some turns up missing. Suspecting the beaver, they set up a night watch. And sure enough the beaver were stealing timber to improve their dam. Upon close examination it was noted that the beaver preferred the fir because it was heaver with pitch.

With the waterwheel flue completed the miners concentrated on digging for the ore bearing sill. To reach the slipped sill they had to cut through a cliff of flag stone. Igor noticed the flag stone was of good consistent quality. He developed a scheme. Igor collected the young men and gave them a proposition. He laid out the collection of pocket knives he had brought from Portland. There were two bladed, three bladed and four bladed knives and scabbards. He offered them to the boys that collected the best flagstone according to size, thickness and configuration. In front of his shop he laid out lots and assigned each boy a lot.

In order to protect the boys from the mining operation he restricted them from gathering during excavation for the sill. The competition was fierce. It wasn't long until Igor had enough stone to build the fireplace he was planning for his new home. Several things were accomplished; first the young men learned that it paid to work second was that competition was esteem building and third was the respect they earned by their accomplishments.

The Salish-Kootenai new comers were well settled in. Working at the saw mill had a hellacious effect on the stalwart braves. The physical activities gave them feelings of expansiveness. Muscular growth aroused physical contact with their wives. Leisure time found them in competitive sports. The script received for their labors enabled them to shop the trade post for desirable items. Their wives expanded their activities to include the basket weaving and pottery. It was a good assimilation of cultures.

The compound for the Sisters of Marialata was nearing completion. Shelter and pasturage for the milk cows and garden space for their personal garden was laid out. Some of the functional buildings still needed completion. The school, clinic and library needed the sisters to add their personal touch. The freight wagon from Portland creaked its way to the village. Wapaxo couldn't believe the abundance of material dropped practically at his door. He hadn't felt the addition of a dairy was necessary until he was told they would make cheese. He had developed a taste for cheese when in San Francisco.

Ivan and Reanna were delighted to hear of the advent of the Nunnery. Since they were Catholic they would have a place to worship. The library would benefit for their many books would not leave with them when they returned to Russia.

The two coaches bearing the Nuns preceded their cargo wagon and arrived without event. Wapaxo and Milliwana, Ivan and Reanna, curious children and the usual trading post hanger-ons were the sum and total of the welcoming committee. The Nuns were just glad to arrive to clean furnished quarters. After freshening up Reanna with the help of Igor's wives served them a delightful dinner. The care of the milk cows seemed to be of most importance. The feeding and milking was given priority. The American natives stood in silence as Mother Superior Anna De Lagracia led the sisters in prayer. She and the sisters knew it would take time for the natives to learn and understand their religion. At the end of the second day of their arrival the Mother Superior presented herself to Wapaxo and was delighted that he spoke some English. Wapaxo couldn't help but believe this advent was part of the owl omen. Thinking about the forthcoming cheese, he asked when they would be making some. Sister Anna could only say soon when she saw his eagerness. God had shown her the way to a man's heart was through his stomach.

Milliwana approached Chief Moose Who Walks on Water's hogan a little unsure of her reception. He was commonly known as Walks on Water. His full name was given him when as a young boy he mistook a camas field as a deep lake and couldn't believe his eyes as a moose walked across it. As was common courtesy she called out "hoy" as she approached.

Showing respect she crouched at his feet placing her hands in her lap and waited his recognition in brevity he asked, "Yes my daughter"? In Camaize he deferred to Wapaxo assuming a lesser social position in recognition of Wapaxo's success in accomplishment of the development of the village and social organization. Milliwana also held an upper class position with the women. She had perceived her father's people preparing to trek to a distant camas field. "Father may I ask why are the Poncos breaking camp?" He answered, "We have a long distance to travel. The upper meadow fields are ready to harvest." "There are fields here to harvest less than a day's ride and we still have a large store of Camas and corn in storage. Why don't you harvest here and save the move?" "This is Wapaxo's territory", he answered." She countered with, "Why don't you ask Wapaxo and agree to furnish help to increase the corn fields? Wapaxo's tribe is small and the Ponocs could add strength by joining with him." You have six hunter scouts. With Beaver Boy, Up River, and Broken Branch, plus the two new Klikitat braves, all equipped with fire arms they would be a formidable protection force." Where would we get the weapons?" asked her father. They would have to work for them," countered Milliwana. "They would be given jobs at the mine, mill or the corn fields." "My warriors would never do women's work," stated her father. "The fire arms are treasured. Wapaxo's warriors are highly regarded and they worked for theirs," said Milliwana. Leaving her father with the thought Milliwana mingled with the Poncos women and gave them hope they wouldn't have to break camp.

That evening when Milliwana was alone with Wapaxo she dug into her memory treasure trove, reminding Wapaxo how grateful she was he had been her savior from the grizzle sow. and how she had nursed him back to good health. With leading conversation she remarked how well off they were but she was worried that bad people could bring troubles with theft now that they had a bank and a trading post store. This led to her asking how they could increase their protection with more scouts like Beaver Boy, Up River and Broken Branch. As she pointed out, they were often away hunting. Wapaxo listened attentively knowing this was leading to something but he knew not what at this stage.

As was a common practice several of the village men including the two Chiefs and a couple of the white men gathered in the evening on the trading post's big porch/veranda. The white men chattered like chipmunks thought Wapaxo and Walks, while the noble Chiefs were noncommittal emitting a grunt every once in a while. An outsider would have been baffled for the conversation was a mixture of English and Shoshone; the grunts could be affirmative or negative. Take your pick. Since this evening gathering was restricted to men the true linguist Reanna missed a royal chance to help them unconfound their attempt to communicate. However since she was a close cohort with Igor's two wives she was lavishly kept abreast of what was going on.

It was three days before Wapaxo and Walks were able to meet without interference. As a result of this meeting Wapaxo called Beaver Boy, Jacque and B.C. Bob to a smoke and meeting with Chief Walks. They agreed that they needed added security in Camaize. They also agreed that the six braves selected from Walks tribe would have to work to earn their riffles and ammunition needed for them to learn to handle the rifles. Their training and subordination was left to Beaver Boy.

The combining of the two tribes created a multitude of problems. Foremost of the problems was the adjudication of disagreements and property rights. It was decided that each chief would administer to their known members. When the conflict involves apposing members both chiefs would administer. Jacque was amazed he had never in his whole life believed that such a transition could take place. Under the tutelage of Milliwana the local Camaize patches became organized cultured fields. Time spent moving from patch to patch was spent improving and expanding the patches near the village. With Ivan's input the corn fields were fertilized and production in this area exploded. Fruit trees were planted and grape vine arbors were established. The dairy was a start. The community still depended on the hunters to provide meat. The next advancement was the establishment of husbandry. The rolling hills North West of Camaize. Wapaxo recalled visiting the Sonoma Ranch at Ft. Ross. It was common knowledge that this ranch had prospered through the theft of southern California cattle. There was no doubt that this nefarious practice was still practiced in this area. In conference with Wapaxo, and Chief Walks, Jacque, B.C. Bob and Beaver Boy it was decided that a seed herd be purchased from the Sonoma Ranch and brought overland to Camaize. White man buffalo would back up the hunter's harvest. Cattle ranching was not an expertise of any of the Camaize population. The Sonoma ranchers were of Mexican extraction. Spanish was their language. Jacque could speak and understand a few words but was hesitant to undertake the negotiations to purchase and hire competent drovers to bring a herd to the Camaize area. Ivan heard of the dilemma and told Wapaxo Reanna was fluent in Spanish. When she was approached with the idea of accompanying the cattle drive her adventuresome spirit was ready but she hesitated when it was brought to light that there was no concept as to the time involved. At first Ivan objected but when Milliwana agreed to accompany her he agreed with the stipulation he would also go.

Beaver Boy would head up the expedition. His first directive was to initiate a hunt planning to have plenty of jerky and pemmican for trail food. Milliwana busied herself preparing camas and corn meal for the trip. Soon it was apparent that they were planning a trading venture and an ox team and wagon was added to the three mules and extra horses. Leaving Up River and Broken Branch to maintain order at Camaize.; Beaver Boy took three of the Poncos braves that had earned their new rifles and two of the young Klikitat braves that had also been checked out on the henry rifles.B.C. Bob had also wanted to go but the mine was beginning to look productive and his expertise was needed to develop the activities in this area.

Taking the familiar route the trip to Wapaxo's Klikitat village was effortless. The road had been slowly made navigable. After trading for salt and smoked/dried salmon they continued on their way. The next pause was at Manny Horses camp. Several of Manny Horses' people joined to increase the safety of numbers. The travel down the coast was slow as a result of the trading stops. However the clams and abalone were enthusiastically devoured. The coastal tribes had experienced a good year in the harvest of sea otters and willingly traded for salmon, vases and baskets.

Fort Ross was a disappointment to the traders. The Russian ships had abandoned the harbor for the more lucrative ports of San Francisco and Los Angeles. Many of the former settlers had left to try their luck in the gold fields. With the loss of the hide trade Rancho Sonoma had extra cow hands they didn't have work for. The ranch was glad to sell off two hundred and fifty head of heifers, cows and bulls. The cattle were gathered and run through chutes and corrals with the new hands selecting the best. Jose Ramirez, forty year old with a wife and two children was selected to be Heffe (boss).of the herders. Two younger married vaqueros made up the cow herder crew. It took five days to assemble the herd and line them out on the trail. The ranch rejoiced at receiving twenty dollars a head paid in gold. The Mexican herders had dogs that proved invaluable in keeping the herd moving The Camaize scouts picked lush meadows to allow the herd to graze as much as possible. Any of the herd that didn't appear to be in top condition were culled out and given to the villages of Klamath and Tillamook tribes in trade for hay.

After the festivities the Sonoma Ranchero conspirators nurturing hangovers began to speculate if the herd buyers had more gold in their possession. In recollection they remembered the pouch from which the gold was dispensed to pay for the cattle didn't look empty. Their larcenous nature took over and they began plans to follow the herd and rob them of their wealth. They had witnessed the shoot- off and skill that the terrible trio had displayed. Only Beaver Boy had been recognized and the new henry rifle bearers were discounted. This was of course a mistake. Beaver Boy had trained them and they were quite proficient. Wanting to keep the raiding party as small as possible they decided twelve raiders should be able to overtake and hit the herders with enough fire power and stealth to secure the gold without real danger to them selves.

Beaver Boy enjoyed his reconnoitering; he was in absolute tune with nature. The chatter of a squirrel told him that he had been noticed. The call of a blue jay confirmed the squirrel's alert. Silently he circled to the east of the trail route. He climbed up a draw to the top of a ridge that gave him an overlook of the entire valley. Staying below the ridge top and occasionally dismounting and scoping the herd's back trail through the bronze telescope that was the prize possession of the Wapaxo tribe. Hanging behind the herd he was able to spy the raider's forward scout. For them to swing to the west would put them into rugged territory that would make it impossible to keep up with the herd so they had to head east if they intended to intercept the head of the herd. It was apparent they were not intent on stealing the cattle. Although Beaver Boy couldn't understand waisachu's gold fever he knew this was their target. The twelve raiders had no knowledge of Beaver Boy's presence. He dropped below the rim and took the best trail to the head of the herd.

He located Ivan, Reanna and Milliwana and told them of his observations. A raid on their camp at an unknown time was of course disconcerting to the women. Beaver Boy told them that the best time to nip this bud was to strike them first when they least expected it. It was agreed that Ivan was to remain with the women and the Wapaxo braves would intercept the raiders. The herders were instructed to cluster the herd in the next valley. Happy to settle into the deep grass without the dogs and drovers the cattle grazed with hearts content. The drovers not knowing what was transpiring accepted the relief from the drive with pleasure.

Beaver Boy assembled his warriors and explained the mission. The best place to intercept the raiders was a half days ride to the south. There was a choke meadow there. It had one problem there was no place for the warriors to conceal themselves. Beaver Boy showed the Braves how to camouflage themselves with sage brush and grease wood. They had just settled in when the raiders entered the valley. Each Brave was told that his target was to be according to their position. Beaver Boy would take the first two the next brave the next two and the following braves would target accordingly. As the raiders came abreast there was one continuous roar and all twelve dropped... The horses and the weapons of the raiders were collected and the corpses were left to the ravens, magpies and other scavengers.

Two of the raiders survived the ambush. They nurtured one another and were able to start their long walk home. When they arrived at Rancho Sonoma the first impulse was to seek revenge. Tequila, pulque, Cerveza, and bravado enlisted forty or fifty eager hot bloods to seek and ride on the raid. The next day when the alcohol wore off the band was reduced to nineteen willing avengers. The ranch cabal that had established the ranch from stolen stock was reluctant to sacrifice more horses and equipment without insurances that they would gain through the theft of the gold from the Camaize drovers. The urge to seek revenge was not strong enough for the remaining raiders with the fervor to launch the raid.

Beaver Boy guided the herd north of Portland to avoid the development and meet the Columbia River as close as possible to the fording beach. The wagons and the traders continued into the town as the herd was bunched in a valley north of Crown Point. Exhausted the cattle were contented to graze and ruminate in the belly deep grass.

The Czarina III was in dock and the crew was glad to see the Camaize traders. Their warehouse was bulging with cargo for the expanding town. There were tons of pipe and fencing; also plumbing fixtures and glass in abundance. Ivan stepped forward and took charge of the freight He found that he would need six more wagons and twenty four more oxen. The gold left over from the cattle purchase would not cover this cost. It was pure luck that Captain Sheppenov was aboard the Czarnia. He went to the new bank in Portland with Ivan and arranged for a draft on the Ursus account. This was a relief for Milliwana and Reanna for they had wanted to shop with the gold reserves.

Beaver Boy his braves and the Mexican drovers were amazed to see the wagon train of oxen and their cargo. It was decided that the oxen wagons would lead the trip to Camaize there- by missing the manure created by the cattle. The big problem facing the drovers was the crossing of the Columbia River. Two hundred forty seven head were left after trading nine crippled cows for hay and six cows coming fresh with healthy calves. The cows with calves were separated out from the herd and held back. Several lead cows were led into the stream and the bulk of the herd crowded behind them. The mother cows followed and the calves were hog tied behind the saddles of the drovers. After crossing the herd was mustered up stream from Wapaxo's home village. Everybody rejoiced, not a single critter was lost to the fast stream. It didn't take the cow calf pairs long to assemble with the main herd. There was plenty of feed and the herd settled in to eating and resting while the traders bartered for as much dried salmon as they could. Three of the braves went with Beaver Boy to the coast for tobacco and salt.

The road leading to Camaize was well developed for forty miles south of the village. The crushed gravel and the slag from the blast furnace had made a good road bed. With the messenger bringing news of the herd and the oxen train was a message from the California Catholic Diocese. Father Remaldo the Diocese Cardinal was coming to inspect and bless the new Monastery. When the tribal members heard of the Priest's visit they speculated that he must be Christ since the Nuns were known to be the "Brides of Christ". A lot of humor grew out of his expected arrival. The younger braves chuckled amongst themselves. The herd was complete as with the dairy herd, "the bull was coming" It wasn't until Reanna arrived that Wapaxo was able to understand the composition of the church organization and the Cardinal's functions. He dampened the jokes and tried to explain the church to the tribal members, to no avail.

Temporary quarters had been set up at the ranch for the three families responsible for the care of the cattle. A new well was dug, a windmill and tank was built and a garden patch was laid out. The Mexicans had brought their chickens with them. There was lumber and fencing to build a chicken pen and hen house.Wapaxo arraigned for the three ranch families to purchase what they needed from the trading center. After thoroughly inspecting the oxen loads Wapaxo called for a conference with Igor and Ivan. The fencing wire, gate hardware, and some of the plumbing articles were unknown to him. The large quantity of pipe intrigued him. After explaining that the wood pipe they had laid from the water tank was only temporary and would have to be replaced. Wapaxo's next questions concerned the fencing. His visit to Fort Ross made him acquainted with fencing and he was happy to have the barriers set to protect his beloved corn.

Ivan had brought a large supply of mangel-wurzel seed, commonly grown throughout Europe as cattle feed. With much difficulty Ivan convinced Wapaxo that some of the valley farmable land should be seeded with this nutritious beet. Ivan also convinced Wapaxo that it would be advantageous to cut niches in a near-by hill to store agriculture harvest. He explained to Wapaxo that the saw dust produced from the mill would be excellent to bed the beets and other plants in to preserve them from roots.Wapaxo was amazed to learn that he could store ice from the lake in saw dust. It wasn't long until the oxen teams were put to work cutting the niches in the hill side and they were filled with saw dust.

With the corn, mangels and garden crops in, the urgent need was for hay. There was no way that the women and children could hand cut and cure enough to take care of the large herd of cattle, mules, horses, and oxen. There were several valleys that were waist deep in rich grass. Mowing and curing this grass into storage hay was the immediate problem. Ivan had seen the harvesting of hay in the Russian Steppes. They needed a mowing machine. With the images in his mind Ivan and Igor set about constructing a mower. The ox cart wheels could provide the power all they needed was the design of a pitman to provide the action needed to slide cutting blades in a horizontal motion to be pulled through the tall meadow grass. By gearing the wagon wheel to drive a disc with an off center piston movement they could drive a flat blade in a shaft, Then all they had to do was equip the flat blade with triangular blades with grass cutting edges. They soon learned that they had to build guards to protect the cutting blades. With a seat mounted above the axel they had a mowing machine. Oxen moved too slowly to be effective. The mules not used to being harnessed were a problem. Beaver Boy had been packing with these mules for years. They understood Beaver Boy and he soon had them working in harness and the hay was properly stacked and stored.

URSES Enterprises was prospering in San Francisco. The telegraph was extended from Sacramento to San Francisco and north to Portland. With the improvement of communications Camaize flourished. Dispatchers were able to accept and deposit the mine's produce direct to URSUS' accounts. The early accrual of land in the San Francisco area proved to be another capital bonanza. The Russian and Mexican influence on desires and wants of the village occupants flooded the trading center. Those willing to work were able to obtain highly desired riches. The strongest restrictions were on the purchase of weapons and ammunition. These had to be with the approval of Wapaxo. Added to the list of controlled items was blasting powder. The mine was curtailing their activities since the ore bearing sill was petering out. All of the smugglers bars except for those secluded by Wapaxo were shipped out. The very composition of the gold bullion aided credence to the assumption of the origination to be the Far East... The bank at Camassia was in a very stable position, however it was without direction and a loan debtor relation was not established. The general population wasn't involved with deposit, withdrawal and savings concepts. Tatjana deeply engrossed in Ursus finances seen a need to intervene. She booked passage on the next ship to Portland and arranged for travel to Camaize. Her arrival was unexpected but joyous. Igor, B.C. Bob and Ivan had been aware of the problems of the banking and monetary system of the Camaize Bank and welcomed her arrival. She brought with her a simple printing devise and sample forms for checks and balance documents. Three of the Nuns from the Convent were educated so she solicited their aid to bring the bank into a functional institution. Wapaxo always alert accompanied by Milliwana called for a conference. With the Wasichue present, Wapaxo asked for advice. B.C. Bob the most educated member of the group spoke up. "The problem we are facing has been growing with the definition of our bartering culture. We haven't established a value of time. When a member of our group performs labor what should he or she receive for their time?" What means you time, "asked Wapaxo. This stumped B. C. Bob. Thinking for a minuet "he said there is daylight time and night time. How you spend this time is your choice. If you hunt, gather your corn, take care of your animals you have spent this time to your needs. If somebody spends their time helping you and you give some of your corn for their help this is called wages. However when you do something for the good of the community as a whole, who should give you wages? In a do or not do society this involved the principle of obligation. In a society that followed the rules of nature as an objective concept the quantities are what is observable. Time is not observable. It can only be associated with accomplishment. I.E what could you have done in this time period? To bring this into Wapaxo's perspective he asked, "How many bushel of corn would you give for a fat buck?" Wapaxo answered, "It depends on which I have the most of, meat or corn". B.C. Bob marveled at the perspective of Wapaxo. He replied, "This is considered supply and demand. We all have an undefined period of time in this life. How we spend it is a matter of free choice if we haven't obligated the time to another. "As an example", said B.C. Bob, "I will water your corn if you will dig this hole for me." "I understand," said Wapaxo. B.C. Bob could see Wapaxo was thinking, "Why don't I just water my corn and you dig your hole?" This opened an entirely different field of discussion. Whose time is the most valuable?

It was the next day that Beaver Boy found Wapaxo surveying his corn field as he sought him out. "Oh Bear Slayer" he greeted in a most formal tone. "I have a big problem. The beaver have moved from their pond. I think it is because of the yellow iron activities and the wind stealing machine, "wind mill". They have moved to the White Owl Valley, two sleeps away by foot. You will always be my Chief, but I am going to move with the beaver. Up River and Broken Branch want to accompany me and I will take the White Owl boy as a son." Seeing the stunned look on Wapaxo's face he said, "Mitwask and Yatum will assume my duties as your strong arm when you need one. They are well trained and proficient with their henry rifles". Beaver Boy assured Wapaxo that he would bring meat every month when it was possible. "Look for me when the moon is full he continued, know also in your heart that if you send for the Terrible Trio we will be here as soon as possible." "I know the valley", said Wapaxo. "At the southern end there is a spring with the coldest water I have ever tasted. Close by is a shelf cliff and cave like Little Foxe's only much smaller. It should give you shelter from the north winds. Your gifts of meat will count as credit in the trading post for what you need when you visit." As they conversed they moved toward Wapaxo's hogan which with sawmill lumber was actually a house. Wapaxo leading the way took Beaver Boy into what he called his water room "Watch" he said as he turned a spigot above a metal sink. At first the spigot regurgitated a sputtering belch of air and water startling both of them. "Angry water" said Beaver Boy, "it no longer belongs to the beaver family. " The water in the White Owl Valley is happy water. At the end of the valley is a stream that is formed by two streams coming together at a rocky channel a marriage that is happy for it sings it's way into the valley. That evening Up River and Broken Branch visited Wapaxo and confirmed that he was still considered to be their Chief. Wapaxo reminisced about the White Owl Valley, remembering the abundance of berries and the good sized stream that was loaded with brook trout. He almost envied them but his reverence for his corn patch outweighed any desire to change locations.

The move of the Beaver Boy clan wasn't the only event of interest in Camaize. One of Igor's wives was pregnant again. Ether it was Diannee or Diannaa? Nobody knew. The problem wasn't with the twin that was pregnant but with the sister. They had religiously regulated their sleeping arrangements so that they had equal time in the big bed with Igor. The diligence with which they performed their wifely duties was often of consternation to Igor. The rapid modernization of Camaize drew heavily of Igor's abilities. His long hours of labor were taxing on his physical being. He needed his sleep. With the advent of one of his wives being pregnant was welcome news to Igor. There was a possibility that bed time would mean sleep time. This wasn't however the case. The twin not pregnant rationalized that it was her lack of insemination that caused her to be barren. If it wasn't her lack of adore it must be that he loved her sister more. This irrational thinking brought about arguments and she chose a position of celibacy. Igor breathed a sigh of relief.

The sister that wasn't pregnant was loosing weight as fast as the pregnant one was gaining. Milliwana observing these conditions became worried. She sent a telegram to Dr. Tatjana care of Ursus in San Francisco. "Dr. Tatjana if possible could you visit Camaize? We have several problems needing your expertise." Milliwana.

Ivan and Tatjana ended their days as usual in their comfortable penthouse on Nob Hill in San Francisco. The usual cocktails were mild and enjoyed. Ivan had become very wealthy by investing in San Francisco Real-estate. Knowing how Ursus planned to move gave him an advantage and he bought low and sold high, very high.

"Darling I have been asked to visit Camaize,"she remarked. Ivan remained silent for a long while." It peculiar that you ask this for I have had thoughts of Camaize for several days now" said Ivan. "There is something calling me back to this idyllic place," he commented.

I have never felt about any other place like this. Russia has its charm and San Francisco has its excitement, but none of them hold a candle to the adventure of the clash of cultures that Camaize has. "If you feel the urge to leave as soon as possible I will join you as soon as I can divert my investments and free myself from this money grabbing culture. It couldn't be more explicit Camaize was it. It took ten days for Tatjana to pack, adjust her hospital position, and pack her household and personal possessions. A Czarinia ship was scheduled to leave on the week end. The schedule was tight but possible. The telegram read: Camaize Milliwana break will arrive Portland aboard Czarnia II July 3, love Tatjana.

Milliwana had a fast coach prepared to meet Tatjana. Knowing she would have additional luggage and personal effects to follow she alerted Ursus in Portland to assist her in every way. Tatjana felt that it was a complete break and she packed all of her medical

Books and equipment this was it! With Ivan it wasn't so simple it took a month for him to be able to follow her. The power of Ursus made it possible. He brought with him twelve of his personal staff. Three of them were construction engineers, three were accountants and three were personnel managers. Carpenters, plumbers and electricians brought the team to completion.

When the dust settled it was a good thing Wapaxo's warehouse was empty. Ivan and Tatjana filled it up. Ivan surveyed the area and decided he was going to be a gentleman rancher. The construction people he had brought with him went immediately to work. Camaize Ranchero remained under the existing supervisors. The wives of the Mexican workers were given positions in the house hold staff. All builders were hastened to work on a huge log home with all of the amenities.

Tatjana didn't wait to get settled to assume the problem of the D. Sister. She visited the Igor home and immediately conferred with the ailing twin. It was apparent to her that this was a psychological problem. She brought her anatomy books with her and sat down with the troubled twin to explain why pregnancy was a complex occurrence. There are many complexities involved with becoming pregnant. None of them involve voluntary actions and result in a multitude of complications. In a few days of consoling the grieving twin relaxed and became her normal self. Upon examining the pregnant twin Tatjana discovered she was carrying twins. This somehow brightened the spirit of the depressed twin.

Wapaxo, Jacque, and Beaver Boy were enjoying some of the good tobacco on the veranda of the trading center when they were joined by Ivan. Beaver Boy had just brought in a fine bull elk. It was a full moon night. The main discussion was on the merits of different meat. Wapaxo's belief was that nothing compared to the quality of young cow Tonka, (buffalo). This brought remembrances of the trip to the Pishkun country. Beaver Boy recalled the problem Wapaxo had re-claiming his spear. And remarked how much easier the hunt would be with rifles, especially buffalo guns like the three 45/70's the tribe owned. "We should return to the Pishkun", declared Wapaxo.

Ivan could see the excitement in the faces of the old time comrades. The corn, camas, stock beets "mangels", and hay are ready for winter. By the time we get there the weather should be cold enough for the harvested buffalo meat that we haven't made into jerky and pemmican should keep. We can make it a trade voyage. So we will have to make a trip to Klikitat and the coast for salmon, salt and tobacco. Wapaxo said, "No women so we will have to take care of the meat ourselves I know this will be hard work for you hogan huggers" When Ivan asked to join them Wapaxo was unenthusiastic, but when considering the efforts Ivan had contributed to the wealth of Camaize he couldn't say no. When Milliwana, Tatjana, and Pillar were told of the hunting expedition plans they were disappointed. This led to a woman's conference. The three ladies conspired to teach the men a lesson. They insisted on going on the trade trip to Klikitat and Portland. Tatjana and Milliwana assured Pillar that she would be surprised at what they could purchase with script from Ursus. The guilt ridden men finally gave in when the women insisted on a light wagon on the trade trip.

A ferry had been installed between the north Columbia shore and Portland so the big shopping spree began.Pilar was overcome. Milliwana and Tatjana were highly amused. It was only their sophisticated experiences gained from exposure to San Francisco that kept Pillar from making foolish purchases. The light cart with two frisky horses was no longer light. Over night at Klikitat and then on their way to Camaize the women chattered gaily. The men grumbled wondering what foolish purchases their wives had made, but they knew better than to complain. The hunting expedition was foremost on their minds.

It was in the first part of November when the hunters lined out. They had four pack mules loaded with trade goods. Each man was armed with a henry rifle and a revolver all with plenty of ammunition. It would have to be a big foolish war party to attempt to interfere with this group. Beaver Boy had left a week ago, planning to stop at Little Foxe's cave village and the Kiowa Camp they had visited on the first Pishkun hunt.

As usual Beaver Boy traveling light, avoiding encounters with anybody was way ahead of the hunting party. With a mystical awareness Beaver Boy observed Mother Nature in all of her glory. Armed with the ships brass telescope he often paused to watch the rutting and sexual practices of the animals he encountered. He never used his fire arms to procure game for food. It was only the steel tipped arrows that changed his equipment from the time he was a tribal young warrior. He recovered all of his arrows except for the one that a skunk had scented when it had beaten him to a rabbit he had shot. Remembering a lesson from Milliwana he scoured a lighting strike burnt spot for morel mushrooms. Service berries and choke cherries were in abundance as were pine nuts.

His arrival at Little Foxe's camp was a joyous occasion. After a smoke, food and entertainment was ordered. When he tried to explain the Wasichue cities of San Francisco and Portland, he was stumped for words. There just weren't any descriptive words for the Whiteman's activities and achievements. His hardest story was to describe the big sailing vessels. Since there hadn't been any hostile activity Beaver Boy decided to remain with Little Fox until the main party of hunters arrived. The white buffalo pelt still hung in its place of honor. Kept spotlessly clean and roped off to keep reverent hands off. He noticed Milliwana's large kettle still had a prominent place in the food preparation of the tribe. He told Little Fox of Milliwana's new kettle and they laughed in joy. The main concern of the tribe was the loss of buffalo. The herds were growing smaller every year and were widely scattered. Beaver Boy inquired about Peelee Denko, "White Tail" "He is on his trap line" answered Little Fox. He will be here late this evening." There had been a bond between Beaver Boy and Peelee since they were both naturalists by nature. As daylight graced the cave entrance Peelee and Beaver Boy were deep in conversation. They were exchanging animal stories. Neena Peelee's wife brought them a delicious tea laced with wild honey. She was truly glad to see Beaver Boy and asked about Gee Gee. She was studying Beaver Boy closely. She finally said "I believe Beaver Boy and Peelee are the same size. She asked Beaver Boy to try on Peelee's Jacket. It was a perfect fit. I have an idea she said. Be sure to stop and see us on your way back from the hunt. Both men speaking at once, said, "Why?" "You will see" she answered coyly, and rejoined the women.

It was mid morning when Wapaxo and the hunters met with Beaver boy at Little Foxe's encampment "We have no knowledge of the whereabouts of our Kiowa friends", Said Wapaxo. "Leave us a message at the big rock of the river that flows (north) up hill". It wasn't an easy job finding the Kiowa. They were elusive in their attempts to out- wit the Black Feet. They had immigrated to the Sun River country, inching toward the Pishkun.

The meeting of Wapaxo and the Kiowa was joyful they were especially interested if the Klikitat/Nez Perc had brought salt. Beaver Boy had mentioned trading goods, but hadn't delineated the trade goods. Wapaxo always thinking asked, "How has your buffalo berry harvest been"? The wise young chief thinking of all of the women's work involved in the making of pemmican planned to gain as much as possible for trade of the highly prized salt. The Kiowa women were masters in making pemmican and there were plenty of them to do the work. This would only leave the jerky for his hunting party to process. Knowing the advantage his party with their buffalo guns had he negotiated for hunting advantages. He arranged for all of the bison downed by his party to be flagged. The yearlings, the most desired kills would be flagged with white flags on their horns. These the Wapaxo hunters would bleed and field dress. The small intestines were cleaned and packed with pemmican by the Kiowa women "It is plain why you are a chief", remarked" Jacque, pleased with the relief of all of the labor required to make pemmican.

The preparations for the hunt were the same the dances and sweat hut were performed. Ivan like most Wasichue considered this all mumbo jumbo. Wapaxo explained, "The wild animals have many times better smelling powers. The balsam smoke and sweating helps us smell different." Ivan was astounded to see the masses of buffalo. When Wapaxo told him of the Pishkun that the ancient natives had used to cripple the beasts for easy slaughter he had to visit it. Beaver Boy took him to the small cliff and explained the strategy involved in the ancients success in maiming and slaughtering their winter's meat.

Ivan developed a new appreciation for the Indian culture and resolved to expand his knowledge before passing any judgments on the primitiveness of ancient Americans. Thankful that they had the instincts to bring a good supply of salt the Wapaxo hunters headed west. With help from the directions of their Kiowa friends the Wapaxo hunters left the headwaters of the Sun River and headed over the continental divide. With elevations between eight and nine thousand feet they were slogging through high snow drifts. It was only when they dipped south that they found the pass (Rogers Pass).As they headed into the Salish-Kootenai (Flathead) country that recalled their friendly visit with the Flat Head tribe and the joyous event of the huckleberry festival. As they approached the Swan Valley they saw in a distance what appeared to be a gathering of Kootenai celebrating a weeks gathering of huckleberries. Scouting carefully they determined that there were six men and six women. Watching from concealment they saw six young braves approach the gathering. The body paint and clothing of the six newcomers was not to Wapaxo's liking. "They are not friendly", he commented. However they were greeted and feasted by the six couples. After eating and drinking the customary huckleberry wine the six painted braves pulled knives and subjugated the six husbands. The six women huddled together as the intruders tied their husbands to six different saplings. After securing the men the renegades each grabbed a woman and had their way with them while the husbands watched helpless. After more wine the nefarious ones gathered the horses, collected the harvested berries, tied the women to their mounts and left leaving the six husbands securely bound. They would surely have perished without help.

Beaver Boy led the mules to the tied up men while Wapaxo and the other hunters intercepted the raiders. Beaver Boy had a hard time convincing the husbands to remain with him. It was only when he showed them his henry rifle did they consent to stay in camp knowing that the bad guys didn't have a chance against the hunters. .

The six raiders were intoxicated and had no remorse about leaving the husbands to die most horribly. When they crossed a little stream and entered a lovely meadow they were completely surprised to find themselves to be facing three fire sticks. Two of them reached for spears only to have them shot from their hands. This display of fire power brought them to a stand still. Jacque soon had them bound as they cowed under the threat of sudden death. What you have done is as bad as possible declared Wapaxo. The women wept with joy when one of them recognized Wapaxo from their last meeting. He assured them that their husbands were being taken care of. "You didn't kill their husbands so I will spare your lives. That you will be known as cowards and for what you have done to these women they shall choose your punishment." Wapaxo took the six quivers belonging to the raiders selected an arrow from each of them. He broke the arrows in half giving a pointed half and a fetched half to each of the women. The balance of the arrows, quivers, bows and spears he put in a pile with some kindling wood and set it on fire. He instructed them that they should drop a fetched half or a pointed half in front of the rouge that had raped them. Those receiving a pointed half would have the tip of their nose cut off. Those receiving a fetched half would have one of their Achilles tendons severed. Upon the choices of the women four noses were to be cutoff and two had the tendons severed. The four to loose the tip of their noses were blind folded and tied to a sapling. The two to have their Achilles tendons severed were hog tied and laid with their faces down. He took the trade knives that he had taken from the rouges and placed the blades in the coals from the fire. As he moved down the line bobbing noses with the super sharp knife made for him by Igor, Jacque cauterized the stubs preventing excessive bleeding, and throwing the knives in the fire as his finished.Wapaxo severed the right tendons of the last two using the hot blades from the fire. "I will leave your horses and suggest that you depart this country as fast as you can" said Wapaxo as he untied the raiders, gathered the stolen horses, stolen huckleberries and women.

It was a joyous time when the wives and husbands were united. The women were all talking at once and laughing as they told of Wapaxo's justice. They were insisting that the hunters take a major portion of their berry harvest. Wapaxo recalled how well they had been treated during their last meeting insisted they accept salt, camas, corn meal and buffalo meat in trade. Wapaxo's justice had erased the shame the women felt for the attacks by the raiders. That evening the berry pickers and the hunters enjoyed warm friendship. Wapaxo said, "Why don't you visit Camaize our growing village with many wonders?" Your kind of people will always be welcome. We are headed for the cave village of Little Fox. Maybe you have heard of the white spirit buffalo hide there? It is about three sleeps south west. We will spend three sleeps there before we continue on to our camp." The berry pickers acknowledged that they knew of the spirit buffalo and the Little Fox tribe. At day break they said their goodbyes and departed in different directions. The trek to the cave was without incident and the greetings were as joyful as always. A substantial portion of the fresh buffalo meat was left with Little Foxe's people. When Neena presented Beaver Boy with the exquisite white buckskin jacket you could see the envy in every body eyes.Peelee explained, that Beaver Boy had given Jacque's Father's traps to him and he had been able to greatly improve his catches from that time on. Wapaxo and Jacque understood. The beaver were spirit kin to Beaver Boy and he couldn't abide the leg traps for this reason alone. Without rancor but lingering envy Wapaxo's hunters prepared to leave for Camaize.

Accustomed to having visitors to see the white buffalo hide Little Foxe's people were only slightly surprised to find six adults with children riding travois coming down a slight grade from the north. The friendly greeting by Wapaxo overrode any apprehension the Little Fox tribe had. When the Flat Head berry pickers told Little Fox about their encounter with the raiders and Wapaxo's method of meting out justice Little Fox's people were delighted and the Chief remarked such wisdom could only come from a great leader. Wapaxo rode higher in the saddle.

Beaver Boy took his position in the lead, scouting the route ahead of the hunters and travelers. When they arrived at the creek that is no more Beaver Boy had a nice young buck killed dressed and hung to cool. The women of the Flat Head soon had a good fire going and the smell of cooking venison wafted the air. The Flat Head women made quick work of the evening meal and immediately started to gather pine nuts. Wapaxo was pleased to see the men also gathering nuts. They would fit into his tribe where everybody worked.

Beaver Boy selected the next stop near a large patch of service berries. A quick meal of left over venison and the travelers' men and women were busy gathering service berries. The women noticed that Wapaxo headed in a different direction carrying several buckskin bags. Curious they asked him what he was gathering. He explained that his wife Milliwana was the tribal medicine woman and he was gathering herbs for her. The oldest of the group said, "Show us we know most of the herbs and plants and we will help you". "Milliwana will be pleased" answered Wapaxo. "She is always too busy to gather her own." The third day's stop was by a favorite camas gathering meadow for Milliwana. Under Wapaxo's watchful eyes the women collected enough to have fresh baked camas for the evening meal. The berries and pine nuts had increased the horse's and mule's loads to capacity. There simply wasn't room for more of anything. The travelers were themselves walking with only the children riding the travois.

The next late afternoon brought them into sight of Camaize. The Flathead visitors looked down at the village with delight. It was like a big city to them. The welcoming committee was almost the entire village. The greetings were cheerful and loud except for Gee Gee. When she saw the beautiful buckskin shirt jacket Beaver Boy was wearing she asked, "What did you have to do to receive your new shirt"? The question was dripping with jealousy. Reading the situation Wapaxo stepped forward and explained about the beaver traps and that Neena had given Beaver Boy the shirt in appreciation for the boon to their existence. It was Milliwana's turn to exclaim about the abundance of herbs and plants Wapaxo had brought her. The eldest of the Flathead women (Belita) stepped forward and exclaimed that she was a medicine woman in her tribe and she hoped her and Milliwana could compare knowledge. An instant bond was formed.

For temporary quarters Wapaxo directed that space be made available in the large storage shed. It was then that he learned that there was two pairs of sisters and that they were all cousins. The name stuck with them for they were known from that time on as the cousins. The next day Wapaxo assembled the men Cousins and showed them the two flat plots that were available away from the blacksmith shop, the hammer mill, and the saw mill and not cultivated. Then came forth the question that Wapaxo knew was on the cousin's minds. The eldest asked, "How can we obtain the fire sticks?" "They will have to be earned," replied Wapaxo. "Beaver Boy will leave for his valley tomorrow. Ask him before he leaves." In this way Beaver Boy retained his status as chief of security. Wapaxo summoned Beaver Boy and explained what he had done. Beaver Boy called for Mitwask and Yatum his deputies in Camaize. They knew the procedure. First the receivers of rifles had to be worthy. Then they had to perform labor equivalent to the value of the weapons. Then they had to receive training on handling and responsibility. Jacque as a ranking sub-chief accepted responsibility and lined the cousins out on their duties and responsibilities. The first task to be accomplished was the building of housing for the new comers. The shipwrights laid out the quarters. Each was to have running water, a sink and outside toilet accommodations. There was lumber and plumbing material available. Each of the cousins was assigned to a Millwright to do what he asked. This was almost a disaster; "the language barrier". Reanna was summoned. With six houses under construction at the same time, it was impossible. They finally decided to combine their forces and do two houses at a time. Four couples would just have to wait until their house was complete. Reanna breathed a sigh of relief and kept the working cousins close to her for ease of communications.

Just in time for the completion of the second cousin's house the stoves arrived. There were two stoves to each dwelling. A small cooking stove and a wood heating stove, stove pipe, roof flashing, and fire proof hearths completed the assembly. The new occupants were instructed on the use and care of the stoves. Never before had early natives been so abruptly introduced to such modern facilities. Furniture had been pre-cut and only assembly was required. The rough floors were covered with reed mats from the trading posts stores. Pots, pans, dishes, and rudimentary utensils were explained demonstrated. The magic of running water bewildered the new home owners. They had to be cautioned that the supply was limited. The first family to move in was the senior brave Tallekot (Tall Man) and Belita with their two children. The tribe assembled and Milliwana and others brought food and helped with the kitchen chores, showing Belita how to light the stove and prepare dinner.

At the blacksmith's house Igor and his two wives were fussing over the twins. They were boys. The twin that had remained barren had recovered from her disappointment over not also haven born a child and mothered the twins as if they were her own. Recognizing Igor's anxiety and pressure Wapaxo visited the blacksmith and practically ordered him to accompany him to a nearby stream. There he introduced Igor to the sport of trout fishing. The relaxing test of man against the wiles of trout enchanted the blacksmith and he was hooked. Prepared for a night out Wapaxo introduced the blacksmith to a campfire dinner of camas/cornmeal bread and trout. Their relationship had in the past been one of respect and appreciation. Igor's life had been centered on the creation and repair of objects. Wapaxo had lived more on a spiritual level. The fishing expedition had been a revitalizing experience. Igor gained insight into the problems of being a Chief and Wapaxo developed an understanding of the blacksmith's pressures. Wapaxo resolved to include Igor in all of the council meetings.

Ivan was rejoicing as a gentleman rancher. His investments and his share of Ursus Enterprises had made him an extremely wealthy man. The telegraph had made it possible for him to order some prize bulls and exotic cattle. With Portland growing there was a big demand for beef. After a short rest he took his wife and headed for Portland taking financial and legal advisors with him. Thinking and planning for the purchase of more cattle he decided to take the ranch boss and family with him.

North East of Portland was a large tract of land available. Ivan was pleased that he could secure twenty thousand acres of pasture land with four running streams. There was only one problem he couldn't find adequate living accommodations in Portland. He solved this by buying the hotel where they were staying. When the land was secured Ivan set up a construction camp. Reanna picked out a home site and drew some simple plans for a house. The fourth day in Portland was hectic. A construction firm established by some of the shipwrights that had come to Portland with one of the Czarina ships took on the job of building the house and out buildings for the ranch.

Ivan, Reanna, the ranch foreman and family left Portland in a comfortable stage coach bound for Fort Ross. The road had been laid out and improved. It was a two day trip with lay overs at two established coach station accommodations. Rancho Sonoma was glad to see them and made them comfortable. That evening Ivan brought up the question, "What should we name the ranch?" Since this wasn't a function or a part of Camaize they decided not to mention the tribal town. However much of Ivan and Reanna's success had help from the gold mine at Camaize, it was concluded that some reference should

be made to credit the gold's contribution. Reanna said,"
Let's keep to the California Spanish tradition with a Spanish
name" It seemed a natural: El Rancho Toro Oro, (Golden Bull
Ranch)."

Rancho Sonoma wasn't able to provide the two thousand
young cattle desired to stock Rancho Toro Oro and there were
no available vaqueros to help move the herd. Ivan decided to
leave Reanna and Jose's family at Rancho Sonoma and he left
with Jose for Los Angeles to purchase a herd and hire vaqueros.
Uninhibited by accompanying family the duo made good time
to Los Angeles territory. Their first task was to hire dependable
ranch hands preferably some that were bilingual. Jose consulted
with the local priest asking his guidance in the selection of
vaqueros. Some of the most desirable men were reluctant to
leave the Los Angeles area. While Jose was interviewing the
future ranch hands Ivan sought out a blacksmith to join the
Rancho Toro Oro. work force. Ursus had a large presence in Los
Angeles which Ivan utilized to locate reputable farm equipment
dealers. Procuring haying equipment was a top priority. Bob
Bellancourt the only blacksmith Ivan could persuade to move
to Oregon Territory was extremely helpful in ordering spare
parts for the equipment needed to keep the planned large
scale haying operations functional. When the Ursus offices
told Ivan that the Czarnia III was in the Los Angeles Harbor he
was elated and went immediately to arrange the transport of
his multitude of purchases to Portland.

With a crew of twenty Vaqueros Jose began the selection
of fifteen hundred two and three year old animals for the drive
north. Mules were purchased to pull the supply wagons and the
chuck- wagon. The mainstay of a successful cattle drive is the
camp cook. With the help of Ursus a former cattle drive cook
that now operated a Mexican restaurant "Manuel Largos" was
persuaded to sign up. His wife and four of their six children
were booked aboard the Czarnia III. The two older boys were
taken on as mule drivers and camp helpers. Under the shrewd
eye of Jose the cattle were mustered. Equipped and supplied,
the herd headed north seventeen days after the arrival of the

Toro Oro duo's arrival in the Los Angeles area. The blacksmith's wagon followed by the cook-wagon preceding the mule/ horse herd was a glorious sight for the first fifty miles then the noise and dust took over. The rough well armed vaqueros prevented any thefts and took care of the mishaps. Arriving at the Rancho Sonoma range was uneventful. Jose inspected the five hundred two year olds and rejected fifty of them. The two wives were glad to greet Ivan And Jose, but hesitant to join the dusty rough bunch until Ivan bought a light spring buckboard for their ride further north.

When the herd approached Portland Reanna and Jose's wife headed for the hotel post haste. Ivan stayed with the herd anxious to see what had been done by the construction crew. There was much to be done but rudimentary accommodations had been completed and the cattle seemed to settle in on the lush meadows near the headquarters. Czarnia III had been in dock for six days when Manuel went to pick them up. The children had fared well but Maria had several days of sea sickness. After four days at the hotel the women moved to the ranch. Some of the families had to rough it for a while living in tents and hauling water and fire wood. Some of the vaqueros had left families in Los Angeles. Ivan sent a telegram to Ursus and arranged for their next passage on a coastal ship bound for Oregon Territory.

The vaqueros well rested were lounging when Jose assembled them for duty assignment. In groups of five man teams he put them to work building fence. Resentment arose they hadn't anticipated working out of a saddle. Czarina III had brought several tons of barbed wire. Needed were the posts to hang it on and the holes to set them in. This was about to become the first fenced ranch on the west coast. The ranch was home to several clusters of cedar trees. Perfect for fence posts the vaqueros tackled the post manufacturing with reluctance. They hadn't anticipated callous earning labor. Ivan sensing the displeasure of his men called for a holiday. A huge barbeque was initiated; cerveza was rolled out by the barrel. A wagon load of young willing ladies from Portland were invited. The next day was of necessity another holiday.

Wapaxo after visiting Camaize ranch was notably concerned. Everything seemed to be in disrepair and the cattle were not properly cared for. The lack of Jose's supervision was evident. Seeking advice Wapaxo visited Igor and told him of his concerns. After consultation they wired Ivan and asked for his and Jose's return to Rancho Camaize. Thanks to the miracle of telegraph Ivan and Jose were there in three days. The problem was evident. Some of the feed corn had been allowed to ferment and the result was distilled into powerful liquor. The problem was boredom. Leaving Jose in charge Ivan returned to Rancho Oro Toro... The next day a wagon load of barbed wire was on its way to Rancho Camaize. Wapaxo had little time to confer. The news of the new ranch at Portland that was extemporary of Camaize disturbed him .Private ownership and actions were not of his understanding.

Wapaxo pondered, "how can man own land?" The land was the center of existence. When Manitou arose from the depths of earth as humans they approached the earth surfaces at different points of the world. Human forms arrived, some in the north some in the south and west and east. The climates and the preceding vegetation and animal life determined how they existed and developed. The humans adjusted to their environments according to their evolution. Those evolving in climates of abundance lived off of the land. Those that appeared in harsh climates developed an approach that accommodated their existence. When Ivan asked to accompany Wapaxo's clan to Camaize he accepted an inclusion to the circumstances and conditions of Wapaxo's rule. How then could he independently establish his own semblance of authority? It wasn't until six months later that Ivan sent an invitation for Wapaxo to visit Rancho Toro Oro that Wapaxo assembled Beaver Boy, B.C. Bob and Igor and asked them to accompany him to Ranch Toro Oro.

With Walks on Water in charge the four delegates of Camaize set out to visit Rancho Oro. The wives were accorded a comfortable coach ride while the men rode horse back. Mules carried the camp equipment and one of the vaqueros from Rancho Camaize tended the live stock. The reception was royal. The vaqueros provided music and a huge barbeque was prepared and exceptionally well laid out. After an extensive tour of the ranch Ivan explained that the idea had come to him when he questioned the marketing of Camaize cattle. It was hard for Wapaxo to grasp the difference between Camaize cattle and Ranch Oro cattle. Ivan explained that Rancho Camaize would exceed the need of Camaize for meat needs. The excess cattle would of necessity have to be sold in Portland where the demand was. With the advent of Rancho Oro there had been established an assembly point for Camaize cattle and assistance in marketing the beef. Bewildered Wapaxo accepted the arrangement and held no resentment. Wapaxo's stoic approach to the separateness of Camaize and Rancho Toro Oro led him to announce that he wanted to visit Portland on his own to collect his thoughts and clear his vision. Ivan brought him to the hotel and gave him simple directions and markers to observe to find his way back to the hotel.

Leaving his scepter at the hotel and dressed in Whiteman's clothes he stepped off in a brisk walk toward the business district. Remaining aloof he observed the populace in their individual activities as they went about the city on separate endeavors. Window shopping was for him a revelation of the abundance of material objects available even when he didn't understand their utilization. He paused at a sidewalk café observing and listening to the understandable requests for service and savoring the smell of coffee and bakery goods. He decided to try the apple coffee he heard a man order and watched him savoring the repast. When he managed to be served he ate and drank slowly as he observed the people eating and passing on the sidewalk. A group of Chinese men and women selected a table next to him and startled his senses with their demeanor and chatter. It was the Negro couple that really attracted his attention. He recognized they were speaking English but heir drawl confused his understanding. As he made his way back to the hotel observing the land marks and different buildings his conscious disturbed his psyche nothing in his past life had prepared him for this onslaught of facts and conditions. Upon his return to Rancho Toro Oro he remained aloof and barely communicative. It was a short trip to his native village of Klikitats. It was doubtful the light coach that had brought the women to Portland could carry all of their purchases to Camaize. The Camaize group split up and conducted their usual trips to trade with the coastal tribes. Upon their return Wapaxo instructed them to leave for Camaize without him for he had some visiting he wanted to do on his own.

The afternoon of the Camaize group's departure found Wapaxo headed for his mountain of puberty enlightenment. He was dressed in only a loin cloth carrying a robe and meager food supplies in his left hand, with his right hand carrying his scepter. When he found his remembered last visits spot he spread the robe and sat cross legged, took a long deep breath, held it until light flickers caused him to exhale. It was as if the boyhood spot rejected him. All he could think of was the high spirit mountain. The next morning he drank sparingly from his water bottle and chewed a small portion of jerky. Gathering his robe and Scepter he departed in the direction of Mt Hood. His trek took him in the direction of his home village. There he regrouped dressed fully, packed more food and rested for the crossing of Mother River and southern up stream hike along the Hood River. Other than his scepter he had his sling tucked into his waist as his only weapon. Even at a brisk pace it was several days walk to reach the piedmont upon reaching a small southerly exposed overhang just below the snow line he stopped and considered the need to camp there. In a primitive fashion he started a small fire to recover from the chill of the breeze blowing down the mountain from the snow covered peak. It was his third day of meditation that the Old Woman appeared to him as he huddled in his robe around his shoulders facing the morning sun. The breeze carried her question in a hushed tone." What do you seek of me my child"? 'Mother I am confused about the origin of man- kind and the differences of their nature", replied Wapaxo. "This has been a question that has baffled mankind throughout their existence The Great Spirit that is the supreme intelligence has not revealed this to us lesser Entities. My position as Mother Earth leads me to believe in the Seed Theory. This is natural with me since my partnership with Father Sun produces all varieties of life on earth. The plants sustain the animals which reciprocate in turn. The Seed Theory states that when Earth was formed the Greater Intelligence collected from the vast beyond, smaller particles shaped them with his will and hands and hurled them into space. One of those particles was earth that sought the protection of the Sun and showed obedience and obeisance by circling in orbit around the source of light. Once established the earth was bombarded by lesser particles carrying seeds, pollen and genomes that became plants and animals. Among the animals so distributed was mankind. Each animal and plant evolved according to the climate and soil conditions. Physical shapes and characteristics were altered to allow for survival to the circumstances of climate and sustenance. The harsher climates forced the animals to exert more energy to compensate for the apposing elements. The presence or lack of water developed creatures with abilities to exist on meager amounts" The sun was setting when the old woman dissolved into the evening haze. It was dark when the bush to the right of the sheltered area began to glow and a very elderly man appeared. "Evening!" Spoke the Elderly Man in fluent Klikitat dialect. Astounded, Wapaxo stood in awe. The Elderly Man bade him to remain seated. "The natural order of world life speaks favorably of your position and adjustments to the changes of order within your purview." Unable to speak Wapaxo only grunted and bowed his head. "The questions you had for Mother Earth are not definable by mortals". "Why"? Asked, a confused Wapaxo. The Old Man Spoke, "Yours is a developing world its future is in a far distant future. Since you have been granted "Free Will" your actions will determine if you continue to exist as a species." Your perfection may be your demise" The glow of the bush diminished and Wapaxo shuddered with the sudden cold. Not exalted but mollified Wapaxo didn't see any further need to remain in the rarefied atmosphere. Stumbling in the dark he headed for the low lands stopping on the banks of the Hood River. When daylight appeared as was his nature it didn't take him long to rig a fishing pole and line. There were trout to be cooked for breakfast. As he finished his breakfast and made ready to hike towards the Mother River he pondered his vision experience. He felt sure that he had been visited by the mountain spirits and regretted that he hadn't thought to ask more questions. His first inclination was to head for his native village but his need to speak to Ivan guided his steps toward Rancho Toro Oro. Three days later he stumbled into the ranch headquarters. After refreshments and the miracle of a good hot shower he asked for a council with Ivan. Mentally going over his experiences Wapaxo was hesitant to tell Ivan a waisachu of his spiritual encounter. Fortunately Ivan had been studying the Klikitat tongue and was able to guide him into a full disclosure. Ivan's experiences with his native associates had shaped his psyche into a belief that in some matters the native people were able to discern a clearer ambience with nature. With careful words he guided Wapaxo's persona to believe that only because he was a chosen leader the spirits chose him to guide his people to accept the differences in cultures and their achievements.

With Ivan's help Wapaxo was able to withdraw sufficient funds from the local Ursus Financial organization; allowing him to make extensive purchases in Portland. With trade goods Wapaxo formed a coastal trade expedition. He purchased large amounts of whale oil and candle fish and of course a goodly quantity of his prized tobacco and salt. He vowed that he would return to the Hood Mountain rendezvous; hoping to make contact with the mountain spirits again bringing tobacco as a gift.

The trip to Camaize was uneventful and fast requiring only two nights on the trail. His arrival was anticipated with the miracle of the telegraph. The two nights on the trail found Wapaxo in deep thought. He was mentally comparing the differences in the relationships of his people and their wives as compared to waisachu couples. The native considered his wife a possession while the waisachu treated his wife as a partner. The matrimony between waisachu couples was a mutual agreement while the acquiring of a wife by a tribal member was often a trade agreement.

Women were often placed in high regard as was noted in the references of important elements of geographical nature such as Mother Earth and Mother River. This had been brought forth in his mind since his experience with the Old Woman Spirit of the mountain.Wapaxo felt a need to expound on his spiritual encounter on the mountain. Since it was the old woman of the mountain who first appeared to him he felt the need to consult Milliwana.Before retiring for the night he called Milliwana to his side and hesitatingly told her of his encounter. Milliwana was taken back. It was the first time Wapaxo had asked for her opinion. She sensed a dramatic change in their relationship. Daylight found Wapaxo in high spirits and full of energy. He dispatched a runner to ask for Beaver Boy, Up River and Broken Branch for conference, allowing them two days to get to Camaize. He then strode off at a vibrant pace to collect Igor and B.C. Bob informing them of the upcoming conference. He set the time for his meeting to give himself a period of conference with the white men before the joint council with Beaver Boy and his cohorts. Sharing some of his good tobacco and a mug of local brew he began with Igor. After a little chatter of small talk, Wapaxo asked Igor what had been his bride price for the twins. His answer to Wapaxo stunned the Chief. There had been no bride price the circumstances of the conjugation had been the result of free will. The words of the Old Woman Mountain Spirit returned to Wapaxo, The seeds had been scattered to the whims of chance.

After greetings and libations followed by a smoke, Wapaxo spoke, " I have recently conferred with the spirits of the mountain and they have enlightened me with the some hints as to the origin of man kind and our destination, giving me as much knowledge in this area as is allotted to mere humans. From this I have come to the conclusion that our wives should be included in conferences on subjects that influence them, this isn't to include decisions of war, hunting or home location. With this in mind when I summon you bring your wife with when possible." This pronouncement left the native members in shock but the white men increased their respect for Wapaxo's sagacity. After further libations and a smoke the council disbanded. Wapaxo pulled B.C. Bob to a side and asked him to stay a little longer. When they were alone Wapaxo asked B.C. Bob, "What means three times three?" It wasn't any shock to B.C. Bob that Wapaxo was confused in the matters of numbers and mathematics. He resolved to teach the Chief the rudiments of mathematics. Asking him to follow he led Wapaxo to a gravely area behind the council house. There he smoothed off a place in the soil, arranged nine pebbles in three rows; covering two of the rows with his handkerchief, he asked Wapaxo, "How many pebbles do you see?" Wapaxo answered, "three". Moving his handkerchief to cover the six pebbles to the right, he asked now how many do you see?" Wapaxo answered, "Three"again.Removing the handkerchief entirely he asked, "now how many do you see?" Wapaxo counted and said, "Nine". "What you have is three rows with three in each row. Thus three times three equals nine. This is written like this said B.C. Bob as he scratched the numbers, times sign and equals sign in the dirt. This was the start of an intense set of classes that wouldn't make Wapaxo a mathematician but it would enable him to handle money and cope with numbers.

In Portland the Czarina III docked and Ivan was there to supervise the unloading of his farm and ranch equipment. One of the passengers was a tall lanky cowboy with a tied down pistol on his hip. He carried a saddle and bridal which he lowered to the dock and approached Ivan and in a deep Texas drawl asked him if he knew where he could buy a horse. Giving him an approving glance Ivan asked if he could speak Mexican. Like a native was his reply. Do you know anything about cattle? asked Ivan. "Hoof, hide, horns, and beller" answered the cowboy ".What is your name?" asked Ivan shoving his hand forward. I am Ivan Utzeph and I own the Golden Bull ranch. I am looking for dependable hands if you're looking for work" ".Depends, answered the cowboy taking his hand in a strong grip, I am Huston Wells. What are you paying"? "How does sixty a month and found, and a substantial increase if you work out", answered Ivan. "I still need a good horse" said Huston. "We have a large remuda come take your pick" said Ivan. "I prefer to buy one or two of your mounts, that way I am not beholden to you if I choose not to stay," said Huston. "Suit yourself" said Ivan. "In the mean time throw your gear in that yellow wagon with the farm equipment and let's go get some chow." With Huston's saddle and other gear taken care of they walked to the now "Golden Bull" hotel and found a seat in the restaurant. Huston couldn't help but notice the excellent service and marveled at the menu." "I couldn't help but notice the hotel has the same name as your ranch," said Huston. "That's because they are both mine," replied Ivan. Huston despite his rugged out doors look seemed at home in the up-scale restaurant. Ivan sensed a mystery around the aura of Huston. Through small talk Ivan learned that Huston was originally from San Antonio. He had been working at different rancheros in the Southern California area when he heard of the Oregon territory and decided to check it out when he learned that passage aboard one of the Czarnia ships was available. "We can head out to the ranch if it is convenient for you" said Ivan. "If I had my druthers I would prefer staying over night said", Huston. They stopped at the front desk and Ivan asked if they had a single room available. When the clerk said they didn't Ivan turned to Huston and said, "I guess we will have to bunk in my suit the hotel seems to be full. I keep permanent accommodations here for me and my family there is two bed rooms."

Huston feeling a little cruddy remarked that he would like to pick up his possessions from the yellow wagon. "I am afraid that won't be possible", said Ivan, "I am sure they are on the road to the ranch." "As far as toiletry items the room is fully equipped. If you need clothing items there is a good general store two doors down." continued Ivan. All I need is underwear and socks" said Huston. They picked up the room keys and stepped out the front door, made a right turn and entered the Emporium. Huston made his purchases which included several boxes of 45 pistol ammunition. "Planning a war?" asked Ivan. "Nope I just like to target practice when I am out on the range", replied Huston. Ivan again had that feeling that there was something mysterious about Huston Wells. Leaving calls for five am the two left for the suit. The furnishings and décor were impressive for Huston. The two bedrooms had their own bath room. Feeling the effects of a long day they hit the sack. The next morning they took a few steps behind the hotel and Ivan led the way to a buckboard that was loaded with packages for the ranch and Reanna. Ivan pointed out the land markings as they traveled the road to the ranch. When he spoke of synclines and anti clines Huston had to ask him about the land formations as they passed by. Ivan apologized and explained the geological terms. When they turned off the road and headed down the lane to the ranch entrance Huston noted the massive gate posts and the huge sign Toro Oro and the figure of a large golden bull. Ivan swung by the bunk house and stopped to make sure Huston's belongings had been dropped off there. They then proceeded to the chow hall and shop area. Past the shop area was a large corral with twenty horses lined up to the feed manger. Ivan called a vaquero tending the horses and told him to cut out the two horses that Huston picked out. Then excusing himself he drove up to the main house. Huston in perfect Mexican introduced himself and started asking questions about the saddle stock. A high spirited, blazed faced sorrel caught his eye. He asked the horse wrangler about him and was told that he was flighty and bucked hard. The sorrel had a rangy look to him and seemed to be ruggedly built with a deep chest and long sturdy legs. Lets turn him out he said and between them they got a rope on him and led him to the stable. His next choice was as different from the sorrel as possible. A medium built stocky mustang seemed a bit feisty toward the other horses and demanded respect from the herd. He was a real problem to corner and subdue. With him in a stall Huston walked to the bunk house, selected a bunk in a corner away from the made up bunks, planked his possessions at the foot of his bunk, made his bed and checked out the latrine. It was a military lay out with a foot locker and hanging rack at the head of his bed. It wasn't long until the cowhands came in from work. They were astounded to see him and more so as he greeted them in fluent Spanish. Jose had just entered when Ivan came into the bunk house and made his introductions. Huston accepted that Jose was foreman and that he would be given his work assignments from him.

Jose wasn't accustomed to ordering Gringos around and hesitated to assign work to Huston. Feeling his reluctance Huston asked if he could have a tour of the ranch before he buckled down to cowboying. His fluency in Mexican lightened Jose's reluctance and he assigned one of the younger men to give Huston a tour. Huston asked if it would be alright if he worked with his chosen horses first. With that being settled they headed for the chow hall. At the chow hall he found out why the hands dug into the food with gusto. It was delicious. Huston was partial to Mexican food and was delighted with the delicious dishes prepared by Manuel Largos.

When the vaqueros learned that Huston was going to ride the loco sorrel they begged to be allowed to watch. Jose told Ivan of the show and he came with Reanna to watch. Huston began to believe the wranglers comments about the horse when he seen the audience gathering. Not wanting to damage the horse's mouth, Huston chose a halter instead of a bridle and bit. He had to cross hobble him to get a saddle on. When he pulled the halter rope from the snubbing post and swung aboard he was able to snuggle into the saddle with no trouble as the big gelding stood stiff legged and humped.

It wasn't until he touched his sides with his spurs that all hell broke loose. The contortions of the fireball were unbelievable. At times it seemed as if he was going to spring completely over onto his back which would have pounded his rider into the ground. When his contortions were to no avail he swung his head around and tried to bite Huston on the leg. He finally settled into a series of crow hops and finally just stopped cold. He snorted 'threw his head high and almost playfully pranced around the corral. Seeing his chance Huston pealed off onto the corral top rail and let the sorrel drag the halter rope around. Huston stepped down hardly able to stand and accepted the back poundings and cheers of the boss and hands. Ivan brought Reanna over introduced her and she laughingly took his hand exclaiming what a wonderful ride he had made. We still have a long ways to go before we are a team he replied with a twinkle in his eye.

It had just broken daylight when Huston roped the sorrel and snubbed him to the post. This time he bridled the big horse and took another pull at the latigo tightening the cinch as tight as possible. Huston was prepared for the sorrels attempt to bite him. He had filled his shirt pocket with bull Durham smoking tobacco as he swung into the saddle he threw a handful into the sorrels eyes when he swung his head around to take a nip. That was the last time this bronco tried that maneuver. After a few serious bucks, a crow hop or two the sorrel settled for a quick step around the corral. Huston steered him to the snubbing post, tied him up short, dismounted and opened the corral gate. Tightening his belt and pulling his hat down he remounted and loosened the tie rope giving the stead his head. The sorrel saw the open gate and didn't make a jump before heading out to open country. When Huston tried to rein him in the sorrel clamped down on the bit and started to buck again. Not wanting to hurt the horses mouth Huston tried yanking back on the reins. This had little effect so he was forced to see-saw the bit in the sorrel's mouth until he loosened his clamp in the bit. Then he gave the powerful beast his head and let him run himself out. Lathered and heaving he finally accepted the control and headed back to the corral. When Huston had him snubbed up close he took off the saddle and bridle and gave the trembling gelding a good rub down with a grain sack. After turning him loose he gave him a portion of oats and watched as he headed for the water trough and took a long drink.

When Huston returned to the bunk house he found that the men had all left for the chow hall. He washed up and joined them. They looked askance of him and he explained that he had been working with the sorrel. They were disappointed that they weren't invited to witness the ride. When they were told how he had broke the bronc's biting trick they laughed and thought it was a splendid idea. Jose assigned Pablo to show Huston the spread.

Pablo and Huston went to corral and saddled their chosen mounts. Since they were planning to overnight in one of the line cabins they took bed rolls and food for several meals. Huston was glad to hear that Pablo's horse was a roping critter since he didn't expect to be able to rope from the sorrel. Pablo rode off in the lead and they paralleled the north south western fence to a high cliff area. They skirted the bottom of the cliff and ended in a lush valley with several young beef feeding in content. Huston asked Pablo to cut out one of the heifers and hog tie it. Pablo with the skill of a top hand had the critter tied in no time at all. He stood by as he watched Huston inspect the critter thoroughly. Huston started with the animal's mouth looking at its teeth, and then he moved to its ears flanks and hoofs. When finished he made some notes in a little note book he was carrying and turned the heifer loose. When Pablo asked what he was looking for he said just the animals general health.

They crossed a beautiful stream and Huston asked for a halt to rest the horses and have some lunch. While Pablo gathered some fire wood to heat some coffee, Huston cut a willow and quickly caught several brook trout. It was a water bug season and the spooky trout dearly loved the insects usually found under stream side rocks.

After inspecting several critters Huston asked Pablo how he would like rabbit for dinner. Pablo said, "sure but we don't have a rifle he had seen the two cotton tails about ten yards off. No problem said Huston and drew his pistol faster than Pablo could see and shot the two rabbits in the head at ten yards. Astounded Pablo stepped down and went to the two rabbits and saw that they had been clean head shots. Shaking his head in disbelief he brought them back to Huston who plucked a knife from his boot and dressed the rabbits in a few seconds. He then walked over to a close by spring and washed the game clean saying, "Fire is your job". ".If we continue on this trail we will be at the south east line cabin in another half - hour and there will be a stove and pans to cook with and bunks to sleep on", replied Pablo. Grunting an approval Huston slung the rabbits behind his saddle and the headed south. The line cabin was larger and better equipped than Huston expected. Water from a small stream allowed the riders to tidy up the cabin. After turning the horses into a small corral Pablo fed them from the adjacent hay shed. Pack rats had fouled much of the hay but hadn't managed to get into the cabin. Several air tight tin canisters yielded flower sugar, salt, coffee and baking powder. Huston fired up the sheep wagon stove and it wasn't long until a dinner of rabbits, gravy and biscuits were ready for the two big appetites. While Pablo cleaned up the dishes Huston cleaned his pistol and added two shells for the ones expended killing the rabbits. Where did you learn to shoot like that? asked Pablo. Huston's answer was, "lots of practice and hundreds of rounds of ammunition". "Have you ever killed anyone?" Pablo. Asked. "I don't talk about that!" replied Huston and Pablo had sense enough to end the conversation. The tone of Huston's comment left a heavy cloud over the former joviality of the relationship. It wasn't until they had packed their gear and headed out the silence between broke when Huston asked light heartedly, "which way?" Pablo sensed the ease of tension, pulled his harmonica from his shirt pocket and began a lilting Mexican tune. "That is great", commented Huston. "I love mariachi music".

The duo continued east along the southern fence stopping every once in a while for Pablo to rope a heifer and Huston to inspect it thoroughly making notes as he did so. Pablo was curious as to why Huston inspected the animal's ears so closely. Finally Huston called him over and showed him a mark in the inner ear. It was an old Indian good luck symbol, (later to become Germany's Nazi party's insignia.). He didn't explain to Pablo that this was a mark branded in the ears of selected cattle by Southern California Cattlemen's Association. When an animal so branded was legally sold a circle was placed around the brand. This was not disclosed to Pablo. Huston wanted to inform Ivan himself when he reported to him after his orientation tour. It was Huston's turn to ask a question. Do any of your punchers ever have problems with poison oak rash?" he asked. "Oh! Very much so Senior Huston," was Pablo's reply. "As you can see the country is lousy with it he continued" as he pointed out the oak shaped leaves of a nearby bush. Our biggest problem is when we have round-up and branding for the cattle have been rubbing against the poison oak when they feed and they pick-up the poison on their hides". Again the note book came out and Huston scribbled another comment. It was an unusual breeze that was blowing from east to west. There wasn't the bite of an approaching storm although the breeze was strong enough that their approach over a ridge was muffled enough that two wolves dragging down a calf didn't detect them by sound or smell. The distance was too great for Huston's pistol but he quickly dismounted pulling his carbine and snapped two shots that dropped the two wolves. Again Pablo was amazed at Huston's skill with weapons. Both wolves were dropped with head shots. The wolves were in good condition but their pelts were in poor shape due to warm weather. Pablo made the comment that they were in far better than the Indians that had butchered two cows earlier in the year. "What happened then?" asked Huston. "Oh we tracked them to their camp and Boss Ivan rode in and confronted them by himself. Noticing the rundown looking camp and the starving people he ordered us to bring two older cows and gave them to the people, saying "You now owe me four wolf hides". Noticing that the people seemed unaffected by poison oak He asked them "why"? The reply from an older man was, "Many snows ago Manitou brought our people to this area and planted the himshatiswa to discourage our pursuers. Since this time we have lived with the himsahtiswa as cohabiters of this land." Boss Ivan tried to hire the natives to help him eradicate Oro Rancho of poison oak, but the men wouldn't work and there was too much for the women do.

Reaching the north east corner of Oro Toro they headed at an angle toward the south west and the home spread. That evening brought them to an intriguing creek. Huston couldn't resist. They camped and after taking care of the horses Ivan sought out a nice long willow and soon and it rigged for trout fishing. Without directions Igor gathered fire wood and kindling and had camp set anxiously awaiting the coming fish dinner that was sure to arrive. Not wanting to be outdone Pablo began gathering wild berries. There was an abundance of service berries and wild strawberries. Smashing this together and adding flour he soon had a fruit pancake ready for the pan. It wasn't long until Huston came ambling into camp with a big string of trout. While dinner was in progress, Huston went to his pack and fetched a pint bottle of good bourbon. Added to a little sweet brook water and they had a couple of good drinks. After dinner Huston gave his steed a good brush down and fed him one of the berry cakes.

Noon the next day they saw the ranch headquarters in the distance. Relaxed they first took care of their mounts, cleaned themselves up and stretched out for a small rest. Pablo couldn't hardly rest he was so full of information about Huston that he was about to burst.

When Huston approached the crew he felt a difference in their attitude. They weren't stand offish but definitely more polite and accommodating. Smiling to himself he piled praises on Pablo saying he was one of the best trail partners he had ever had. He couldn't help but notice the glances to the colt he still wore. He knew that Pablo had expounded about his powers with the pistol and rifle. In a way he was glad for it would prevent a future contest where he would have to kill somebody. After taking care of his horse he made an appointment with the blacksmith to have his horse shod properly. That evening he approached the big house with his notebook to brief his employer about his expedition about the ranch and what he had found. Upon being greeted at the door by a Chinese Butler he glanced around taking in the opulence with a little disdain. He would rather have a more common- place domiciliary. Ivan rose and greeted him as the butler issued him into the study. The warmth of the greeting was appreciated by Huston but he still felt a little uneasy at the opulence. With a bid to make himself comfortable Huston cleared his throat and said, "Before I give you my report I feel that I should properly introduce myself." Taking a wallet from his pocket he produced documents showing he was an investigator for the Southern California Cattlemen's Association. "I knew there was something special about you when we first met", said Ivan. "So I am glad the plate is cleared." "My duty to you and the association requires me to inform you that you have several head of stolen cattle on your range." Huston Said. Ivan rose and walked over to his office safe and brought out a packet of documents, i.e. bills of sale. Huston accepted them and said," This is very interesting. You purchased your seed herd from Rancho Sonoma. We have long suspected them as being the receivers of stolen cattle from the Los Angeles area. If you will allow me to have copies of these documents I think we can proceed against them and leave you in the clear." That should be no problem," said Ivan. "I will first have to clear it with my lawyers" "That finished" said Huston, I am happy to inform you that you have a wonderful ranch with adequate water and bountiful feed. I see two problems. First and foremost you should dip your cattle they are having problems with parasites. Second you have way too much poison oak shrubbery. Pablo has told me of your experience with getting the Indians to clear the shrubs. In California some of the ranchers with this problem have been able to solve the problem by leading the braves to believe that removing the shrubs is like counting coup. Try awarding the highest receivers in some notable way. Old military medals and knives sometimes work well. Rifles work the best but this is not always good." The problem of rewarding each individual by the number of plants harvested is that they don't recognize boundaries and will take plants from outside the ranch lands to achieve a good score". I would suggest that you send somebody out with a bucket of paint and daub some on the plants you want removed. This way a plant with a splash of lets say yellow would count a coup and receive award credit." "Brilliant", exclaimed Ivan. Now! let's talk about something more important. Are you planning upon staying with the association or are you open to another offer?" "Depends upon what you have in mind," says Huston. My present foreman is just on loan to me from the Camaize Ranch. He is a good foremen but I am looking for full manager willing to sign a contract for $500 a month plus a percentage of the net profits at the end of each shipping schedule." "I would be open to an agreement like that if I can have separate quarters. Eating with the hands would be acceptable but I need to have time to myself when I work a crew. What would you offer as a fair percentage?" " I think five percent for the first year and an increase each year for ten years if the ranch is profitable," replied Ivan. Huston pondered for a while and answered, "You are going to have to clear the marked cows in your herd first. Since I was in your employ when I discovered the suspected pilfered cattle you should be able to claim a finder's fee. This plus five to ten dollars per head should clean the slate for you. The additional money is negotiable and I think you can bargain hard for the former owners will not want to undergo the expense of bringing the animals back." "I'll drink to that", said Ivan and stepped over to an ornate cabinet, opened the doors and dazzled Huston with a varied display of whiskey, liquors and aperitifs. "Make mine bourbon neat", said Huston. "I'll take the same" replied Ivan and splashed two Texas shot glasses full. They toasted each other and shook hands. It was a done deal ". I had anticipated hiring a married man as a manager so I have a bungalow ready for you." said Ivan. What do you say to me making Pablo a straw boss?" asked Huston. He is young but he is energetic and sharp." "You' r the boss" replied Ivan. "Come on" said Ivan as he preceded Huston out the door. A short distance, actually half way between the bunk house and the big house symbolic of the status of the new occupant was a small but complete bungalow. Actually it had never been occupied. Huston stepped in and voiced his approval upon seeing a shower. He hadn't had a good shower since leaving the Los Angles area. Even the Golden Bull only had a bath tub. "I would like to move in right away if it is ok with you. First I want to visit with the blacksmith my horse needs shoes and I am particular about this." "I'll go with you and explain to Bob Bellancourt your position as general manager. You'll like Bob he seems a little cultured for the job but he is an excellent blacksmith. He was a great help in picking out my new haying equipment." It was a brisk walk past the corrals to the blacksmith shop that had living quarters attached. The familiar clang- clang was heard as they approached. Bob was shaping a horse shoe for a stocky built mustang. Bob dropped the shoe in a tub of water and turned to Ivan and asked, "What can I do for you boss?" Here is somebody I would like you to meet" said Ivan. "This is Huston Wells. I have just hired him to manage this ranch the whole shit and caboodle. Hue this is the best iron pounder in this neck of the woods Bob Bellancourt". "Glad to meet you", they said simultaneously and shook hands. "I guess I'll be taking orders and instructions from you. You can start with the instruction on how to make this ornery critter stand for me while I fit him with new foot wear."" Which hoof are you working on? Asked Huston. "The left rear," answered Bob. Huston walked around the mustang and Picked up a lariat tied one end just above the left rear hock lopped it through the halter and tied it to the right front hoof. "Now give it a try," he said. Bob took the cooled shoe out of the water Put the hoof between his knees and grabbed the hammer and nails. The mustang attempted to pull his foot away and received a jerk on his neck for his effort. Bob grabbed a mouth full of nails and hammered away. "That wasn't bad at all I'll remember that. What I really hate is when a large work horse sits on you." He commented. "I know what you mean," My father fired me as a blacksmith when I brought one of the county's percherons up with a blow to the ribs with a shoeing hammer. A lasting friendship was formed with this encounter. Ivan feeling good with the introduction headed for the big house while Huston and Bob continued talking. "I need to get my horse shod and if you don't mind I would like to do it myself." "I heard about your ride and please be my guest. That hellion is all yours" he said with a chuckle.

Huston stopped by the dinning room and walked into the kitchen. Manuel couldn't get over Huston speaking fluent Mexican and greeted him like a long lost friend. "Do you want something to eat" he asked. "What have you got?" "I have a fresh baked apple pie and some cheese" said Manuel. I don't know who said it first but I truly believe that (Apple Pie Without Cheese is Like a Kiss Without a Squeeze). They laughed and Huston asked if you haven't used all of the apples could I have a couple? Manuel laughed and said," You are going to spoil that devil horse of yours aren't you?" Manuel wiggled his corpulent frame out of the chair and disappeared to return with a small bag of apples. Smacking his lips and rubbing his belly Huston headed for the bunk house to gather his belongings. and settle into his bungalow. He noticed a hushed acceptance without cordiality. Pablo had expounded on his fire arms skills and had given him respect out of recognition of his ability to overcome any position of confrontation. Leaving Ivan to announce his new authority he quietly departed for his new digs. Selecting one bed room for an office he dumped his belongings in the back bed room. Tomorrow when he accompanied Ivan to the lawyer's office he would broach the need of a desk and file cabinet. Then a wicked thought entered his mind, why not a young beautiful secretary? Slow down big boy he told himself.

After breakfast Ivan summoned everybody on the ranch to a meeting at the chow- hall. The only cowboys (vaqueros) not present were line riders. They would get their orders from Pablo the next day. Jose had already been informed that he could take a wagon and driver to Camaze ranch. Ivan had put together a packet of papers for Chief Wapaxo.

Wednesday Ivan Reanna and Huston settled into the Studebaker wagon drawn by two beautiful palominos and headed for Portland. First stop was the Golden Bull hotel where Reanna disembarked and Huston carried her luggage to their suit. Rejoining Ivan he asked.

"What is our first stop?" Ivan answered "Like you said we had better clear the ranch of any suspicion of cattle theft. I want you to explain to the lawyers about the special; markings of the suspected cattle and the possibility of finders fees. After we have secured a per head price to gain clear title we will accept on offer to turn over the cattle to whomever they choose. We will make it clear to them that we intend to round-up all of our stock dip them and check for markings before we can settle the score" ".Sounds like a good plan. In the mean time I will wire the association, give them my report and resignation. I will also inform them of my employment by you. That way every thing is above board. I will also give them my word that the count will be accurate and advise them to make an equitable settlement." The conference with the lawyers lasted for three hours and left Huston wrung out. He just wasn't use to all of the legal mumbo jumbo. There was just enough time left to establish Huston with the Ursus bank and pick out the office furniture he expected to need.

Reanna informed them that they would be having dinner together and that the lady that managed the hotel for them would be joining them at six pm sharp. Like a good husband Ivan winked at Huston and said "Yes Mother!". Reanna like all women was match making. Roselina was an outstanding beauty.

Her mother was of German extraction and her father Castilian. She had graduated from a university in Germany specializing in Hostelry Management. She had met Ivan and Reanna aboard one of the Czarina ships before they had bought the hotel now named The Golden Bull. They had hunted her down and employed her to help get the re-decorated hotel up and running. Under her tutelage the hotel had prospered beyond imagination. Huston was immediately under her spell. In his opinion she was the most beautiful woman in the world. He had thought Reanna extremely lovely but she couldn't hold a candle to Roselina in his opinion. He would look at her and feel extremely uncomfortable, tugging at his collar hoping to relieve his discomfort. He had worn his normal go-to-town clothes but now they felt completely inadequate. If you asked him how the food was he couldn't even think of what he was eating and mumbled some incoherent reply.Reanna seen what was happening and was extremely amused fighting herself to keep from bursting out loud with laughter. Finally Huston was completely beyond himself He muttered something about rest room and excused himself and headed for the bar. He needed some liquid courage. A double shot of Old Thunder Bolt seemed to do the trick. He stepped into the men's rest room and dashed his face with cold water. Feeling somewhat composed he made it back to the dinning room just as Ivan and the two ladies were finishing up,Roselina said " It is so nice out let's go out on the garden deck and have a margarita." This was great until Roselina hooked her arm in Huston's elbow and started out the door. If she felt Huston tighten up and almost stumble she didn't let on as she signaled a waiter. Maybe she didn't notice but Reanna sure did and was again amused beyond words. She whispered to Ivan, "If you ever loose Roselina you will loose Huston and visa versa. She knew that as tough and impervious as he appeared he was definitely not stoic. Speaking loud enough to overcome the ringing in Huston's ears, she asked Ivan, " Do you think Roselina would enjoy the dunking party you are planning as a reward for the hard work the hands are going to do to complete the round-up and baptism?" "It should be fun". "What do you think?" Asked Ivan. Turning to Roselina. Her reply; in a flirtatious way as she turned to Huston and stated" you will of course be there; I would love to attend." The hook was set "I'll send a coach for you," said Ivan. With all of the business done; Ivan called for the coach, ordered the office furniture delivered and they paused to say goodbye and see you at the dunking party.

Ivan and Reanna stopped at the dinning hall with Huston to say goodbye to Jose and family as they prepared to head out for Camaze. "I wish I could keep you here" stated Ivan but Chief Wapaxo needs you. With everybody in good spirits Jose and family turned toward the gate on their way to Camaze.

In Camaze there was excitement over the pending visit of Chief Little Fox and his cave tribe. Beaver Boy had been dispatched to meet the travelers and guide them in. Chief Wapaxo was anxiously awaiting Chief Little Foxe's report of his encounter with the White Man's Army. There was also anticipation of the gifts they knew were forth coming.

The reception for the Little Fox's group was riotous. Milliwana had prepared a delicious feast of small game and vegetables in her large cast iron kettle. After giving his guests a chance to rest and refresh Chief Wapaxo conducted a tour of Camaize.The cave dwellers were astounded at the richness of the village. The trading post was of special interest to Neena. She could hardly wait to purchase sewing notions and cloth. In a special ceremony Peelee and Neena presented Chief Wapaxo with a beautiful white buckskin suit. Because he had been cautioned by B.C. Bob not to let anybody know of his successes in the recovery of yellow iron Peelee called B.C. Bob to a side and showed him the two large buckskin pokes of placer gold. B.C. Bob was amazed to see the nuggets as large as garden pea kernels. Calling Jacque over he showed the gold to him and again there was excitement in his acknowledgement. The fact that some of the nuggets were unsymmetrical was an indication that the mother load was close by. The nuggets hadn't washed very far or they would be rounder in shape. B.C. Bob had given Peelee a gold pan and a crevasse tool when he had last visited the cave clan. With Chief Wapaxo changing into his new suit and the high spirits of everybody at the festivities Peelee, B.C. Bob, Jacque and Igor slipped down to the blacksmiths shop where he dug out his balance scales and weighed the gold. Rough calculations showed over $20,000 worth. They rounded it off to $20,000.oo and gave a receipt to Peelee and told him to meet them at the teller's cage in the trading post to receive credit for that amount at the retail counters. Peelee was glad to hear that Chief Little Fox would be able to purchase twenty henry rifles and plenty of ammunition. Neena could go wild in the dry goods section.

With the festivities over the women, children and unofficial braves were excused and the council at Chief Wapaxo's bidding smoked and clustered around Chief Little fox to hear of his encounter with the white mans army.

"It was an early autumn morning with a hint of frost on the shrubbery and the ground, when six pony soldiers rode up to the cave entrance and demanded to speak with the Chief. Sub Chief Runs Faster refused them entrance and had several of his braves with rifles surround the soldiers. Through a scout interpreter; the troop leader advised the sub chief that he didn't want to go down this path. He asked the sub chief to accompany him to the plateau over the cave where they could scan the valley below. The troop leader took one man with him. This man had two flags on sticks. When Runs Faster saw the large body of pony horses below him he just grunted. Believing that the cave could hold them at bay since they had fire arms. The trooper with the two flags stepped to the front on the edge of the overhanging lip of the cave and waved the flags. There was a loud explosion and a huge tree high on a hill past the cave's entrance disappeared in a cloud of flying rocks, dirt and dust. Seeing the implication Runs Faster led the troop leader to the cave entrance and conducted him to me", said Chief Little Fox. "What is this?" Wapaxo asked Jacque. "These big guns are called artillery," answered Jacque. "This would be light artillery accompanying horse soldiers" Their only disadvantage is they require a work team to haul them around. You made a good decision not to confront them any good gunner would at a maximum of three shots put one right into the entrance of the cave and devastate everything in there." "All they wanted from us was information" said Little Fox. "They wanted to know if any of Chief Joseph's war party had been in this area. When I told them the only strangers we have seen were Black Feet. They moved on

"How can my people achieve this prosperity?" asked Little Fox?" Accepting a nod from Wapaxo, Jacque said," You only have to convince your braves that it is honorable to work with their hands and not leave everything for their women to do. B.C. Bob and I will return with you and get you started. You are going to get the twenty rifles you asked for and lots of ammunition. For a start your braves must work to get a rifle and work more to get ammunition." Beaver Boy said, "I will come also and teach your braves how to care for and use their rifles". No mention was made of their gold strike.

As Little Foxe's people were getting ready to leave for home Jose and his family arrived. Chief Wapaxo encouraged Chief Little Fox to stay one more day and take a tour of Camaze Ranch. The concept of ranching was new to Little Fox and his people. It was the first time he saw white man's buffalo. Wapaxo had loaded them up with beef sausage and jerky for their trip home. Here was another example of men doing men's work. Little Fox had heard stories of and seen white men's slaughter of the big buffalo herds. He reasoned that they wanted the land for their tame buffalo. Chief Little Fox was thinking of the famine of the White Buffalo year. How wonderful it would have been to be able to slaughter a white man's buffalo?

The travelers left at day break. Everybody was in good spirits except for the young braves that thought they would be carrying their own rifles. Jacque, B.C. Bob and Beaver Boy had rifles and some of them had pistols on their belts. Jacque was the first to notice the discontent and worried that there would be trouble. Calling B.C.Bob and Beaver boy to the side he told them of his fears. "Simple" said Beaver Boy "lets us give them a simple demonstration and let each of them try to duplicate it." The evening of the first day on the trail ended by a beautiful stream and while the women set up camp Jacque, Beaver Boy and B.C. Bob walked over a close by knoll calling the four braves to accompany them. They picked up some large pine cones, placed them on a leaning log and stepped off twenty paces drew a line and. called one of the braves over handed him a rifle and a shell and asked him to shoot the cone off the log. Being the oldest of the four he accepted the rifle and shell and studied the rifle for a few minuets, looked at the end of the rifle turned it around and finally completely confused looked with askance of Beaver Boy who stepped forward, jacked the lever inserted the bullet, set the safety handled the rifle to the shooter and stepped back The tension was high as the arrogant brave raised the rifle pointed it towards and pine cone pulled the trigger and when nothing happened lowered the rifle and fumbled with the lever jacking out the unfired cartridge and looked dumbfound. Beaver Boy took the rifle from him loaded it and blasted the cone from the log.

Those following the first brave had an advantage but they didn't observe the safety set. The second would be shooter ejected the cartridge re inserted it and again leveled on the pine cone and couldn't fire. This time Jacque took the rifle and inserted a second cartridge and shot two cones off the log. The third brave having the advantage of seeing two failures had observed the safety lever and proceeded to insert the cartridge and fire holding his nose against his fist as he squeezed the trigger. The result was a bloody nose and of course he missed the pine cone. Number four stepped forward accepted the cartridge inserted it raised the rifle confidently and fired a shot God only knows only where.

Jacque confronts the four braves. A rifle is like a good woman it belongs to her owner and will perform correctly only for the one that it belongs to. To own and learn about a rifle you have to work for it and with it only lots of practice can make you into a true rifleman. Before you stand three true and tried real riflemen. Pick any one of us and your choice will show you what we are talking about .The four would be rifle owners picked Beaver Boy since he was not waisachu. Beaver boy placed four pine cones on the log and shot all four off in rapid fire. He then handed B.C. Bob three cones stepped back as the three cones were thrown high into the air. As the cones reached their apex Beaver boy blasted them apart in rapid fire before any could fall to the ground. The demonstration made believers out of the young braves. The next test would be the proof that the would-be rifle owners will be willing to do physical work to acquire the weapons. Jacque, B.C. Bob and Beaver Boy were anxious to see the stream Peelee had worked for the placer gold.

Arriving at the cave was a joyous occasion. Neena was eager to show off her purchases of cloth and cooking utensils. At daylight the next day Peelee led off leading a pack horse followed by Beaver Boy a pack horse, Jacque and B.C. Bob. The climb out of the valley was arduous. The trail went along a narrow cliff that had a steep drop off and only room for one horse at a time.Peelee turned a bend got off his horse and led the animal up a small incline strewn with fist sized boulders. The rest of the group followed suit each awaiting his turn at avoiding the falling boulders as they made their way. At the top of the incline Peelee entered a steep walled defile that opened onto a small valley with a bubbling stream flowing through it. "How in the world did you ever find this place," asked Jacque. "I was following a lynx that I had wounded", replied Peelee. Wait we are not through yet" he added as he guided his horse into the stream wading up stream through a small canyon that opened into a larger valley. "We will camp here, he said. There is color in this creek." "I don't think we will ever find the mother load," said B.C. Bob as he cast a calculating educated eye at the topography. "Let's eat" Jacque remarked as he gathered some dry brush to make a fire. "This is as good a camping spot as we can find", said Peelee as he unloaded and hobbled his animals.

"If Wapaxo were here he would have us a meal of trout by now", remarked a laughing Jacque.

After a breakfast of trout and camas/corn bread the four men hurried to the stream with their pans. Just working the gravel there was a lot of color. Jacque moved a little to the left and probed a large crack in the bed rock. Whoee! He exclaimed as the pan revealed a half dozen large nuggets. We wont have to do any hard rock mining to give us and Little Foxe's cave tribe a handsome reward. There was one big problem. The water was so cold it should have been ice. The only solution was to spend short periods of panning followed be a stand at the fire. At present the fire was the most important. Everybody gathered wood and slowly turned themselves before the bonfire.

B.C. Bob walked over to the hill side of the stream and studied the stream. Just as he had surmised the stream had at one time ran along side of the opposite cliff. Earth movement had shifted the streams course toward the center of the valley. The base of the cliff had at one time been an oxbow lake.

A flock of mountain grouse provided a change of diet and the hungry frozen miners were glad for the repast and rest from the cold water. After cleaning up the dishes the men sat and lit up their smokes. "The way I see it, said B.C. Bob, We will not be able to fight the cold water for a week and walk out of here. We are going to need to build a sluice and divert some of the water from the little falls at the head of the valley for a sluice-way. The longer we can make the sluice-way the shorter distance we are going to have to haul the gravel

Jacque unpacked the saws and axes, summoned the two braves to follow him and walked to a path that led to the timber half way up the slope of the valley.B.C. Bob paced and measured the route to build the sluice-way. Peelee Denko thought everybody had gone crazy. Beaver Boy explained that this is what had made Camaze so prosperous. "What would you be willing to do for six fine horses of any color you wanted?" he asked. "Almost anything," replied Peelee. "If you listen to

Jacque and B.C.Bob you will have them and more when we leave here," said Beaver Boy.

After driving stakes to mark the position of the sluice box and sluice B.C. Bob hiked to what he guessed the middle of the small former oxbow lake was. Dug down through the overburden to the bed rock and them dug all of the gravel he could carry after tossing the larger stones. He dumped it along side of the stream and began washing it with his pan. He was right there was good color. He knew that nobody could spend many hours in the extremely cold water and not suffer severe damage to their muscular and circulatory systems of their legs.

It took them five days to finish the sluice box and sluice way. They were able to lengthen the sluiceway forty feet by using two downed tree trunks that were rotten in the core. As hard as the work was digging out the bed rock gravel and hauling it to the sluice box they didn't have to withstand the chilling water.

When the day came for them to leave the hidden valley Jacque started his lectures about yellow iron. He cautioned Peelee he should never talk about it where waisachu were present or where they could over hear. White men go crazy over yellow iron (gold).They will do anything to possess it he said. And I do mean anything including murder of a close friend or family member. We will help you trade your share or you will be cheated and lied to. Never show this place to anybody. We will break down our sluice and burn it. If you slip up on this you could be tortured to death for what you know. They stopped at the trails end and made camp. As they smoked Jacque again lectured Peelee and told him very bad spirits accompany yellow iron and these spirits are especially dangerous to white men. Neena is going to ask questions. You must caution her about the bad medicine. Never show anybody any of the yellow iron. It is best if you come with us to Camaize, bring Neena with but be careful that your good luck doesn't turn into bad luck.

Departure day was joyous. Peelee had told Neena that she could make a list of wants from her friends without any promises. Chief Little Fox was asked by B.C. Bob what he could send back for himself and his tribe. His wants and needs were small. Beaver Boy led off. He picked a way that he thought a small wagon could go. Peelee picked Runs Faster to accompany him. He had earned his rifle and the Camaize group promised to teach him the proper care and use of it. Neena was glad he brought his woman with as company for her. Delika was young and vibrant and had no children a special gift for Milliwana was a large quantity of buffalo berries. The pemmican she made with the berries and beef was extraordinary. For Wapaxo there was a gift of a bear claw necklace. It had been a huge bear; the claws were five inches long.

Runs faster and Peelee became fast friends on their trip to Camaize. Runs Faster had observed the gold exchange and made no comment. He had been cautioned not to speak of it and complied with Peelee's wish completely. He had never seen such wealth as was displayed in the trading post store. After the festivities the Little Fox group prepared to depart. For himself Runs Fast had selected one of Igor's exquisite knives. Peelee took what tools he would need to rebuild the flume and sluice boxes. On a long stretch where Peelee and Runs Faster were way ahead of the women Runs Faster asked Peelee if he could ask some questions since there was no body to overhear them. "Why is the yellow iron so powerful to the white man?" "I don't know answered Peelee. I think it is an evil spirit called greed" "Can you explain what greed is?" asked Runs Faster. "It can only be a desire to be important through the possession of material things", answered Peelee. A long silence between them ensued. Peelee was burdened with a huge problem. How could he close the gap of poverty between the Little Fox Tribe and the affluent Camaize village? He knew that yellow iron was the solution. This created another problem. How was he going to extract the yellow iron secretly? It would take a minimum of three men to successfully operate the placer claim. Upon their return home Peelee and Runs Faster were greeted in style, but not so much as Delika was welcomed with their gifts for the tribe's women. Little Fox called Peelee aside and asked him, "Why is your heart so troubled my son?" "As you have observed, the Camaize village is wealthy while we are poor. In the winter time we struggle to feed our selves. I believe that our biggest problem is the men of our tribe are not willing to do physical work. They leave the manual chores to the women. The women are overburdened. "How can we encourage our warriors to plant corn and help raise camas?"

"You are wise beyond your years. I have asked Chief Wapaxo these questions. He told me that it has been the influence of the waisachu that has helped him. We have some friends among his white tribal members but we have none as members of our tribe and I am not sure we want any. All of the white men I have known excluding Wapaxo's people have been too arrogant and superior acting. Wapaxo with his accomplishments like slaying the great bear has overcome the influences. I have no such accomplishments." "But you have", said Peelee, "it was your tracking of the White Buffalo that saved us all from starvation". "I have learned something from the white man's curse. It is greed. We all want something, a good wife, a fast horse, a rifle, or honor. All we need to do is to teach our tribal members and friends that they can achieve their wants through labor. Do you know any of our tribe that would be inclined to work for some of their wants or desires"? Peelee asked.

"The only one that I can think of is Rabbit Runner. And maybe his cousin Spotted Deer" replied Chief Little Fox.

With something to think about Peelee left Little Fox wondering about this conversation and what Peelee was planning. He had observed the white man tools Peelee had brought back from Camaize. The next hurdle Peelee had to overcome was getting Neena to make buckskin pokes for dust and nuggets without disclosing what he wanted them for. He was sure he could count on Runs Faster but it would take at least four workers to work enough gravel to make the trip worth while. Calling Runs Faster aside he asked him to find out what he could about Rabbit Runner and Spotted Deer. Without letting them know anything. It was the middle of August and October in the lynx creek valley could find them snowed in. He had to work fast.

At Rancho Toro Oro plans for a wedding were under way. There had been no need to worry about a replacement for Rosalina. She had been grooming her best clerk to take the job of managing the Golden Bull hotel. Huston and Roselina were planning on a honeymoon on board one of the large Czarnia Russian ships to Los Angeles and El Paso Texas. Where Huston planned to purchase three Brahma Bulls and arrange for their transport back to Rancho Toro Oro. A stop over at San Francisco was planned to allow Roselina to purchase furniture and household needs. Huston had been here before and the only difference was this time he was accompanied by Roselina and a letter of credit for the Ursus bank. With Huston and Roselina both being bilingual they picked Spanish or English in their conversations according to who may be able to overhear them. Their preference for Mexican food made good business for the better Mexican restaurants. Huston couldn't remember the name of the Restaurant in El Paso but he knew where it was and that it had the best Mexican food he had ever eaten. A trip to E Paso wouldn't be complete without slipping over the border to Juarez for a shopping spree. Pottery and leather goods were extremely inexpensive. With their purchases and luggage they were going to have a tough time getting transportation back to San Diego. They discussed their problem and decided to buy a light spring buckboard and a good team and drive them selves. They could save time with the short cuts Huston knew and travel at their own pace. The only problem was renegade Indians. It was Comanche territory. When Roselina informed Huston that she could handle a rifle better than most men they went to the livery barn to bicker for a wagon and horses, two barrels, bailed hay and oats. Huston was making sure the buckboard was well greased when he heard a gruff voice growling: "Is that you Huston you old saddle sore bronco stomping cow chasing scoundrel?" Roselina couldn't believe such a rough voice could come from such a dried up little man that didn't look large enough to use the big revolver hanging low in his left hand holster. "Skamper, when did you get out of Yuma?" Queried Huston and stepped over the shake the diminutive cowhand's preferred paw. "Oh they pardoned me when their witness declared the hold-up man had been over six feet tall." When Huston introduced Roselina Skamper devoured her with his eyes as he took off his sombrero. "I thought I saw you dickering for a wagon, horses and water barrels. Where you heading?"

"San Diego and Los Angeles", answered Huston. "So are we, I'm traveling with Luke and Fred. You know Luke, Fred and I worked on the Broken Wheel together" added Skamper. "When are you leaving? We should travel together that is rough and dangerous country. Be much better in a larger party. I can vouch for Luke and Fred", continued Skamper. "Four rifles would be better than one or three." "Make that five." Said Huston My wife is a better shot than most men. We are planning to be on the road at day break, planning to halt during the middle of the day and travel as late in the evening as possible." " Sounds good we'll be here at day break since this is the route out of town." "Done deal, see you at day break; I am going to rig some canvas for sun shelter". Huston had been apprehensive about traveling with Roselina in this dangerous country. Four armed men would deter even a large party of hostiles. The three capable riders leading two pack horses were waiting when Huston and Roselina pulled up; after brief introductions they headed out. The first day cloud cover allowed them to travel all day without stopping to avoid the hot mid day sun. Tying the pack horses to the buckboard allowed the three riders to range out to watch for hostile scouts. When they neared Yuma Skamper said, "I would like to avoid Yuma if you don't mind. If we veer north there is a spring; water is a little brackish but the horses won't mind. Huston winked and said, "I thought you said you were pardoned?" "I was replied Skamper but the place still gives me the willies." "Suits me fine; you probably know this country far better than I do anyhow," said Huston.

It was the sixth day out that the newly weds headed the wagon into a large draw. Skamper had marked the trail good so they boldly followed the dry bed ahead. Huston was wondering where the riders were they hadn't seen them since early this morning. A puff of dust ahead alerted Huston and sent a cold chill up his back as he saw the approach of twenty or so riders up ahead. They were without a doubt Comancheros distinguishable by their mixture of Indians, Mexicans and renegade white men; all disreputable in appearance and reputation. Huston took off his hat and waved them away. They laughed and milled around. Knowing their reputation and sure of their intent, Huston fired a shot into the trail in front of the leaders. Again they just laughed and edged forward. Out in the open Huston felt helpless. He made up his mind that he would die fighting before he would allow them to molest Roselina. There was a large boulder fifty feet in front of them to his right. If they continued to advance he was determined to kill as many as possible when they reached the boulder. Arrogant and boisterous they came forward. The large fat one seemed to be in charge as he turned to his group and raised his hand to signal them to swing around the wagon. With a look of surprise he lowered his hand as he crumpled from the saddle and as he hit the ground the rest scattered as a volley of fire from the surrounding rocks brought eight others out of their saddles. Huston stepped from the wagon and proceeded to empty three more saddles. In complete disarray the remaining riders departed to the left and the right completely demoralized by the intense and accurate rifle fire from the rocks from their right and left and their rear. They were scrambling for their lives with no idea of the size of the force attacking them. Roselina was kept busy controlling the wagon team Huston took over and headed the team up the swale and into the narrow part of the draw.

Luke Fred and Skamper didn't show themselves until the wagon and its occupants were safe in the narrow gulch. Luke stepped off his horse and approached saying, "we must have killed at least twelve of them Are you folks OK?" Damned Comancheros, the worst of the trash in this neck of the woods". Roselina replied, "No damned horses, they kept me busy and I didn't get off a single shot." Good for you, because of you're keeping the horses steady Huston was able to nail Pablo Deperro. He was the fat one out front and was and I emphasize he WAS, the worst of the terrible. He has uncounted murder and rape counts against him. They have no idea of the size of the force against them so they won't be back. They rode together up the defile until they came to the alkali spring. "This doesn't taste too bad my advice is don't drink it unless you have to. It won't bother the horses but you will be making frequent brush stops if you do." Fortunately they had plenty of water in the barrels. It was time to camp. They had a communal fire and after a meal of rabbit and beans the riders moved off to the brush and left the newly weds to sleep in the wagon after shuffling the load around.

As they approached San Diego they made their goodbyes and the wagon headed to the metropolis. Roselina was looking forward to a night and a bath at one of the good hotels. Huston Made a quick visit to the local law enforcement and reported the encounter with Pablo Deperro. This generated a flurry of telegraph messages about the location and condition of the gang With the dispatch of their purchases Huston sold the wagon and team and the couple took a coach to Los Angles and was welcomed at the Golden Grizzly Hotel in L.A. The final leg of their travels would be aboard one of the Czarinia flag ships.

Rancho Camassia had missed Jose's leadership. The ranch had need of repairs and the cattle had to be worked to bring proper use of the pasture. This big problem appeared to be over consumption of alcohol. One of the Mexican hands had been the son of a bootlegger on one of the big Los Angeles rancheros. After watching his father make a mash brew out of corn and fruit he began to wonder if the mixture of corn and camas wouldn't give the necessary results. Camas was noted for its sweetness and had been used as a food sweetener by the Native Americans for centuries. One of the niches cut into the hill above Camassia that had been used to store vegetables and mangles made a perfect place to set his large vases of mash to ferment. Copper tubing was part of Igor's stock of metals. After drawing the brew off it was a small step to distilling the alcohol. The canning jars brought from Portland served as acceptable containers for the potent brew. Jose discovered the set up when he set about to inventory his ranch's winter stock of hay and stock feed. Since he himself wasn't a teetotaler he didn't take harsh measures with the culprit, but he did take control. The concoction was put under lock and key and drinks were rationed.

When B.C. Bob heard of Jose actions he visited him and asked to be shown the still and to see how the alcohol was distilled. It had been a boon to Scotland and distilled spirits had become a leading industry there. The use of copper tubing without soldered connections showed that the manufacturer knew the dangers of lead poisoning. Taking note of the ingredients he discerned that there should be no reason to be wary of the product. He tasted the liquor and found it to be delightful. The mash consisted of two thirds corn and one third camas with a natural ferment. . The result was a mild nutty tasting concoction with a smooth elixir flavor. He took some to Wapaxo and explained to him the problems associated with the consumption of the potent brew. Wapaxo knew of the problems Native Americans had with alcohol consumption and reinforced Jose's control over the substance.

B.C. Bob and one of Milliwana's older sisters had looked at one another and liked what they saw. B.C. Bob was rough around the edges and his refinements and education didn't show through his appearance. Oleta wasn't the beauty that Milliwana was but she was comely and well built with the right proportions. She had excelled in the classes of language, reading and mathematics that The Sisters of Charity had been conducting.B.C.Bob had noticed her when he taught classes for The Sisters of Charity. She was by far the most advanced and sought him out after classes with questions that amazed him with their foresight and clarity. It was when B.C. Bob asked Oleta to accompany him to Oro Toro Rancho that the bonding was recognized. Wapaxo was consulted and he in character with his new position on inclusion of wives in decisions informed Milliwana. Delighted Milliwana could picture them as a couple and approved wholeheartedly.

The light spring wagon was about as comfortable ride as one could expect on a trip to Portland's. C. Bob was a little uncomfortable on the first night out as he made up a bed for Oleta in the wagon and one for himself on the ground nearby. While B.C. Bob was picketing the horses Oleta rearranged the wagon bed to a double bed and led him to the wagon. Human needs took over and they spent a gratifying night together.Oleta assumed the leading roll in preparing a campfire breakfast and with light spirits they were on the road again.

In Portland B.C. Bob sought out the Golden Bull Hotel secured a room and took Oleta to the local court house where they procured a marriage license and sought out a Justice of Peace for the ceremony. This way they could feel comfortable to drive to the ranch the next day as man and wife. Ivan and Reanna rolled out the red carpet, invited Huston and Roselina to dinner and proceeded to celebrate. Huston was immediately enthralled with the acquaintance of Dr Mckamey and wife. Roselina (Now shortened to Rose) Gushed in approval of the guest's recent marriage and choice of Rancho Oro Toro as a honeymoon visit. After dinner the men strolled out to the veranda" Besides wanting to visit your ranch I have another agenda," said Dr. McKamey. Upon announcing this B.C. Bob reached for his valise that he had brought with him and extracted a bottle of the Camassia liquor. Ivan stepped in the door and asked Reanna to bring them three glasses. B.C. Bob poured a liberal portion in each glass and said, "taste then salute". My God that is good exclaimed Ivan and Huston nodded his approval. "I suggest we create a liquor company based on this formula. I am willing to invest a hundred thousand and Huston is welcome to join in if he desires", said B.C. bob. I'm in said Ivan and I'll advance Huston his portion if he wishes," said Ivan. "I have fifty thousand "said Huston. They shook hands and the deal was made. "Now for the formula said," Ivan. "Simple," said B.C. Bob. It is sixty six percent corn mash and thirty three percent

Camass. "I think a good brewers yeast would improve it", said Ivan. "The biggest problem", said B.C. Bob is the procurement of Camass it is guarded by the local tribes and wars have been fought over it. ". Before we go any further let's ask the women their opinion," suggested B. C. Bob. The three men filed into the drawing room and asked for three more glasses and poured another round, this of course making it their second drink the women looked in askance, being offered a drink of straight liquor? As they each gingerly took a sip, they rolled their eyes and eagerly downed the rest .What is this they queried?

"It is a secret formula that we have agreed to market. Do you agree"? Asked Ivan. "Of course", they answered! "It should be a smash hit"." Several questions come to my mind," said Ivan. "(1) what should we name the drink? (2) Where should we make it? (3) How should we market it?' "I can help with one of the questions" said Huston. In the north east of the upper forty is a spring of the purest water in the world." That settles the where," said Ivan "Who would object to calling it Golden Bull?" he asked. "Ursus has several hotels in a California Territory, why don't we target them as a starter" asked? B.C. Bob. Always the clear minded one, Reanna suggested that all of their agreements should be legalized and signed with everything but the formula codified. They assumed a task. Huston would develop the spring and start on construction of a brewery/distillery. B.C. Bob tool charge of procurement of Camassia. Ivan would research the equipment needed and procure same. He also would initiate the distribution process.

Tomorrow being a big day they halted the celebrations and called it a night. Bob and Oleta accepted the owner's suit at the Golden Bull for their Honeymoon night.

The legal documents were simple and the Ursus Bank acknowledged the account of the Golden Bull Beverage Company.Reanna accepted the duty of temporary secretary for the company.

Bob and Oleta decided to board the Czarnia ship in harbor for a trip to San Francisco. The need for housekeeping goods was evident. A telegram to Wapaxo asked him to facilitate new quarters for the newlyweds.Oleta was deathly ill with sea sickness during the trip. Bob the practical one arranged for coach travel back to Portland .The opulence and hectic activity of San Francisco overwhelmed Oleta.She had no idea of the wealth of Bob and was amazed at his approval of her purchases and consent to her desires. On Bob's part he had never known the warmth of love and cherished every moment with her. The accumulation of wealth had never been a goal of Bob's his drives had always been seeking knowledge and solving everyday problems. He analyzed his exposures seeking to determine the basics of all experiences. To him all of life deserved close scrutiny.

Golden Bull Liquor was an instant success even though it was the most expensive. Bob laughed to him self when he thought of the effort and expense men endured to seek and mine gold only to gladly throw it away on expensive liquor. Golden Bull was without a doubt the best gold mine there ever was and the labor to produce was the least arduous.

Huston was so delighted with the north forty spring's water that he bottled it and brought it home for Ivan and his household to drink. He had convinced himself that the Golden Bull liquor was superior to that produced in Camassia because of the water. By agreement a percentage of the liquor produced was forwarded to Wapaxo as tribute. The first shipment to Camassia was to be delivered by B.C. Bob, (now shortened to just plain Bob).Another name shortening was Roselina to just Rose. When she learned of Bob's trip home she asked Huston if they could go also. She had heard so much about the Indian town she was anxious to see it. With Ivan's approval and the arrival of the bulls Huston had shipped to Toro Oro, Ivan decided to share one of the huge Brahma critters with Rancho Camassia. The trip was planned. It was going to be a slow journey since the lead wagon was a double yoked oxen freight wagon loaded with goods for the village. Bob drove the light spring buckboard while Huston rode outrigger with his high stepping saddle horse. Their arrival was anxiously awaited by Beaver Boy, Up River and Broken Branch. They had heard rumors of Huston's expertise with fire arms and were anxious to challenge him in a contest.

As was usual the arrival was an opportunity to celebrate. Not to be out done Huston had brought with a package of Chinese fire works. Wapaxo had taken an instant liking to Huston and had acquiesced to permitting the children of the village to remain in the commons area to observe the fire works, not knowing what they consisted of. The bang and sparkle of the rockets brought fear to the simple natives. Wapaxo expected the Gods to intervene and punish them for disturbing the Heavens. Bob stepped in and explained that the display was only what happened when they used fire sticks (rifles) the difference being the explosions were visible instead of being contained by the barrels. Somewhat mollified Wapaxo remained stoic for the rest of the evening after the children had been sent to their beds.

The next day Beaver Boy broached the proposal to Huston of a weapons contest. Huston declined not wanting to create an atmosphere of confrontation. Again it was Bob who cleared the atmosphere explaining to Huston that these braves needed to learn that no matter how good they thought they were there could be somebody better. Seeing the logic Huston agreed. To prevent the possibility of their being an accident the four contestants went to a small pasture below a bluff and set up some targets. In the fixed target contest it wasn't possible to determine the best shot on points they all held high scores. When it came to the draw and shooting of flying objects the Braves were left slack jawed in wonder. Huston was so much faster it wasn't even a contest. He complimented the Braves and answered their questions of why he was so good with the answer, "it just takes practice". Remember the toughest target is the one that shoots back.

Jose greeted Huston at ranch Camassia. It was difficult for Huston to figure out who actually owned the ranch. Jose explained that the tribe occasionally asked for a beef and he delivered it to the trading post without receiving any receipt or acknowledgement of the transaction. However when he needed supplies, he only had to sign for them. This held true for his ranch hands. Again Bob came to the rescue and explained that the trading post and Ursus bank kept records of all transactions giving credits to accounts jointly to the ranch and individuals. He walked off muttering to himself, "what ever works".

Huston left baffled, how was he going to show Ivan and Rancho Toro Oro that he had delivered the bull?

Rose found the community delightful. She especially enjoyed her visit with The Sisters of Charity, their school and library. The blending of cultures and religions seemed flawless. That the children spoke English and were able to read, write and do simple math was remarkable. It was only when she was given council with Wapaxo that she discovered the wisdom from which this miracle sprang. Her next encounter was with the wives of Igor. The confusion of identity with the two women changed her belief of the cultural taboo of bigamy. The question of under what rules or law would society separates the two women? The harmony of family accord and the efficiency of divisions of labor were remarkable. She walked away thinking "I could write a book about this". It was when she met Igor that she understood the glue that made this possible. He was dynamic, strong and amicable. When asked if he could tell his wives apart he merely shrugged.

The procurement of camass had run into a snag. There just wasn't enough to supply the food needs and supply the burgeoning Golden Bull malting enterprise. The main stumbling block was Milliwana. She prized the camass as a food supply and derided the use of the food plant to supply a malting/liquor enterprise. Huston asked to see the camass plots and mentally reconnoitered his knowledge of Rancho Toro's vast domain. The best he could recollect there were over a hundred acres that would support the low land damp acreage needed to grow camass.Milliwana considering his dilemma offered to supply him with seed to plant camass on the ranch. She also suggested that he contact the California Hupa tribe, telling him that they had an abundance of camass. She also told him that they had plants that were often in seed production and that he might be able to gather enough to start his own fields. Concerned that they might harvest white flowered (toxic) camass she asked Wapaxo's permission to accompany Huston's group to the Hupa region. Thinking of the delicious flavor of the Golden Bull liquor he consented.

Milliwana and Rose formed an instant friendship. When she learned that Milliwana was going to accompany Huston to the Hupa tribes region she immediately decided to accompany. The trip back to Toro Oro was a delightful experience for the two women. Huston delegated duties for the ranch and prepared for the camas gathering trip. Planning to bring as many intermediate sized bulbs as possible, Huston selected an intermediate wagon to make the trip with. The plans for a camass field put an additional burden on the farm boss. He yoked up oxen and went to the areas Huston told him about and began preparing the ground for bulb transplant. The return trip was slow with the wagon loaded with mature bulbs needed for immediate preparation of the mash.

Golden Bull Liquor was an immediate success. The demand was burgeoning the elite cliental was clamoring for more.

Huston found himself overburdened and suggested that Ivan seek a manager for the Golden Bull beverage enterprise. Ivan consulted the Ursus consortium and they came up with a man named Hienrich Kaltner. He was recent immigrant from Germany and had managed a large brewery in the Sudetenland. Heinrich's credentials were impeccable. He brought with him a beautiful blond wife who immediately fell in love with Huston. Huston felt the vibrations and innuendos. He was deeply in love with Rose and the feelings made him very uncomfortable. Heinrich caught the obvious flirtations of his wife and was deeply disturbed. There was no fooling with Rose she spotted the action in the first meeting. Her biggest mistake was blaming Huston. He couldn't help but notice the advances, but he did his best to deflect them. It was Reanna that came to the rescue.Ginelle Kaltner's flirtatious advances to Huston were grossly open and offensive to Reanna.How to halt these advances became a determined goal of this highly moral woman.

Peelee gathered his crew making sure that they understood that their moves was to be kept secret and that they were going to be doing some rough travel and extremely hard work. The trail across the slide area before the entrance to lynx creek valley was almost impassable. At first it seemed that the Little Fox braves were going to be amicable to the hard work of washing and hauling of gravel for the collection of the tiny bits of yellow iron. On this particular day it was cold and rainy. The cold drizzle was reason enough to huddle around a fire and complain. Peelee sympathized with the weary men but he knew that this rain would soon turn into snow and the rock slide trail out of the lynx valley would become impassible. He picked up his henry rifle and hesitatingly loaded the magazine with the maximum five rounds and proceeded to put on a demonstration of marksmanship. With eager concentration his three companions observed as he shot five times in rapid demolition of five pine cones at east twenty yards off. A much greater feat than the best bow shot could have been made. He continued by expounding on the need to practice and the need for many rounds of ammunition for the acquiring of the rifle and skill. It is only the yellow iron that can give you this advantage he told them. Come let's go to work we don't many days of good weather left to waste. Eager to gain the rifles and skills they grudgingly scrambled to the gravel and sluice boxes feeling an important eagerness as they encountered large flecks and nuggets of gold. It was five days later that the drizzle turned to snow. They broke camp and headed out of the valley. It was the will of Manitou that they had just passed the huge slide hill when a deafening roar told them that the trail was no longer passable. It probably wasn't necessary for Peelee to insist that they never speak to anybody about this trip. He simply told them that bad Wasichue would kill for the chance to do what they have done. Luck was with them for they encountered a herd of elk on their way back to the cave and were able to bring a big load of fresh meat to the village. The reason for their trip was furnished. It was with bitter disappointment that they had to postpone their trading trip to Camaize. Winter had arrived in the high country.

The quarters for the north forty spring brewery's workers and the home for Heinrich had been completed and furnished. The wonderful spring water was contained and every drop was reserved for the brewing of Golden Bull Liquor. The camas fields of Toro Oro were constantly expanded and corn grew in profusion.

Portland was growing by leaps and bounds. The demand for rough and finished lumber exceeded the capacity of the present saw mills. In locating cedar posts for the rancho's fences Huston had noted the large amount of mature cedar trees available to navigable streams. It was mind boggling. Thinking of the crude sawmill at Camaize he visualized a bigger much more sophisticated mill on Toro Oro.

It was a glorious day on Rancho Toro. The sky was scattered with medium and small cumulus clouds with the sun peaking through adding warmth to the slight breeze that caressed the trees and shrubs. It was a Friday and Reanna was readying herself for a shopping trip to Portland. The cook and the small trading post for the families and ranch hands, would add their lists to the needs of the blacksmith. Ivan was in Portland at an Ursus meeting as Chairman of the Board. Huston and Rose would accompany her. Ginelle was not invited. After a busy day of shopping the purchases were assembled at The Golden Bull Inn where they were to meet Ivan for dinner and drinks. The cocktail lounge and dinning room was entertained by a very handsome Troubadour playing his guitar and singing lovely Mexican love songs. You could almost see the idea flash over Reanna's beautiful coffure.She would give a party hire the Troubadour and encourage him to make open advances toward Ginelle, concentrating on her for his romantic repertoire. Bursting with mischievousness she confided in Rose. Ivan and Huston thought their wives had lost their senses as they giggled It was all the way home.

Huston and Ivan discussed and mentally planned for a saw mill on Toro Oro. The next day Ivan sent a cable to Bob at Camaze. "Need to consult with builders of saw mill at Camaze" Ivan. The answer was: "Will be at Toro Oro in one Week" Bob. "Meet at Golden Bull Inn on Thursday next" Ivan. The next morning Huston and Ivan saddled up and rode to the South West forty. Taking a large bundle of painted stakes and food for over night they headed for the line cabin. In the morning they rode to a small canyon near the ranches southern border. They rode up stream for approximately two miles and climbed out of the canyon. They mentally surveyed the landscape and determined that the lower portion of the little canyon would be the place for a dam. The source for a water wheel driven saw mill was noted. They carefully staked out their survey and headed home.

With the advent of spring and the opening of the mountain passes, Peelee took his Lynx Creek workers to Camaze. Because he didn't understand the money exchange procedures Peelee contacted Bob and consulted him on how to exchange the collected gold for needed and wanted items. Even with great trust he wouldn't disclose the placer operations, only stating that more wouldn't be possible because of inaccessibility. Because of the quantity and size of the nuggets Bob was sure the mother load was close to the stream that was the source of the placer operations. He accompanied Peelee to the Ursus financial center and observed the weighing and calculating processes. The grand total rounded off to $30,000.00.

This figure meant nothing to Peelee and the others. When Peelee stated that they wanted guns and ammunition Bob told them that gun sales were controlled by Wapaxo and he would have to be consulted. Bob collared one of the young braves and asked him to locate Wapaxo.The young brave reported that Wapaxo was at the blacksmiths so Peelee and his group accompanied Bob to the shop. When Wapaxo learned that these were Little Foxes' people he was inclined to let them purchase henrys and ammunition, but first they had to have training from Up River and Broken Branch.

While Up River and Broken Branch were getting ready to indoctrinate the Little Fox braves in the use and care of the henrys they traveled to Rancho Camaze where they selected several fine horses and credit was transferred to the rancho's account. The orientation, care and use of the henry rifles should have taken only a few days, but the Little Fox braves were too child- like and eager to start shooting up the country side. It was only through tight control of the ammunition was Up River able to control the reckless use of the dangerous weapons. Early every morning he assembled the Little Fox braves and had them line up for inspection. He examined each rifle carefully and scolded them unmercifully for the least indication of poor care or dirt. They had to learn to conserve ammunition for it will be a long trip to Camaize to replenish their supplies.

It was a happy day when the Little Fox band departed Camaize. They rode sitting their new mounts straight and fanciful as they led three heavily burdened mules loaded with supplies and gifts for the home tribe.

The need to transfer the gold to Ursus- Portland was an excuse for launching a trading expedition to the coast and Wapaxo's home village.Igor and his family led the trek two days before the Wapaxo group and their light wagons proceeded on the Road.Up River and Broken Branch supervised the loading of the strong box on Igor's lead oxen cart. They accompanied the oxen wagons for two days before they circled around and joined the Wapaxo group with the light wagons and the second strong box. The strong box on the oxen wagon was a decoy.

One of the young braves of Wapaxo's tribe had developed a sense of rejection. He had always been tall for his age as a result of a birth deformity. His legs were extremely long in proportion to the rest of his body. This had resulted in ridicule from his contemporaries who had nick named him stork legs. The jibes and laughter led him to seek solitude. He spent most of his time afield hunting. This led to more ridicule as he seldom brought home game. His excursions had resulted in associations with some of the Nez Perce braves that had been rejected from the Wapaxo tribe for their failure to accept manual labor as part of the Wapaxo culture. Their mutual rejection led to counter actions like petty thefts and conspiracy. When information about the transfer of gold and money to Ursus-Portland reached Stork Legs' ears he and his cohorts began planning a hold up. They envisioned the purchase of rifles and ammunition from the wealth of the strong box. Wapaxo had anticipated an attempt of this sort and had elaborated the loading of the large cumbersome strong box on Igor's wagon with instructions that Igor should make no attempt to protect the box. The smaller strong box with the gold was loaded on one of the wagons in Wapaxo's group which was guarded by Up River and Broken Branch. Without a shot fired the nefarious ones unloaded the strong box and drug it off behind their horses where they proceeded to break into the box using stone hammers. Igor and his family were allowed to continue down the trail. Igor had built the box so that it was almost impregnable. The time spent by the robbers trying to open the box gave Igor a comfortable travel distance from the robbers.

Stork Legs was actually quite intelligent and perceptive. He remembered that there had been some of the bamboo charges buried after the closure of the mine at beaver lake. The robbers were at first determined to chase the blacksmith down and make him open the strong box. When he told his Nez Perce conspirators about the explosives they saw the possibilities and proceeded to the mine site in search of the buried explosives. It had been three winters since the beaver lake mine had ceased operations and the exact location of the bamboo charges was unknown. Examining the different cuts and slope mine openings turned out to be far more work than the would-be robbers had anticipated. Their indolence precluded any real hard labor required to open the shafts and tunnels. It was only failure of some wood closures the turned lucky for them and they uncovered the blasting charges. All of the traders had reached Portland before they returned to the hidden strong box. With a dozen charges beneath the box the fuse was lit. There was a loud bang and the box unopened was lifted several feet into the air and landed unopened. Of the twelve charges set only one of them actually exploded the others had been rendered harmless by moisture.

The arrival of the Camaze traders was noted with a runner sent to Toro Oro. The visit was a call for celebration. Included in Igor's cargo was a large measure of corn and camass. The formula for the Golden Bull liquor had just about depleted the brewery's supplies. It was Wapaxo that asked for a tour of the saw mill and brewery operations.Dr Mckamey (Bob), spoke up and asked if he could be included in the tour. The first object of the tour was a trip to the saw mill which was near completion. Ivan had business to attend to so it was up to Huston to conduct the tour. When the normally reticent Wapaxo began asking questions that were very technical in nature; Bob was astonished. It hadn't occurred to him before and it struck him like a bolt of lightning; Wapaxo had the uncanny gift of a photographic memory. Without fully understanding the principals of the working saw mill at Camaize he had mentally catalogued the details of the plans. Looking at Wapaxo with a different set of eyes and values he suddenly realized why a so relatively younger chief was so sagacious. It was hidden from Wapaxo's associates by his typically clipped speech and lack of verbosity common to Native Americans. Huston was impressed and elaborated further. He detailed the problems he had encountered hoping Wapaxo could guide him in his future operations. Wapaxo returned to silence unable to postulate and anticipate functional problems

The fields of corn and beds of camass re-kindled Wapaxo's interest and the sprayed poison oak amused him for he understood the tribes interest in milking the white man's ranch for all they could. It reminded him of a story he told them about a tribe that claimed immunity to poison oak and a young brave the wanting to prove this chewed some of the leaves and choked the death. The tour of the brewery and distillery was delightfull.The delicate flavor of the Red Bull Liquor was noted and appreciated.

Wapaxo had a problem. He couldn't understand the fence and boundaries of the ranch. How can you own land when you can't take it with you? Bob accepted the challenge, "Chief, where your hogan sits is it your plot of ground?" he asked. "How about two feet from your hogan is that also your plot of ground?" "I think you have the idea. It isn't the ownership of the ground it is the control of the use of it." Wapaxo showed his grasp by answering," This is also the idea of renting", he said. Bob glowed with acknowledgment. "Now you have the idea the renter doesn't own the plot he only controls it for a specified time."Wapaxo hunkered down into his normal contemplative mood and there was silence between the two for a long period of time.

With all of their purchases and supplies loaded for the return trip to Camaize the villagers settled in for an early bed time in order to be prepared to leave at the break of dawn. Wapaxo spoke up. "I will not be returning with you he said. I am going to visit the Mountain Spirit". When the travelers mustered for the trip Wapaxo was gone.

Having planned ahead Wapaxo was equipped to hike to Mt Hood. It was a clear crisp morning when Wapaxo struck out on his journey. He headed north east to a point where he could cross the Hood River. And then follow it up stream to the base of the mountain. The river was too fast where he had planned to cross so he headed up river hoping to fine a more suitable crossing About to giver up for the day he spotted a snag floating he way, He stepped into the ice cold water, hoisted his pack into the branches and began paddling toward. the east shore. Shivering, he gathered some moss and dry. Twigs that allowed him to build a roaring fire in minutes. Warm and dry

Wapaxo hunkered down and dined on pemmican and camass bread He awoke to a drizzling rain. He began to wonder if his psyche was playing tricks on him. Had he really had a vision of meeting with the mountain spirit? His memory reminded him that he had doubted himself before the last visit and brought to question how much was fact and what was fantasy? A cold blast of wind from the mountain reminded him that he was a mere mortal and nature had the ability to destroy him in an instant. It was dusk and close to night fall before Wapaxo hunkered down for the night. He gave Himself the luxury of a rose hip tea with his jerky and camass bread supper. The next day he doggedly scaled the rocks and snow until he reached the overhang that he remembered from his last visit. With his back to the small cliff he faced the south west with only the small bush outlined by the setting sun the restricting his vision of the mountain base. Hunger pangs reminded him that he hadn't eaten in several hours. As the sun was giving off its last light the bush again appeared to be on fire? A slight breeze stirred the branches of the bush and the old woman appeared. "Greetings my son, she said, " I have been waiting for you" "I sent the snag down the river to aid you to cross." I apologies for the coldness of the river. That is not in my preview. The river belongs to the realm of the Mountain Father" Where is the Mountain Father?" asked Wapaxo ".He is conference with the Core Foundation.; about something to do with tectonic plates, whatever they are"? You are here for human reasons which are in my preview".

"You have been given a wonderful gift. A photographic memory, which is the ability to retain images and facts but isn't inclusive of reasoning power, Reasoning power is a subsequence of enculturation or simply a multiple exposure to problems of a human nature. I am bringing you this information for the betterment of your people. Not that you will be able to achieve anything in your life span but to inform you that your son Buffalo Hunter has inherited your gift. Use the white man contacts you have to educate and groom your son.

The sun set in the west and the little bush lost its glow and the old woman faded away there was still enough light for Wapaxo to see the large wolf at the edge of his clearing. He stood and the wolf walked away. When he stopped the wolf returned and sat on his haunches. There wasn't any recognition at first just a feeling. Wapaxo spoke, "Is that you Horse Wolf"? he asked. Still leery the wolf advanced a few steps and stopped. When Wapaxo didn't move the wolf came back, looked at him and again walked off a short distance. Determining that the wolf wanted him to follow Wapaxo cautiously approached and the wolf led off. After about fifteen minuets of scrambling to keep up with the wolf Wapaxo found himself confronted by a much lighter, smaller wolf bristling and growling. Horse Wolf rushed between Wapaxo and the obviously agitated female snarled and snapped at her without actually making contact. Horse Wolf then led Wapaxo to a small depression there cuddled in a grass nest were four fuzzy puppies. "You have done well", said Wapaxo as he avoided the still snarling mother. He adjusted his pack and stepped briskly down the path. There was a ghost of a smile on his face as he mentally gave thanks to Manitou

The full moon gave Wapaxo enough light to allow him to select a long slender willow which he soon and equipped with a line, hook and sinker, few grass hoppers and half a dozen skillful casts and a trout evening meal was ready for the fire. With a full belly he hunkered down at the base of a huge ponderosa pine after raking the nearby needles into a comfortable bed. As he dosed the images of the wolf family brought a smile and contentment as he contemplated The Mountain Woman's admonition concerning the enlightenment and cultivation of Buffalo Hunter's gift of photographic memory. He recalled the multitude of times that B.C. Bob had helped him solve problems of barter and the understanding of dealing with money and the value of gold. He knew the old woman's advice to be sound.

The sun was up and gave promise of a wonderful day as Wapaxo broke camp and headed down stream. A beaver slapped its tail giving warning to all of the river denizens of his approach. He circled a small lake, forded the stream outlet and struck out on a game trail that headed in the direction that would return him to Toro Oro. It took him all of the daylight hours of three days to reach the ranch headquarters. The evening meal was over but the cook was able to feed Wapaxo fully with left overs. Huston was inquisitive as to Wapaxo's sojourn but felt it would be impolite to question the Chief. Impressed with Huston's efficiency, Wapxo asked if he could send the thirteen year old to work under the ranch manager to learn the cattle business and improve his Spanish. He like his father was large for his age and should be able to do a man's work.

On a good horse Wapaxo made good time on the way home. He stopped at he junction where Stork Legs and his friends had accosted the blacksmiths party. Reading the sign he quickly found the battered strong box. It hadn't been opened. Wapaxo couldn't make up his mind if this was good or bad? If they had opened the strong box they would have learned that they had been snookered. This way they just felt inept. He decided that he would pass the word of a sizable loss and see if additional attempts would be made on opening the box.

The return of the Chief was reason for celebration. Roasting fires were started. The big kettle was with Milliwana's supervision cooking three different types of meat and six different vegetables. When Milliwana learned of Wapaxo's decision to apprentice Buffalo Hunter at the Toro Oro ranch she became apprehensive. This caused Wapaxo to tell her of his encounter with the Woman of The Mountain and Buffalo Boy's gift of photographic memory. He made no mention of his encounter with horse wolf fearing it might bring ridicule upon him.Milliwana had known that Buffalo Boy was exceptional but she hadn't linked it to his retention abilities.Wapaxo had a plan. He organized a hunting trip that included Beaver Boy, Up River and Broken Branch. He instructed his long time friends and cohorts to each of them to concentrate on teaching Buffalo Boy about animals, hunting and survival. He spent his time instructing Buffalo Boy on sharpening his skills on observation and memory. This is when he told him that he was going as a spy to learn all that he can from Wasichue. He was to learn to speak English and Mexican languages. He told him that he was to think of himself as a warrior.that would someday bring the native people to the forefront. Confident that they would be successful the hunting party brought four mules to pack the meat out.

Beaver Boy took over the first teaching assignment. He sidled over to Buffalo Hunter and told him. "This is the stupid season for elk. They have only one drive; to mate. Their instincts and urges are governed by smell and sound. A rutting cow will give out an odor that she is ready. She will flair her posterity fringe hair as if to say here it is. This is of course when she has smelt the presence of a bull. When the bull has determined the presence of an available cow he begins to bugle to bring her to him. She in turn keeping her independent attitude gives off a series of grunts as she stomps her foot. You only have to remain down wind and keep the cow under surveillance. In the advent that the couple haven't found one another, to encourage the bull try stomping and grunting. The tact was successful. A few grunts and stomps brought a big well antlered bull running. Buffalo Hunter was about to shoot when Beaver Boy silently laid his hand on Buffalo Boy's arm and said "let's let him do his job first. This will ensure a spring calf. The bull almost looked ridiculous as he slobbered over the cow as she pranced with her rump hair flared out. The bull needed no further invitation. He mounted her and did his thing. Finished he strutted as if to say I am the king. Beaver Boy said. "Now! And Buffalo Boy dropped him in his tracks. The startled cow sprang into the tall shrubs and disappeared. Beaver Boy continued his instructions. "There is another animal that is important for a hunter to understand. It is the pronghorn antelope. There not any in our area, but there are many of them in the area where you were born. They cluster in medium sized bands in open country. In the rutting (mating) season they act similar to deer. They have fantastic vision and hearing capabilities but they lack the smelling abilities of most other prey. They have a strong curiosity drive and an urge to investigate observed unnatural objects, especially those of a light color. If you spot a herd in a distance you can conceal yourself, hang a light buckskin flag on a branch and they will come to investigate. Stay concealed and they will approach to within shooting distance.

You are learning the nature of large animals, but the smaller animals are also of importance to survival of the hunter. You are skilled in the use of the sling, but what do you know about the most abundant of preys, the rabbit. There are in our area four distinct rabbits species. The jack rabbit, the snow shoe rabbit, the cottontail and the bush rabbit. The predominant being the cottontail. One aspect of the rabbit family is their deceases. Upon killing a rabbit feel its back bone. If there are lumps there discard this animal for it is carrying the larva of the bot fly. This rabbit is unhealthy. Also inspect the liver and if this has white spots the rabbit is unhealthy do not save. Up River and Broken Branch each took their turns in instructing Buffalo Hunter in their learned skills as nature observers.

Upon the hunters return B.C. Bob (Dr. Mckamey) took over and began a series of question and answer sessions to establish a lesson plan. The Nuns of the Sisters of Charity had already observed that Buffalo Boy had special abilities. They coached Dr Mckamey and helped him direct Buffalo Boy's concentrated education. When Buffalo Boy was due to depart for Toro Oro Dr. Mc Kamey grave him a long letter for Huston outlining the plan for the super student.

The big roan horse pranced as it stepped into the roadway toward the Mother River country. With his head held high and his back as straight as a ramrod Buff Hunter, (Buffalo Hunters nick name), felt the exuberance of the powerful animal. It was as if they were communicating on a higher plane. There wasn't the ruffling of a leaf or the scurrying of an animal that they missed in their excited state of awareness. Buff had named him Gallant and gallant he was. His mother was the Wapaxo's large white Arabian and his father a spirited stud from the Rancho Camaize herd. Buff and Gallant had been constant companions since his birth. He had gentled him and broke him to ride at the tender age of three.

After ten hours of leisurely traversing the glades and breaks along Mother River they came to lush little meadow beside a sparkling creek. Buff dismounted and Gallant began to graze while Buff gave him a thorough brushing and rub down. He didn't bother to hobble or tether him, they were inseparable. At daybreak Buff was gently awakened by the nudging of Gallant. After a brisk wash in the creek they shared a few camass/corn muffins and Buff washed down some jerky while Gallant continued his grazing. A sharp whistle brought Gallant on the run he didn't give in to the bridle easily as he wanted to continue grazing. By-passing his father's village Buff headed for the ford and crossed Mother River turning south toward Rancho Toro Oro.

Buff dismounted at the water trough stripped his saddle and bridle from Gallant and began brushing him as he drank. In near fluent Spanish Buff asked one of the curious lads to notify Huston that he was here. It took a good half hour to locate Huston. Not knowing what to expect Huston was impressed with the tall young man with a decent hair cut. He rode up on a lathered buckskin gelding, stepped down, shoved out his hand and said, "I understand you're the new hand, what I call you?" "I am Buffalo Hunter but I prefer to be called Buff for short". "Great, do you want to grain your horse before we turn him into the corral?" asked Huston. "I don't know if he will mix with your horses, he is kind of pushy," replied Buff. "Don't worry they will sort things out," answered Huston as he took a halter from the corral rail and offered it to Buff. "I don't need the halter", said Buff. He placed his hand on Gallant's velvet nose and said, "come" and headed toward the barn. Gallant nudged him in recognition and followed Buff into the barn and a large stall. Buff saw that the stall was large enough for Gallant to lie down and asked if it would be ok to leave him here over night. Huston said, "Sure" and forked some hay into the manger.

"We have been expecting you. We are invited to the boss's house for dinner. Bring your tuck and Ill show you to your bunk." I have put you in the bunk house with the other hands. I hope this is ok with you?" Most of them speak Mexican, can you handle that?" Buff said, "I am fair at Spanish it is the language of the Camaize ranch." Answered Buff... "This will all be new to you," said Huston, "Especially dinning at the boss's table. I will be sitting opposite from you just copy what I do and you'll make out ok. The way I understand it your position here is like a school assignment and we are all going to try and bring you into the Whiteman's world". He showed Buff the shower-toilet room and instructed him in the use of the shower, told him he would be back to bring him to the big house in a half hour.

Buff reveled in the shower and hated to step out and dry off. After dressing in his best buckskins shirt and trousers, he took a smaller heavy buckskin package from his bed roll and laid it at the foot of his bed. When Huston came through the bunkhouse door Buff picked up the heavy buckskin package and followed him out the door. Huston saw this and decided not to ask him about it. They went first to Huston's house where Roselina joined them. When Huston introduced them he was delighted when Buff replied "my pleasure madam." Buffs sophistication was unexpected. When they arrived at the Rancho's main house there were no introductions needed for Buff remembered the owners from their visit to Camaze. He handed the buckskin package to Ivan and said, "My father the Chief asked me to give you this and say that I will need new clothes and some books. He told me that you would know how to convert this to spend able money". Ivan un-wrapped the buckskin package revealing six gold smugglers bars and said," This should outfit you royally."

When they were all seated Ivan asked that they joined hands and he offered a prayer in almost flawless Shoshone. He looked up and smiled saying, "Your father and grand father were good instructors." Buff followed Huston's moves exactly from the moment that he put his napkin on his lap and remove it to wipe his mouth.

Rose and Huston climbed into the covered buckboard along side of Buff leaving him the driver's job. They checked into The Golden Bull hotel and had lunch before heading to the store.Buff was clothed from boots to hat. Occasionally Rose made selections and Buff was surprised when Huston deferred to her. Their last selection was a suit case. He looked in askance and Rose replied that he would be going to San Francisco when he left the ranch.

The morning after returning from Portland everybody was awakened by loud whinnying from the corral. Gallant was calling Buff at day break at the same time as the roosters were announcing the new day. Buff sprang from his bunk and made for the shower. Huston himself really loved his shower so he asked for one for the bunk house when he was hired. This was a luxury Buff took advantage of at every opportunity. Before breakfast he was graining and brushing Gallant when Huston took him to the dinning hall. As they entered Buff noted that Pablo was seated at one of the smaller tables by himself. Huston approached and introduced Buff. Saturdays is always special for the cook. He makes an enchilada omelet that is out of this world. Occasionally Rose joins me for Saturday breakfasts it's that good. Huston speaks up. Pablo Buff is one of the hands, you're still the boss but I would like you to treat him as a student. Explain what and why you are doing when he is working for you. It should be no problem since his Spanish is superb. Si Heffe replied Pablo mucho gusto Buff...

Time flew and Buff's sixteenth birthday found him not only familiar with the ranch work but also capable doing any of the saw -mill and distillery jobs. Every evening Buff spent his time reading when he wasn't grooming and taking care of gallant. . He had exhausted the ranches library on sawmill and distillery operations the first two months that he had been there.

What had started out being a normal monthly dinner meeting for Ivan the boss and Huston his manager? The subject was Buff. They all agreed that he was an outstanding individual. "What is your opinion Hue, asked Ivan, "Should we push this wunderkind forward"? Reanna and Rose almost spoke in union. "We must, the nation needs a Native American idol and Buff is a wonderful opportunity for them to have one." The opinion was a consensus. It was decided that Ivan and Reanna would accompany Buff to San Francisco and enroll him in a local university. It was decided with Huston left in charge of all of the ranches activities Ivan and Reanna would accompany Buff to San Francisco, get him established and enrolled.

The stage coach ride from Portland to San Francisco was grueling with two overnight stops. Upon arrival in the city it was easy for Ivan to establish contact with Ursus and arrange for lodging at a Grizzly Hotel and transportation.

Wide eyed Buff took in the wonders of the city and remained quiet and respective. After adjoining rooms were booked and the travelers were able to refresh themselves they met for dinner. Dressed in his new city clothes Buff was glad for the introduction to American eating habits and protocol. Ivan explained the menu to Buff and ordered for himself and Buff; he then ordered drinks of "Red Bull" of course; one for himself and Reanna and an empty glass for Buff .He poured a small amount of the liquor into Buff's glass and explained that it was not allowed for anyone under 21 to be served alcohol. He further explained that he wanted for Buff to see where the Ranches distillery product ended up.

The next day being a Monday it was a good time to locate permanent housing for Buff. Ursus had their own corporate real estate office so they stopped in and made inquiries. They were looking for some place that could take care of all of Buff's needs. The boarding house of Momma Molly was ideal. It could do Buffs laundry and furnished two meals a day. Molly a rotund smiling Irish woman with a sparkling personality was delighted with the new arrival and the assurance that Ursus would pay all bills. An added bonus was the nearness of the library. Ivan knew of Buff's penchant for reading everything he could get his hands on. The next stop was the library where Ivan introduced Buff to the availability of books and procured a library card for him and an endless supply of reading material, making sure he understood the rules. The next stop was the Ursus Bank where Buff opened a checking account as astute as he was Buff's head was in a spin. A Chinese restaurant gave Buff the first chance to write a check and a problem arose. He didn't have any identification. At first Ivan was stumped but Reanna asked why not get him a job with Ursus and an identity card showing this. Ivan asked to see the bank manager and explained the problem. Since Buff was going to be a full time student the only answer was an apprentice position. Knowing Buff's abilities Ivan had no doubts that he could enroll in San Francisco's Technical College. This turned out to be a bigger problem than anticipated. Buff had no diplomas or certificates of formal learning. The college's rules with this requirement were a complete block to his enrolment. The only avenue available was a dispensation from the state government signed by the Governor. Ursus headquarters was delighted with Ivan's visit and the directors called a small conference to address Buff's problems.

Sutter's Fort now Sacramento had been chosen as California's capitol. The Ursus council voted to petition the Governor to intervene in Buff's behalf if he was able to pass entrance tests. The big day came and Buff's scores in all subjects except history and vocabulary were outstanding. An intensive tutoring campaign was put in motion and Buff was quickly brought up to grade in his lacking subjects. Re-testing results were exclamatory; Buff excelled in all subjects and was admitted. The young female employees of Ursus adopted Buff and soon he had more scholastic help than he could use and found it hard to find peace and quiet. Marta Bella Gustafson the daughter of the President of Ursus International found his weak spot his Achilles heel. Buff loved the ocean and her father had a sailing schooner

Buff's popularity and academic skills piqued the interest of the Governor and he began requesting monthly reports on the young Braves achievements. Buff's.credit workload shortened his matriculation and he graduated with a B.A. in threes years.

Graduate school in the new University of California finally tested the metal of the new scholar. He majored in political science and minored in American Native studies. The Governor had just what he wanted, somebody to head his Native American Council.

Buff's return to Camaize was joyous and sad at the same time for he told his family and friends that he felt his position with the state government were important to the development of Native American assimilation and betterment. He had found his calling. Every where he went he had a following of young people eager to hear his stories of the wonders he had seen and experienced. The governor had inculcated in Buff the urgency of closing the gap created by the demise of the Spanish/Mexican control over the Native Americans. The advanced weapons of the exploiters had subdued the natives and brought the mission system into being. Cattle and agriculture industries had to be assimilated by the tribes that they might advance,

The most joyous reunion was with Gallant when he visited Toro Oro on his way beck to San Francisco and Sacramento. The bond that had formed between this horse and man was remarkable and rarely duplicated. When Buff took a walk Gallant followed like a puppy dog. Occasionally nuzzling Buff as they strolled about as if to say can't you go faster? It was only when Gallant spotted a particularly good looking bunch of grass that he left Buff to chow down. Try as he might Buff couldn't escape his feelings of obligation to his native brothers. His new position in life didn't have room for Gallant.

It was going to happen sooner or later. Buff was in a respectable restaurant lounge in Sacramento, dressed in a business suit and seated by his own self when three roughly clad rowdies approached him. The largest unshaven lout reached over to Buff pulled out his tie and exclaimed, "Well lookit here if we don't have a snooty red skin thinking he is good enough to eat with white folks. He jerked Buff up by his tie and pulled a knife and held it to Buff's throat. Buff grabbed the knife hand where it joined the wrist squeezed until the man dropped the knife which Buff picked up ,looked at it and said "a trade knife the only problem is they break easy" and he snapped the blade off. of the handle and dropped it to the floor. This display of strength was enough, the trio shuffled away and left Buff to order and eat in peace. When attending the University of California Buff had spent many hours in the gym and taken judo courses. He was not one to be messed with. The loneliness brought by his concentration of bettering the welfare of his kindred folk left his physical needs as a man lacking. The very attractive cashier at the lounges register smiled in an inviting way. He had noticed that she never wore a ring indicating that she was single. She was a brunet with large attractive brown eyes that seemed to be inviting. Encouraged Buff asked her what her name was stating that he had noticed her the times that he had frequented this dinner. With aplomb, she answered "Sally". Encouraged by her frankness he told her, I am a stranger here and sure would appreciate somebody that would show me around to take advantage of this city. She smiled and answered, "I am free in an hour if you would like we can take in a play that I want to see." That would be great. I am called Buff Hunter and I will be here in an hour."

They met at the front of the dinner named the "Embarcadero" and the positive vibes couldn't be more electric. She took Buff's arm and walked out the door. "I have to ask" said Sally. "The name Buff is unusual and I need to know does it have a special meaning or derivation?" "As a matter of fact it does. Replied Buff "My full name according to our culture is: Buffalo Hunter – Son of Chief Wapaxo". "This is too much to write and understand at an introduction. Therefore I have shortened it to simply Buff Hunter". "We make a good pair, Said Sally, "My name is actually Tercilla Ann Hendrix. I shortened it for the same reasons you had". They laughed and took off in healthy steps toward the local Play House/ Theater. Not knowing what to expect Buff paid for the tickets and followed Sally's lead to seats half way down the center of the half circle rows around a stage. The title of the play was "Much About Nothing". An ochestra was playing a soft melody when a disturbance broke out in one of the balcony sections. A man swooped up a young well dressed lady in his arms and threw her over the railing where she was caught on a trampoline, bouncing off and curtesying to the audience.

The music stopped and a nattily dressed young man stepped forward cleared his throat and began to recite a lyrical poem when two women seated at preferred seats around a small table interrupted his recitation by screaming at one another throwing punches and began pulling each others hair. Finally they separated each holding a wig from the other with flesh colored nets holding their natural hair close their heads. They bowed and the orchestra started up with lively a military tune. This time the band was allowed to complete their repertoire. They were followed by an opera singer who had began an aria when a maiden dressed as a milk maid came down the isle leading a cow and carrying a bucket and a milk stool. She stopped in front of the stage and started to milk her cow. A man stuffily dressed stood up and began berating the milk maid. He screamed, "You cannot bring that beast in here this is no barn." The maid kept on milking. When she finished she took her bucket over to the complainer and dumped it over his head. It was filled with confetti. The opera singer finished her aria and received a standing ovation.

Buff escorted Sally home to her maiden aunt's house. They settled down on one of the wicker settees on the big porch. "When will I see you again?" asked Sally. "Not for a while" replied Buff. I have to visit several Missions for the Governor." "It is my jobs to help the Indians like me adjust to the Whiteman's life and culture. It is my plan to change the Mission Indian's image to one of dignity. And eradicate the derogatory aspect of the

"Mission Indian" being a nary-do-well". They warmly embraced and Sally said hurry back I will be waiting.

Buff left early the next morning. His first stop was Monterey. He made good time with his spirited team of palominos and his light spring buggy. His destination was a convent of the Sisters of Marialata Charity, a branch of the convent in Camaize where he had started learning the white man's culture. There he hoped to form a roving educational group that would instruct Mission Indians in white man's ways. Once they learned the basics of reading, writing and numbers he hoped to inculcate them in the ideas of collective bartering. Their present haphazard bartering of their handy craft left them open to exploitation by unscrupulois traders. Buff left after arranging the Nuns and giving them their tasks. He went to the different tribal areas conferred with the tribal leaders encouraging them to participate in the educational program by offering them promises of money and incentives to encourage the tribal leaders to facilitate his plan. In conference with Ursus Buff was able to create an account for the newly formed tribal commercial group. They assigned a coordinator to assist in the transactions. The area concerned was huge. It took Buff a month to accomplish the task of pushing the Indians into a modern transaction arrangement.

Excited about seeing Sally Buff hurried to make himself presentable and headed for the Embarcadero. He stopped at the cashier's cage and Sally hurriedly told him that she didn't get off for an hour. I am a slow eater quipped Buff. The waitress knowingly asked," can I start you off with a cup of coffee and a menu? "Perfect" answered Buff and returned her warm smile. Then it hit him like a bolt of lightening. He hadn't even thought to ask Sally if she had eaten and where she would like to go. Seeing that she didn't have any customers at the register he scooted over and asked her. "How thoughtful" she remarked. "Do you like Chinese?" "I don't know replied," Buff, "I have never tried it". "There is a little bar two doors down the street. I will meet you there in about thirty minutes," said Sally.

Buff spotted the bar and in a few steps was in the door. He laid a five dollar bill on the bar and said in English, "a bottle of El Porto please." The bar tender smirked and told him that they couldn't serve Indians. At first Buff was angry but he shook it off and repeated his request in perfect Mexican, saying I am no more Indian than you". He had pegged him just right and the beer was served with haste. When he was about half way through the beer Sally walked through the door and couldn't help feeling the lust in the bartenders eyes. She said, "I see you have met Pedro. He is a frequent customer of our diner." Buff couldn't help himself when he asked," You mean you serve Mexicans" and laughed at Sally's startled look. He explained as he took her arm and walked out the door.

The Chinese cuisine excited Buff and his introduction these culinary delights almost dimmed the delightful experience he was enjoying in Sally's presence. When he pulled the buggy through the gate to the extremely large almost mansion home he could only surmise that Sally's aunt must be a very wealth person. He almost expected a livered butler to answer the door. When it was Sally's aunt Martha Buff was immediately taken with her plain but aristocratic appearance. Sally excused herself and left Buff in Aunt Martha's care. She said, "I know that Sally has told you that she is staying with me but this isn't absolutely true, she owns this house and 90% of the dinning establishment where you met her. She inherited it all when her parents were killed in a boating accident five years ago.

Sally came in and took Buff's arm leading him to the rear porch. She turned to him and melted into his arms and they embraced lovingly. Buff couldn't explain to himself what he was feeling but he knew that he wanted the feeling to continue. He had heard about white-man's explanation of love and guessed this was it. The feeling of helplessness was new to him he had always been in control of his personal affairs. He extricated himself and apologized for his forwardness. Sally quickly reached out to him saying "Buff this was meant to be. I have been looking for you all of my life." They embraced again. "It is late I must be going." Said Buff . "Please stay answered",

Sally there are six bedrooms in this house Aunt Martha will show you to one." "I have to see to the horses" said Buff. "I have already seen to that" answered Sally. "The yard man has stabled them and fed them. Our family has always taken care of the livestock first." Aunt Martha showed Buff to his room. It was elegant and included his private bathroom. Buff and Sally met again on the veranda. They spent several hours story telling about their families and childhood years. They embraced and agreed that it would be awkward for them to allow their feelings to lead them to love making.

The next morning they arose early and Sally headed off to work and Buff started his journey to the capital to report to the Governor on his accomplishments with the Mission Indians. Before parting Buff asked Sally if she could accompany him at The Grizzly Inn for the annual Ursus meeting where she would get a chance to meet his parents and the Ursus conglomerate. It was a date ". I hope it won't inconvenience you but I want you to know the social functions following the business meeting will be formal. I mean by this dress and décor. "No problem", said Sally I will be ready with flourishes and bells".

Ursus had an annual meeting with a revolving delegated Chief Administrator. It was Wapaxo's turn to conduct the meeting. It would be an excellent time to introduce Sally.

After reporting to the Governor Buff collected his notes on commercial bargaining and organized them into a workable lesson plan for the Sisters to use with the classes they were conducting to bring the Mission Indians up to snuff on trade transactions and keep them from being short changed and cheated. He also arranged a collective council to establish fair prices and keep everyone abreast of going rates. Buff managed to return to Sacramento in time to clear his time off for the Ursus conference that the Governor would be attending as an honored guest. It was the Governor's wife that Buff eagerly looked forward to conferring with. Lady Helen was delighted with Buff's questions and counseled him in a conspiratorial fashion. She even went with him to pick out an engagement ring. She didn't know Buff had a substantial allowance from his father and was surprised when he picked out a half carrot diamond.

Sally had arranged to have several days off as cashier and book keeper at the Embarcadero Restaurant. It was an electric moment when Buff called for her and they headed for San Francisco and the Grizzly Arms Hotel. As they approached the city Buff pulled over at a beautiful spot that is now Golden Gate Park and said, "There is something I want to show you" he produced the ring and said, "Will you marries me?" Sally gasped and began to cry. Buff couldn't fathom this and asked, "Why are you crying?" She replied these are tears of joy, I was beginning to believe that I was going to have to ask you". "You mean you would have"? He asked. "Definitely" she replied. At the hotel Buff was expected and his instructions for two adjoining rooms had been followed to the tee. As it turned out only one room was required. Buff was curious when Sally brought one of the large bath towels to the bed. Sally told him, "I am a virgin and the first time is messy."

It was fortunate First Lady Helen was at the check in desk and when she saw the ring on Sally's finger she gave her a hug and said we are so happy for you he is a remarkable man and will go far in this world. Since the Governor was not an Ursus staff member they. Had time to accompany Sally during the business portions of the Ursus meeting. Lady Helen asked, "You are Tercilla Hendrix, daughter of Drs. Wayne Hendrix and Elizabeth Hendrix and an only child are you not"? Sally answered, "I am but I like to be called Sally". "The governor and I were close friends of your departed parents and were shocked at the event of their deaths." As I remember they were swamped and crashed into a reef of rocks off the Faralon Islands. The summary of the Coast Guard report said the accident was the result of a micro burst followed by a rip tide that carried your family yacht with your parents and a crew of four of which there was no sign of any survivors." Oh I am so sorry" continued Lady Helen, I shouldn't have brought this up it was so tragic." "No I am glad you did I never had the nerve to read the report at the time" replied Sally.

The arrival of Chief Wapaxo and Milliwana was without fanfare but the respect and condescension of the hotel staff reflected their importance. They stepped out of their coach, Wapaxo leading and Milliwana following. They were both dressed in almost snow white buckskin. Milliwana's suit was more flamboyantly beaded. Wapaxo's right hand clutched his spear scepter. Inter mingled with the feathers below the spear head, were four ivory cobs of corn. They had been carved from walrus tusks and presented to Wapaxo as tribute from one of the coastal tribal chiefs and were highly prized byWapaxo. Buff with Sally at his side was waiting just inside the lobby. Buff had explained that his father didn't shake hands and a simple nod is acknowledgement by him. When Wapaxo transferred his scepter from his right hand to his left hand and brought his right hand in a loose fist to his left breast Buff was almost open mouthed startled. This was almost condescension by the Noble Chief. When Buff announced that Sally was his betrothed Wapaxo declared that the wedding "will be at Camaize and he would perform the ceremony. Sally was a little taken back at Wapaxo's dictatorial position Buff whispered to her, "Remember in his world and to his people he ranks somewhere between God and the Pope." Sally's bright smile and chuckle pleased Wapaxo immensely. Later when she had the opportunity Milliwana hugged Sally and advised her that to marry Buff was a solemn obligation. He will some day replace his father as Chief of the Camaize a Sub Tribe of the Nez Perce Indians. His position will equal that of a Governor of a state under treaty laws of the United States. Sally felt a little tinge of fear of the possibilities of responsibility. It was only when Buff brought Huston over and introduced her to him and the lovely Rose. That Sally couldn't help but feel a warm flush at their exuberant approval of her especially when Buff called Huston his mentor.

Ivan and Tatjana arrived on the scene and another introduction added to Sally's warmth. When Sally asked

Tatjana about Ursus she received a concise history of the large investment and capital organization. She also learned more about Huston who Ivan had made a partner in Toro Oro. She explained that Huston had brought all of the separate entities of Toro Oro to a point of high yield and efficiency while Ivan was occupied with Ursus expansions. Huston called Rose over and asked her to do a favor for him and keep Sally occupied for a half hour or so. Rose glided through the crowd and up to Sally, taking her by the arm affectionately. "Please tell me how you managed to corral Buff"? She asked.

"It was hunger and destiny", chortled Sally. I was fortunate to be working when Buff came in to eat and there was an immediate attraction. This is actually only our second date. We went to a play together and had a platonic evening at my home that I share with a maiden aunt. It was truly love at first sight. Rose told her of Buff's apprenticeship under the tutelage of Huston at Toro Oro. Sally told Rose how she had inherited her parent's restaurant, The Embarcadero. Do you have a lounge in the restaurant?" asked Rose. "No", replied Sally, "But I am negotiating to purchase the building next to the dinning room with the intent of adding an upscale lounge to our facility. "Have you tasted the Grizzly Inn's Golden Bull liquor" asked Rose. When Sally replied in the negative Rose led her through the lobby to the cocktail lounge and ordered two cocktails and watched Sally's face light up when she tasted the delicious concoction. "Oh! I must stock this", she exclaimed. "You might be able to with your connections the distribution is very limited. The Grizzly is the only dealer in San Francisco, but with your restaurant being in Sacramento I am sure it can be arranged", said Sally.

Sally thought it odd that Wapaxo insisted that the wedding should be held in the fall at the same time as the corn harvest. Buff told her of his father's introduction of corn cultivation to his people and what it meant to him. The delay was disappointing to her, seeing her disappointment Buff told her that They could have a justice of peace wedding quietly before the tribal formal wedding and he would move in with her after the Ursus function. Meanwhile Wapaxo telegraphed Camaze instructing the millwrights to build a honeymoon cabin for the newlyweds.

Huston managed to pry Buff away from his father and Ivan and led him to the back veranda. "You my young friend are in serious danger. Your success with helping the Mission Indians in getting a handle on their income producing handy work has made you several very nasty enemies. The scum that has been exploiting your people are feeling the pinch in their pocketbooks. I have spoken to the Governor and he has allowed me to have some of your time. I still have connections in California law enforcement. Tomorrow we are going to the Justice hall I want you to look at some pictures and I have a gift for you. Now let's join our women and work out a schedule that will keep them happy.

Rose and Sally were enjoying each others company when Huston and Buff strolled into the lounge." I'll bet a dollar Rose is corrupting your bride to- be with Golden Eagle liquor," quipped Huston. "Can you stay three more days here", asked Huston. "Sally laughed; I think that can be arranged since I am the boss. But I don't know about Buff," she added. "I have already taken care of that," said Huston. "What's up"? Asked Rose. "Nothing important" replied Huston, but his eyes carried a message of don't ask. "I just want to acquaint Buff with some of the records in the Justice Hall that pertain to his work with the Mission Indians. We will have to be there at 8 am sharp," said Huston. "You ladies will just have to be on your own. Sally would probably appreciate a tour of the shopping centers here in Frisco", he added. Rose could read Huston like a book and sparkled at the chance to leave the men to proceed with some nefarious plan.

Meanwhile as the two couples joined the rest of the URSUS congregation for the evening banquet; in Monterey a different gathering was huddled in a dusky tavern in a cloud of tobacco smoke. Here the attire was rough work clothes except for one decently dressed swarthy man chewing on a foul smelling cigar. Who said, "We got to make it look like an accident or we will stir up a hornet's nest of state law officials," he grunted. An extremely thin greasy haired man said, "For a hundred thousand smacks we should be able to make it look like anything you want" Everybody had something to say except for a short guy with shoulders so broad that he almost seemed square. He was dressed like a long shore man and seemed to be more of a listener than a verbose ruffian. They were discussing the planned demise of Buff. There were six of them sitting away from the general crowd, with their heads forward to properly hear the discussions in low voices. Everything was discussed, from an arrow shot to a bear attack. "If we only knew what his itinerary was it would be a snap. I hear he never carries a gun only a knife", interjected a small weasel character with a bandana over his head. The bar maid stopped at the table and took their orders for drinks. She wouldn't stand out in a crowd, not a beauty, but comely and pleasant looking. In appearance she didn't fit the scene. She wore very little make-up and was conservatively dressed so that she solicited no advances. The meeting broke up without any definite plans for the murder of Buff.

It was a Tuesday morning and Huston and Buff were admitted to the reception desk of the justice building. A pert young receptionist greeted Huston with, "Good morning Mr. Wells, I am sorry but I have to see some identification of your companion." Without hesitation Buff presented his URSUS employee card and his University student identification both of which had a photo on them.

You're expected gentlemen she said as she pushed the electronic locking device. Upon entering a small reception area Huston again had to produce his Identification. It was perfunctory and they were admitted to a large file room. Huston asked the file clerk for the Black Eagle Files and they only had to wait for a few minutes for them to be placed on a waist high table for their perusal "Study these closely " instructed Huston; we cannot take anything from this room. " Some of these I have seen before,"said Buff .Huston identified each of the pictures and gave a brief history of their activities. When Buff had sufficient time to acquaint himself with his adversaries, Huston asked the clerk for the agents file.

The clerk was a little hesitant and Huston had to specify which agents he wanted Buff to Peruse. "Some of these may startle you", said Huston. The first one definitely did startle Buff it was Pedro the bartender that questioned his Indian status almost refusing to serve him until he spoke to him in fluent Spanish. That's Pedro the bartender replied Buff," "Yes he is status four but he is considered highly reliable," Replied Huston. The next picture was the waitress Betty. . "I think I have seen her before", said Buff. "Never show that you recognize her if you happened to meet. She is deep in cover and it would compromise her if you should recognize her". The last picture of importance was the short guy with the exceptionally broad shoulders. "This agent is your undercover body guard", said Huston, ".Do not recognize him but be aware that he is there for you". "Has Sally told you of her plans to expand her restaurant by adding a lounge?" "No we haven't discussed this admitted Buff." "Well I believe she is intending to hire Pedro as managing bartender. He will be your contact. When you go in there he will offer you a menu. Inside the menu will be a sheet of paper. If it is white and blank call me; if it is red be on alert an attempt will be made on your life soon.

After leaving the Justice Hall they drove out of town to a shooting range. Huston opened a brief case he had been carrying and withdrew a colt revolver which he presented to Buff. He set up some targets and demonstrated it to Buff with several bulls eye; shots." It is a common belief that only practice is needed to become a good pistol shot. This is fiction. Practice doesn't mean perfection. The accurate handling of a pistol is a science and no matter how much you shoot you cannot master the art without the knowledge of some basic facts. He unloaded the revolver and told Buff to pull the trigger several times. Then he took a tablet from his brief case and took out a blank tablet that he drew some diagrams on. A human hair measures roughly one hundredth of an inch. We will suppose your target is twenty feet away. Now if your aim is one hundredth of an inch off at the muzzle how far is it off twenty feet away? It is easy to see you have missed your target. This is the result of your trigger pull. One hundredth of an inch at the muzzle has multiplied to several feet of deflection. It is all due to trigger pull because of the trigger fingers connections to the wrist. To prove a point I am going to wrap a slender board to the back of your hand so you can see the improvement of your aim with your wrist rigid. All this will do for you is to teach you to pull the trigger not squeeze it. From here out it will be practice. After several shots Buff was amazed at the improvement of his accuracy.

After Buff had been three days with Huston Sally could feel a tension about him. When she questioned him about what was the matter, not wanting to tell her about his newly discovered danger he replied, "Maybe it is the sudden thoughts of marriage." This was the wrong answer. Sally with tearful eyes, said that had better be a cruel joke and these are not tears of joy". He took her in his arms and said ", I agree that was a careless remark and I am sorry. I am full of joy with the thought of having you as my wife". Lets us go for our license and have Aunt Martha stand up for us today". Aunt Martha was delighted and understood the necessity of the J.P. wedding preceding the formal affair performed by Buff's father the Chief.

Buff and Sally had their moments of bliss but Buff couldn't shake the apprehensions of danger after being briefed by Huston. He headed for the shooting range as often as possible clandestinely, not wanting to alarm Sally with his knowledge of danger.

Each time he drew the pistol he imagined the feel of the brace Huston had attached to his wrist and was pleased with the increased accuracy of his shots. Huston had emphasized that accuracy was far more important than speed.

Another scenario was playing out in the Indian country around the Sierra De Salinas area. A band of Mestizos cattle thieves had hidden fifty head of beef in a secluded little valley;

blocked the entrances to the valley and scattered, planning to recover them when the heat of the endeavor had abated. After a week had passed they returned to find the entire herd had died or were sick. Not wanting to loose their ill-gotten gains they set about skinning the animals, scraping the hides and stretching them to dry. They loaded the hides on a wagon and hauled them to a warehouse in Monterey. None of this activity had escaped the Black Eagle gang. Except for Delano (the square built undercover agent); they were in deep conference. They were planning on stealing the hides from the Monterey warehouse. They already had over a hundred hides that they had short changed the local tribes out of. Loading the hides and hauling them to the loading dock and a ship destined for the Orient was more work than this group was accustomed to. Even the husky cigar smoking leader handled the hides, mainly, inspecting; delighted to see the quality and care they had received. It was several days until their poor sanitary habits brought them to a stand still. The stolen hides had come from cattle with anthrax. They had been stolen from a health herd but the valley had been contaminated by a few contagious wild cows and animals. Anthrax is a deadly disease and the contact with the diseased hides was a death sentence for the slovenly thieves. Agents of the California Justice bureau reported the deaths of the thieves and a big load was lifted from Buff's anxiety level. This didn't cause him to decrease his weapon handling and target practice.

Sally was wrapped up in the new lounge adventure. She found the inventory of Golden Bull Liquor was responsible for an increase in upper class business. The high price asked for this exotic drink turned it into a status symbol indicating a consumers elevated financial or social status. The hectic business activity helped her suppress her anxiety over her up-coming formal wedding performed by her father-in-law the Chief.

The day was set. What to wear and what to pack was foremost on her mind. With the business of running the restaurant and lounge turned over to subordinates she began to fuss over selecting a wedding dress. Aunt Martha accompanied her to the local dress shops and they were engaged in trying on the gowns when Buff tracked them down. With a flurry Sally rushed to a back room before Buff could see her in a wedding dress. Out of breath she explained to Buff that it was unlucky for the groom to see his intended in her wedding gown before the ceremony. "I am sure glad I caught you before you bought something," he exclaimed. "My mother will have the appropriate dress for you when we get there. It is our tradition."

The stage coach ride to Portland was rough and dusty. In a true pioneer woman tradition there was little complaining from Aunt Martha and Sally. However they found the accommodations at The Golden Bull Inn were excellent and were they were glad for the chance to freshen up. Sally found Portland to be refreshing and would like to have spent more time there. Buff promised her that she would get a chance to explore the area when they returned home. There was a rather large coach to take them to the ranch. For economy purposes trips to town were as usual, an event of restocking the ranch and the coach was loaded with ranch goods. The driver welcomed Buff as an old friend and the ride to Toro Oro was refreshing and not arduous. The driver stopped at the main house and Ivan and Tatjana were there to greet them.

Sally noticed that Buff was treated as part of the Family and there were plenty of accommodations in the six bed room mansion. Huston and Rose were there for dinner. The women clustered around the bride and attempted to answer all of her questions about Wapaxo, Milliwana and Camaze. Sally was glad to hear that Tatjana and Rose would be at the wedding. The next day Sally accompanied by Tatjana and Rose took a tour of the distillery where the famous Red Bull liquor was produced. Ivan, Huston and Buff spent their time inspecting some of the high bred cattle after Gallant and Buff became re-united. It was remarkable how the big gelding showed his affection for his old master. Buff resolved that he would bring Gallant back to California.

Sally couldn't help but feel apprehensive at the fuss that was made over her and Buff as the little caravan made ready for the trip to Camaze. She tried find out from the ladies about Buff's rejection of a bridal gown. All they would say is," you will see". Two hours from the edge of the village the caravan stopped by a clear mountain stream and everybody took advantage of the wonderful water to refresh. Sally had been made to feel exceptional it was the little things like making her feel protective during their necessary stops. As the caravan approached the village the tension grew in her fright, fearing unacceptance by Buff's family.

When they rode into the village they were greeted by a covey of singing children mostly little girls singing in English songs of welcome. The Convent fronting the community square was her first cultural shock. The buildings were so solid and artfully arranged. She had to ask, what this collection of structures was". It is the Convent, School, and Clinic/ hospital answered Buff. "And what is the big commercial looking building across from the Convent? He answered, "The commissary/ Store.

Only Ivan had knew of the approaching convey bearing the Governor of California, his entourage and guards. Buff had extended the invitation, but had not known if the Governor could accept or not due to his responsibilities. Ivan met and escorted the Governor to Wapaxo. Introduction was not necessary they had met at the last general meeting of Ursus in San Francisco. Wapaxo knew of the importance of this powerful man and felt gladdened that his son was being so honored.

In her studies of Anthropology at The University of San Francisco she had absorbed the belief that the present day American Indians was the result of tens of thousands of years of hunters and gathers culture. The modern structures, commercial achievements and social progress were completely different from her expectations. It is no wonder the Chief Wapaxo was considered as almost a Deity. It was through his insistence that the tribe had become horticulturists. They no longer suffered through hunger times in the winter. He had also been able to inculcate in the young men's beliefs that it was honorable to perform manual labor and that there was dignity in cultivating storable plants and vegetables.

Sally surrounded by her traveling companions, Milliwana and other ladies of the community was hustled off to Milliwania's house where she was offered refreshments. The women gestured and Milliwana came forth carrying a white deerskin dress that was ornately decorated with fringe and artistically covered with beads. It was exceptionally beautiful. To Sally's surprise it fit her perfectly. Now she knew why she had been prevented from purchasing the selected wedding dress. The whole affair made her feel as if she was royalty. The chapel of the monastery was chosen as the wedding hall. In the presence of a selected assembly Wapaxo asked, "Who gives this woman in matrimony?" The Governor of California stepped forward and said," I, as a close friend of the departed parents accepts this honor". Wapaxo speaking reverently said, "It Is proper in the order of nature that those of opposite sex should by coupled for the preservation of the species. So " be it" go forth and multiply." In Whiteman's way Buff kissed his bride. As the celebrants cheered, Igor Stepped forward and handed Buff a cleverly designed box depicting camass blue blossoms that had been created by the artistic hand's of his wives. When Buff opened the box he found nestled in fine down a golden chain linking four gold and platinum kernels of corn

Buff fastened the necklace around Sally's throat and another burst of applause and clapping ended the ceremony.

There never had been and probably never will be another feast as Camassia experienced for the next three days. The Governor and his entourage could not stay any longer that the wedding day and the following one.

Before departure the Governor called Buff aside and they had a long discussion on the state of affairs in California. He told Buff that there would soon be an election and that he intended to seek reelection and asked Buff if he would run as his second in command as Lt Governor. Astounded Buff could hardly reply. He stumbled' asking, "Do you think I qualify"? The Governor's answer was, "more than any person I know. Your work with the betterment of the Mission Indians shows you have organizational ability, you show compassion and use you time effectively in the performance of assignments. These are exceptional abilities essential in governing a state as large and diversified as California.

In an amorphous state of mind Buff sought His father Wapaxo for guidance. When he blurted out the governor's offer, Wapaxo was stunned to silence. All he could utter was that he had hoped Buff would replace him as chief of the Camaize Tribe and leader of the community. Having traveled California as far as San Francisco and been appraised of its size and complexity he knew his small domain was insignificant in comparison. To be offered the position of Lt. Governor was indeed a great honor> It was both painful and gratifying to have his son so recognized.

Wapaxo and Buff had noticed the above average warrior in the fringe of the wedding reception He wasn't wearing war paint but he was carrying a bow and spear with a quiver of arrows. He stiffened as he notice Wapaxo and Buff approaching. "I don't recognize you?" declared Wapaxo. The ever alert Broken Branch and Up River moved into flanking positions covering Wapaxo protectively. Their maneuvers were noted by the strange warrior as covetously saw their ready rifles. "I am called Front Runner a warrior of the main Tribe of The Nez Perc; I come with greetings from Chief Wolf Stalker." "Why haven't you come forth?" queried Wapaxo. "We are all Nez Perc". "There are no waisachu (white men) in the Nez Perc tribe" retorted Front runner. When he spoke waisachu was spat out like a cuss word. The hackles rose on Wapaxo's neck. He replied, "The white men you see here are learned men that have brought wisdom to me and my people. Ask yourself how many babies, young and old people die from hunger in the winter?" You claim to be warriors yet you cannot fight and win the battle of hunger. You live on a false belief that work is beneath you and that it is only for squaws. He turned to Up River and asked him to fetch him a large ear of corn. When Up River brought the cob he presented it to Front Runner and told him this can be the salvation of your people. The true strength in leadership is knowledge. Have your MEN, plant this in the spring and if they are great warriors in the fall you will receive the benefits of waisachu wisdom. Leave it to the squaws to plant and I will not provide further seed.

It was almost laughable what Front Runner reported to Chief Wolf Stalker. Oh! Chief he exclaimed. There is no need to concern yourself with Wapaxo or his son aspiring to your tribal leadership. They are all squaw men and poor selectors of women. Buffalo Hunter's wife while attractive of face was spindly, light of frame and build, she could never bring in a winters supply of wood and could never dress or skin an elk. He never produced the ear of corn or mentioned Wapaxo's lecture on the starving times.

Front Runners words drifted back to Camaize and they did provoke humor. With the frivolity over, the guests departed. Golden bull welcomed back the wedding guests and the newly weds departed for Sacramento.

Twenty years later Buff and Sally were enjoying their three teen aged children. They had been brilliant students and social successes. Buff as the head executive of Ursus was extremely wealthy and Sally had opened a chain of busy restaurant- lounges. The impact of Wapaxo's guidance was being felt throughout the Native American cultures.Electricty and telephones had been introduced and Camaize was leading in modernization of the west.

Not the End but the beginning of a new era.